JACKIE'S
NEW YORK

A NOVEL

MERCEDES KING

BOOKS BY MERCEDES KING

The Jacqueline Bouvier Kennedy Onassis Collection

Jackie's Paris

Jackie's Camelot

Jackie's Greece

Jackie's New York

Historical Fiction Titles

A Dream Called Marilyn

Plantation Nation

Crime Fiction / Mysteries

Every Little Secret

Grave Secrets

Columbus Noir

Newsletter subscribers receive a FREE e-book for joining. Sign-up here.

For everyone who found strength and inspiration from Jacqueline Bouvier Kennedy Onassis through the decades and across generations

PROLOGUE

Lee didn't hate her sister. Not really. But lately, she couldn't stand her. Part of it had to do with the passing of Aristotle Onassis, Jackie's second husband—and Lee's former lover. She could never admit to Jackie that she hadn't forgiven her sister for marrying him. But Jackie wasn't capable of doing anything wrong, was she?

Despite being married when their torrid affair began, Lee had quickly fallen in love with Ari. During their years together, he was patient with her, never pushing or insisting on more than she could give. Ari seemed to understand her dilemma. Leaving Stas and dismantling her marriage, especially with children to consider, couldn't be done carelessly. Or, in her mind, without reassurances that Ari would one day marry her.

Ari compensated by seeing other women, namely Maria Callas.

However, the dynamic between Lee and Ari only began to change after an assassin's bullet made Jackie a widow. Ari slowly but surely exchanged Lee for Jackie. Discarded her and left her in the wind because something better came along. That was exactly how Lee felt!

She divorced Stas anyway—when Peter Beard came along. But the passion that brought them together became their undoing. Betrayal ended their affair, and Lee found herself alone and battling financial insecurity.

Then, seven years after his union with Jackie, Ari died. The tragic loss of his son combined with his own deteriorating health ushered him into the grave. For Lee, it meant their relationship would remain unfinished. That she would never know if they could have made it as a couple. What might have been haunted her.

She didn't attend Ari's funeral. Heartsick as she was over the man's death, she listened to Jackie, who believed it was for the best, knowing the press would be relentless enough since Jackie hadn't been at Ari's bedside at the American Hospital of Paris when he passed. There was enough upheaval for her to contend with, she claimed.

After the funeral, rumors blazed that Ari's daughter Christina held great animosity toward Jackie for marrying her father in the first place and intended to protect her father's substantial assets from "that gold-digger." If one believed the tabloid stories. But months later, Jackie not only attended Christina's wedding but also reached a settlement agreement, through her team of lawyers and Christina's team of lawyers, that enabled her to bag twenty-six-million dollars from Ari's estate.

A fortune that could have been mine!

Lee refused to think about it. She had an exciting life and her own adventures to focus on. Such as her upcoming travels with Truman Capote. New Orleans and Mexico awaited. Though it was true her affection for Truman had waned since he proved to be a whiny bore when they toured with the Rolling Stones, she hoped he would be entertaining and not awash in vodka and numb on tranquilizers.

Lee decided she needed more direction in her life. A project of some sort that would deliver her from Jackie's shadow, even though she'd spent her life picking up Jackie's scraps and always coming in second place to her sister. Lee could hear the echo in the halls of her mind from teachers at Miss Porter's. Those breathless exclamations of, *"Oh, is Jacqueline your sister? She's so witty and intelligent."* But any interest or zeal they had in Lee faded, only to be mixed with profound disappointment, once her lackluster academic performance prevailed.

She wasn't Jackie. An unspoken yet repeated cadence throughout her life that tainted others' expectations of her.

So she grew a thick skin. She had to. Because she was her own person, gifted with robust talents, striking beauty, and charms. Unique and worthy of being loved.

Lee doubted she could tolerate Jackie's current state of smugness much longer. Or prevent that seed of bitterness from sprouting into full-grown hatred.

Pain throbbed in her chest when she thought about how their relationship had deteriorated. Not so long ago, their sisterhood had been similar to a vibrant garden, lush with healthy, colorful blooms and plump, choice fruits. But in recent years the landscape had become unrecognizable. Bare, parched earth, brittle and cracked from neglect.

But whatever gripes she had against Jackie they couldn't be justified. Because Lee had betrayed her sister in the worst way and deserved the shackles of shame. Regret began to surface, as it often did when she became riled over Jackie's success and triumphs. That prickly reminder that Lee held damaging secrets.

One secret in particular had the potential to permanently scorch and destroy whatever was left between them. Lee had learned to live with the deceit. But her instinct to protect Jackie and to do what was best for their relationship had grown threadbare. She didn't know how much longer she could keep the betrayal to herself—and if it was worth it anymore. Because these days, she didn't care about Jackie getting a taste of the hurt she'd endured for years.

ONE

August 1975

"**J**ackie, you have to agree that me hiring you as an editor is a bit preposterous. Critics are going to come out of the woodwork—for me *and* for you. Surely you realize that."

Jackie forced a grin while clenching her napkin under the table as Tom Guinzburg, president and editor of Viking Press, mildly laughed at her. Petty as it was, her need for retaliation stemmed from the fact they were lunching at the Knickerbocker Club, on full public display. Onlookers might recognize her and note her sudden tension.

Good friends as she and Tom were, she gave a moment's thought to marching out the door. How could he sit there and laugh? Was it really *preposterous*, approaching him with an interest in working at a publishing house? After all, Dorothy Schiff had offered her the chance to write a column for *The New York Post* recently. Intrigued, Jackie considered it. Even toured the *Post*'s offices. But the fear of having to produce new writing on a consistent basis spoiled her romantic notions. So did the fact that Eleanor Roosevelt held the position previously. Jackie preferred blazing her own unique trail.

After she'd passed on the offer, friends Letitia Baldrige and Nancy Tuckerman suggested the role of an editor might suit her better. Though, truth be told, she couldn't deny her naivety at what the position would demand.

Tom coughed and cleared his throat, seeming to note her irritation. A benefit to their long-standing friendship.

"Who am I kidding, Jackie? I never could hold a poker face. It should go without saying that Viking Press would do just about anything to have you on board—but in a limited capacity at the start."

Jackie's aggravation lifted. "Really?"

"Well, I'm sure they want me to play the cards close to the vest, but we've known each other for how long? Twenty years?"

"At least." Longer, if she had to do the math. Tom had been in her social circles as far back as she could remember. He had roomed in the same dorm at Yale as Yusha, her stepbrother, and always seemed to be somewhere on the periphery of Jackie's life. Another reason she'd reached out to Tom, hopeful that securing such a job might be possible at this juncture in her life.

"Viking knows that you'd bring so much to the company, even though you have no experience in publishing. We're keenly aware of how well-educated you are, and your love for reading is undeniable. I will tell you that my bosses are nearly salivating at the prospective clients you may bring in. Celebrity biographies are revered in this industry."

Jackie recoiled inwardly but kept a neutral expression.

"Oh, Tom, I don't want to busy myself with simply helping the likes of pampered movie stars parlay their drunken escapades into a book." She stopped herself, suddenly concerned she'd made an incorrect assumption about an editor's responsibility. Tom's comment also made her consider, quickly, the degree of concession she was willing to make for the position.

He nodded. "I understand you don't want to attach your name to certain endeavors, but publishing is a fierce business. One way of looking at it is to treat it like a compromise. The projects you edit, one day, will benefit from your support. You won't have to participate in a march or a sit-in at city hall, but you want subject matter that attracts readers and dollars. As much as Viking cares about having you on board, they care even more about their bottom line." He leaned back in his chair. "There's a bit of risk in hiring you."

"It's rare I consider myself a liability." She was nervous enough, putting herself out there for consideration and potential rejection. Tom wasn't easing her fears.

He grinned. "I'm pushing it, but not by much. The public scrutiny of a former First Lady—well, let's be honest, the country's most *beloved* First Lady—going to work and taking a job she isn't qualified for is going to become a news item. Viking Press will have to answer the critics and naysayers, and so will you. How will you handle that?"

Jackie's face heated, first at his praise and then at his warning. "With as few words as possible."

Jackie thought back to her time in the White House. Aside from hosting state dinners, special events, and working on the restoration, she chose a private life. Instead of heading committees and welcoming ladies to tea, she retreated to the countryside with her young children. And when it came to press conferences, she instructed her press secretary, Pamela Turnure, "I want minimum information given with maximum politeness." A motto Jackie adhered to long after leaving her role.

Tom winked. "That's the kind of gusto this is going to take for this to work."

"I'm not afraid to learn new things, or to put critics and naysayers in their place. Politely, of course."

Projecting confidence was important and helped waylay the apprehension of what she'd gotten herself into.

DAYS LATER, when she was scheduled to meet her mother and Lee for lunch at La Grenouille, one of her favorite French restaurants in Manhattan, Jackie decided not to reveal that she was on the verge of becoming a working woman. Details still needed finalizing, though she made no fuss over the salary of ten thousand a year or the fact that she would start out in a dumpy little cubicle, like every new hire. Since she wasn't accustomed to keeping a daily routine or being around dozens of strangers regularly, Tom had agreed to her proposed schedule of working three days a week in the office. It was a means of self-preservation for her introverted nature.

Maybe she would wait a month or two before telling Janet and Lee. She wanted time to settle in, craft her groove—and see if she could in fact fit into the environment and could fulfill the new demands upon her.

For today's lunch, she hoped her excitement about the position wouldn't cause her to slip and say something that gave away a hint and required her to elaborate. On the other hand, keeping mum on a sensitive topic was her specialty.

When Jackie arrived at La Grenouille, Lee was already seated and waiting.

Jackie steeled herself with a subtle yet deep breath. Since Ari's passing, their relationship suffered an undeniable shift. Had she been wrong to discourage Lee from attending the funeral? Jackie thought she'd done them both a favor and saved them from potentially embarrassing headlines, such as, "Sisters Grieve the Loss of Shared Lover." Or some such incestuous-flavored bit. Protecting Lee had been her priority.

But Jackie suspected Lee didn't see it that way. She worried Lee was harboring a grudge for being nudged out of the spotlight—and Ari's will.

As an aside, she hoped Christina would view the gesture as an extending of an olive branch, of sorts, since various sources had informed her that while Christina didn't like Jackie, she loathed Lee (and vehemently detested Maria Callas). Jackie had hoped that keeping the two women out of Christina's sights for her father's burial would make her more pliable when it came to Jackie's settlement. Though the legal haggling wasn't finished, and Jackie had yet to receive a check, her theory seemed to have worked. Proceedings were moving along.

Now, as she took the seat across from her sister, Jackie wondered what it would take to repair the breach.

Probably half the money, her mind answered.

They sipped coffee, chatted about their children, and smoked while awaiting Janet's arrival. Their polished cordiality reminded Jackie how much she missed the ease of being with her sister. The deep dives into social gossip and exchanges of their old inside jokes. Of course, Ari and his passing weren't to blame. Not entirely. Jackie knew they had created a tattered patchwork of moments like this, where both sensed the disconnect but neither would address it.

A variety of factors had widened the chasm. They didn't see each other as much as they used to. Didn't travel together like they used to. And didn't commit to holidays together like they had when their children were young.

Jackie also couldn't discount the envy she suspected was festering within Lee, knowing a windfall of funds was on Jackie's horizon. She could overlook such resentment, though, because she truly missed their closeness.

When thirty minutes had passed and Janet still hadn't joined them, Jackie looked at the restaurant's entrance for the umpteenth time.

"It's not like Mummy to be late. Punctuality is a beatitude for her, and she's never missed a luncheon."

Lee glanced at the door as well. "Do you think something's happened? Perhaps Hughdie isn't well."

Alarm gripped Jackie. Remembering her stepfather's recent struggles with emphysema, she slipped from the booth. "I'll go call Hammersmith Farm."

The maitre'd hastened to her right away. She explained her need for a telephone, and he ushered her to a private alcove where she dialed the Auchincloss estate. After a brief conversation, she returned to the table.

"What is it?" Lee must have read the dumbfounded expression on her face.

"I spoke with Marguerite. She said Hughdie is fine. They're both fine. In fact, they're out strolling the garden together."

Lee scowled. "Mummy's in Newport then and didn't come to Manhattan."

Jackie nodded, unable to curtail her concern. "She must have forgotten. I told Marguerite not to bother them."

Jackie knew just as well as Lee that their mother lived and breathed according to her social calendar. She was never late, and she *never* forgot.

Lee sighed. "I was on the telephone with her the other day, and she called me by your name. Twice."

So it wasn't just Jackie's imagination. "The last time I was with her in Newport, she misplaced her reading glasses. It turned out they were in her pocket."

Lee stamped out her cigarette in the ashtray on the table. "I suppose she *is* getting older."

The reality landed too harshly for Jackie. "Perhaps we shouldn't worry ourselves about it. Everyone forgets something now and then. Let's enjoy our lunch together."

"You're right. I suppose I can go ahead and share my news." Lee clasped her hands together and smiled. "I'm starting an interior design business."

Jackie grinned also. "Pekes, that's wonderful! Oh, I'm thrilled for you."

"I've always had a passion for making a home come to life with personality. I should've done this ages ago. It's such a part of who I am."

"I couldn't agree more. Do you have your first commission?"

"It's in the works." Lee pursed her lips. "I considered working with Mark Hampton, but as you can imagine, it's just too complicated. He's established and has a distinct point of view and a solid reputation. There's no need for him to consider a collaboration with me."

Jackie nodded. She couldn't envision that mix of egos leading to a successful venture anyway. Each of them too distinct in their tastes and foreign to the art of compromise.

"You should invest in me now, Jacks. Friends have arranged for me to meet with Mario di Genova, the head of the Americana Hotel chain. Can you imagine where that might lead?"

"I'm so excited for you." Jackie truly meant it and hoped that, for once, Lee's endeavor would prove fruitful. Unlike her critically panned attempt at acting and her failure to produce a memoir for publication. If Lee finally found a measure of success, perhaps it would help mend their relationship.

"Apart from learning the business ropes," Lee sighed, "my only other concern right now is Tina."

"Is she not doing well in school?"

"School is fine. It's when she's home...and around me that things get prickly."

"It's part of being a teenager, I suspect. Remember how anxious we were to grow up and escape Mummy's heavy hand?" Jackie kept from flinching as flashes of her mother slapping her reeled through her head. Slaps that Janet dished out as correction. Or when her frustrations simply boiled over. A heavy hand indeed.

Lee's expression sobered. "I hardly parent like Mummy."

"Of course not." Jackie said it in a convincing tone. While she knew her sister didn't strike her youngest child, Jackie had heard Lee speak bluntly to Tina and warn her—more than a fifteen-year-old girl needed to hear—about her weight and her appearance. If Jackie had to pinpoint the cause of the friction between the two, she would lay blame on Lee's divorce from Stas. The break-up turned Tina's world upside-down, with Tina moving with Lee to America and Anthony staying with his father in London. The separation proved difficult for the tight-knit siblings.

"Why don't you have Tina come and stay with me for a while?" Jackie suggested. "Until you get things off the ground with your business. Caroline is leaving for London soon, and John is often busy with his tutor. I could use the company so it would really be a favor to me."

Lee seemed to consider the idea as she produced another cigarette. "A small change might be good for the girl. She adores you, and perhaps she'll listen more to you when it comes to tapering her figure."

Jackie nodded, although not completely innocent on the subject. She had suspended Caroline's credit card when she learned her daughter had developed a slight obsession with spareribs from Mr. Chow's and had ordered two pounds. At length she warned Caroline to guard her waistline, and she didn't reinstate the charge account until Caroline agreed to go jogging with her regularly in the park. For added measure, Jackie instructed Marta, her governess-turned-house-keeper-cook, to scale back desserts.

When it came to Tina, though, Jackie didn't want Lee's straight-forward approach to nudge the girl into anorexia, a condition that had plagued Lee for years. How Lee was oblivious to such a danger, baffled Jackie.

The conversation suddenly served as a sharp reminder for Jackie. She needed to be careful about staying in her sister's good graces. A false word or notion could light the fuse for an outburst or cause Lee to pull away and not speak to her. Jackie could only attribute it to an unknown resentment Lee harbored. Thin ice to waltz upon.

As Jackie peered across the table at her sister, she didn't know whether she should mine the issue and bring it to light, or if she should simply leave it alone. They had both lost so much since Ari's passing, especially in the vein of their camaraderie. Part of her believed repairing the rift between them was impossible now. They were a far cry from the little girls who'd grown up on Long Island,

and even more distanced from the ladies who traveled together on a goodwill trip to India and Pakistan with the world watching in 1962.

Still, she had to try. Jackie would schedule a visit with André Meyer and instruct her financial advisor to send funds to Lee's business account. She'd discuss with him what might be a reasonable amount to contribute, with no expectation of a return. Five thousand, in her view, was a generous investment.

Not that Lee would appreciate it. If anything, she might criticize the amount, telling André, "What a paltry sum. Jackie can afford to be much more supportive than that. But what does she know about running a business?"

No. Jackie refused to get steamed and ruffled by her imaginations. Lee could surprise her with an uptick of gratefulness in her attitude. Jackie couldn't count it out. But going forward, and unlike in years past, she wouldn't bear the brunt of Lee's moodiness for the sake of peace. Surely it wasn't unreasonable for Jackie to believe her little sister craved harmony as much as she did.

INSTEAD OF LETTING her worries get the best of her, Jackie determined to focus on making her long weekend with Caroline and John memorable and relaxing. In the coming weeks, Caroline, having been accepted into Sotheby's art history internship for two semesters, would soon be leaving for London to live with Hugh Fraser, a long-time friend of Jackie, and his daughters. John would be returning to the Collegiate School shortly, and life would resume that busy pace that didn't allow as much time for reading and dabbling with paints. The last bit of summer was starting to slip away.

Adding to the changes would be Jackie's new position as a consulting editor with Viking Press. Caroline and John had seemed receptive to their mother taking a job, though none of them could guess how it would impact their lives. Making the life-altering decision to reenter the workforce at forty-six-years-old thrilled her, along with the fact she didn't *need* the job, thanks to her pending settlement from Ari's estate. Even though she was committing to a work schedule, she'd never known such freedom. Going forward, in any venture for the rest of her life, she could say the same. No limitations could dictate to her, and the social demands of securing a husband no longer existed.

Packed into her forest-green BMW, a gift from Ari, she couldn't have been happier as the three of them headed to her secluded home in Peapack, New Jersey—or Peapack-Gladstone, if one wanted to be proper. An hour outside of Manhattan the area boasted more acreage and rolling hills than people. It was an alcove of privacy, in the heart of the Essex Fox Hounds Hunt that provided the perfect setting for horseback riding, watersports, and lounging in each other's company. And fabulous stables for her horses, Winchester and Sadar.

As they bustled from the car and into the house after arriving, Jackie couldn't shake a troubling thought. Over the course of the weekend, she would need to find a moment to broach an uncomfortable topic. Nude pictures of her that had appeared in the Italian magazine *Playmen* last year had recently been published in *Hustler* and branded with the banner, "Billion Dollar Bush."

She could already imagine John's classmates wiggling a copy of the magazine in front of him and taunting him with rude comments. Teenage boys often proved crude and had a worthless talent for harassing John. The best she could do was prepare him.

With help from others, like Nancy Tuckerman, a personal friend dating back to her days at Miss Porter's who had served as her secretary since the White House, Jackie did her best to monitor items in the press that could be hurtful to her children. When reports about their father's womanizing ways made it into print, she circumvented specifics, keeping their ages in mind—seventeen and fourteen until their November birthdays—and canonizing him as a leader while humanizing him as their father.

Little things, she found, pleased them most, such as hearing her retelling stories about how Buttons became his nickname for Caroline. "From the day you were born your father said you were cute as a button," she'd told Caroline. And she shared with John how he would nearly throw a tantrum whenever his father teasingly called him Sam. "'Come over here, Sam. Where are you, Sam?' And every time you would stomp your little foot and say, 'That's not my name.'"

She abandoned references to Camelot.

"Daddy made mistakes, just as we all do, but he loved you very much," became her primary mantra.

Now that the children were older, however, there would come a greater need for them to understand the man they hardly remembered but were forever connected to. Even more complicated for them would be maturing into the people they wanted to be while political expectations hung over them.

Intent on making the weekend enjoyable, Jackie put away discouraging thoughts as she went out back with Caroline and John.

Caroline wanted to take the horses out for a ride and stretch, which Jackie readily agreed to. John went along with the plan, even though he wasn't as comfortable and skilled in the saddle. Through the years, Jackie had attempted to remedy his poor horsemanship but didn't force it. He could hold his own, and that had to be good enough for her.

Because when it came to John, Jackie had to be careful. Gentleness was her nature, but John needed a firm hand. He was gangly and sometimes clumsy, but never short on curiosities or questions. Knowing that he needed to be active to work out his abundant energy, and preferred being outdoors, she never discouraged him from climbing too high in trees or from swimming too far out. Such risks, she hoped, would build his confidence as he grew into a man. His need for adventure was surely a trait gifted to him from his father.

Later that evening, after their ride and spaghetti for dinner, Jackie asked John to join her in the living room after Caroline slipped off to her room to finish reading a book.

"Is this going to be one of our talks?" he asked.

"Yes." She sat on the sofa and couldn't tell offhand how tolerant he would be. Sitting and listening weren't among his favorite things to do. "I wanted you to know how proud I am of you, working so hard this summer at the Bronx Zoo. You were so responsible, setting your own alarm and riding the subway by yourself."

John gave a half-grin. "The monkeys were the worst. One of them threw poop at me."

"I remember you telling me that." Jackie giggled. "You said their aim was terrible."

With his hands stuffed into his pants pockets, he twisted from side to side. "So is that it? Can I go to my room now?"

She sighed. "Not yet. You're about to start school again, and I want you to feel prepared."

The beginning of the new school year ramped her concerns for him. John struggled academically, and she knew the coming years would prove even more challenging, especially the closer he got to college. Teachers and counselors shared the same observations: "He's bright and outgoing but easily distracted. His Latin is subpar, and his mathematical scores demand remediation." Precisely why Jackie had hired a tutor for him over the summer.

"Your classes are only going to get harder." She didn't mean the comment as a slight.

Standing behind the couch now, perhaps as a futile attempt to escape, John bent over it and placed his head on the seat cushion, then summersaulted and landed on the floor. "Did you see that?"

Jackie adored his silliness but wanted him to better discern when it was and wasn't appropriate. She couldn't be harsh with him, though, knowing he was still recovering from Ari's death. When John hadn't been away at school, Ari had made time for him. They often took out the speedboat Ari had bought for him, and Ari educated him on every aspect of the *Christina*, the luxury yacht Ari preferred as his home. There were numerous travels, including an excursion in Egypt where they rode camels and toured the pyramids in Giza, and occasional trips to Shea Stadium to watch the Mets play. Ari's love for John was genuine, and he became the only father John knew.

Jackie focused and eased into her concerns about his academics. He said he would try hard, which was the best she could ask for. Before she let him run off to bed, she warned him about the nude pictures in the magazine. Having to explain such a thing to her son stoked an ember of ire for Ari, who had paid a paparazzi to snatch those bare candids of Jackie while she sunbathed.

John nodded but kept his head down and didn't ask questions.

Jackie cracked a smile as he danced off to his room, snapping his fingers and singing, "Get Down, Get Down," drawl and all.

September 1975

PERHAPS SHE WAS WRONG, but the last time Jackie recalled being a tangle of nerves was the night of the inaugural balls. Back then, she had to adjust to the fact that her privacy would be further compromised as First Lady. Exhaustion was also having its way with her that night since she was still recovering from John's premature birth and a caesarean. She only made it to two of the five balls before nearly collapsing. Fortunately, no reporters ended up immortalizing her slip with a photograph, and Jack, who stayed out most of the night enjoying the revelry, was understanding.

Today, as she walked into the offices of Viking Press as a new hire, she relived that excitement from fourteen years ago—and felt the sharp contrast between the woman she was and the woman she was dedicated to becoming.

Viking Press had released a statement the previous week as a proactive measure, according to Tom, with the goal of lessening the hysteria of Jackie Onassis getting a job. Aside from confirming her employment and role, few details were given. In response, the press lined the sidewalk outside the building on Madison Avenue determined to capture an image of her arrival.

Jackie used an underground entrance and foiled their plans.

Although a few pictures were taken for posterity's sake, one with Tom talking to Jackie in Viking's library and one with Jackie in her workspace, much of her first day seemed to mirror the experience of any new employee. She got acquainted with coworkers and staff, sat in on meetings, and settled in at her desk.

When Tom called her into his office and closed the door, she welcomed the reprieve. Despite years of being under the glare of flashbulbs for numerous events and milestone occasions, Jackie still preferred a quiet, private life. Being around a flux of people regularly, even on a part-time basis, would take getting used to.

Tom perched on the corner of his desk while Jackie sat across from him. "You've got the office on edge, Jackie. I can't remember the last time I've seen everyone so sharply dressed and buttoned up. They're scared of you."

She smiled. "Well, I gave up biting people on the playground when I was seven. That should offer comfort."

Tom laughed. "It's going to take a bit for them to loosen up around you, and who knows how long it might take for them to get used to your wit. But let's assume they've all seen the *Hustler* pictures. You're the most famous, glamorous woman in the world and now you're one of them, reading books in their office space."

Jackie knew she had to prove herself. Hopefully her coworkers would give her a fair chance and not treat her like an exotic bird in a gilded cage.

"There's one other thing I want you to keep in mind." A more serious tic laced his tone. "Your safety. There's no telling how far someone might go to get close to you."

Somehow, Jackie kept from doubling over with laughter. Tom had no idea the antics she had endured from Ron Galella, the ever-persistent paparazzi who went to unusual lengths to capture images of her. From jumping out of bushes, to hiding in a coat check area, to attempting to date one of Jackie's maids, the man respected no limits. Although Jackie won a restraining order against him, he violated it four times.

"Security has been notified, of course," Tom continued, "and don't hate me for saying this, but I almost wish you still had a Secret Service agent."

Upon marrying Ari, Jackie had forfeited protection. Caroline's protection detail had expired when she turned sixteen, and John's would do the same.

The pesky photographer aside, Jackie had learned to accept that threats would rise up against her and her family. After Jack became president-elect in November of 1960—and after newborn John was stout enough to be released from the hospital after his early arrival—the family kept to their tradition of heading to Palm Beach for the holidays. Jackie craved rest. Recuperating from childbirth never came easy for her. But when Jack said they should attend Sunday mass as a family, especially with the press noting their every move, Jackie wasted no energy protesting. She managed to pull herself together and not look haggard. The children behaved well, and Jack was pleased.

Days later, Richard Paul Pavlick was arrested for plotting to kill Jack. With a carload of dynamite, Pavlick planned to crash into Jack's limo when he left the Kennedy estate that Sunday morning. However, when Pavlick saw Jackie and the children join Jack, he decided to wait until he caught Jack alone. His hesitation cost him. Stellar work by the Secret Service and law enforcement, who had been tipped off, led to Pavlick's apprehension before he could make good on his plan.

"Now, I don't want you to worry," Tom continued, "but we have been getting phone calls with threats. I only want you made aware. Something tells me you've had to get used to this kind of thing."

Jackie snapped from the memory and didn't bat an eye. Living in a city of millions helped ensure her privacy, but like most urban areas, crime was a constant. When John, at just thirteen years old, was robbed of his bicycle and tennis racket last year in Central Park, she considered a move but only for a fleeting moment. Manhattan was their home. "It doesn't frighten me. I've chosen to live above any fear. Otherwise, I would never leave my apartment." She sighed. "But I hate the idea of anyone else being upset or put in any danger because of me. I'll comply with whatever measures you think are wise."

"It won't come to anything extreme. As long as you feel safe, that's what I care about." Tom stood. "I still can't believe you're actually here, doing this. Punching the clock, so to speak."

A burst of glee hit Jackie. Somehow, she'd done it. Secured her own job. She just hoped the euphoria would sustain her when doubts crept in, because if she failed at learning to be an editor, she had no other recourse in mind. No other pursuits to fall back on. She knew neither Jack nor Ari would have supported her crafting a career in any fashion, and she intended to keep that in mind.

TWO

October 1975

Just as Jackie was finding a tempo in her new position, just as John was carving a rhythm at Collegiate and doing well, Jackie received a call that nearly brought her to her knees.

"Caroline's fine. We're all fine. Well...not all of us." Those words came from Hugh Fraser on the morning of the 23rd. "Gordon, my neighbor...he happened to be walking past as the car exploded. My God, if we'd gone out to the car five minutes later..."

Jackie held her breath, not wanting to imagine but unable to escape thinking how different the call could have been.

Last summer, she had agreed to let Caroline attend a year-long course by Sotheby's auction house in London. Much like her own studies abroad in Paris, Jackie viewed it as a chance for Caroline to grow into her own while staying with the Frasers, a family she knew and trusted. Hugh, a lifelong politician and father to six children, two of them near Caroline's age, and his wife, Lady Antonia, had welcomed the chance to host. Jackie had every confidence that nestled in the suburb of Campden Hill Square among friends, Caroline would be safe—until today.

"We were headed to the car, on our way to Sotheby's, but my housekeeper called me back in to the telephone. I took the call, and then I saw Gordon, walking his dogs...My Jaguar is toast. Not that I give a scrap about that, but it shows me what could've happened—" He choked out the last few words and took another moment to recover. "I suspect it's the IRA. They probably meant to target me, but I doubt that really matters."

"It's not enough that there are men with rifles out there. Now they're using bombs."

Naturally, the incident took Jackie back to the motorcade in Dallas when Jack was shot. She saw it all over again. His face. Blood everywhere.

"Should I come to London?" Jackie had spoken to Caroline, who offered repeated assurances that she was fine. Knowing her daughter's quiet nature, Jackie worried she was only parlaying what a worried mother wanted to hear.

"No, Jackie. I don't think that's a good idea right now. Caroline was a bit shaken up, but she's completely fine."

Jackie despised that her seventeen-year-old knew how to portray fine. That she'd learned and refined such a skill alongside the caskets of her slain father and uncle.

Jackie twisted the telephone cord tighter around her fingers. "At least let me call David and Pamela. Caroline should stay elsewhere for a few days."

"That would be helpful. The police will want a thorough investigation, so it might be best for her to find relief from this scene."

She suspected this was Hugh's way of letting her do something since an ocean and thousands of miles currently separated her from her daughter. If arrangements could be made with the Ormsby-Gores, it allowed her a fraction of peace.

Caroline returned to the receiver, with generous reassurances she was safe and all right before Jackie finally ended the call. Her hands trembled as she reached for her address book by the telephone. Tears blurred her vision as she flipped through the pages, trying to find David's number.

Dear God, if ever there was a prayer I needed answered more than anything, it would be that my children would be spared from tragedy.

GROWING up and being away at boarding school, Jackie became familiar with the adage that it's better to beg for forgiveness than to ask for permission. She found it useful, especially when she was sitting in the head mistress's office a time or two after masterminding pranks and getting caught. Through the years, she sharpened her craftiness and evaded capture.

Now, she found herself in a similar situation with her mother and Lee. In her mind, a just-right opportunity never presented itself for her to tell them about her job at Viking, and instead of hearing it from Jackie, they learned about it through the company's press releases and a mention on the evening news.

When her mother called to rant and scold her, Jackie diffused her anger by inviting her to New York for a holiday shopping excursion. Her treat. Janet accepted.

Lee, on the other hand, said nothing.

But Jackie heard, through Tom, that her sister had been furious.

"We were seated next to each other at a party the other night, and she had daggers for me the moment she sat," he told her. "I asked her what was wrong, and she snapped at me. Told me she shouldn't even be speaking to me since I hadn't bothered to phone and tell her I'd hired you. I was completely shocked, because it didn't cross my mind that you didn't mention it to her—and how was I supposed to know that? I think she wanted to slap me."

Jackie apologized for putting Tom in such a predicament.

But she had no idea how to approach Lee on the matter. Once again, Jackie was in the position of having upset and offended her sister. Putting forth an apology and making it up to Lee was on her shoulders, but Jackie almost didn't care. Why was placating and soothing Lee her responsibility? Wasn't it clear to Lee that their sisterhood was fractured? That they were no longer sharing the details of their lives like they used to? Lee's response was to lash out at Tom, their mutual friend who would report back to Jackie. Where was Lee's concern—her heartache—over the chasm growing between them? Did Lee find more satisfaction nursing her wounded pride and embarrassing Jackie? And yet the brunt of blame fell squarely on Jackie?

There were days she was certain Lee would never change, and their relationship was beyond saving. Just as there were days when she didn't even flinch from the notion.

December 1975

HAD Jackie been a younger version of herself, with her identity saturated in her husband, current revelations would've badgered her and struck her down with a migraine and a desire for copious amounts of vodka. However, she had shed the skin of the woman who retreated to her bed and neglected commitments and entertaining because she thought Jack's infidelities reflected on her.

But the latest allegations were shocking and salacious enough to rattle her resolve.

A month prior, *The Washington Post* reported that Evelyn Lincoln's logbook documented seventy calls from Judith Campbell Exner to Jack in the Oval Office over an eleven-month period. Jackie knew about Jack's romps with Judith and held a particular distaste for the woman after she found a pair of Judith's panties—yellow satin underwear with white ruffles—in her bed.

But the article—and the logbook—substantiated the affair. Making matters worse was the well-known fact that Judith had also been involved with Sam Giancana, former Chicago mob boss, during the same time period she was slipping into the White House to see Jack. Wire taps, released by the CIA, revealed that Judith had made calls to the White House from Sam's home in Oak Park, Illinois. Further conjecture suggested Giancana had swayed the city's voting results in 1960, and that Judith played messenger-courier between the men.

In response to the article, Judith gave a press conference in San Diego. She confirmed having a "relationship of a close personal nature" with Jack, whom she met in 1960 while she was in Las Vegas with "a mutual friend." No one had difficulty concluding the friend was Frank Sinatra since he was connected to both men and formerly owned the infamous Cal-Nev Lodge & Casino where mobsters were known to frequent.

Shortly after the news broke, and Jackie's phone at Viking had to be taken off the hook several times a day, Teddy reached out to her. Concerned, he said, over the coverage, he urged Jackie to bring the children and join him and other Kennedy members at the Snowbird Resort in Utah for a getaway.

Jackie hesitated at first. Running to the Kennedys was no longer her style. Over the years, especially after the loss of Bobby, she had done the subtle yet undeniable work of keeping a disciplined distance. But being cloistered with Kennedys would provide a temporary refuge from the press's onslaught, especially for the children.

After arriving at the snowcapped resort, Jackie spent the day on the slopes, appearing content and enjoying her children as photographers, kept at bay, snapped away. She appreciated that Ethel, Jean, Stephen, Joan, and the rest of the family treated her pleasantly, as they always did, and made no mention of the upheaval.

That night after dinner, Jackie popped into Teddy's suite. Joan was already asleep. Eased back in a recliner with a drink in one hand and the *Post* in the other, Teddy read the article aloud. Much to Jackie's discomfort.

He then tossed the paper aside and took a hearty drink from his glass of Scotch. "They're just going to keep coming."

Jackie had endured years of tabloid reports about Jack's philandering, but this was different. The logbook provided evidence and had been made public. If a Senate committee formed, an investigation was launched, and a hearing took place, Secret Service agents from the Kennedy detail would be required to provide sworn testimony. Details, essentially, about how they enabled the president to conduct the affair. Jackie's head swam with possibilities as she inhaled her cigarette with fierce desperation.

"At that press conference Judith said she'd been contracted to write a book." Teddy pointed his finger. "We'll have to see what we can do legally to stop that."

Jackie nodded but recalled how their efforts against *The Death of a President* proved fruitless. Though she later regretted the storm she created over William Manchester's well-written, accurate tome, that wouldn't be the case with anything Judith penned.

"It's all about money for her, I'm sure."

And notoriety. The mistress that destroyed Camelot.

"You know she'll share intimate details about sleeping with Jack. Same with Sam. And it won't matter, what's true or not." Teddy set his empty glass on his chest and leaned his head back.

As he closed his eyes, a flare of hatred scorched Jackie. With his father and brothers in their graves, Teddy had become the family patriarch by default. As far as Jackie was concerned, he was the weakest of the Kennedy men in character, leadership, and charisma. She would never say it, but she suspected Teddy enjoyed watching Jack's legacy become tarnished. That it made him look better, the more secrets that came forth, as if it lessened the taint of his own egregious mistakes. The true consequences of which never seemed to catch up with him.

Simmering over circumstances she couldn't change didn't help her now.

Neither did the dread that seeped over her when she thought of all the books in the last eleven years that had found their way to publication. Each offered insights into Jack's flaws, his health, and his genius. Jackie counted each of them as a betrayal, from Maud Shaw, the children's former nanny to the most recent from Ben Bradlee, once a dear friend but now the executive editor of *The Washington Post*.

Jackie's stalwart intent to craft and protect Jack's image for history had become ashes.

"Yes, there's no stopping the things people will say. No accountability for what's written, and no respect given to Jack's memory." Hopeless resignation never sat well with Jackie.

Teddy opened his eyes. "If you're agreeable to the idea, we'll let Dave handle all public commentary on the family's behalf. We'll shore up his talking points. Maybe we can swing some of the publicity in our favor, use it to gain attention for the library."

Jackie nodded, thinking of Dave Powers, the former Special Assistant to Jack, and one of the devotees who helped Jack campaign for the seat in the Eleventh Congressional District in 1946. He now served as museum curator for the library. An ideal role for him since he had been by Jack's side for most of his career, keeping secrets safe. Dave also took to the role of Kennedy family spokesperson as needed. When it came to Judith he mildly stated, "The name doesn't ring a bell."

Perhaps it was a gift Jackie should've admired more, Teddy's ability to distract and turn attention to matters that served him. She thought it was a tired, foolish tactic but could offer no better alternative.

"Dave has a way about him." Detachment laced Jackie's words. She knew Dave was also responsible for ushering various women into the White House for Jack. Not that it mattered now.

Of all the Kennedy men, Teddy, arguably, had proven to be the most scandalous. Primarily for having escaped any legal and moral responsibility for the death of Mary Jo Kopechne.

In 1968, Mary Jo had been an integral part of Bobby Kennedy's campaign team. Smart and a devout Catholic, she worked tirelessly as one of the Boiler Room Girls, a nickname given to the secretaries who became accustomed to working late hours in a cramped, hot, windowless office space. One of her main contributions had been in helping draft Bobby's speech announcing his bid to run for the presidency.

When Bobby was assassinated in June 1968, Mary Jo, like so many, was shattered. Although she briefly considered leaving politics, she stayed true to her passion.

On July 18, 1969, a reunion party was held in honor of the Boiler Room Girls on Chappaquiddick Island, off the coast of Martha's Vineyard. Mary Jo and her former co-workers enjoyed a carefree night. Talk naturally drifted to the topic of Teddy one day running for president. Teddy, who was also in attendance, made no promises but commended everyone for their hard work and dedication to his brother.

Later that night, Teddy offered to give Mary Jo a ride so she could catch the last ferry of the night, and get back to Edgartown, where she was staying. During the drive, Teddy, probably inebriated from the party, drove his Oldsmobile off a narrow, unlit bridge. The car sailed into Poucha Pond and flipped onto its roof. Teddy managed to get out of the car but left Mary Jo inside.

Since Teddy failed to go for help immediately, she eventually drowned.

Authorities, the press, family members—everyone—was baffled when they learned Teddy didn't report the accident until the next day.

A week later, Teddy pleaded guilty to leaving the scene of an accident and had his driver's license suspended for two months. The Kopechnes buried their only child and claimed Teddy never apologized to them for his involvement in their daughter's death.

The Chappaquiddick incident had tainted Jackie's view of Teddy. She never let on, because she loved the man, but the full, blind trust she put in him was cracked and mauled.

Seemingly learning nothing—and impervious to dedicating

himself to true servitude or redemption—the father-uncle of Bobby's children imposed no rules on the brood at the Kennedy Compound at Hyannis. The younger generation had embraced the lifestyle of rich party kids, which was one of the reasons Jackie had kept Caroline and John from their cousins and their influence as much as possible.

Further eroding her respect for Teddy was his treatment of Joan. He cared little for hiding his dalliances with other women and portrayed a callous attitude toward her struggles with alcohol. Two years ago, when she was arrested and had her license suspended for drunk driving, he'd treated her with disgust and had her committed to McLean Hospital in Belmont, Massachusetts, to address her alcohol addiction.

Excusing his behavior in the past had been characteristic of Jackie and other Kennedy wives. Jackie held him accountable but only in her mind. She couldn't disconnect herself permanently from him, and to a degree, he deserved a place in Caroline's and John's lives. Even if it was primarily a role of title rather than function.

Jackie, tired of the deluge of bad memories, finished off her cigarette and decided to change the subject with Teddy. If he was still awake.

"Since you mentioned the library, you should know we're in a predicament," she sighed, but not so Teddy would hear. "Funds are dwindling, and we haven't resolved the matter of the site."

He turned his head toward her. "Harvard still won't budge?"

"They're standing by their refusal to host the site because they don't want the campus disturbed by a tourist attraction."

Teddy nodded. "I can understand that."

"It leaves us with the harrowing task of finding enough land in the area for the build. If we have to purchase land...well, I don't have to tell you how disastrous that could be for us financially."

His eyelids began to flutter as he nodded faintly. An instant later his eyes were closed. His chin dipped toward his chest. It was possible the Scotch and the warm fire had lulled him to sleep, but Jackie was inclined to blame his all-day drinking at the lodge.

"Teddy?" Her tone was firm but without frustration.

He lifted his head and his eyebrows jumped, slitting his eyes open. "I'll—I'll make a call when we get back." His hazy state took over, and he seemed helpless against it.

Jackie wouldn't fight him. In truth, she doubted Teddy could wield the kind of sway she needed, and she already suspected that constructing a shrine to Jack meant little to him.

The insufficient amount of money bothered her most. But just like she'd already done, she'd find a way. Second only to raising their children, overseeing the design, construction, and opening of the library would be her greatest gift to Jack. Infidelities or not, family support or not, she would do whatever was necessary to see the project through.

THREE

February 1976

A dinner cruise in February?

Jackie nearly cackled when she received Lee's invitation for a party aboard a chartered yacht on the Hudson River. Days later, when Lee called to ensure she was coming, Jackie expected a haughty attitude, having spoken little since Jackie started working, but her sister surprised her. When Jackie accepted, Lee asked her to bring their mother while refusing to divulge too many details regarding the occasion.

"Dress as you would for any party, Jacks," was all Lee gave her over the telephone. "We're celebrating, and I want to make it an unforgettable night."

Jackie didn't stir up a fuss about serving as her mother's chaperone. Perhaps it would be best anyway. She could make sure Janet traveled safely since Hughdie, who no longer ventured out much and especially not at night in the cold, wouldn't be accompanying her. Looking after Janet would also safeguard her against any potential bouts of confusion that might arise.

When Jackie boarded the gleaming ship, with her mother by her side, she soon realized few guests were there. She saw Liz Smith but planned to avoid the gossip columnist. Lee's hairdresser and a few uptown-looking matrons—going by their heavy make-up and full-length mink and sable coats—were there, along with other people Jackie didn't know or recognize.

When Jackie noticed Truman Capote boarding, anger blazed within her. In November, *Esquire* magazine had published his article, "La Côte Basque 1965," which offered a preview of his yet to be finished and yet to be published book, *Answered Prayers*. Previously unknown to Jackie and "the Swans"—Truman's nickname for the rich, beautiful socialites he constantly mingled, dined, and partied with—his latest work was a collection of revelations aimed at exposing various secrets the Swans had shared with him over the years.

Lee, seemingly his favorite among the Swans, was mentioned by name in the article and not referenced by a phony code name like the others had been. Truman also didn't expose any of Lee's secrets or disparage her the way he had Babe Paley, wife of CBS executive Bill Paley. Among others.

However, Truman wrote a searing observation about Jackie, claiming she was little more than a drag queen persona.

Par for the course when it came to Truman. Gossip served as his primary currency among his famous friends, and when Jackie was a young wife learning the political and social ropes in Georgetown years ago, she assumed that she deserved immunity against his silver tongue. A mistake she didn't make twice.

Though she cut off communication with him, Truman went on to forge a deep, almost inseparable friendship with Lee and became an instrumental catalyst in her efforts to launch an acting career. Her off-Broadway play and TV movie failed miserably, despite his financial support and endless public praise about Lee's talents.

Seeing him now explained Lee's evasiveness.

Truman trip-stumbled onto the yacht, causing Jackie to suspect he was already intoxicated. With that in mind, she pictured how easy it might be to nudge him over the ship's railing and into the frigid waters. A grin ticked the corner of her mouth at the thought, until she wondered if Lee had invited him intentionally to bristle her. If that were so, Jackie knew better than to let her irritation show.

Catching an aside moment with Lee, Jackie whispered, "What's he doing here?"

Lee glanced over at Truman, who was at the bar worsening his inebriated state with a martini. "I thought I might get a last gasp of use out of the old worm. He's certainly no good for anything else these days."

"Use? For what?"

Lee shook her head. "No getting ahead of ourselves, Jacks. That wouldn't be fair to the other party goers."

Considering the time and the scant amount of guests who were present, Jackie couldn't help asking, "Did the others discover Truman was coming? Is that why they're not here?"

"Snarky as ever, I see." Lee paired her words with a smile. "Oh, have you met Peter Tufo? I'll introduce you."

Lee ushered her to Peter's side and made introductions.

"He's a partner in a wildly successful firm here in New York, and last year, he was appointed Chairman of the Board of Corrections by the mayor. You may have seen his name in the paper, because he played a vital role in ending the prison riot on Rikers Island back in November. A hero to the city."

"She likes to brag." Peter said as if it were an inside joke between him and Jackie. "I will say I've heard a great deal of bragging about you. Lee's had nothing but exceptional things to say about you."

Whether he was being truthful or had been encourage by Lee to pour on compliments, Jackie liked the man. Even when he kissed the top of her hand. He cut a fine, trim figure in his sharply tailored suit. Though he matched Jackie in height, he was strikingly handsome with dark hair and cheekbones most women would kill for. Jackie immediately suspected he and Lee were dating.

"Excuse me." Lee continued to make her rounds.

For a change, Jackie didn't mind being left with a stranger. She and Peter engaged in pleasant small talk. Then right before Jackie felt brazen enough to ask how *close* he and Lee were, Janet joined them.

"Peter, how wonderful to see you," she said.

He matched her enthusiasm and pecked her cheek.

As Jackie watched, Lee welcomed each of her guests and made sure all had a flute of champagne. Then she helped herself to the middle of the room. Peter tapped on the side of his glass to call everyone to attention. Jackie figured a throat-clearing would have sufficed.

"I've invited you all here for a very special reason," Lee began. "Instead of running a story in the newspaper, I wanted to tell you in person that I'm officially launching my very own interior design business."

A happy gasp escaped Janet, and Jackie wondered if the whole set up was meant as a barb at her for not making a similar to-do when she secured her position at Viking. Not that it was worth getting riled over.

"Peter and several others have helped me work through the jungle of legal red tape, and I'm proud to announce that I've already started work on the prestigious project of designing suites for the Americana Hotel. I'll be designing rooms at several of their locations. One in Bal Harbour, Florida, one at their resort in Acapulco, and another at their Palm Springs location." She put a hand to her cheek. "Heavens, what have I gotten myself into?"

The crowd responded with a courtesy laugh.

"First though, I'm going to cut my teeth, so to speak, by doing a room at Lord and Taylor's Manhattan store. They've invited me to participate in their Celebrity Decorated Rooms for Summer campaign—"

Janet clapped, seemingly unaware of having interrupted her daughter. "Cheers to you, Lee! How wonderful! I always knew you would become a wonderful success."

"Yes, congratulations, Pekes." Jackie, in an awkward attempt to cover for her mother, held up her glass of champagne.

"Well, I for one am not entirely surprised." Truman slurred the last word. "It's not enough anymore for a woman to just be. She has to be attached to something these days, whether there's real value in it or not."

"There's undeniable value in all the money she's going to make." Peter pointed out.

"My Lee has always had extraordinary talents. Extraordinary!" Janet, her hand on her chest, took a deep breath.

"You're going to be a sensation, Lee, and in no time at all," Jackie added, deciding to smother Truman's negativity with praise for Lee. "I remember the time you decorated Yusha's apartment. It was so stylish, wasn't it, Mummy?"

Janet scowled. "What? I don't recall Lee ever furbishing Yusha's apartment."

"It was years ago but was a fantastic test-run," Lee said.

"No, no, no." Janet shook her head. "You're both mistaken. Oh, I gather that's what happens when you spend too much time nipping on champagne."

Silence invaded and hung until Truman erupted with obnoxious laughter.

Jackie caught Lee's fiery stare, one that demanded she salvage the situation.

"Well, as it just so happens, I have news to share as well."

Truman's boisterousness subsided and all eyes focused on Jackie.

"I'm going to Russia. It's research for an exciting book I'm a part of. I'll be traveling with Thomas Hoving from the Met and Diana Vreeland."

"Really?" Lee didn't hide her surprise.

Jackie nodded. "It seems impossible, I know, and it's such an undertaking since I'm still so new to publishing. Yet here I am, preparing to launch into this project with Diana, who was your first boss all those years ago—"

"Oh, I'll never forget my time with Diana. She had such an impact on my sensibilities and helped to broaden my horizons when it came to fashion. Jackie, at some point, you must tell us more about this. For now, let's move into the dining room. Dinner will be served shortly, and I can share what I have in mind for the commissions I'll be working on."

Jackie kept her grin in place. She should've known Lee wouldn't appreciate her effort to rescue them from Janet's embarrassing outburst. Shifting the focus onto herself had also been a cardinal sin, according to Lee Radziwill party etiquette. Lee was allowed to slight Jackie or any of her party guests, but such behavior from others wasn't tolerated.

Jackie let it go, the way she always did. Next time, she'd leave it up to Lee to handle Janet's ramblings or Truman's drunken tirade and see how *that* played out for her.

June 1976

WHEN JACKIE HUNG up the telephone, she sank into the chair beside the nook, certain she would faint from the news. Stas was dead. Her beloved brother-in-law had succumbed to a heart attack before retiring to bed and was found on the hallway floor the next morning. He'd been staying with friends in Essex since those who were closest to him knew he hadn't been well in recent months.

Since his divorce from Lee in 1974, Jackie had seen little of Stas. He kept to London but made a point to dine with Jackie at the Ritz whenever she traveled across the pond. Stas had custody of his son Anthony, who attended the prestigious Millfield School. By all appearances, he had moved on from his relationship with Lee and of late was seeing Christine Weckert, a pretty but shy brunette who was markedly younger than Stas.

With Lee in a state of shock, Jackie took care of making travel arrangements. Stas's funeral, held in St. Anne's Church, the very building Stas had commissioned for his mother and other family members' burial at Fawley Court in England, drew a sizable crowd. Lee was asked to light the candle intended to burn for the night, a sentiment to acknowledge his Polish heritage.

After the service, Lee wanted to slip back into the church and sit a while longer with Stas's coffin. Jackie understood and said she would meet her back at the hotel, but Lee reached for Jackie's hand.

"Stay with me. Please."

Jackie nodded. She turned to Caroline and told her to stick with John and her cousins, then walked back inside with Lee. The honey-spice aroma of the chrysanthemum bouquets gave a pleasant tone to the atmosphere. Jackie thought Stas would have been pleased with the service and honored that his casket was draped in the Radziwill family flag, which was on loan from a museum in Warsaw. Various friends and family members had shared touching recollections and flattering stories during the service, making the ache of losing Stas acutely worse for Jackie. She could only imagine Lee's heartbreak.

Together, they sat in the first pew.

Tender silence followed, and Jackie reflected on one of her favorite memories with Stas—the fifty-mile walk.

In February of 1963, Stas and Chuck Spaulding, one of Jack's long-time advisors, decided to take up the challenge Jack had proposed. Concerned that too many Americans were getting soft in the middle and out of shape, he encouraged everyone around the country to participate in a fifty-mile walk. After a month of preparation, Stas and Chuck were ready.

They selected the Sunshine Highway, a newly constructed roadway that stretched from Miami to Fort Pierce that wasn't opened to traffic yet and began walking at midnight. Twenty hours later, unable to best Bobby Kennedy's time of seventeen hours, they completed the trek—with blisters and body aches to show for it. Jackie, Lee, and Jack had checked on them periodically, then celebrated afterward with a round of champagne.

"You think I made a mistake, don't you?" Lee swallowed hard and didn't look at Jackie. "That I never should've left Stas for Peter."

Jackie didn't want to have this conversation. Not now, and not with Stas's casket before them.

But she knew lashing out was easier for Lee than simply weeping and wailing. Lee deserved to vent her feelings. She was angry—they both were—about losing a man they loved. Jackie wasn't going to fall into a useless argument though.

When Lee had begun her affair with Peter in 1972, Jackie aired her disapproval. Saving her marriage to Stas would be a better use of her energies, she'd said. But Lee fed her passions for the adventurous wildlife photographer, who was several years younger than her. In some ways, Jackie couldn't blame her. Artistic, devastatingly handsome, and one to live by his own rules, Peter had charms that were hard to resist. Had he made advances at her, Jackie believed she would have caved to temptation.

"Everyone has regrets, Lee," she said softly. "Don't torture yourself now. It won't do you any good, and it won't bring back Stas."

Back then, Lee gave up everything to be with Peter. Her marriage, fabulous homes, and custody of her son Anthony, to a degree, and in exchange lived with Peter in a beachside cottage in Montauk, New York. She constantly claimed she had never been happier or more in-tune with her curiosities. Whether Lee and Peter ever spoke about marriage, Jackie didn't know, but a year after her divorce from Stas was finalized, Lee ended their affair after she caught Peter in bed with a twentysomething model.

Lee wept quietly beside her now, and Jackie knew how much she needed the release, having upheld a stoic veneer since they left New York. Honestly, she wasn't sure if Lee had the strength for the reception. Perhaps sitting in the church also served as a delay tactic. If so, Jackie couldn't blame her. She wouldn't rush her.

Stas's candle sputtered and flickered, and Jackie liked to think he was with them.

When Lee finally tucked her handkerchief back into her purse, streaked with make-up and damp from tears, she pinched the clasp closed and sighed.

Jackie waited a moment before she spoke. "Stas never stopped loving you, Pekes. No matter what happened between you, I know he loved you."

"Do you really think so?" Her voice was little more than a whisper. "I...I've made so many missteps..."

Jackie gripped her hand. "We all have, Lee. We all have."

NINE MONTHS INTO HER POSITION, Jackie had earned a small office. Nancy had also landed an administrative position at Viking, complete with her own office nearby. She still culled and took care of correspondence that came in for the former First Lady and kept up with her new duties as well. Naturally, the arrangement pleased Jackie.

"These arrived first thing this morning." Nancy held out a packet as she swept into Jackie's office.

Jackie took the envelope and opened it. Pride swelled in her at the discovery of a stack of pictures. She shuffled through the images of John and his cousin, Timothy, serving with the Peace Corps in Rabinal, Guatemala. The region had been struck by an earthquake, and John was part of the team dispatched to aid with rebuilding efforts and food distribution.

"No longer little John-John, is he?" Nancy peeped the snapshots over Jackie's shoulder.

Jackie pursed her lips. "I always hated that name. It was such a sham too. Jack never called him that, but one reporter misinterpreted what he overheard, and John got branded with that horrible nickname. There's no undoing it. Reporters should be held to a higher accountability though."

Nancy snickered. "Some people would say the same about certain politicians."

Whether Nancy's jab was aimed at Jack, due to the avalanche of revelations about his unfaithfulness, or at Teddy for the death of Mary Jo Kopechne, Jackie didn't know. She ignored Nancy's stare and decided not to engage on the subject.

But the thought ratcheted the regular unease Jackie dealt with, enhanced back in March when the *National Enquirer* had released a story about Mary Pinchot Meyer. According to her friends, who were the sources for the article, Mary had enjoyed an on-going affair with Jack from the time he became president. She also told her so-called friends that Jack smoked pot with her during their trysts in her Georgetown home. A former CIA agent confirmed the on-going, two-year affair by acknowledging that Mary's phone had been tapped. When she visited the White House, she was recognized as a friend of the family, being the sister-in-law of Ben Bradlee, a savvy, respected journalist who had been friends with Jack since the 1950's. Mary even accompanied the gathering of friends and family aboard the presidential yacht, *Sequoia*, for Jack's forty-sixth, and last, birthday celebration.

Incidentally, in the fall of 1964, Mary was shot and killed while walking a towpath near her home. The crime, still unsolved, served as another log on the fire when it came to the inferno of burning conspiracy theories surrounding Jack.

Jackie *despised* when salacious accounts from personal, close acquaintances made front page *news*.

Even so, she wouldn't let the thought make her cross with Nancy or sour her mood.

Her focus returned to a picture of John. Dirt smeared the side of his face. Thick, unruly curls shaded his eyes. She would always do everything she could to protect him, but when it came to the press, she held no power. The best she could do was teach and remind him how best to deal with the public's insatiable interest in him, and the media's determination to deliver.

But she couldn't escape wondering if her love and support would be enough to keep him from turning out like his father—or worse, like his uncle Teddy. He was nearing the age when girls would pique his interest, and she felt woefully unprepared when it came to discussing sex with her teenage son. How did a mother teach her son to balance and control his sexual urges while treating young ladies with the utmost respect?

Not only that, but John needed to guard himself against women with less than honorable intentions. Jackie didn't want him used for a story or—God forbid—a baby he wasn't ready for.

Yet, he was only fifteen. Jackie knew she was jumping ahead—far ahead—but was she? John cared about others and wasn't flippant when it came to people's feelings. Qualities that came from the Kennedy women—Eunice in particular, who not only believed in compassion but also demonstrated it with her involvement in the Special Olympics.

"You're such a worry wart."

Nancy's remark broke Jackie from her trance of imagination tinged with concentration.

"It shows on your face, but only when it comes to John. You must hide it better or simply have less worries with Caroline." She leaned over and tapped the picture of John in Jackie's hand. "You've seen it for yourself. He's fine, Mum."

He's fine. For now. But how would that change as he grew into a man?

JACKIE COULDN'T HAVE BEEN MORE surprised when Lee readily agreed to her suggestion of having Stas's will reviewed by her advisors. Part of her expected push-back from Lee, even though her sister was not fond of juggling and tallying numbers. On the other hand, Jackie was relieved. Lee would be in good hands, and the fact she acquiesced gave Jackie a glimmer of hope about the strengthening of their relationship.

She set up the meeting at Alexander Forger's office. Having

served as one of Jackie's attorneys for years, Forger welcomed the chance to comb through the legal details. Also in attendance were André Meyer and Maurice Tempelsman, one of Jackie's newer advisors. Peter Tufo accompanied Lee.

Once introductions were complete and cigarettes lit, Jackie, Lee, and the men took their seats as coffees were poured and served.

"Lee, how familiar were you with your husband's business dealings?" Alexander began.

"Since our divorce I would say not at all."

"I was afraid as much. You see, and this may come as a surprise to you, Stas was nearly broke. I see from his financial records that you received a settlement and a monthly allowance. That there's a trust fund for your children's education, but it's in danger of being depleted. The bulk of his earnings went to keeping his company afloat, and quite honestly, that endeavor was nearing doom."

Lee seemed to shrink in the leather chair.

"But Anthony is set to move back here and continue his studies at Choate in Connecticut." She looked at Jackie. Desperation filled her eyes. "What will I do if he can't attend? Oh, what will I tell him?"

Jackie placed her hand on top of Lee's. "Don't worry, Pekes. We'll see to it that everything's taken care of."

"Yes, I apologize, Ms. Radziwill," Alexander continued, "I don't mean to distress you. My objective is to give you a straightforward, albeit stark, lay of the land up front. We'll work our way through with the aim of making sure your needs are addressed."

Lee nodded weakly, her disbelief and anxiety apparent as her chin dipped.

Jackie could guess what she was thinking. *What about me? Will I be left destitute?* Nerves struck her because she felt an immediate responsibility to take care of her younger sister while at the same time fearing that supporting Lee might be the equivalent of filling a bag with holes in it.

Alexander went on to cover a lengthy list of costs and expenditures, which meant little to Jackie and Lee, then he read the will.

Personal items were bequeathed to Stas's children, including John, his oldest son from his first marriage, but the majority of his estate would be split between Anthony and Tina. Or at least what remained after debts were settled. Money for Lee would also be on the table, if anything was left—a stipulation that affirmed what Jackie already knew, Stas still loved Lee.

After the proceedings, everyone stood and exchanged handshakes all around. If Jackie were pressed to describe the mood, she would say it was somber yet hopeful, but she didn't know if Lee would agree.

Maurice approached Jackie and Lee.

"Please allow me to extend my sympathies to you and your children, Ms. Radziwill." His Belgian accent tinged his words as he took Lee's hand. "I know today has been difficult, but don't lose heart. I'm sure we will work hard to rectify the situation and will see to it that your financial needs are met."

Lee nodded. "I thank you kindly, sir. Despite today's circumstances, it has been a pleasure to meet you."

"I echo the sentiment." He looked to Jackie. "May I invite you both to dine with me this evening?"

Pettiness flared in Jackie. She didn't want Maurice to like Lee more than her, though she couldn't say why. His refined manners dazzled her, and in some ways, she wanted him to reserve all his charms for her, even though he was a married man.

"You two should go," Lee said. "Forgive me, please, for not joining. I'm sure you can understand."

"Of course." Maurice squeezed her hand before releasing it. "Another time then."

Lee nodded and Peter stepped to her side. She looked at Jackie, "We'll wait for you in the lobby."

After Lee and Peter departed, Maurice looked at Jackie. "Quite a strong lady."

Jackie quickly considered Lee's difficulties. Two divorces. Falling out with various friends and socialites. Lovers who came and went.

Being separated from Anthony while he attended school in London. Through it all, Lee took the hits and managed to go on.

"She can be resilient." Jackie suppressed the temptation to point out that some of Lee's misfortunes were her own doing.

"Would it be all right if we dined together tonight? There are a few matters I would like to review with you, because I have exceptional news about your investments and tax shelters." He glanced at Lee as she waved her final goodbyes. "It may not be for me to say, but if you had any intention of looking after your sister financially, at least while she gets past this hump, I can assure you that you're in a position to do so."

"Oh?" She suddenly prickled with delight. The idea of her wealth increasing gave her a sense of power, a feeling she wanted to become accustomed to.

Maurice nodded. "It might sound crazy but, just as I anticipated, the price of gold has soared. The money invested on your behalf has grown exponentially. You're poised to become a very wealthy woman, Jackie. A couple years from now, that inheritance from Aristotle will seem like a drop in the bucket. Not to mention, the funds we put into those three supermarkets, it's going to function as a tax shelter, a loss, if you will, for several years to come, which will help safeguard your bottom line."

Whatever Maurice may have lacked, in the traditional sense, of being handsome or suave, he made up for with his business savvy and slightly mysterious ways. Though he was pudgy around the middle—what man wasn't at forty-seven—balding, and had the beginnings of sagging jowls, Jackie wasn't repulsed by him. An interesting man intrigued her more than a handsome man. Not that it mattered since they weren't dating or involved.

Much like André Meyer and Alexander Forger, Maurice had mingled in Jackie's world for decades. He and his wife attended functions at the White House during her tenure as First Lady. Jackie couldn't recall the exact details about how Maurice slipped into that inner circle of acquaintances, but believed it had to do with his political persuasions and the business connections he cultivated in Africa as a diamond merchant. Someday she would ask him about it. In the meantime, she appreciated his astute financial knowledge and the comfort of familiarity his presence brought.

Maurice didn't invite André or Alexander to join them. A detail that likely meant nothing, she decided, but having Maurice to herself for an evening gave her a touch of delight.

FOUR

July 1976

Arrangements for Jackie's trip to Russia involved more details and compromises than she was accustomed to. For one thing, her lady-in-waiting, Provi, who'd been part of her personal staff for decades, was not permitted to travel with her. And when she reviewed the itinerary, Jackie marveled at the planned efficiency but kept concerns to herself. As much as she was at odds with her celebrity, she couldn't deny the privileges it afforded for international travels.

However, this would be a business trip, not a goodwill excursion. She was going as an aside. Practically as a peon, still learning the publishing industry. Thomas Hoving, the director of the Metropolitan of the Arts had cultivated a slow but steady working relationship with the curators at the Hermitage Museum in Leningrad over the last several years. In recent months, Hoving had convinced the executives to loan various historical costumes for a traveling exhibit in the United States.

Above all, Jackie had Diana Vreeland to thank for the opportunity. In the world of fashion, DV, as she was sometimes known, was considered a goddess. Her career as an editor, for both *Harper's Bazaar* and *Vogue*, spanned decades, and she had been instrumental in connecting Jackie to Oleg Cassini, who became her courtier during her White House years. More recently, Diana had become Jackie's mentor, helping her navigate and mix the modern-day world of news, culture, and fashion. Many revered DV, so when she suggested to Jackie that they should work together to create a coffee table-style book to serve as a companion piece to the exhibit, executives at Doubleday were easily persuaded when Jackie made the pitch.

She couldn't have been more thrilled with the project—and the chance to visit Russia, even if she wouldn't be fawned over, meet heads of state, or be lavished with gifts.

When she, Diana, and Thomas spent the day at the Hermitage, Jackie felt as though she had stepped into a fairy tale. Seeing and touching the garments worn by Peter the Great and the long line of tsars through the ages humbled her. Immersing herself in the history and evolution of military dress, coronation looks, boots, headpieces, jewelry, and medallions, transported her to battlefields, bitterly cold winters, and grand balls of long ago.

Jackie credited her enthusiasm for winning favor with the museum's director. With care, he draped a red shawl from the 1820s around her, then watched her eyes alight as he shared how such a piece, comprised of fleece from Tibetan goats and Saiga antelopes, was constructed by serfs for ladies of the aristocracy, took three years to craft, and might cost a hundred thousand gold rubles.

Soon after her return from Russia, Jackie and the children flew to Round Hill, Jamaica, with Tom Guinzburg and his children, which they had done sporadically throughout the years. Not only did it allow a relaxing getaway, but the vacation also gave Jackie the chance to thoroughly share about her experience in Russia.

When she returned to New York, it came as no surprise when she saw photos of her and Tom on a tabloid cover with the headline,

"Jackie Dates Her Boss!" It was a rare occasion where faulty gossip gave her a good laugh.

July 1976

BITTERNESS ROSE WITHIN HER, but Jackie bottled every ounce of resentment and stashed it deep inside her heart when she attended the Democratic Convention. She had no love for political conventions, primarily because they reminded her of Jack and one of the worst tragedies of her life.

Back in the dreadfully hot summer of 1956, she'd accompanied Jack to the Democratic Convention in Chicago. He swayed her into going, claiming that delegates wouldn't be able to resist a young, forward-thinking congressman and his pregnant wife. Pressure from fellow Kennedy wives, Ethel in particular, surrounded her. Jackie went, despite her doctor's advice that the summer heat and the stamina needed for such an event would prove too much for her fragile condition.

Jack ended up losing the vice-presidential nomination vote to Senator Estes Kefauver of Tennessee and didn't become Adlai Stevenson's running mate.

After they returned from the convention, Jack, moody as ever and sulky, decided to stick to his annual getaway and left Jackie, eight months pregnant, for the French Riviera with his parents and Teddy.

Jackie retreated to Hammersmith Farm. Exhaustion steamrolled her, as did a looming sense of doom. The onset of premature labor in the middle of the night meant being rushed to the hospital. An emergency caesarean was performed, and Jackie's precious baby, Arabella, was stillborn.

Jack, sailing somewhere on the Mediterranean, couldn't be reached for days. By the time Bobby Kennedy got a hold of his brother, Arabella had been buried—under a nameless marker since she wasn't baptized—while Jackie began her slow recovery, having almost died from blood loss.

Although Jack's win of the presidential nomination in 1960 brought a happier association, she could never forget Arabella. She attended a luncheon during the 1964 convention but did not make an appearance inside Boardwalk Hall, the main hub of the event. In 1968 and in 1972 she stayed away altogether.

Now, for the current convention, no Kennedys were on the ticket. Sargent Shriver, Eunice's husband, made a short-lived presidential bid but dropped out of the race early in the primaries. For Sarge, as the family called him, it marked his second defeat in the political ring. Back in 1972, he replaced Senator Thomas Eagleton, who withdrew nineteen days after the convention, when it came to light that the senator had undergone treatments for his mental health, including electroshock therapy.

Jackie liked Sarge. Always had, but he didn't exude the same charisma as Jack or Bobby. Or even Teddy. She knew Sarge was honest, upright, and—possibly because he wasn't a *true* Kennedy—didn't have to answer for a litany of scandals.

Tonight, her appearance at the convention had a purpose. She had entered the hall with Eugene Kennedy, who was a former priest, journalist, and professor at Loyola University in Chicago—and no relation to the Kennedy family. Jackie, and a fellow editor, had recruited Eugene to write a biography about Richard J. Daley, Chicago's mayor since 1955. Having such a lengthy career, he was a political powerhouse and was once well-connected to Joe Kennedy. Naturally, he and Jackie were acquaintances.

When Jackie entered the hall on Eugene's arm, and took her seat in a reserved box, the crowd erupted with cheers and applause. Knowing that she was practically putting herself on the center stage, she had invited Lee to sit with her, thinking the gesture would be well received and a healthy move for their relationship since they struggled to find common ground. Ecstatic, Lee accepted and asked if Peter and Anthony might accompany her, which Jackie agreed to.

Hugh Fraser also joined their party. Having recently been left by his wife, Jackie hoped the evening at least provided a distraction for him.

Later that night, after speeches and delegates began to wind down, Jackie and Eugene were escorted to a private area in the underbelly of Madison Square Garden. Richard Daley awaited and greeted Jackie and Eugene warmly. She wasted no time in telling the mayor that Eugene had been commissioned by her to write his biography. While Daley didn't seem pleased, he listened respectfully. Jackie expressed her confidence in Eugene to handle the project fairly and thoroughly and raved about an article Eugene had written last year, which focused on spending St. Patrick's Day with Daley throughout the city's festivities. The piece also served as Eugene's point of inspiration, having found Daley to be quite the figure.

They parted cordially, but Jackie didn't know Daley well enough to discern if he was outraged or not.

SINCE THE CONVENTION didn't provide an ideal setting for conversation, at least not on the main floor, Lee asked Jackie to have a drink with her at a nearby rooftop bar. Both Peter and Anthony had early morning obligations and couldn't join them. Lee's invite allowed Jackie to gladly bid goodnight to Hugh. He had become too flirtatious for Jackie's taste and, in her opinion, was taking advantage of their friendship. Compassionate as she was for his situation, she had no interest in falling into bed with him, which seemed to be exactly what he wanted.

Jackie and Lee were seated along the railing of the bar, ten stories high. With the night air striking the perfect balance of refreshing crispness and the beauty of the New York skyline in lights, she began to relax as she sipped her wine spritzer.

"Do you realize we've hardly spoken since our meeting at Forger's office? With all your globetrotting it's hard to pin you down, Jacks."

"It has been a whirlwind of a summer." Her biggest complaint would be that she hadn't spent enough time with Caroline and John. Both were busy, with Caroline working as an intern in Teddy's senatorial campaign office, and John, having returned from Guatemala, volunteering at a non-profit in Harlem and preparing to attend Philips Academy in the fall.

Soon after her evening with Maurice, Jackie had made sure that André and Alexander both understood her wishes for a trust to be established to ensure Anthony's and Tina's educations were paid for in full. Not that she would mention it to Lee. Just like with her donation to Lee Radziwill Incorporated, Jackie would let André make a call to Lee's advisors. Ladies of their upbringing rarely discussed money outright.

"Did you and Maurice have dinner together that night?" Lee exhaled her cigarette smoke over the railing and flashed a Cheshire cat-like grin.

The question struck Jackie as odd. Why had such an insignificant detail been the first thing for Lee to ask about?

"Yes."

"Alone?" Lee drew out the word with a suggestive tone.

Jackie gave a squinty stare. "Are you up to something, Pekes?"

"Of course not. But I had the distinct impression that Maurice is madly in love with you."

The declaration surprised Jackie more than Lee's question. Her cheeks tinted, and she didn't want Lee to notice.

"Whatever gave you that notion?"

Lee shrugged. "I'm accustomed to men becoming infatuated with you and losing their senses around you. Maurice seemed awed yet able to retain his dignity."

"You gathered that from such a brief encounter?" Whether it was true or not, Jackie liked the idea of Maurice being secretly infatuated with her.

"Jacks, I'm overly gifted when it comes to reading people in a social setting, especially men."

"Your radar must be faulty then. Maurice is a brilliant financial advisor, and a trusted friend. Nothing more." Not that she would admit it, but in recent months Jackie had enjoyed the pleasures and freedom of indulging in romantic trysts rather than one steady relationship. Though not as tawdry as it seemed, she kept to men she already knew well and was seen in public with infrequently.

When it came to Maurice, a flutter of emotions stirred. She bit the inside of her lower lip, regretting the last part of her comment and not wanting to leave it on what sounded like a disrespectful note. Plus, she didn't want to sound defensive. "Besides, you know he's married."

"From what I hear he's more *separated* than married. He and his wife haven't lived together for ages."

Jackie served a playful sneer. "Should I bother asking what's behind all this? Are you moonlighting as a private detective?"

Lee huffed. "As if I have the time these days. Between Peter and my design business, I'm stretched more than saltwater taffy at Coney Island."

"You and Peter do seem co-dependent."

"Smirk all you want. You're not entirely wrong. We've enjoyed traveling and being together. Our ski trip to Switzerland was particularly wonderful." Lee sipped her drink as if to suppress the smile on her face. "But it is strange, dating when you're older, and I have to work much harder at this whole love game than you do. Passions are still there, but it's just as important to make sure you don't bore each other, which can be a chore at times. If it bothers me too much, I concentrate on my commissions and I'm simply not available for several days. It's good for him to miss me a while."

Listening to Lee, Jackie realized she didn't miss the emotional work that went into sustaining a relationship.

"And speaking of which," Lee went on, "I'm not ashamed to tell you I'm already turning commissions away. Part of the blame goes to

Lord & Taylor. The unveiling of the room I designed was a smash hit, and I wasn't prepared for the publicity it brought me. People were calling for a solid month wanting me to redesign this or redo that. Don't get me wrong, I want the money and the prestige, but for the love of God I didn't want to give up my life for it."

"You have an incredible eye for dressing a room to perfection, Pekes. A real knack for it." Thick as the compliment was, Jackie meant it.

Lee seemed to bask in her sister's approval. "Perhaps I shouldn't care as much as I do about what you think," she darted a glance at Jackie, "but I really do. I can't escape it, I suppose."

So much is entangled in those words. Our love and rivalry for each other, looped and twisted like a Christmas bow torn from a present...

———

JACKIE BASKED in the praise and adulation her coworkers extended as they filed out of the conference room. When she was at last alone in the room with Tom, she leaned back in her chair and sighed. She'd done it. Her first project with Viking Press was moving forward, fueled by contagious excitement.

Remembering the Ladies and *Sally Hemings, A Novel* nonfiction and fiction works respectively, were other books she had in the pipeline, but *In the Russian Style* had been hers since its inception and held her heart.

Tom stood on the opposite side of the room, leaning against the credenza with his legs stretched out and crossed at the ankles. His arms were folded across his chest.

"If that isn't a feather in your cap, then I don't know what is."

She smiled. Not her usual camera-ready smile, but one that reflected the giddiness threatening to erupt in her soul. At today's meeting she shared a sample of the layout, complete with pictures, illustrations, and one of the captions she'd written. She also shared how support from both Thomas Hoving and Diana Vreeland would give the book a marketing boost, along with the traveling costume exhibit sponsored by the Met.

"I'll admit, I may have had my own doubts about how this venture might work out." Tom pressed his lips together. "But now, I can breathe easier."

Jackie eyed him. "Are you talking about the book or the risk you took in hiring me?"

"Well, I am wondering how much longer I'll have to wait for you to reel in a memoir by Sinatra, but otherwise, it's apparent that hiring you was one of the best moves I made. You knocked their socks off today."

She gave a slight nod as a gesture of thanks. Today's meeting had boosted her confidence, and she could forget the murmurs of gossip that had infected the office. Whispers of how *privileged* she was to travel to Russia. Now, she could let it roll off her back.

"Does that mean you'll support me next month when I propose an autobiography by Philippe Petit?"

He cocked his head sideways and squinted one eye shut. "The guy who finagled a tightrope between the Twin Towers?"

Jackie nodded.

"I remember that. He spent about an hour up there, right? Walked back and forth six or seven times, did some tricks. One of the craziest things I'd ever heard about. Still can't believe he and a few other guys managed that whole set up without getting caught—and without the city's permission. Don't get your hopes up on that project though. I doubt it would drum up enough interest to make it a commercial success."

Disappointment prodded, but Jackie wouldn't let that diminish the wind in her sails.

Tom took a seat, then laced his fingers on the tabletop and looked pointedly at Jackie.

"There is another matter I needed to discuss with you."

"If you're still angling for me to talk to Rose about writing a book—"

"No, it's not that." He cleared his throat. "We're taking on a book that you might not like. It's tentatively titled *Shall We Tell the President?* It's written by one of our British authors, Jeffrey Archer. He's famous for his political fiction, which is exactly what this book is, but the plot has me concerned about you."

Her muscles stiffened. Had this man written about her?

"In a nutshell," Tom continued, "the story revolves around a plot to assassinate a senator turned president. Ted is the president."

Jackie's breath caught. "He wrote a book about killing Teddy?"

"It's fictional, but yes, one of the characters, an FBI agent, works to foil the plan of the would-be assassins."

She closed her eyes and chased away the image of Teddy, hoisted up and waving to a cheering crowd, only to be struck in the chest by a bullet. Her anger sparked at how effortlessly her mind contrived such images.

"There's no decency in this world anymore."

"I know you don't like it, Jackie, and I'm not wild about the whole idea either. But no one's asking me. This is the ugly trade-off, the give and take, when it comes to publishing. Sweet children's books on one end, some graphic material that someone labels as art on the other."

She knew Tom was right. What some people considered art, others found vulgar. What she considered crossing a line, especially after having her husband's blood splattered on her, others used as inspiration for entertainment. Perhaps she had valid points for a protest, but what good would it do? Ultimately, her disapproval could harm the tender shoots of camaraderie she'd just established with her colleagues.

"Even if Viking decided to pass on the book—"

"Which they won't," Tom interjected.

Jackie nodded. "Even if they did, another publisher would pick it up."

"Yes. Any way you look at it, that book is going to print."

"Because publishing is a business." A phrase she had drilled into her during her training sessions. "A money-making business."

"We wouldn't be here otherwise."

Jackie stole a quick breath. "Will I have to read it?"

"No. You won't have to see it. If that's any consolation."

It wasn't. But she'd absorb the injustice, like she had so many times before, and put it out of her mind. What choice did she have?

"I'm sorry, Jackie. I know this is a hard one to take."

"It's not your fault, Tom, and I appreciate you telling me."

"I wanted you to know. When it comes out, we'll be sure to make a statement emphasizing the fact you had no involvement with the book."

"Thank you." She knew it was bound to happen, books and subject matter she didn't like. Tom had a business to run and couldn't coddle her. It would be up to her to cope with the discomfort, outside the office.

But what do I do when a book comes along about Jack?

FIVE

September 1976

Spending September at Hammersmith Farm had become Jackie's annual tradition years ago. Sweltering temperatures were gone, and the air turned crisp, especially in the mornings, which made it ideal for a gallop on horseback through the meadow and across her mother and stepfather's Newport estate. The scenery was enhanced with the leaves changing into their colorful autumn wardrobe. Narragansett Bay proved too chilly for Jackie to even dip her toes in, but Caroline and John didn't hesitate to plunge into the water when they took the boat out.

Today, with Caroline and John up early and off to Bailey's Beach Club for the day, Jackie decided to enjoy breakfast with Janet and Hughdie. Situated on the deck as the sun stretched and blazed across the horizon, Jackie read sections of *The Newport Daily News* to Hughdie. In recent months, his emphysema had worsened. He now required a wheelchair for mobility and full-time oxygen. Jackie found it difficult, seeing him robbed of his vigor and strong business acumen, but she found endearment in watching her mother care for him. A nurse visited daily to monitor his stats, administer medications, and to assist and relieve Janet, but it was hard for Jackie to watch her stepfather decline.

As stepfathers went, Hughdie had been a treasure to Jackie. Walking her down the aisle for both marriages, always generous and loving, he trumped her father, Jack Bouvier, in more ways than she cared to admit.

Since Hughdie received care and treatments in Washington DC, he and Janet spent ample time at their Georgetown home, but Jackie appreciated that they stayed faithful to their Septembers in Newport.

She had just finished reading over the numbers on the market exchange page when Janet rolled a serving cart onto the deck. The sizeable staff that once ran and maintained Hammersmith Farm had been drastically reduced. Those still left, who had been with the couple for decades, primarily tended to the house and grounds. A change, Jackie knew, that was hard for her mother.

"I found this box of lemon cookies in the pantry." Janet carefully poured the cookies onto a platter and quickly arranged them. "I do hope they aren't stale."

Old habits, Jackie thought.

"They'll be fine, Mummy." Jackie took it upon herself to pour the coffees. "Oh, we're short a spoon."

"What?" Janet swept her gaze over the tray and up to her daughter. "Surely not."

Jackie tensed, watching her mother's anxiety ramp up. She regretted the mention of the forgotten utensil.

"It's nothing to worry about." Jackie hoped to redirect her mother's attention. "I won't even use one. Why don't you serve Hughdie first?" Along with the cookies, a plate held a stack of buttered toast, and a bowl cradled a handful of strawberries. Jackie should have known better than to address a missing spoon.

"Of course." Janet helped her husband hold the cup as he took several sips, then placed a cookie in his hand.

"Thank you, my dear." His voice shallow and ragged.

She patted his forearm, then sat and took up her own cup. "Should we tell Jacqueline our news?"

Hughdie nodded.

"It's taken some doing, but we think we've finally sold the house."

"I suppose that's a relief after all this time. And difficult as well." Relief and apprehension mingled within Jackie. Selling Hammersmith Farm had been a sensitive topic for the family.

"Indeed." Janet pressed her lips together. "We...just can't manage the estate anymore. The new owners have agreed to certain allowances. Hughdie and I will move into the Castle, and we'll maintain some of the land. I'm not sure how the details will iron out since they plan to turn this into a museum—"

"A museum?"

"Yes. The new owners are businessmen. They see an opportunity here and want to transform it into a historical site. Open it for tours so people can see the house and grounds where the former First Lady grew up. Something to that effect."

"Oh, Mummy, you can't let that happen." Though it hadn't been her home for decades, Jackie cringed at the idea of swarms of strangers walking through the house and grounds. To her, it felt like an invasion of privacy.

"Jacqueline, there are a number of issues that are out of my hands. This is one of them."

Silence gripped Jackie. As did guilt. A couple of years ago, her mother had asked her to purchase the property before they put it on the market. At the time, Jackie said she would need to speak with Ari since she personally lacked the funds needed to save their home. However, given the deteriorating state of her marriage and Ari's own health issues, she never mentioned it to him. Deep down, she knew she was using Ari as an excuse and had no intention of rescuing them financially. A vengeful side of her, she knew. One she thought she might overcome.

"Oh, but our dear Lee," Janet put her hand to her chest, then began to fiddle with the charm on her necklace. "She was so upset when I told her. Why, she wanted to run to that bank and take out a mortgage in her name. Even said she would put her business up as collateral if they'd let her. Oh, that dear." She paused for a moment, apparently giving the memory its reverence. "But I told her not to. I insisted. Didn't I?" She looked to Hughdie who grunted and nodded.

Jackie bit into the cookie—stale as could be—and carefully ground it to bits. Janet plated three strawberries, and no one touched the toast.

Janet sighed. "Besides, she shouldn't spend the money she received on us. It's practically all she has, and it wouldn't be right."

Although she hadn't finished her bite, Jackie had to ask, "What money?"

"From the estate. Haven't you spoken to her?"

Jackie shook her head.

"It turned out that after the debts were paid, Lee ended up with half a million dollars. Not enough to save Hammersmith Farm, obviously, but she was dear to offer. On the other hand, I can't say I approve of how she intends to spend that money."

With artificial lemon seeping into her taste buds, Jackie could only imagine.

"She has her eye on a beach house in Southampton. Off Gin Lane, I believe she said, and not far from those kooky Bouvier women. Apparently, the mother isn't well."

Janet's disdain for her ex-husband's family had remained solid since her divorce in 1940. Edith Beale and her daughter, Little Edie, lived together at Grey Gardens. Little Edie left her successful modeling career in New York City and returned home to tend to her mother, who was recovering from eye surgery. Over the next twenty-five years, they evolved into recluses as their seaside house fell into disrepair and became overrun with cats and raccoons.

When Lee became aware of her relatives' living conditions, she contacted Ari, who shelled out over thirty thousand dollars for immediate repairs. Money was also set aside for the Beales' living expenses since their funds—Big Edie's divorce settlement and Little Edie's trust fund—had dried up years prior.

Aware of Ari's generosity, Janet believed, being his mother-in-law at the time, that she was also entitled to such financial help, though none came, which added to her ire.

But now, Jackie couldn't believe what she was hearing. That Lee would funnel her new-found wealth into a secondary home. Near the Beales.

Although Jackie had visited her aunt and cousin during the clean-up phase, she had not kept in regular touch. Apparently, Lee had. But Jackie was nearly appalled that Lee was buying a home she didn't need rather than investing the sum and finally building wealth. Why hadn't she called and asked Jackie to put her in touch with Maurice?

I'll never understand her.

August 1955

LEE WAS WORRIED. Aside from holidays, she hadn't made a point in recent years to see her father much. When he called and proposed taking a vacation, the five of them, she loved the idea. He had been longing for a getaway with his two smashing daughters and the scamps they'd married. His words.

But later, after the plans were set and their bags packed, she feared her father might badger her with reminders that they didn't see each other enough anymore. That an awkwardness might descend and spoil the trip.

Since she and Jackie had married, Black Jack Bouvier

complained that he had lost his girls and no longer had a place in their lives. He had a way with dramatics and criticisms, undoubtedly learned from his own father, but Lee couldn't deny that she rarely made time for telephone calls, which were a necessity now that she lived in London. Her father had once been everything and now he existed in the crevices of her life. She imagined Jackie faced similar challenges sustaining a relationship with him as well. Because while Black Jack was quick to complain and play on one's emotions, he was also adept at denial. Never was he one to apologize for missing a planned dinner or family get-together because he ended up drunk and passed out, or drunk and consumed by his losing streak at the track.

However, when the man came through, as he had for this adventure on the island of Corsica, he came through.

Lee couldn't have imagined a better setting or better company. Jackie seemed quieter than usual, but Michael, Lee's husband, was making a grand effort engaging with both her and Jack. Lee loved him even more for it because it created a relaxed ease among them and seemed to erase the fact they hadn't spent much time together since their weddings two years ago.

Black Jack's jovial mood also dissipated her concerns.

They chartered a boat to spend the morning sailing the Gulf of Porto. Their craft was small enough to navigate through the red rocks of Capo Rosso and allowed them to approach several caves. Though Lee could tell it wasn't the sea adventure Jack had enjoyed during his time in the Navy, he joined Michael and Jackie in jumping off a few rock formations and swimming in the water. Soon, he was coaxing Lee to jump in. She abandoned her fear and plunged into the crystal-blue waters. Seeing Jack pleased with her made it worth it.

After their sail, they explored the village of Girolata, where they ate a light lunch and popped into shops. For some reason, Jack seemed especially attentive toward her. She liked it and didn't mind his occasional hand on her lower back or when he swiped her windswept hair from her face with his fingertips. Lee couldn't have planned a more perfect day, and she was certain they all felt the same.

When they returned to their villa, her father excused himself to take a nap. Jackie complained of a light headache and said she wanted to lie down before dinner. Too much wine and too much sun, she said. Michael admitted the day's activities had caught up with him also and asked if Lee would forgive him for stealing away for a short rest. She didn't object.

Jack, on the other hand, said he felt invigorated and wanted to enjoy the villa's pool. Lee said she would join him.

In the water, Jack challenged her to a race, even promised her a head start. She laughed and agreed and didn't mind when he beat her to the edge. Again and again. But Jack overestimated his energy and found himself petered out.

"I think I may have aggravated my back," he said, after leaving the pool and easing onto a lounge chair.

Lee was well-aware of his ailment, one that hadn't been curable with medications or risky surgeries. She suspected he was guarding his expression. Jack Kennedy was the type of man who always hid— even ignored—the extent of his pain and discomfort.

"I suppose leaping from the boat and the rocks today didn't help matters," he added.

"You should know your limits." She joined him on the lounge chair, making sure her bum only took up a small part of the edge.

"A man has no limits when he's hoping to impress a woman."

The glint in his eye made her blush and confirmed that she had not been imagining his flirtatious ways.

He leaned his head back and closed his eyes. Was it an indication that his pain had increased?

"Let me get you an aspirin." She started to stand.

Jack caught her by the wrist.

"It'll pass. Stay."

She sank back down.

"If you rub my leg, that will distract me from the pain."

Lee couldn't help looking at him. His bare legs, speckled with water. His gray swim trunks, housing his...

She took a deep breath and stood again. But immediately, she knew she had to keep the playfulness going.

"Such a cad. We already know what a dashing hero you are, Jack. There's no need to be miserable." She let her eyes return to his trunks and linger a moment because she couldn't afford to upset him or have him think she was put off by his suggestion. Even though a part of her was. "I'll get you that aspirin."

Turning to walk back into the villa, she thought her heart might burst from her chest it was pounding so hard. Every inch of her felt electrified by Jack's desire-filled touch. A vicious thought zipped through her mind.

Wouldn't it be delicious to ruin Jackie this way?

But she didn't let it go further. She couldn't. If she crossed that line—if she slept with Jack—she would never escape the guilt and shame. Her loyalty to Jackie needed to rise and squash the sudden temptation.

Deep breaths helped her clear head and calm her desires. In the kitchen, she found her father, pouring himself an orange juice. He claimed he couldn't sleep. Relief grounded her.

"You know, I think I might lie down after all." Lee touched her forehead as if she needed to emphasize the point.

"Yes, my pet. Catch a rest if you can."

She hesitated. "Oh, Daddy, would you mind getting some aspirin to Jack? He's out by the pool. Seems his back is aggravated."

A smirk threatened when she pictured Jack's face. She suspected he'd be upset about more than his back when Black Jack joined him. Knowing she'd hoodwinked him gave her a rush of delight.

September 1976

Dear Jackie,

I just wanted to dash off a quick note of thanks. As always, your presence at board meetings for MAS is appreciated. Nothing seems to fuel the fight and elevate our members' passions more than when you're in the room with us.

You may have heard that the lawsuit Penn Central filed to have Grand Central Terminal's landmark status revoked and removed is continuing up legal channels. Of course, we will continue our work to stop them from demolishing our beloved GCT in favor of a new high-rise skyscraper of soulless office space. At last year's press conference, when we announced our plans to battle for preservation, you said that great effort even at the eleventh hour can succeed. I wholeheartedly agree and believe it may come down to that if the case goes before the Supreme Court for decision.

Your association with this project—and your undeniable dedication to keep much-loved structures reflecting the past—has helped to strengthen and legitimize our cause.

It hasn't been a quick or easy issue, and there are days I worry we might lose to "progress". When the "little people" go up against the big money of the Railroad, they rarely win. In the meantime, I wanted to reiterate how integral you have become to this fight. We can't imagine doing this without you, and we wouldn't want to.

Sincerely,
Frederick Papert
Committee to Save Grand Central

Municipal Arts Society

November 1976

WHEN HUGHDIE PASSED, Jackie worried endlessly for her mother. What would Janet do now that she didn't have her husband of thirty-four years and the responsibility of caring for him? Janet's own health, at least mentally, was another concern for Jackie. Slips of forgetfulness, the inability to find the right word when she was talking sometimes, and occasional moments when she simply paused, as if a switch had been thrown and frozen her in place for a few seconds troubled Jackie. Her tender approaches toward the subject and suggestion that Janet needed to see her doctor were met with enough hostility to discourage her. For now.

Instead, she kept to her mother's side and helped her carry out the plans for the funeral arrangements. Janet insisted upon two services, one in DC and the other in Newport. Jackie felt two services were unnecessary, but rather than upset her mother, she went along.

Further complicating matters was the fact she and Lee weren't speaking. Sort of. Jackie was still miffed that Lee hadn't told her about the money from Stas's estate and that she didn't reach out to Jackie for financial guidance.

During the funeral, she and Lee sat together in Trinity Church, packed in a pew and surrounded by step-siblings, Yusha, Nina, Tommy, and their half-siblings, Janet Jr and Jamie. But Jackie sensed that Lee was making an effort not to talk to her beyond obligatory conversation topics. Naturally, she questioned herself and thought she was being too sensitive or crafting drama where none existed.

Back at Hammersmith Farm for the funeral reception, Lee mingled casually with everyone. Unusual, Jackie thought. The crowd consisted mostly of Hughdie's family members, business associates and contacts. People Lee had little history with.

Jackie preferred Janet Jr's company, since her younger sister lived in Hong Kong and Jackie rarely had the chance to visit with her and her three children. They settled in a corner of Hughdie's study, not completely apart from those gathered but enough that they could converse privately.

"The last time I saw Daddy was September of last year. When Mummy called with the news," a breath escaped Janet Jr, "I didn't know his condition had worsened so." Fresh tears glistened in her already puffy eyes. "I talked to him on the phone a couple weeks ago, but still." She dabbed her eyes with a scrunched tissue.

"I wonder if Mummy was trying to protect you from what was coming. She wouldn't want you to worry so, especially when there's nothing you could've done."

Janet Jr sniffled and shook her head. "I could've been here."

"Mummy took wonderful care of him, and it would've pained you terribly to watch him fade away. I'm sure he didn't want that to be your last memory of him. You know what a proud man he was."

Janet Jr seemed to consider that and nodded. "Daddy was always so upright and could handle anything." She glanced toward their mother, who stood in the hallway chatting with others. "I don't know what she's going to do without him."

Jackie had to agree. She thought about sharing her concerns over their mother's mental decline but decided it wasn't worth upsetting her sister further with another situation she couldn't help with or remedy.

Janet Jr caught her eye. "Is there something going on between you and Lee?"

The unexpected shift caught Jackie off guard. "What do you mean?"

"You two are usually thick as thieves, but I don't think I've seen you together for more than five minutes."

So Jackie wasn't out of her mind. Janet Jr had picked up on the awkward behavior too.

"Nothing serious." She didn't know what else to say on the subject. "We haven't seen each other a great deal since we're both working." She could only imagine how contrived that sounded.

"And everything is upside-down at the moment," Janet Jr added.

Jackie released a slow sigh, grateful her half-sister didn't want to devote her strength to figuring out the rift.

Later, their mother and Lee joined them.

"Jacqueline, there's a matter you and Lee must tend to for me."

"Yes, Mummy. What is it?"

"The house in Georgetown. I want it sold immediately. It will need to be thoroughly cleaned and made ready. First and foremost, you'll have to go through everything in the attic. There's no doubt in my mind that will be the biggest task, and I can't imagine what all you may find up there. I can't have strangers going through it. Not such personal things. The ideal solution is for the two of you to do it together."

Considering Janet's urgency and emphasis, Jackie wondered if the task served as some sort of set-up.

She looked to Lee, who responded, as if on cue, "Don't worry, Mummy. Jackie and I will see to it. Together."

Jackie couldn't tell if a glimmer of hope or a flash of caution accompanied her smile. Either way, she welcomed the chance to have Lee to herself, even though they were the least suited for what was sure to be a dirty task. But if swiping away cobwebs and being trapped in a haze of dust was what it took to bring them together, so be it.

SIX

January 1977

Winter winds howled, dusting Jackie and Lee in flurries as they entered Janet's home on O Street in Georgetown. Inside, stomping and shaking off what snow they could, both remarked how fiercely cold and miserable the season had been so far.

After the chill had subsided, Jackie shivered at the empty feel of the house. While furniture and belongings still abounded, it was almost as if the place knew Hughdie was gone, and Janet was widowed. Never one for ghosts or superstitions, though, Jackie knew that *she* was the one haunted. That the house served as another reminder that she would never see Hughdie again.

The Auchinclosses had purchased the home after Jack was elected president. Janet envisioned having a grand role in social affairs, as the mother of the First Lady. Jackie didn't mind their proximity, although she never hosted a dinner at the White House specifically for them. Janet's ambitions were fulfilled, though, when she acted as hostess for Jackie on several occasions. It wasn't uncommon for Jackie to shrug certain duties and dash off to her rented home in the countryside.

Jackie rarely visited DC anymore. The memories and tragedies of her old life were still too vivid and disturbing. Standing in her mother's house now, perhaps inspired by the heavy somberness, she thought back to Jack's assassination. The children had been here, staying with Janet and Hughdie while she and Jack traveled to Texas. After the unimaginable happened, Jackie telephoned Nancy and told her that she wanted them back at the White House, and for them to be told, as delicately as possible, that their father was gone. Janet saw to it, but when it came to talking to Caroline and John, she faltered and let the task fall to Maud, the children's nanny, instead.

"It already feels so final." Lee ran her hands up and down the sleeves of her angora sweater as if she were still cold.

"Yes." Jackie found the thermostat and dialed up the heat.

She and Lee hadn't seen or spoken to each other since the holidays, which had been somber and perfunctory with Hughdie's passing too recent for the family to feel festive.

But the loss of Hughdie aside, Jackie felt she and Lee had only grown farther apart, and in reality, she was unsure what she wanted to accomplish with this venture.

Jackie made coffee, a sure-fire way to warm them up and ready them for the task at hand. After a steaming cup and a smoke, they headed to the attic.

The stairs creaked under their feet. Though she didn't frequent the attic, Jackie found the wall switch and clicked on the lone, bare bulb attached to a rafter. Hardly enough light to luminate the space, but Jackie wondered if that was for the best. Steamer trunks, hat boxes, racks of clothes sheathed in clear dry-cleaner garment covers, and shelves filled with more boxes, trinkets and books lined the walls.

"How are we ever going to get through all this?" Jackie gave serious thought to phoning her mother and telling her there was no way she and Lee could manage.

"Mummy must have no idea how much is up here." Lee moved

toward a shelf holding rows of shoe boxes. She peeked inside a lid and gasped with delight. "Oh, Jacks, look!" She withdrew a handful of photographs. With her mouth hung open and eyes wide, she rifled through the stack. "It's from the time we went to the county fair with Grampy and Grandma Maude."

Jackie took the pictures as Lee handed them over. Moments later they were both transfixed by the captured memories.

"This was the year I won that rabbit."

"The one you named Ruffles?"

"Yes!" Jackie hadn't thought about that pet for decades. "I kept him at Lasata, remember?"

"Didn't Daddy try to build a pen for him, so the cats in the stables couldn't get him?"

"Oh, he tried."

Jackie and Lee's tailspin back into their childhood and long-forgotten memories deepened with each box and trunk they peered into. There were furs Janet wore religiously during the early years of her marriage to Black Jack. Costume jewelry. Shoes, dresses, suitcases. Pictures and mirrors in gilded frames. Even postcards Janet had mailed to the girls from her travels.

Jackie suggested they make a system. One pile would be for donations, and they'd set aside a few items Janet might want to keep. Jackie could envision much of it going to the trash heap though.

But when she came upon two dress boxes, she froze when she read the handwritten labels.

Jackie's Wedding Dress, September 12, 1953
Jackie's Dress, November 22, 1963

Dallas. The second box contained her bloodstained raspberry-pink Chanel suit. Most likely, everything she'd worn that day. The navy blouse, hose, pumps, purse. But her matching hat had gone missing. She'd given the ensemble to her mother after she'd taken it off—

somewhere in the early morning hours of the 23rd, after Jack's autopsy had been completed at Bethesda Naval Hospital and she returned to the White House officially a widow. Of course, she hadn't laid eyes on it after she removed it, but Janet told her it was inventoried and taken care of.

Lee stepped to Jackie's side and read the label. Her face paled.

Morbid curiosity sparked in Jackie, and she reached for the dress box.

"No, Jacks." Lee snatched Jackie's hands. "I won't let you do this to yourself."

That fateful day flashed through her mind. Exhaust fumes from the motorcade. The crack of the gunshot. Jack struggling beside her, then cascading onto her lap while Governor Connelly was yelling, *"They're going to kill us all!"* from his seat in front of them.

Lee gave her a firm shake. "Don't. Don't go back there."

"You're right." Trembling, she withdrew from the box.

"Let's get out of here." Lee took her by the hand and wrapped her other hand around Jackie's forearm. "We've done enough for now. And don't give another thought to the dresses. I'll speak with Mummy, and we'll take care of them."

"Thank you, Pekes." Jackie returned to her senses. Stabilized herself, though her heart pounded in her chest. "I...I don't know what I would've done if you weren't here."

Lee flashed a half-hearted smile.

They left the attic and made their way downstairs. Jackie's legs felt shaky on the descend, causing her to grip the handrail. Back in the kitchen, Lee grabbed her into a quick but fierce embrace. Sighs escaped them both.

Despite the lingering, mild friction between them, Jackie was grateful Lee had been with her in the attic, facing those dress boxes. If it had been a member of the housekeeping staff instead, Jackie might have popped the lid. What would it have done to her, seeing the smeared bloodstains from her husband's gunshot wound on her beloved Chanel suit? She pushed away the images swirling in her mind.

March 1977

"JACQUELINE, you mustn't concern yourself over the pink suit. I made arrangements and the box was taken to the National Archives. We'll still have legal documents to contend with, but I was adamant that the contents are to be sealed, kept from viewing, and above all, never to be on public display."

Janet's deftness at handling the matter reminded Jackie that her mother still had her wits about her. Perhaps she'd been wrong about her mother's mental state after all?

Weeks after their tag-team effort to clear out the attic, Lee called Jackie with the sad news that their Aunt Edith had passed. Their cousin, Little Edie, who had taken care of her mother for years, was now planning to sell Grey Gardens and move to Florida.

Jackie and Lee attended the funeral together.

Shortly after, Jackie's professional world was rocked by two items appearing in newspapers. The first was a review by John Leonard in the *New York Times*. Having read an advanced copy of the forthcoming *Shall We Tell the President?*, he capped his scathing review with: "There is a word for such a book. The word is trash. Anybody associated with its publication should be ashamed of herself."

Other criticisms followed and echoed a similar sentiment.

The second blow came when Tom Guinzburg was interviewed by the *Boston Globe* about Jackie's involvement with the book. He was quoted as saying, "Jackie knew about the book."

On the heels of Tom's comment, Jackie phoned Nancy Tuckerman and urged her to come to her apartment at 1040.

"I absolutely can't believe he implicated me, as if I gave approval for that awful story to be published. All the years of friendship we shared, and he cast me aside for a profit."

"Is it really all that bad?" Nancy picked up the newspaper with Leonard's review and looked it over. "It's just a book. A made-up story."

"What's most infuriating is Tom's betrayal." Jackie folded her arms across her chest. "He told me he would issue a statement and make certain that the press knew I had nothing to do with that book."

"You should talk to him."

"Are you out of your mind? What could he possibly say that would make a difference?" Jackie stiffened and huffed. "I can't ever step foot inside Viking again. I'll write my letter of resignation, and I need you to deliver it for me. My things will also need to be collected from my desk."

Sadness crept over Jackie. Was she really letting her job go? A job she excelled at. That she'd grown to love more than she thought possible.

"Is that really what you want?" Nancy's words were soft and tentative.

"No." The grip of her anger laxed. "But this is humiliating."

"Have you spoken to Teddy about any of this?"

"Only briefly over the phone. He told me I shouldn't worry about it, that these things are like a sparkler and burn out quickly."

"For once, I agree with him."

Jackie looked at Nancy and couldn't resist a burst of laughter at her smug expression.

"Oh, why did this have to happen, Tucky? This book has ruined everything."

"Hmm. I seem to recall a few other books you were upset about over the years. All containing material you didn't like. And I believe you admitted, well, not publicly but to others, that you may have overreacted when it came to a particular book."

Her remark miffed Jackie. She knew Nancy was referring to William Manchester's *The Death of a President*. Concerned about information she had shared with Manchester during their two lengthy sessions where he recorded his interviews with her, Jackie objected to certain sections being included in the book. Bobby tried to discourage her from going so far as to file a lawsuit but lost that battle. In the end, a few passages were redacted, but Manchester won the right to publish the book. After she read the carefully detailed account the former professor had crafted, Jackie was captivated and realized she had been wrong to launch such disapproval.

"Why do I put up with you?"

A smug yet cheery grin crossed Nancy's face. "Because you know you can't live without me."

Despite the release in tension, Jackie went through with her resignation from Viking Press. Tom relayed a note to Jackie via Nancy, part of which read, *I told the Globe you knew about the book but had nothing to do with it. They didn't print the last part of my statement. As your friend and boss, I beg you to reconsider your stance on this and return. I will keep your desk ready. Please, Jackie, come back to work.*

After she had time to calm down, she read and reread Tom's note. Jackie believed him. She knew Tom well enough to know the sincerity in those words rang true. However, she couldn't go back. Returning to Viking would only deepen her humiliation. Nancy told her that she was likely the only one who would see it that way. Jackie didn't disagree, but she was willing to live with the fact her hasty decision had cost her. And in that vein, there was no need for her to accept Tom's phone calls.

Ultimately, she blamed the press. Once again, they had invaded and spoiled a beautiful part of her life. Giving up her position brought a dark cloud. Nancy lovingly reminded her that there were dozens of publishers out there and not to lose heart.

One thing is certain. I'll get no sympathy from Lee.

A HIATUS. Or a sabbatical. That's what Jackie told herself. She was taking time off to figure out what she wanted to do next. Of course, now that she had some experience under her belt, her passion for the publishing industry had grown exponentially. Though she enjoyed writing, she didn't enjoy the agony that came with having to produce. Writing also meant putting herself out there for criticisms. Another layer of agony she preferred to avoid. Editing was her niche. She mulled over whether she should move on to another publishing house or pursue a position elsewhere but held back making an immediate decision.

In the meantime, the press showed no mercy regarding her departure. Jackie didn't bother addressing the matter with Lee or her mother. Luck, perhaps, was on Jackie's side, as Lee was occupied on the West Coast.

Working on a commission in San Franciso had also kept Lee from further helping Janet pare her life down into one house. That responsibility fell on Jackie's shoulders. Together, she and Janet finished clearing out Janet's Georgetown home.

Once on the market, the home sold quickly. Though Janet was living off money she inherited from her father, Jackie was relieved that her mother now had more funds to cushion her bottom line. She mentioned nothing about investing the sum.

After finding a groove in streamlining Janet's belongings from her DC home, Jackie applied that same efficiency when it came to moving her things from the main house at Hammersmith Farm and into the Castle. The home was markedly smaller, but Jackie considered that a good thing. Less for Janet to manage.

On their second day of arranging furniture and readying boxes for donation, an unfamiliar voice echoed through the house.

"Hello, hello. Anyone around?"

When she went to the entryway, Jackie saw a man, straw hat in hand, wearing overalls and angling his head as he looked up the staircase, until he spotted her.

"May I help you?"

His smile revealed a row of wide teeth. Lanky, spectacled, and crowned with gray hair, he approached with his hand sticking out. "You must be Jacqueline. No doubt about that. A striking beauty like your mother."

Jackie hesitated but shook his hand. "And you are?"

"Bingham Willing Morris. Friends call me Booch. Sometimes Bing. Makes no difference to me."

"Oh, Bingham, you're here!" Janet exclaimed as she approached. "Wonderful. I could use a man to move a couple nightstands upstairs for me. They're currently in the dining room."

"I'll get right on that." He tossed his hat onto the console near the door and slapped his hands together.

Janet directed him where to go, then turned to Jackie.

"Do you remember Mr. Morris? I believe you've met before."

"I don't think so." Jackie darted a glance at the hat and wondered if she could sneak it into one of the outgoing donation boxes. The overalls needed to go too.

"Well, no matter. I'm sure you'll get the chance to visit more later. He's staying for dinner."

"Dinner? Who is he, Mummy?"

Janet glanced down the hallway, as if to make sure he wasn't listening.

"He's an old beau of mine. Oh, it must have been nearly fifty years ago when we courted. Nothing serious, of course, but we remained friends a while. His wife was one of my bridesmaids when I married your father, if you can believe it. Naturally, we lost touch for many years, but he read in the papers about Hughdie's passing and stopped by for a visit one afternoon. His wife, Mary, bless her soul, has endured her own health issues of late. Oh, we had so much to catch up on, and he's been magnanimous with helping me move my things."

Jackie struggled to control her facial expression, which was torn between dumbfounded paralysis and a fit of laughter. Not in a thousand lifetimes could she have pictured her mother finding common ground with a man decked in overalls, which Janet didn't seem to notice. But with all the life-changing chaos Janet seemed to be handling well, Jackie couldn't fault her for finding a friend.

Although she had no idea how she would refrain from giggling if her mother called him *Booch* at the dinner table.

SEVEN

June 1977

Although she knew a long road lay ahead, Jackie welcomed the nearly tangible anticipation that defined the ground-breaking ceremony on Columbia Point. She didn't stab the earth and lift a hearty scoop of dirt, not like John, Caroline, and Teddy. Even Rose made a better show of it than she did, but Jackie was never one for competing with the Kennedys. Construction of the John F. Kennedy Presidential Library and Museum had officially commenced, and that was what she cared about.

Her immediate view was hampered by a mob of clustering, angling photographers, but she looked beyond them to the sweeping views of the Thompson Islands and the Boston skyline. The water-front location made up for losing the site at Harvard Square. She could picture Jack skippering the *Honey Fitz* or the *Victura* on the waters of Dorchester Bay.

Deepening her satisfaction was the fact that the University of Massachusetts Boston had donated the nine and a half acres for the building site. Money saved that would be utilized for construction and design. And after helplessly watching funds dwindle for too many years, Jackie was elated that the Kennedy Library Corporation, under the tutelage of Stephen Smith, Jean's husband, had raised over twenty million dollars. More than enough to cover projected building costs and future operating expenses.

Jackie glimpsed her children. She was grateful for their ease under the lenses of dozens of cameras. It was a level of comfort she had yet to achieve, though she doubted that would ever happen. Her breath was also taken away by their growth. She hadn't paused enough lately to appreciate the transformation, as unavoidable as it was glorious. John was taller than her now, and Caroline excelled at her studies at Radcliffe College Harvard. Jackie's tender littles had been replaced by confident, curious, intelligent young people who were certain to add to their father's legacy.

Taking in those sweet revelations in a moment the press couldn't intrude upon, with the sun shining down like a radiant smile from Jack's vantage point in Heaven, she reveled inwardly. Today marked the beginning of the completion of the only two things that held her heart together after Dallas—raising the children well and building the library.

You would be proud today, Jack.

July 1977

SINCE ITS INCEPTION, by Ethel in the early 1970s, the RFK Pro-Celebrity Tennis Tournament had attracted a plethora of politicians, athletes, and celebrities each year, both as participants and attendees. Though Jackie considered her tennis game above par, she passed on the offer to play but made attending a priority. Caroline and John also loved the tournament since much of their Kennedy family took part in it.

Held in the Forest Hills Stadium in New York, the event raised money for the RFK Foundation, which kept Bobby's memory and mission alive with its donations to children of low-income families.

Arnold Schwarzenegger, Rosie Grier, Walter Mondale, Dustin Hoffman, and Clint Eastwood were among the notable attendees, but Jackie was more interested in connecting with an old friend. An old lover, truth be told.

When Jack Warnecke slipped into the aisle and sat beside her on the steel bleacher, a school-girl-like excitement fluttered in her chest. Bobby had been her first lover after the assassination, but Warnecke was her first relationship. Her time with Bobby didn't qualify as a relationship in her mind since there was no real chance they could end up married or together in a permanent sense. What they shared was outside the bounds of convention or explanation, as far as she was concerned.

That hadn't been the case with Warnecke. They had known each other for several years before they became romantically involved, with Warnecke having met Jack back in 1941 when he audited classes at Warnecke's alma mater, Stanford.

After she hired him to design Jack's gravesite at Arlington, she and Warnecke spent an ample amount of time together. Every detail mattered to Jackie. Her stamp of approval touched every rock, inscription, and blade of grass. Throughout the eighteen-month process, her involvement remained steady while Bobby pulled back, having a particular disdain toward Warnecke, though Jackie never understood why. Their meetings became one-on-one, and eventually, Warnecke found the gusto to let his personal interest in her be known.

She liked him, both in bed and professionally, but she ended their relationship after the site's unveiling because she couldn't envision marrying the man who designed her first husband's grave.

Now, though she had no interest in marriage, she wondered what it could mean to have him back in her life.

He sat close. The skin-to-skin contact of their legs touching, in the full heat and humidity of summer, brought its own sexual charge for Jackie. Though his hair had grayed, his trim physique still turned her on. Memories of his body on top of hers threatened her concentration, as did the sliver of sweat beading on her leg.

He leaned closer. "I may not be the first to say it, but I'm disappointed I won't get to see you and Ethel out on the court together, whacking it out."

"You and every reporter and photographer here." That was one of the primary reasons she wouldn't play, knowing the crowd might have a thirst for watching the two widows pitted against each other.

"I don't get out to the East Coast as much these days, so it's good to see you."

Jackie looked at him. "From what I hear, you're seeing a great deal of my sister."

"How about that? Almost unbelievable, isn't it? Lee transforming into a businesswoman and going bi-costal as well. She's putting that office of mine to good use, I'll say that for her. And her new commission seems to have enhanced her love life."

"What do you mean?"

Warnecke reared back. "With the man she's seeing. Newton Cope. Hasn't she mentioned him?"

"Not at great length." Lying never suited Jackie, but the truth, when it came to Lee, rubbed her the wrong way more than the deception. "She's in San Francisco so much for one thing."

"Is that your way of telling me you two don't speak much?"

Jackie gave a casual shoulder shrug. "We're both too frugal to spend time or money on long-distance calls." She paired the comment with a grin, hoping to seem unaffected by his observation.

"I've worked with Newton. He's still broken over losing his wife. Understandable, since she passed just last year. But when we had lunch together a few weeks ago, he couldn't stop talking about Lee. They haven't known each other long, but I got the definite impression he was smitten. To hear him talk, he might be done for. It wouldn't surprise me if their relationship developed very quickly. But maybe that's just the romantic in me talking."

As much as Lee enjoyed her jabs at Jackie—*Must every man fall in love with you*—Lee had her own powerful charms. For the most part, Lee attracted men with a debonaire flair. Her husbands Michael and Stas, even Peter Beard, were the epitome of suave—though not without an element of playboy in them. Jackie, on the other hand, gravitated toward charismatic men with money and power—and a shameless, incurable penchant for infidelity, it seemed.

Jackie tried not to react to Warnecke's revelation and wondered if the infatuation was one-sided. That could explain why Jackie knew nothing about their relationship. On the other hand, if the attraction was mutual and a romance was in bloom, would she tell Jackie? Or was their sisterhood so frayed that it was best to keep personal developments private?

And what happened to her and Peter Tufo?

"So," Warnecke said, leaning in closer, "seeing anyone these days?"

"Don't you keep tabs on me through the tabloids? They probably know more about my private life than me." How she loved to tease.

"You have no excuse to turn down my invite to dinner then?"

"I might consider it."

"Because you know what it does to me, seeing you? I've never stopped thinking about you, Jackie. I only wish I would've fought harder for us, because I've always been in love with you."

She smiled, and in a breathy, flirtatious voice asked, "What time is dinner?"

———

JACKIE WOKE EARLY the next morning and carefully slipped from the sheets of Warnecke's bed. Mindful, too, of the empty champagne bottle on the floor. Warnecke stirred, but she had already zipped back into her jumpsuit by the time he was fully awake and focusing on her.

He propped up on his elbows. "I could order up breakfast."

The sex had been as glorious as she remembered, perhaps even better, but she knew Warnecke well enough to know that he wasn't a man just after sex. Kindling their romance would ignite his desire for an attachment.

Her impishness mixed with her afterglow. "Better make it for one then."

January 1978

NOT LONG AFTER Nancy began her new position in the public relations department at Doubleday Publishing, she encouraged Jackie to consider joining the company and continuing her path as an editor.

Jackie was hesitant. She didn't want to go through another embarrassing mishap or deal with another book that maligned her efforts. But no other pursuits invigorated her like working with books. Although she'd been offered a board position with the American Ballet Theatre, and was lending it serious consideration, it wouldn't allow her to tap into her creative abilities the way editing had. Her two years at Viking had forced her to sharpen her critical eye as a reader and mentor. She had learned not only how to improve a manuscript but also how to coax the best out of authors.

Jackie mustered up the courage and telephoned John Turner Sargent, Doubleday's current president. Although he was delighted to speak with her, since they'd known each other for years, he explained that the company was in a bit of flux. He was stepping down as president and planning to hand over the reins in the coming year to Nelson Doubleday, Jr. It pained him to admit it, but he wasn't sure what kind of job security he could offer Jackie since the company's financials were currently in shambles. Even so, he invited Jackie to lunch.

By the end of that late afternoon meeting at the Four Seasons,

Jackie accepted the offer to join the publisher as an associate editor and would begin in February.

She dismissed her inner concerns that the house was in trouble and possibly heading toward bankruptcy. Instead, she chose to focus on what—and who—she could bring to the company to bolster sales and hoped to find ways to improve Doubleday's lackluster reputation for poor quality books.

But if her new endeavor tanked, Jackie had no idea how she would handle the criticism or what on earth she would do next.

DESPITE THE BITING cold and heavy snowfall blanketing the city, Jackie's niece Tina stopped by unexpectedly. When the doorman called up to let Jackie know about Tina's arrival, he mentioned that Tina looked distressed. Mild trepidation zipped through Jackie as she waited at her apartment's entrance to receive Tina.

When the elevator opened, Jackie held out her arms.

"Tina, dear, what's wrong?"

"I need to get away from Mummy for a while. She's..." Tina embraced Jackie.

"Come in." Jackie put her arm around her as she led her into the living room. "Can I get you anything?"

Tina shook her head, seemingly on the brink of tears.

Jackie, relieved that it was a family crisis rather than a tragedy to deal with, gave her a sympathetic grin as they sat. "I might have something to cheer you up. I'll be right back."

She slipped into the kitchen and took a can of orange Crush from the refrigerator and a pack of vanilla wafers from the pantry. Two of Tina's sugary favorites since childhood, Jackie always kept them on hand, along with strawberry Pop-Tarts and Sprite for Anthony. Because no matter how old her niece and nephew were, she always wanted her home to be a place of comfort and goodies.

While she made up a tray, Jackie mentioned to Marta that Tina had popped in and would be joining them for lunch. Jackie kept it simple with linen napkins and a China plate for the wafers. A glass with ice for the Crush and a skinny vase with one perky daisy. Jackie took the tray out to Tina, who yielded a faint smile when she saw it.

"John will be home soon for lunch, and you can join us. A little snack beforehand won't hurt though."

"Thanks, Aunt Jackie." Tina reached for a wafer and took a nibble.

"Now, what's going on with you and your mother?"

Tina sighed as she tossed the cookie back onto the plate. "It's like there's always a part of her life that's in chaos. She's gone all the time, either to San Francisco or to one party or event or something when she's here. I hardly see her, and when I do, she starts riding me about something. 'Tina, why are your clothes so disheveled?' Or, 'Can't you do a better job with your make-up?' Or, 'Why isn't your hair more stylish?' And she doesn't seem to care that Papa is gone."

The last words croaked out as Tina began to cry.

Jackie reached for her and held her close. Hearing Tina now, she realized the poor girl still harbored trauma from her parents' divorce and from losing her father's unexpected passing. A budding teenager at the time of the split, Tina had to adjust to not seeing her brother, whom she adored, and her beloved father on a regular basis. Their relationships became regulated to holidays and occasional weekends. Resentment had surely invaded Tina's heart, especially since Lee seemed to focus on her own love life or now her design business more than her daughter.

"Of course she cares about losing your father. She loved him dearly. I imagine that's why she seems so impossible at times. It's hard to know what to do with such grief." Jackie had to catch a breath. Not only because of Tina's fierce embrace but also because her own sorrow for Stas stirred. "Your father was a unique and wonderful man. None of us will ever get over losing him."

Tina leaned away and grabbed tissues from a box on the side

table. "It's not like before though, when I had Papa. Mummy is so... critical now. Papa used to tell me that she got it from her mother and that she couldn't help it. He said she didn't really mean the things she said and not to take the harsh comments to heart. But Papa's not here anymore. He always knew how to soothe her, and I can't do it... I just want some space from her."

"You're probably right. Some space would do you both good. You can stay here as long as you like. I'll have Marta set up your room. And don't worry about your mother. She's going through a difficult time. She'll get through it because she's strong like that, but she won't realize the things she's said that have hurt you."

Defending Lee came easier than she expected. Over the years there had been plenty of times when Jackie was appalled and flabber-gasted when she heard Lee speak the same reproaches over Tina that Janet had dished out. How could Lee be so unaware and repeat that awful element of their upbringing? At least Lee didn't strike her chil-dren across the face with that wicked-sharp slap, a strange skill Janet was particularly proficient at.

"And I think your father was right about her being like grandma at times. Your mother can't quite help it." Jackie stopped herself. Her niece needed rescued from a beat-down to her self-confidence, not a worthless psychoanalysis of their family dynamics.

"Christmas was awful." Tina reached for the wafer and snagged another bite. "Mummy acted like it would be so great, going to Santo Domingo with Peter and all but it was miserable." She sighed. "Mummy and Peter fought most of the time. Something about him seeing pictures of her with another guy. They didn't argue in front of me and Anthony, but we heard them. I think they broke up, but I don't know for sure."

So that's it!

Nancy had shown Jackie a couple pages inside some tabloids featuring Lee with Newton Cope, a San Francisco-based busi-nessman and hotelier who'd hired Lee to revamp some rooms at his establishment The Huntington Hotel. Newton was the man Jack

Warnecke had referred to last summer as being smitten with Lee. The pictures Jackie had seen showed Lee and Newton leaving a restaurant together, but they weren't holding hands and didn't appear to look like a couple. But was that intentional?

Had Lee gone back to her ways of two-timing men? The way she had when she was married to Stas and carrying on with Ari? It boggled Jackie's mind.

However, Lee taking out her aggravations on others, especially those who were innocent and not directly involved in her situation, was par for the course. If she and Peter had broken up over Christmas, because Lee was seeing Newton, it made sense that Tina had been caught in the crosshairs of Lee's frustrations.

"I'm sorry to hear about Christmas." Jackie would've welcomed more details but wouldn't put Tina in that position. "I'm glad you're here, Tina, and I say we get your mind off everything to do with your mother for a while. You can help with planning John's graduation party if you like. Then next weekend, we'll go out to Peapack. The horses could always use a good stretch, even in the cold. Perhaps we can do some shopping." Once more, Jackie realized she was getting carried away. This was Tina. Much like Caroline, she found satisfaction in simple pleasures and didn't require constant entertainment.

Jackie back pedaled. "You know, the morning light is perfect for reading in the library, and with a fire going, you might not want to leave your chair all day. And wait till you see all the new books I have for you to read."

A tentative smile returned to Tina's face. "Thanks, Aunt Jackie. I'm so glad I have you."

No other words could've made Jackie's heart feel so light.

LATER THAT EVENING, Lee telephoned, exasperated that Tina had left her a note about her leaving instead of talking to her.

"It was better this way," Jackie assured her. "Neither of you said anything you might regret, and when the time is right for both of you, which certainly won't be long, Tina will return home."

Lee huffed. "I am just spent when it comes to that girl."

Jackie bit back a sudden desire to reprimand Lee. *Spent?* Surely her sister had to be joking. Tina hadn't done anything wrong and had been nearly a perfect child growing up. She revered her parents and wanted nothing but their love and affection. Tina never gave back-talk, disobeyed, threw parties while her parents were out, or associated with people of ill-repute. Lee's complaints about her daughter weren't justified, and in Jackie's view, they lacked foundation.

As much as she wanted Lee to realize this—along with the fact that if anyone had a right to complain about being *spent*, it was Tina —how could she convey that without igniting Lee's temper? If Lee wasn't more careful with the way she treated Tina, Jackie feared the girl could spiral into self-destruction.

"You've had some trying times recently, Pekes." Jackie continued her tactic of soothing Lee. "It's no wonder you're easily ruffled."

"I only have her very best interest at heart. Why she cares to be so rebellious, I'll never understand."

How many times had their mother uttered the same sentiment about Lee when they were growing up? Jackie's concerns elevated. What would it take for Lee to confront and admit how brutal and unfair she was toward Tina? More importantly, how would these two ever connect and find a way to nurture a healthy relationship, with one so distant and out of touch and the other a sort of shrinking violet? It was beyond Jackie.

She refused to allow hopelessness to take root though. As long as she had breath in her body, Jackie would protect Tina and, to the best of her abilities, placate Lee in hopes that one day strengthening her bond with Tina would mean everything to her.

June 1978

JACKIE HAD to postpone dinner plans with a friend because an evening of celebration with her colleagues at the Municipal Arts Society was called for. The Supreme Court had ruled in favor of Grand Central Terminal's status as a preserved historical site, which meant the city of New York could reject the proposed plans by New Haven Railroad to erect a fifty-story tower on the site. She and the other committee members could not have been happier.

Now if only we could get that tacky Kodak Colorama display removed....

EIGHT

February 1979

As soon as Jackie hung up her coat after returning home for the evening, Marta greeted her.

"Madam, John is on the balcony."

"Wonderful." The elation never dulled for her, even though John returned home from Philips Academy almost every weekend. Fortunately, the new school had been good for him. Located in Andover, Massachusetts, it afforded him more privacy. For one thing, Ron Galella, the photographer obsessed with capturing pictures of Jackie and her children, wasn't tailing him nonstop.

But Jackie noted the worry etched in Marta's expression and her tightly clasped hands. "Is something wrong?"

"I could not tell for certain, but," Marta leaned in and whispered, "he took beer from the refrigerator."

That prickled Jackie's attention. At eighteen, John proved responsible, and while Jackie could only imagine what teenage boys did together, she was confident John made good choices. Through the years she had cautioned him religiously that every behavior and every decision he made was under scrutiny. He seemed to understand, but to her, he was still impressionable. And she warned him that not every friend he made would be genuine.

Still, she couldn't recall him ever showing an interest in alcohol before, and his having a drink at home didn't worry her as much as why. Jackie suspected Marta's instincts matched her own, which prompted her to say something.

"I see. Well, I'll speak to him. Thank you, Marta, for letting me know."

Marta nodded and returned to her duties while Jackie walked out to the balcony.

An icy wind slapped her cheeks as she stepped outside. Snow dusted the ledge and the balcony's concrete base. She immediately regretted not grabbing her coat and crossed her arms over her chest. John, still wearing his school's crested blazer, turned to her and flashed a lackluster smile. Jackie took it as confirmation that something was amiss, along with the half-empty bottle of Yuengling in one hand and a paper in the other.

"I'm not sure a wintery terrace is the best place for solemn thinking," she said, somehow managing to keep her teeth from chattering and her voice from quivering.

That coaxed a real smile from him.

"You're probably right, Mummy." He took in the skyline, sparkling against the orange-tinted twilight. "This makes me miss the weekends we spent skiing."

When Caroline and John were younger, and school ties and commitments were less demanding, Jackie often took them to Hunter Mountain in Upstate New York. Hearing him long for more childhood days gave Jackie a subtle affirmation that she'd done a good thing. Getaways to places like Hunter Mountain and the Peapack house had allowed them time to reconnect and knit their family bond even tighter.

"Is that something we should discuss?" She glanced at the paper he held.

John handed it to her. "I got accepted into Harvard."

"Oh, John, I'm so very proud." Reading the letter, seeing John's name somewhat affiliated with his father's alma mater warmed her slightly. Elated, she pressed the paper against her chest.

"I can't go." He shrugged so that his shoulders nearly touched his ears. "I can't go to Harvard."

Jackie didn't have a ready response, but she didn't feel blindsided by John's admission.

"I know it's expected of me. That I'm supposed to go to Harvard, just like my father...and *be* just like my father."

She had long dreaded the day John would come to the realization that the world wanted him to step into his father's footsteps and resume the mantle left behind. That no one would care about or seek to nurture John's own gifts and individuality. However, Jackie knew, ages ago, that John was destined to become his own man.

When he was a tyke, she'd worried that her husband might be disappointed in the boy, as he showed signs of being a slow learner. Jack's love for his son never faltered, though, and he'd once told Jackie, "Above all else, we must build his confidence and teach him to trust himself." She'd known Jack was right.

"I wanted to get in," John continued, "but I never wanted to go. It won't be right for me."

She looked into his eyes. "It's your decision to make, John."

"Do you mean that?" His forehead crinkled.

"If you're asking if I'm upset about it, the answer is no. Your struggle with grades has been a constant. I know what an intelligent young man you are, John. High-brow academics demand a rigidity that conflicts with who you are. The system adheres to a strict learning format, but you're one who learns best by doing. Tests don't always lend to your strengths or demonstrate what you know. I've always believed that."

Not that she would mention it, but John also had a terrible habit of losing his crested blazer, part of his school uniform, at least three times every year.

He also carried the weight of being compared to Caroline, who was currently attending Radcliffe, Harvard's sister college, and excelling in most subjects, just as she always had. Jackie knew part of that had to do with Caroline's quiet nature. Like Jackie, she absorbed books and cared more about teachers' approval and high marks than she did about having an overly active social life. John, on the other hand, was often corrected for talking too much and not paying attention. And rousing the classroom with his spot-on imitations of Mick Jagger.

As his mother, Jackie had spent ample time in the offices of his advisors, counselors, and tutors over the years. Each one repeated the same evaluation. "John processes knowledge differently than his peers. Standard education doesn't allow the room John needs to express what he's learned in a more creative manner."

"Do you have another university in mind?" She treaded carefully with the question, fully expecting John to reiterate how hard school was for him and that he needed time off.

"I think I like Yale. Maybe Brown."

"We'll explore them both and see what other options you may have." Although part of her wanted him to commit and devote himself thoroughly to achieving the goal of becoming a Harvard graduate, like his father, she sensed it wouldn't work. Despite his best efforts, John might fail, or worse, spiral into misery trying to please her and live up to public expectations. She wouldn't subject him to that. This decision was better, knowing from the get-go that Harvard wouldn't be an option.

"What about Grandma and Uncle Teddy?" he asked.

"They will support you no matter what."

"And you won't be disappointed?"

"Only if you wanted to attend Vassar."

Laughter burst from him, and Jackie knew it was what they both needed.

April 1979

"YOU WON'T BELIEVE THIS, Jackie darling, but I'm engaged!"

Jackie squeezed the telephone receiver in her hand tighter, so she wouldn't drop it. "Lee, did you say you're engaged?"

"Yes! And we're getting married next month. At our age there's no sense in waiting and no need for an extravagant ceremony."

"But who are you marrying?" The gut-punch of disbelief had left her breathless.

"Newton Cope, of course." Lee's excitement ticked into exasperation.

So Jack Warnecke had not overstated Lee and Newton's involvement. But how could Lee be engaged to a man Jackie hadn't met?

"I wasn't aware the relationship was so serious. Isn't this all rather sudden? And why rush?"

"Well, isn't it obvious, Jacks? We're madly in love."

Jackie poked her cheek with her tongue. Who was she to dispute her sister's feelings?

"Has he met Mummy and your children?"

"No, he lives in San Francisco, and with running the hotel his schedule can be tumultuous. You know Mummy doesn't travel much these days, and the children are in school." Since graduating from Choate Rosemary Hall, Anthony had been studying broadcast journalism at Boston University while Tina had transferred from the Hewitt School to Brearley, where she graduated from. Presently, she seemed to waffle between traveling and committing to a college.

"Then why don't you let me host a party for you two here in Manhattan? It could be like an engagement party and perhaps give us all a chance to meet him."

"I think that's a fabulous idea."

Jackie jotted notes for flowers and catering. She also agreed to make arrangements for Janet and to discuss matters with Anthony and Tina. Her chasing and scattering thoughts made it difficult to focus though. In the space of a few minutes, she'd gone from little communication with her sister to suddenly planning a party for her upcoming wedding. And apparently, the insanity of it all was lost on Lee.

"Lee, have you already taken care of the prenup?"

A pause. "Why, no. I hadn't really thought about it."

"Oh, you should. I hear it makes things easier these days. You'll want to protect your assets and make sure that you're taken care of."

Another pause. "I'm not sure, Jacks. You *know* how men get when you talk about touching their money."

Yes, Jackie knew. At the same time, she no longer believed it was taboo or unreasonable for a woman of Lee's class and stature to have monetary expectations—and an arrangement in place—and in writing before one committed to anything.

"Marriage is all about women becoming the property of men. He's a wealthy man, and it's not unreasonable for you to look out for yourself."

She considered pointing out Lee's nearly dire financial status but was in no mood to spark an altercation. Lee had sold her 5th Avenue duplex, to Jackie's dismay, and didn't net as much profit as she could have if she'd waited for an up-turn in the market. Lee still had her home in Southampton but rented an apartment in Manhattan, which Jackie covered. That was a matter they never discussed, but as a multimillionaire and older sister, Jackie believed looking out for Lee was her duty. Regardless of the ebb and flow of their complicated relationship.

"I'll telephone Alexander and have him call you. Then he can work out the details with Newton. He may be captivated by you but he's also a businessman. He'll understand."

"Well," Lee hesitated, "if you think it's best."

Jackie knew it was a risk, bringing up money and encouraging her sister to nudge the topic to the forefront with Newton. But in all likelihood, she assumed, he had to be a reasonable man. And if he knew Lee at all, he had to know that marrying a woman of her notoriety would come with stipulations.

"At this point in one's life," Jackie said, "you want to make sure you're financially secure. Nothing matters more, especially if you want to live happily ever after."

———

THOUGH SHE DIDN'T HAVE much time for planning, Jackie hosted a simple yet elegant dinner for Lee and Newton. Anthony and Tina seemed agreeable with the man, and it wasn't long into the evening before Lee was encouraging Tina and Newton's daughters, Marguerite and Isabelle, to travel together after they started talking about wanting to explore Russia and Spain. Janet also took quickly to Newton, thanks in part to his easy charms. Along with Alexander Forger, Jackie had invited Maurice. André Meyer would've completed her trio of financial advisors, but he had to decline, being out of town.

While she had enjoyed Maurice's company on occasion, as an escort to the ballet or an opening exhibit, Jackie felt she didn't know Maurice as well as Alexander and André, but his company always proved amusing and stellar. For tonight, she made sure his invite included his wife, but Maurice arrived alone.

Usually, Jackie wasn't one who found it difficult to converse with new people. At least in a comfortable setting. Being an editor, she'd slowly grown accustomed to meeting writers, who were often introverted or eccentric. Establishing a rapport, she discovered, was largely her responsibility and could influence the success of their working relationship.

With Newton, however, she felt stunted but aimed to make a valiant effort.

Before the dessert course, Jackie allowed her guests an intermission from the table. Some refreshed in the bathroom. Others made brief phone calls. Jackie invited Newton to join her on the balcony for a smoke, since the evening air was unseasonably warm and the view spectacular. She had phoned the Met earlier and asked them to light the Temple of Dandur exhibit, which could be seen from her vantage point atop 1040.

"It's hard to believe you'll be marrying my sister in a few short weeks." Her words felt awkward and forced.

"Are you...distrusting of her decision?"

His direct remark took her aback. Perhaps it was due to not knowing him well enough, or possibly because she wanted to be the one to set the tone of their interaction.

"Even if I vehemently disapproved, which I don't, there's no telling my sister what to do. But I'm sure you'll make each other very happy." She sipped her champagne, worried she was about to launch into a rambling mess of what a delightful future they had ahead.

But she had to give Newton credit. Upon meeting her he didn't put on what she called royal airs, and he didn't over compliment her. She was accustomed to it and partially immune. To meet someone who didn't have her branded in his mind as "America's Queen" or "That Poor Widow" was as rare as it was refreshing.

"Do you have any advice for me? How might I ensure a long-lasting relationship?"

She suddenly thought of Peter Tufo and how he had inexplicably been replaced by Newton. Jackie's devilish side threatened to deliver a snide remark that Newton should beware of Lee's fickleness.

"That's easy." Jackie couldn't suppress her smirk. "Be overly generous with your prenuptial arrangement."

May 1979

Jackie,

I am sending you a letter to confirm that we are on track to finish construction of the library in the next five months. You may plan for the opening ceremony in October as we discussed shortly after the groundbreaking.

I cannot fully express what this project and your faith in me has meant. I know some people tried to discourage you from taking a chance on me because they thought I lacked the experience to undertake a building of such significance.

I also count it fortunate that you did not hold against me the fact that one of my designs was considered for the replacement of Grand Central Terminal. My vision—my Hyperboloid— would have set a new standard in New York architecture. You must admit that a hundred-and two-story building—one to rival the Empire State Building no less—would have secured its own iconic status, especially with my unique cylindrical design. Perhaps one day, I may construct it elsewhere.

Today, I thank you greatly for this opportunity.

Sincerely,
I.M. Pei

May 1979

ON A WHIM, and because no other family members would be present, Jackie joined Lee in San Francisco shortly before her wedding. She hadn't spent much time on the West Coast and felt out of place. The weather proved pleasant enough, but otherwise, she already looked forward to returning home. But perhaps it had more to do with circumstances than the location.

Jackie had accepted that her sister was going through with the nuptials despite the fact a prenup hadn't been signed. She decided it was no longer her place to mention it. There was no way she would risk causing a disturbance so close to the ceremony.

The night before, Lee had tried on her wedding dress. A shimmering ivory column dress Jackie adored. Chic and simple. Jackie glimpsed traces of hesitation in Lee's expression but said nothing. If Lee had misgivings, she could bring it up.

The day of the wedding, Jackie accompanied Lee to a chic salon where they had an appointment to get their hair and nails done before the ceremony.

"I feel good about this, Jacks."

Jackie couldn't help feeling as though Lee was trying to convince her. Almost as if Lee had to hear the words in order to believe them. Earlier in the morning, Jackie had watched her drain a glass of vodka. She didn't intervene and warn Lee that getting tipsy before reciting her vows could be a poor decision. If Lee's aim was to calm her nerves, Jackie could understand. On the other hand, if Lee was attempting to dull her reservations, Jackie had no recourse to offer. She would focus on her commitment to stand by her. The only thing she could do.

"It's sure to be an unforgettable day."

"I just hope," Lee paused before they entered, and as she scarfed a breath, Jackie thought she might crack. "I just hope everyone will be comfortable."

Whether the remark was influenced by Lee's alcohol consumption—though Jackie didn't know if Lee had more than one drink—or a veiled concern, Jackie couldn't tell. Lee had mastered the art of evasiveness years ago when she began seeing Ari.

Jackie followed her sister inside, where they were immediately welcomed, and a message was handed to Lee.

After reading the note, her face paled.

"It's from Mr. Forger. He needs me to telephone at once."

Lee wasted no time in dialing the attorney from the telephone on the receptionist's desk.

Jackie stepped aside with the staff members who had greeted

them upon their arrival. She hoped to hold their attention and down-play that Lee was dealing with the unexpected.

Minutes later, Lee appeared at her side. Jackie recognized her expression—she was rattled but working to hide it.

"Will there be champagne?" Lee forced a smile. The staff moved to serve her.

Now able to speak without being overheard, she locked her gaze with Jackie's. "Mr. Forger said Newton hasn't agreed to the terms of the prenup. He refuses to ensure a monthly allowance of fifteen thou-sand for me. I found the sum quite reasonable for my lifestyle and his means, but Newton doesn't want to budge beyond ten thousand. I'm flummoxed he's proving so stubborn."

Jackie tensed, certain Lee would blame her. "What are you going to do?"

"What can I do? I'm getting married in six hours." She touched her forehead as if she were fighting back a headache. "I told Mr. Forger to push, but not to let Newton know I wanted him to push." She corrected her slouching posture. "For now, let's get our hair done."

Jackie agreed that their only immediate option was to keep up appearances—by having their appearance enhanced. She gave Lee credit as she watched her sister plunge into the role of pampered bride-to-be. After two hours of primping, they left, with Lee exuding her gratefulness, and returned to the Huntington Hotel.

Newton awaited them. He asked Jackie to pardon them as he ushered Lee into a private room.

Jackie retreated to her own suite.

An hour later, Lee joined her.

"We've decided to postpone the wedding."

"Because of the prenup?"

"Newton doesn't think our wedding day is the appropriate time to be hammering out a legal document, and I agree. The stress hampers the joy. He suggested we plan for a ceremony in the fall, and that way we'll have time to arrange for our families to be part of the day. I must say, he's been quite the rock and a gentleman through this ordeal."

"Guests have started to arrive." Jackie stared out the window, feeling an empathetic anxiety for Lee. And a sense of guilt. Was this her fault?

"Newton is on the telephone, taking care of canceling everything. I was with him as he spoke to Stanley Bass, you know, the judge from the Supreme Court who was set to officiate. He told Newton he was just preparing to put on his robe. Newton will have his hands full, informing everyone of our decision. But I'm off to finish packing."

"Are you heading back to New York already?"

She flashed Jackie an arched eyebrow and a wry grin. "We're still going on our honeymoon. After this hectic day, we both could use the getaway, and not even postponing my wedding is going to discourage me from going to St. Martin. A soak in the Caribbean Sea is exactly what I need to recover."

July 1965

LEE KNEW about the gifts Ari sent Jackie. The deluge of flowers he sent when she moved from the White House to the Harrimans' house in Georgetown. A bike for John, which he was too little to ride. Bejeweled hair combs for Caroline. Giving was Ari's nature, especially to those he cared about. And especially, it seemed, to Jackie.

Lee wondered if she was partly to blame for the genuine friendship that evolved between the two. Lee had been the one who suggested a two-week cruise aboard the *Christina* would be good for Jackie. She needed rest and recuperation, and more importantly, she needed the chance to heal, having suffered the loss of her baby Patrick. During that vacation, Ari kept a mindful distance. Other guests had joined them, and Jackie spent most of her time with Lee and the others aboard, but when Ari was around, he couldn't have been more charming and attentive to Jackie.

Lee knew if she mentioned Jackie and the gifts, it would taint her in Ari's eyes. A woman prone to jealousy was hardly attractive. But was she supposed to sit back and risk him falling for Jackie?

One afternoon, as they sunbathed on the top deck of the yacht, she reached over and took his hand.

"We could sail away together. Not tell anyone. We could even get married one day. Maybe at an exotic port, like Tahiti or the Falkland Islands."

For a moment, Ari said nothing. Then, "Such a child." He snorted. "What does marriage mean to you?"

She released his hand.

Whether he meant it as a tease or an insult, she couldn't tell, but she knew Ari was right. She wasn't free to elope on a whim. And though she found herself at odds with parenting at times, she needed to consider her children.

But even if she worked it out—divorced Stas and retained custody of the children—there was another matter between them.

"Why do you invite Maria?" Her skin prickled just mentioning her name.

He grinned, and she knew he wouldn't answer her. He didn't need to. Maria served as a decoy of sorts, keeping Lee's affair with Ari under wraps. At the same time, Lee couldn't deny the chemistry and attraction between Ari and Maria. He liked having Maria around. She understood him in ways others never would—a factor that suddenly made Lee wonder if she could ever truly have Ari to herself. What were the chances of Maria going quietly from the foreground to the background of Ari's life?

What hope was there of one day becoming his wife? But what she didn't know for certain was whether or not the personal cost would be worth it. Or was the role as his not-so-secret mistress enough? And how long would it last? Lee suddenly worried that they had sabotaged any chance of a meaningful future with the current arrangement.

And wasn't Maria in the same position? What had it been, six years since Maria left her husband for Ari? Why hadn't all that chemistry and attraction led them down the aisle?

Lee's head began to ache. She couldn't make sense out of it, and she couldn't cultivate the answers she wanted.

She slicked on more oil and resituated herself on her lounge chair. Perhaps it was best to only focus on the present. Lee was the one Ari snuck into his cabin and made love to—practically under Maria's nose. She was with Ari, and he wanted her at his side. For now, she decided that was enough.

And there was no need to concern herself about Ari and Jackie. Ari had plenty to occupy him when it came to women, and Jackie was entangled in an affair with Bobby. They were unlikely to see each other since Ari preferred life on his yacht and Jackie didn't socialize much these days. Lee couldn't help laughing to herself when she pictured them as a couple. Ari would never settle for the scraps of Jack Kennedy's life. Surely, it was beneath him. And after all the humiliation Jackie had endured in her marriage to Jack, there was no chance she might consider Ari as an upgrade. Like Jack, he shared no interest in horses, the ballet, or fidelity.

What a disaster they would be together!

NINE

June 1979

J ackie settled into her new office space, and among her new colleagues, at Doubleday with greater ease than she thought possible. Perhaps the rousing success of *In the Russian Style* and *Sally Hemings, A Novel* had not only helped legitimize her ability to learn the publishing ropes and to oversee commercially successful projects, but also demonstrated her work ethic and professional drive.

Regardless, she was ecstatic for another chance to pursue the career she'd fallen in love with. Though she kept the same schedule she had at Viking, only going into the office three days a week, she worked on projects from home. Nancy, with an office next to hers, continued to juggle her duties as both Jackie's assistant and personal secretary while fulfilling her role at Doubleday. Jackie couldn't have asked for a better situation.

Her at-work routine continued with eating her sack lunch at her desk most days and sitting cross-legged on the floor while she played with the potential layout of a book. Attending launch parties was the aspect of her job she enjoyed the least. However, she understood the power and exposure her celebrity brought to an author and the book, so she usually made a point to stay for the duration. When she could stand it. And when the press played nice.

Her strength, she found, was encouraging her authors. Difficulties were certain to pop up for every author and during every project. Jackie never criticized their work. Instead, if the writing or direction wasn't working, she used the power of gentle, positive words.

One morning, after Jackie had just sat down with her first cup of coffee, Nancy poked her head into the office.

"You might want to see this."

She followed Nancy into the staff lounge where the TV was on and tuned in to the *Stanley Siegel Show*, which Jackie recognized from the set décor. The camera focused on the day's guest, Truman Capote, who appeared to be giving a monologue.

Nancy spoke into Jackie's ear. "Not sure if he's drunk or high on something, but he's delivering quite the performance."

"I will say that it is the most shocking thing," Truman said, "to endure the betrayal of someone you once loved. But who am I these days to the *principessa Lee Radziwilla*? I'm just an old Southern fag. But there's one thing you can always say about us Southern fags. *We is mean.* If she detests homosexuals, though, I don't know why she's had me as her confidant for over a decade, but times certainly do change.

"Take the princess herself for example. Why, she's practically broke from what I hear, and whether it's Peter Tufo or that hoity Newton Cope, she can't nail down a man anymore. Maybe it's because she lost all her charms after Peter Beard left her for a younger gal, with much fewer miles on her. Men are only interested in her so they can ride on her coattails and boost their notoriety. Which she owes to Jackie, of course.

He put a hand to his cheek. "Shall we dare talk about Lee and the untouchable Jackie Onassis?"

Jackie stiffened, especially when her co-workers darted glances her way. She kept her focus on the TV and Truman.

"Those two may be sisters, but they're not equals." He wagged a finger. "Oh, no, no, no. Jackie is the queen of all, and Lee is a pauper at best. It's probably no surprise but Lee is stuffed with jealousy and intimidation. She's afraid of Jackie and can't stand her. She wants to show her up and craves her approval all at the same time. And let's be honest, Lee probably hasn't gotten over Jackie taking away Onassis from her. Can't you just imagine those two, sitting across from each other while bobbing up and down on Ari's boat. One was his trophy and the other his discarded mistress. But don't worry about poor Lee, knowing what she's done to Jackie, she had *that* one coming."

***

JACKIE, stoic and resolute, left the lounge when the broadcast broke for a commercial. She stayed in her office for the rest of the morning and tried to focus on work, useless as it was. More convincing, she hoped, was the façade she put forth with her fixed smile—her trademark, some might say—and unbothered disposition. Things that were still in her control.

What had Truman meant when he said, "knowing what she's done to Jackie"? Was he just rambling, or did a deeper meaning lie beneath his words?

Either way, Lee must've been frantic.

Jackie took a cab from the office to 1040, but not a minute before her normal departure. Entering her home, she expected Marta to be waiting, with Lee either already on the phone or having left several messages. But Marta, busy with the ironing while her daytime soaps played in the background, didn't mention Lee.

Jackie casually retreated to her room, momentarily relieved that Marta must have missed the broadcast.

But Jackie couldn't sit idly by, flummoxed and thinking about Lee. After a few minutes, Jackie rang Lee's number.

Lee answered immediately.

"I suppose you've heard what Truman did?"

Jackie thought her sister's voice sounded gravely, as though she'd been talking for hours, but didn't address it. She shared how she and some of her co-workers caught part of the broadcast.

Lee paused, as if taking a drag on a cigarette. "Well, I'm glad I didn't watch it, but I was told everything he said. That Liz Smith wasted no time in calling me up. Why, she had even taken notes so she could relay every harsh remark. According to her, a few people knew he was going to go off like a nuclear bomb on me. Can you believe Stanley gave that little worm the airtime?"

"But I want to know why, Lee. What on earth was Truman seeking to accomplish?" Jackie bit her thumbnail to work out her anxiety. Tabloids and gossip outlets were sure to recap the spectacle for those who missed the live performance.

"You know it's because of that other worm, Gore Vidal. They've both tried to use me for their ridiculous squabble."

Known by others for his writing, his failed attempts to run for elected office, and his penchant to spark feuds with other noted writers, Gore Vidal seemed to thrive on stirring up conflict. Jackie and Lee couldn't stand him, even though he had a connection to their family. A stepson to their beloved Hughdie from his second marriage to Nina Gore, he'd joined the Army and was off for his enlistment by the time Jackie and Lee moved into Hammersmith Farm. Not that there had been hope of them forming an amiable relationship in the first place. Jackie's disdain for the man sprang from his compulsion to engage in public confrontations and quarrels.

"Wasn't that over years ago?" Jackie asked.

"No. I testified on the matter last year. Well, it wasn't a testimony per se. I merely gave my statement."

In a 1975 interview for *Playgirl* magazine, Truman had stated that Gore Vidal got drunk at a White House dinner party in 1961 that Jackie was hosting in honor of Lee and her husband Stas. When Gore became unruly, he was physically removed from the party.

Thrown out were the words Truman used in his retelling. The whole story, Truman said, came from Lee. Enraged, Gore retaliated by filing a million-dollar lawsuit against Truman for libel. Gore clarified that he was not *thrown out* but asked to leave, which he did. Truman wanted Lee to testify on his behalf, that she had told him the story exactly as he had told it to *Playgirl*. Lee refused to get involved or to side with either of them.

However, when she was subpoenaed in late 1977 by Gore's attorney, she agreed to submit an affidavit and stated, "I do not recall ever discussing with Truman Capote the incident or evening which I understand is the subject of his lawsuit."

"But Truman's rant today," Lee continued, "is all because of Liz Smith. She said she asked Truman, just recently, if things had changed between us since I gave that statement. According to her, that was the first Truman knew about it and he blew his top. He planned this whole live-TV debacle so he could get revenge on me."

Then why couldn't he keep me out of it? Jackie wondered. She fought back exasperation and asked, "What are you going to do, Pekes?"

"You know there's only one thing to do. Say nothing. I suppose I can hope that people will see the whole thing as Truman spiraling out of control because of his addictions. Or maybe they'll think he's finally lost his mind. It wasn't enough what he did with that *Esquire* article, and maybe this will finish him off." Lee sighed heavily. "I'm sorry you got dragged into this, Jackie, and I hope you don't give a thought to the malicious things he said about us."

Jackie's insides coiled and tightened. She suspected there was a thread of truth in Truman's description of Lee's feelings toward her. Especially when it came to Ari. Considering the verbal lashing Lee had taken today, Jackie decided to tread carefully. For now.

"I think you're right, Lee. Everyone will see he's falling apart. It was a vile display of his character and not worth giving attention to."

Lee huffed.

"I can guarantee you one thing, Jacks. Even if he manages to come out of this and straighten up his life, I never intend to speak to Truman again or to trust him with a grocery list."

July 1979

ALTHOUGH INTRIGUE PULSED through her when Maurice invited her to join him for an afternoon cruise aboard his yacht to discuss recent matters, Jackie couldn't deny an equal tug of hesitation. For years, they had spent time together, mainly in formal settings, and lately, their friendship had deepened. But Maurice was still a bit of a mystery to her. Apart from their business dealings, she didn't know a great deal about him. Not personally. She knew he was married, of course, and a father to three grown, successful children, but otherwise Maurice Tempelsman was an enigma. As one who prided herself on maintaining her own privacy as much as possible, she marveled at his ability to do the same.

"Ah, Jacqueline, you've arrived," Maurice declared as she approached the yacht. Dressed in khakis and a casual button-down shirt with the top buttons unfastened, he raised his hands in the air. "Welcome to the *Relemar*." He took her hand as she stepped aboard.

Memories of her time on the *Christina*, Ari's luxurious yacht, invaded. Of course she didn't expect to find the outrageous opulence here that Ari had adorned his ship with—fixtures made of gold, a mosaic dance floor that lowered and converted into a pool at the touch of a button, and those ridiculous barstools covered in whale foreskins.

Maurice gave her the tour, which didn't take long. Seating on the flybridge promised elevated, clear views but wouldn't accommodate more than a handful of people. Below deck were a main salon, the kitchen, an aft deck for dining, a master stateroom, a guest room, and modest cabins for the crew. Not as stately or as roomy as Jack's *Honey*

Fitz or the presidential yacht, the *USS Sequoia*, but the *Relemar* was cozy and equipped with every modern amenity.

"I crafted the name using my children's names. Rena, Leon, and Marcy," he shared with a twinkle of pride in his eyes.

"How ingenious. It's very endearing." Although she wished the craft afforded more privacy, Jackie allowed Maurice's gentle nature to put her at ease.

"I agree. Shall we enjoy drinks on the flybridge? The breeze is wonderful up top."

Jackie nodded and they climbed their way up the tight, narrow stairs. She tied on a head scarf as drinks were poured.

"We could move inside if you like."

"I don't mind an angry wind, but my hair is another matter." Jackie also wanted to put him at ease and enjoy the afternoon. They tapped their glasses in cheers. "This is spectacular, Maurice." A lifelong lover of the outdoors and the ocean, it took little for her to fall in love with her surroundings. "What a wonderful setting for our lunch. Thank you for arranging this."

"I'm glad you accepted my invitation, although I hope it's not too early for champagne."

"Of course not." Jackie liked seeing him a bit awkward. The care he always took to ensure she was comfortable touched her and stirred butterflies in her stomach.

After they enjoyed fresh crab cakes, Maurice reviewed the performance of her stocks and investments, which had quadrupled her money. Jackie was impressed and exceedingly grateful for his expertise.

"That's truly incredible, Maurice. You're so clever and astute."

He smiled. "It makes me happy, knowing you'll never have a financial worry the rest of your life."

She returned the grin and was thrilled by how he had created a perfect segue for her to share her plans. "What would you say if I had an idea for spending some of that money?"

"Well, I'd say I'm quite intrigued. Does this idea involve fashion?"

His question was a mild letdown. "No. I'm not obsessed with clothes and stuffing my closet."

"That's not what I meant. It's only that I could see you investing in a young designer and helping launch a new career."

"Oh." Her cheeks flushed at her slight overreaction. "Perhaps I'm not as noble as you think."

"Impossible. I know about the work you've done with Grand Central and the Bedford-Stuyvesant project."

Her grin and a dose of confidence returned.

"Please, what is it you have in mind?"

Jackie withdrew papers from her Gucci satchel and unfolded them across the table. Loosely drawn plans, done by her, showed a house on an expansive property.

"You're the first to see this, Maurice. I'm anxious to share it with André, but it will have to wait since he's in Switzerland."

"Yes, I know. He prefers as much time as he can get at his summer home. Can't say that I blame him. It's beautiful there." Maurice donned a pair of glasses and began reading over the real estate listing Jackie handed him. "What do we have here?"

"It's a property I want to buy. The land is what I really want because there's only a small cottage there now. Turning it into what I envision will take some doing, but I've already sketched out a few ideas. I think this could be my dream home."

He whistled. "Quite a chunk of land, three hundred and forty acres. According to the listing, it's mostly raw, and on the southwestern tip of Martha's Vineyard. You'll have to educate me about the geography. How far does that put you from...relatives?"

"Roughly two hours from Cape Cod and a bit more from Newport. Close enough for emergencies, God forbid, but not close enough for casual visits."

Maurice nodded. "Ideal then."

Jackie pointed out the features she found enticing, such as the mile of private beachfront, the rolling dunes, and two freshwater ponds.

"You've sold me." He tapped her drawings. "I'm in full support and think you should move ahead with the purchase. The price seems reasonable, but we should see if they'll budge a little lower. I can get the wheels in motion, if you like, unless you prefer to have André look things over first."

Jackie's interest piqued at the slight hitch in his voice with the mention of André. An indication of jealousy? Was he worried that André's support carried more weight? Maurice had no way of knowing, but Jackie wasn't seeking any man's approval.

"Perhaps I should've been more forthright," she said. "I've already had my offer accepted. But I will need you to make sure the funds are transferred."

To her surprise, Maurice lit up.

"A woman who knows what she wants and goes after it. Rather modern of you, and a very attractive quality if I may be so bold."

His adulation made her face color again.

"Jackie, there is a little something I wanted you to know. My wife and I, we've been separated for years now. We're cordial, which has been nice for the children, but the truth of the matter is that what we had wasn't meant to last a lifetime. She's a wonderful woman, don't misunderstand, but our union came as a result of both our families leaving Belgium to escape the war. One could say it was just short of an arranged marriage. It was inevitable that we grew apart, to no one's fault."

Jackie understood. A degree of compromise had been at the altar with her both times. Not that she begrudged either of her choices.

"Now my intent in sharing this is not to rouse your pity, but I wanted you to have a clear picture of my personal life, because Jackie," he cleared his throat, "I would very much like for you to be part of my personal life."

She couldn't resist the chance to tease him. "What do you propose?"

He reddened. "Well, I doubt that you're in the habit of seeing married men, but I'm only married by way of legal documents. Essentially, I'm free to pursue anyone I like, but in truth, there's only one woman I desire to know intimately, and that's you, Jackie."

Warmth spilled over her. Not in a way that stirred her carnal desires, but in a way that boosted her ego.

"I'm very flattered, Maurice."

"I fear there may be a dreadful *but* accompanying this."

She laughed mildly. "Well, I could be assuming too much, but I only think it's fair to warn you that I don't want to get married again." Should she also admit to him that she currently liked being unattached? Being in an exclusive relationship wasn't appealing, but she ventured that sharing those tidbits would prove too much for now.

He nodded. "I won't be in a position to ask anytime soon."

She liked that he didn't hesitate to tease right back.

"Now, before I forget." He retrieved a present from the wet bar cabinet. "I knew your birthday was coming up and I wanted to get you something."

"Oh, how thoughtful!" She tore through the wrapping and found *Poemes Saturniens* by Paul Verlaine. "*Poems Under Saturn.*"

"Yes, I went off the assumption that you probably possess a robust collection of works by Baudelaire, and that maybe you could find room on a shelf for something new. Well, Verlaine may not be new to you, knowing your extensive love for poetry, but..." Seemingly out of words, he capped it with a shrug.

Jackie adored his rambling. "I always have room for poetry." She wasn't about to admit she already had a copy of the book because now she would reread the poems with Maurice in mind.

A sigh of relief softened his expression. "May I call on you and see you socially?" He posed the question in French, to Jackie's surprised delight.

"*Oui.*"

On the other hand, she had no qualms about Maurice falling for

her. She liked that he seemed receptive to an unrestrained relationship. There had been other men who enjoyed seeing her socially and
probably wanted more, but when it came to them—André and Hugh
Fraser in particular—she never developed a romantic desire. Would
the same thing happen with Maurice? Was he destined to become
another caretaker of sorts? She didn't know, but for now, she chose to
see Maurice, and considered herself open to any possibility.

August 1979

WHEN JANET REACHED out to Jackie to schedule a mother-
daughter lunch with her and Lee, Jackie suggested they meet at
Janet's home. Her mother seemed agreeable to the switch. Jackie was
relieved, especially since she didn't want Janet to experience a bout
of confusion while in Manhattan, although she did note that being
easily agreeable wasn't typical of her mother.

Among Jackie's list of worries, Janet's living arrangements ranked
at the top. She wondered if Janet would be happy living in the Castle.
Although the space was adequate, the home had once been servants'
quarters. Jackie was certain her mother would express despondency
over being reduced to living there, despite there being no traces of
such a past. The Castle was a more manageable space than the main
house, but would letting go of her old life prove too much?

Those thoughts accompanied her as she entered Janet's home.

Lee was already there. Quiche and caprese salad awaited for
lunch. Jackie hardly had a chance to settle in and finish plating her
serving before Janet commanded their attention.

"I'm glad you're both here. There's something I want to tell you."

Jackie exchanged a curious glance with Lee.

Janet reached out and placed a hand atop each of her daughters'.
"I'm getting married."

Silence followed as Jackie absorbed the declaration.

"Married?" She almost couldn't form the word. "To whom?"

"Oh, Jacqueline, don't be silly. Why, Bingham, of course."

"You're going to marry Bingham Morris?" Lee apparently needed clarification.

"Yes." Janet withdrew her hands and took up her cup of tea. "We've discussed it at length. There's no reason either of us should be alone, but we'll each keep our houses. He adores Southampton, naturally, and wants to have a place for his children and grandchildren, and my reasons for staying here match his." She sighed as she set her teacup on its saucer. "This has been my home for decades, and I can't imagine living anywhere else."

"If that's the case, Mummy, you don't need to get married."

"Nonsense, Jacqueline! We must do what is right in God's sight. Having a man come and go into my home would not look proper. A woman's reputation is everything."

"But what on earth do you have in common with Bing?" Lee seemed on the brink of laughter until she caught her mother's side stare. "His nickname is *Booch* for God's sake and he's...uncultured."

"Let me remind you he's a member of the Hasty Pudding Club, and he's sailed around the world."

"That's...nice, Mummy, but Lee has a point. You and Bing don't seem...well-suited for each other."

"With all due respect, I believe you're wrong." Janet's posture stiffened. "We've known each other practically our whole lives, that accounts for something. And he's not a man about town. Since his Mary passed last year, he's not the type who's out every night with a different woman on his arm. I rather like that and find it rare in a man these days." She finished her remark with a firm nod.

"But what about money? Has he agreed to provide for you and sign a prenup?"

"Bingham is quite wealthy, which I'm sure you know. He had a very successful career as an investment banker."

Jackie waited, but Janet didn't elaborate further or give a direct answer to the question. Her mind quickly moved to her mother's health issues. Though Janet might be quick to deny any reasons for concerns, Jackie knew better, and worse, she didn't know what it would mean for her mother down the road. Had Bing been on the other side of one of her mood swings? Or observed her frustration when a bout of confusion struck?

"Bingham and I may have details to work out, but we're going through with it. We plan to get married, here at the Castle in October."

Lee scowled. "Why the rush?"

"Well, that's the last thing I expected from you, Lee. Weren't you the one rushing to the altar a few months ago? Speaking of which, what happened to all that? Is there a ceremony in the works I don't know about?"

Lee dipped her chin. "No, although I don't think this is the proper time to discuss my situation with Newton. You marrying Bing is a more pressing matter."

Janet eyed her. "For whom, dear? It has little to do with you."

"Making someone a permanent part of the family does affect us, Mummy." Jackie kept her tone civil, respectful. "Maybe not in the same way as when you married Hughdie, but he'll become part of our lives."

Jackie's mind unboxed her first memories of Hughdie. When she arrived at Hammersmith Farm for the first time, after the nuptials had been exchanged, he was soft-spoken and welcoming. As much as she didn't want a stepfather and hated that her parents had divorced, Jackie couldn't afford to be rebellious since the arrangement crushed Lee even more. She behaved for Lee's sake, but Hughdie wasn't overbearing and didn't try too hard to win them over with gifts or superfluous attention. He gave them space to settle and adjust on their own. Over time, she grew to love Hughdie, as did Lee.

But if Janet married Bing, circumstances would be different. He would have no influence in her life—and no hope of endearing himself to Jackie. Still, she didn't like it. Her imagination crafted a picture of Bing, standing at the entrance to the Castle, a smoldering cigar held between his teethy grin, and his arms open wide as he stood there shirtless in ragged overalls. She shuddered to erase the vision.

"It thrills me to hear you say that, Jacqueline. Yes, I want Bingham to be part of your lives and to be welcomed by you both."

"Well, I don't completely understand your insistence to marry him." Discouraged, Jackie tried a new tactic. "Have you talked to Janet Jr about this?"

"I have. She won't be able to attend the ceremony, which I didn't expect her to anyway, but she has given me her blessing."

Of course she has.

Jackie's shoulders slumped hearing those words. What recourse did she have left?

Stealing a glimpse of Lee, Jackie's heart ached for her as she sat there, withdrawn and looking as though she was coddling an injury. Had Janet's comments cut that deeply? Jackie didn't know the current state of her relationship with Newton or whether or not they still intended to marry. With the way Lee had gone from seeing Peter Tufo to seeing Newton, Jackie could only imagine what a man went through to be with Lee.

But now wasn't the time to focus on Lee. Her mother's admission had already made her head swim. Was there a way to dissuade her from going through with what Jackie considered a poor decision? Or had Janet discovered a new way to slap Jackie—and Lee—in the face?

September 1979

WHEN JACKIE'S old friend Ros Gilpatric telephoned her at her Peapack home, just after her ride with the Essex Hunt Club, she was elated to hear his voice. She couldn't recall the last time they'd spoken, but Ros had cemented a place in her history. Gossip columnists would say he was the man who came between her and Ari, though not because of a torrid affair but thanks to a collection of letters she'd written to Ros that were stolen from his office and published in newspapers. The last letter she had sent him, which espoused—*I hope you know all you were and are and will ever be to me—With my love, Jackie*—ignited a firestorm because it was written on stationary from the *Christina* during her honeymoon with Ari. Humiliated by the exposure, Ari became incensed. He paid no attention when Jackie gently reminded him she only saw Ros casually before she and Ari had married.

Though the letters contributed to the further decay of her union with the Greek tycoon, Jackie didn't blame Ros. He suffered his own fallout at the time when his wife filed for divorce the day the letters were released.

Jackie and Ros salvaged a friendship through the debris, mainly, Jackie believed, because they hadn't been involved sexually. Although pictures from their trip to Mexico in the spring of 1968 provided a different impression, Jackie and Ros lacked chemistry in the sheets. It was one of the traits she appreciated about him—his ability to play the romantic when the press was watching then laugh about it with her later behind closed doors.

"Ros, how good to hear from you."

"It's a pleasure to hear your voice, too, Jackie, but I'm afraid I have terrible news."

She braced herself, knowing it was a worthless effort. "What?"

"André Meyer has died in Switzerland."

Ros went on to explain that after falling ill, André had succumbed, though doctors were uncertain of the precise cause of his decline but attributed it to his circulatory system. From what they said, that could mean any number of causes. Blood clots, stroke, even a heart attack.

"Forgive me for sounding callous, but it doesn't matter now. He's gone, and I'm sorry, Jackie. I've made arrangements for us to fly to Paris for the memorial service and burial."

"Have you spoken to Maurice?" She didn't care to mention that she and Maurice had grown close, knowing it would inspire the question of exactly how close they were.

"Not directly. He's out of the country conducting business in Africa. His secretary promised to inform him and to make sure flowers were sent on his behalf."

Speechlessness gripped her. Jackie wanted Maurice by her side since he knew André well. She also suspected he would be a great comfort to her, but she couldn't cast Ros aside. Or let on that she and Maurice had a budding friendship. For all she knew, Maurice could end up in the same category as Ros. A man she liked, found to be interesting and good company, but one who didn't spark her sexual desires.

She stashed away her thoughts, though she didn't like that Maurice wasn't readily accessible. Especially since it seemed the older she got, the more death had a say over the ones she cared about. Not that loss was new, but the suddenness and the mounting weight of grief were difficult to bear.

She'd survived what she considered the worst. The loss of two husbands and two infants. Even Bobby's death took a great toll. The worst that could befall her now was if something happened to Caroline or John. She thought about it, of course, because life had not been kind. Not always.

Painful as it was to lose another dear friend, what she couldn't dare consider was crafting a life without one of her children. Of all the tragedies she'd endured and learned to live with, a life without Caroline or John wasn't possible for her.

TEN

October 1979

With her children by her side, Jackie beamed as she took her place atop the platform for the opening ceremony of the official dedication of the John F. Kennedy Presidential Library and Museum. She'd almost abandoned hope that it would happen. In the first year or so after Jack's death, twenty-seven million dollars was raised, but over time, the sum was pecked down to a third of what they'd started with, mainly due to the site research since Harvard refused to allow a building. The decline of prestige in the Kennedy name, which had once been a formidable element in getting things done, discouraged donations.

But standing outside the modern structure, not far from where Rose Kennedy had been born, Jackie, wearing a full-length gray overcoat and withstanding the stern wind, believed every struggle had been worth it.

She had commended architect I.M Pei during their final tour inside the building several days ago. From the replicated Oval Office to the large glass pavilion, she assured him that he had brought her vision for the project to fruition, and that Jack would have loved every inch of the space.

Today, her function was minimal. She was mainly fodder for the cameras.

After she took her place next to John, the announcer welcomed the hundreds who had gathered and then outlined the ceremony's agenda. The Boston Pops orchestra began to play "Hail to the Chief," and President Carter, with Rosalyn by his side, marched up the steps and greeted everyone with a quick handshake. When he came to Jackie, he kissed her on the cheek, just as he had Joan Kennedy and the other ladies along the faux receiving line. Jackie instinctually recoiled, but rebounded swiftly, knowing the press would feast on any hint of discomfort.

She forgave him for the too-personal gesture because he endeared himself to Teddy and the audience with anecdotes and jokes. Though he wouldn't have been her first choice to herald the day, he was the president, and despite his abysmal approval ratings, he was well-received.

Jackie's favorite moments of the day were when Caroline and John took turns at the podium. Caroline welcomed visitors and John read the poem, "I Think Continually of Those Who Were Truly Great."

Teddy delivered a standard yet satisfying speech on the library's legacy while Bobby's oldest son, Joseph Kennedy II, roused the Kennedy grandchildren and die-hards with a speech he entitled, "The Unfinished Business of Robert Kennedy." In her mind it was just shy of a spectacle, the way the clustered-together grandchildren and children kept cheering and hollering and applauding as Joseph called for moral courage and the like. And she knew, or at least suspected, some reporter somewhere would label her behavior as aloof or not thoroughly supportive or some such rubbish.

When the speeches were over, and the Kennedy crowd had calmed, visitors were welcomed inside. Jackie and her children made a subtle exit. Perhaps the press would give her flack for that too, leaving and not mingling with those who were there to honor Jack's memory.

But nothing could dull her inner joy. She'd done it. Almost fifteen years had passed since she'd first sat down with I.M. Pei on that cold December day, when her wounds from losing Jack were still raw and relentless, and they had talked about building Jack's library. At that lowly moment in time for her, the only goals that saw her through each day were raising Caroline and John and completing the library.

Not only that, but before Jack died, they managed to acquire the personal papers of Ernest Hemmingway to add to the library's collection. A unique distinction, Jackie thought.

She could let Bobby's children, mostly young adults and products of a slack upbringing, ride Jack's coattails. What else did they have in hopes of immortalizing their father's memory and the issues he stood for? She certainly held no confidence, based on what she'd witnessed today, that the older ones would pave the way in future politics.

On the other hand, she could've been petty and bitter. Angry, even, that Bobby's son had hijacked the event for his own gain and to lay the groundwork for building his own reputation. But long ago, Jackie had made peace with the fact the Kennedy name would be synonymous with politics. As expected as it was inescapable. Complaining about it or responding to it meant little.

She wondered what it might mean for John though. Seeing the next generation, raw and rambunctious, would they push John aside if he wasn't radical enough for them in both his views and actions? Was he encouraged by what he witnessed, or did he feel a deepening of a divide between himself and his cousins?

Jackie would employ her usual tactic when it came to John and the personal development of his politics. She wouldn't attempt to sway or criticize his budding ideals. He was old enough now to dig deep into his father's speeches and writings on his own, without prompting or verbal footnotes from men like Arthur Schlesinger and Ted Sorenson. Mostly, she would remind herself to trust that she had raised him well, and one day, if the Kennedys tried to press her to get John to step into his legacy and political inheritance, she wouldn't get involved.

———————

November 1979

FOR THE MOST PART, Jackie prided herself on being able to conceal her true emotions. Tonight, however, would test her resolve. As she drove up to the Castle, with Caroline, John, and Tina with her, angst swelled within. How was she going to greet her mother—now Mrs. Bingham Morris—genuinely, without a trace of her discomfort showing through? While it was true Bingham was welcoming and boisterous at the civil ceremony just weeks ago, his attitude failed to convince Jackie that this new marriage was for the best.

Thankfully, her children and Tina seemed unaware of her inner dilemma.

But once she was inside the Castle, a hint of cheerfulness sparked. Janet, lively as ever, embraced her grandchildren and became absorbed as they shared details about their lives, while Bingham, wearing a dress shirt and dress pants, saw to it that everyone had a refreshment in hand. Anthony also arrived, as did Bingham's children, adding to the merriment.

"I'm told dinner will be ready shortly," Bingham announced, his voice carrying above the noise.

Janet looked around. "Well, I certainly hope Lee isn't going to be late. No one likes when the mashed potatoes have to sit."

Her mother's distress brought a pinch of a grin to the corner of Jackie's mouth, but when she considered that she hadn't spoken to Lee since Janet's nuptials, regret invaded. Perhaps she and Lee should have discussed some sort of game plan, one intended to somehow remove Bingham Morris from their family.

Jackie thought back to the last lengthy conversation she had with

Lee. Had it been the day she called her about Truman's rant? Surely not! There had been a few phone calls in between, she was certain, but Jackie was also convinced time passed faster now than it used to. That was the only explanation. Along with the fact that Lee was running her business and traveling frequently to San Francisco.

Her train of thought derailed when Lee flounced in, wrapped in a stark-white fur coat. And alone. A detail that piqued Jackie's curiosity, even though it was highly possible Newton was enjoying the holiday with his family in California.

With Lee's arrival, Janet invited everyone to find a seat at the table. Jackie ended up closer to Bing than she wanted. After they settled in, he led grace, then the food was served.

Jackie used the first bite of the turkey to predict the meal's quality.

Not too dry but rather bland.

"I suppose you heard the announcement." Bingham spoke while still chewing. "That Teddy's running for president."

"He hopes to," John interjected. "First he has to win the Democratic nomination."

"You mean steal it from Carter," Anthony added.

"Something like that." John winked.

"I imagine you'll be helping him out." Bingham looked to Jackie and John.

"Oh, I can picture it already." Lee piped up before Jackie had a chance to respond. "She'll be perched on every podium, right by Teddy's side, up and down the East Coast from now until next November. But that lush hasn't got a chance, you know. Not even with your support."

Similar thoughts had crossed Jackie's mind. She was worried what it would mean, lending herself as a Kennedy pawn and attaching herself to all the problems that followed Teddy. Would it jeopardize her position at Doubleday and mar the relationships she'd built among her associates?

Putting those concerns aside, she focused on the more distressing matter—Lee. She had breezed in and only greeted her children, briefly, before sitting at the table, then she exchanged her dinner plate for an ashtray and began smoking. Judging from the tone and timber of her voice, she was tipsy.

"And I for one hope he doesn't have a chance of winning," Lee went on. "Carter is no prize, I'll say that, but Ted Kennedy is a bore and a disgrace. It's unfortunate that you can't exercise better taste, Jackie. You have no choice in the matter. If that pathetic man is running, then your support is expected. But I don't care to even look at him anymore. Not after the terrible things he's done. I'm sure you don't mind, and you've probably missed all the attention and the crowds ready to worship at your feet."

Everyone sat paralyzed in silence as they stared at Lee.

"Campaigning is my least favorite thing, and you know it, Lee. People shoving and clamoring to touch you—or worse—is hardly a form of worship. And I find it awful, when complete strangers talk to you as if they know you because they've read about you."

Lee laughed. "What on earth are you jabbering about, Jackie? No one cares. I'm talking about the way you treat people. Men in particular. No matter what they've done, rarely do you hold them to the same strict standard of unforgiveness. We all know how you can pocket a grudge."

Embarrassment scorched through Jackie, and she hardly knew what to say but managed, "Is something wrong, Pekes?"

"What could possibly be wrong?" Lee flailed her arms then stamped out what remained of her cigarette. "I have the most perfect sister in the world. Nothing else matters, does it?"

Without warning, she bolted from her chair and left the table.

"What on earth is going on?" Janet looked at Jackie. "Dare I ask what you've done to upset your sister so?"

Jackie resisted sneering at her mother. "I don't know what's gotten into her."

"Well, you had best address it this instant, Jacqueline. I won't have our Thanksgiving ruined over some petty disagreement between you two."

Under the circumstances, Jackie didn't mind being cast from the table. But chasing after Lee chiseled her pride. Lee had created the scene and yet Jackie was held responsible. When would it ever be enough, tending to Lee and placating her whims and fits and outbursts? Perhaps there was no release from the curse of being the older sister.

Knowing it was too cold for Lee to simply retreat outside, Jackie checked the Windmill, the four-story structure that had been rebuilt by Jackie's former love, Jack Warnecke, after a fire. Once upon a time, the Windmill supplied electricity to Hammersmith Farm when it was a working farm, providing food supplies for the nearby naval base during the war. When Jackie and Lee arrived as young teenagers, the Windmill was ideal for hide and seek.

Lee was at the top tier, nicknamed the observation deck, arms tightly folded across her chest and looking stiff-necked. Jackie wanted to leave her right there. Let her stew in whatever convoluted straightjacket of anger she'd worked herself into. But she knew it didn't work that way in her family. Never had. Taking care of Lee always fell on her shoulders. She made her way up to Lee and tried to steel herself against the brisk wind.

"If you're hoping for sympathy from me, forget it," Lee said.

Leave it to Lee to make an awkward situation worse...

"You've rattled Mummy."

"*She's* rattled?" Lee huffed.

"What's going on, Pekes?"

"I'm tired of the whole thing. Of every single thing. I can't stand it anymore. Every election. Every Kennedy." She faced Jackie. "And you. When I look at you, I feel so angry I just want to spit."

The bitterness of Lee's words made Jackie want to melt into the earth, but she wouldn't let Lee know she was shaken.

Their history had taught Jackie that Lee served up biting remarks when she needed to vent her frustrations. Whittling down to the root of the issue, however, often proved impossible. Lee rarely admitted to mistakes she made or owned up to hurtful actions—such as disrupting Thanksgiving dinner—which forced Jackie into the role of punching bag. But Jackie wanted to know why.

"It's Tina, isn't it? You're upset with me that Tina prefers to live with me over you."

Lee regarded her with a frankness Jackie hadn't seen before.

"Why don't you simply cut out my heart. That would be less painful."

"She loves you, Lee. Don't ruin your relationship with her to spite me. She needs you, and if you were only more patient with her, it would go a long way."

"Of course you know how to parent my child better than me."

Jackie held her eyes closed for a moment, unsure how much more she could take of Lee's vitriol. "Why are you so determined to bicker?"

"Because you infuriate me!" Lee slapped her palms against the railing. "Everything in your life comes easy for you."

Easy? The word landed like a nuclear bomb to her gut.

"Having two headstones in place of two of my children didn't come easy, in case you've forgotten." Jack flashed through her mind. The spray of blood from his wound. Hands at his throat as he fell onto the lap of her pristine Chanel suit.

Easy.

A word she couldn't relate to. One that only Lee would see fit to harass her with.

Calmer, Lee said, "I know you've suffered, Jacks. We all have. But I can't take it anymore. I can't take *you* anymore." She sighed and suddenly seemed to shrink in stature and confidence. "This has nothing to do with Tina, but I don't want to live with it anymore."

"What, Lee?"

Jackie saw the tears building in her eyes, but she was on the brink of not caring. What could her sister possibly say that might excuse her rude behavior and harsh words?

Lee shook her head as tears spilled onto her cheeks. "I never meant for it to happen, but I'm sure there's no way of ever making you believe that."

Her heart suddenly pounding, Jackie waited.

"I slept with him. I...I slept with Jack."

June 1963

EXHAUSTION THREATENED to buckle Lee at the knees. Thankfully, she was about to take her seat, along with a dozen or so officials, military personnel, dignitaries and what not as Jack prepared to begin his speech.

Months ago, when Jackie asked her to accompany Jack on this international trip, she'd hesitated at first. Who wanted to go to Germany of all places? But when Jackie said they'd also be going to Ireland to visit Jack's relatives and ancestorial homesites, well, that grabbed her attention. She'd never been. And like the Kennedys, much of her family's history was tied to the Emerald Isle.

"But, Jacks, why on earth are you asking me to go?" Lee had asked. "You adore Ireland. That month you and Yusha spent traveling the country, why, that was all you talked about when you got back. Hardly a peep about Paris in comparison."

Though the press often criticized Jackie's fondness for French cuisine and fashion, and attributed her propensity to her heritage, Jackie and Lee's bloodline contained more Irish lineage than French. Ever since that trip in 1950, Lee had been envious.

"I would love to go. Jack has talked about visiting Ireland for as long as I've known him. The trip will mean everything to him.

There's only one little thing that's keeping me from going." A broad smile lit up Jackie's face. "Or perhaps I should say a little *someone*."

When the news took hold, Lee squealed with joy and embraced Jackie.

Another baby!

They talked about Jackie's pregnancy and due date before returning to the main topic.

"So I can't go to Ireland with Jack."

Lee understood. Pregnancy and childbirth had never been easy for either of them, but ever since the stillbirth of Arabella in 1956, Jackie took extra precautions and care when she was expecting. Her activities and duties were pared down, and international travel was out of the question.

"Then of course I'll go, Jacks." She'd squeezed Jackie's hands lovingly. "Anything for you and that precious baby."

'Anything' had included more than Lee bargained for. She'd been having a fabulous time sailing the Italian coast aboard the *Christina* with Ari, Stas, Randolph Churchill, and some Italian friends. Even Maria Callas, who was also there, had been pleasant. Or at least tolerable for Lee—though she could do without Maria's frequent side glares. Was it her fault that Ari found wonder and amusement in everything she said? Her fault that Maria had caught them making love—because Ari was lax when it came to locking doors and didn't mind being watched?

At any rate, the shopping, swimming, alfresco dining, wine, and dancing that filled their days proved glorious. When they left Naples for Fiumicino so she could depart for Germany, she considered changing her mind. Why break the spell of cheer and good fun against a glorious Mediterranean backdrop and exchange it for stuffy men in suits.

Why? Because she'd promised Jackie.

That was the only thing that propelled her forward. Got her off the yacht and onto the plane for Bonn, where she joined Jack and his entourage. The next two days became a blur as they visited Bonn,

Cologne, Frankfurt, and Wiesbaden. Her feet and stamina held up, and the weather had been kind. Not the scorching summer heat she had expected.

This morning, they arrived in West Berlin, the main focus of their tour. Much anticipation had gone into this very moment. For Jack's appearance, a platform had been specially built at the Brandenburg Gate on the steps of city hall and in front of the Berlin Wall. The elevation allowed him to address the immediate crowd and to look into East Berlin at the same time. With his usual charisma, he delivered a short speech that enthralled the thousands of people who came to hear the American president.

"Ich bin ein Berliner!" resounded from the crowd and through the streets. Afterward, a small reception followed inside city hall. Lee was surprised to find oxtail soup and potato dumplings among the offerings. Convinced they were too heavy for a summer meal, and for such an informal gathering, which amounted to little more than Jack meeting various men and shaking hands while she was left to wander and mingle alone, Lee kept it light. Crackers with a dainty serving of Obatzda cheese butter spread suited her. As she was taking in the building's architecture and nibbling a cracker, she was approached by one of Jack's Secret Service Agents.

"Mrs. Radziwill, we were scheduled to depart in Air Force One within the hour, however, there seems to be a mechanical issue. It's going to take time to resolve, along with a thorough inspection for good measure. We're going to secure accommodations for you and the President since it looks like we'll be here for the night."

Lee sighed. She was anxious for Ireland, but there was nothing she could do. Delays and problems were part and parcel when it came to extensive travel.

After they were settled in at a nearby hotel, Jack informed her the city's mayor had invited them to a private dinner. She appreciated a more relaxed evening, void of the fanfare they'd been saturated in since their arrival. But the food proved too heavy and troublesome for her gut. She kept to boiled chicken and a simple salad, a discipline she should've applied that night to her drinking as well.

Back at the hotel in their connecting suites, Lee was eager to be alone. A warm soak in the tub might do her good. Or perhaps she'd go straight to bed.

But Jack was riled. Just like he always was after a state dinner or a function where he'd been the center of attention.

"Can you believe the size of that crowd today?" Jack undid the top button of his shirt and removed his dinner jacket. "The mayor said they estimated about 150,000 people were there today."

"It was staggering, and you certainly had them cheering." That dried up her useful commentary, since she wasn't one to pay close attention to Jack's speeches—God help her, there were so many—let alone have an ounce of understanding what his words could possibly mean to a hard-pressed throng of Germans.

But providing commentary wasn't her role. She was a stand-in for Jackie and required to do little more than a store mannequin. Smile and look stylish. Clap when appropriate. And after the crowds had dispersed and duties were done for the day, help Jack relax from the day's tensions.

"Brevity is the key." Jack held up a finger, as if emphasizing his point. "That and giving them a sense of hope."

Shouldn't he call for Ted Sorenson or Dave Powers if he's going to repeat his performance and give another speech? I'm in no mood.

She smiled and nodded her agreement. As she was about to put her hand on her head and feign a headache so she could retire to her suite for the night, Jack said, "We should have a toast."

Lee grinned her approval, though she was already wobbly from the two—or was it three—cocktails she enjoyed at dinner. Had her head been clearer, she would've thought the gesture unusual since Jack rarely drank.

He handed her a glass. "There isn't a better place in the world to be kicking back a dose of Jägermeisters. Wouldn't you agree?"

She much preferred gluhwein over the hard liqueur but knew better than to say so and accepted the glass while playing along.

Jack touched his glass to hers. "To Germany and *Ich bin ein Berliner.*"

Still uncertain what the phrase meant, she gave her girlish nod and drank.

"We made history today, kid."

"That seems to happen with every appearance you make, Jack." She didn't want to expose her ignorance and ask him to explain what he meant. What had he changed with a ten-minute oration? Was that just his way of trying to impress her or remind her that he happened to be the most powerful man on earth?

Lee finished her drink, and Jack immediately splashed the bottom of her glass with more of the herbal liqueur. Down the hatch it went, and she wondered if subconsciously she was trying to plunge herself into oblivion. Part of her would argue that she was desperate to loosen up, that she was hoping to soften the inexplicable edge of discomfort.

"Just wait till tomorrow—Ireland. I've waited my whole life for the chance to walk on those green hills and breathe the air where my ancestors came from."

Dublin, Wexford, Cork, Galway, and Limerick, according to an itinerary she'd peaked at. Then a quick stop in England. Jack wanted to visit his sister's grave at Chatsworth. Kathleen, known as Kick, had been Jack's favorite sister, and her death in a plane crash in 1948 had crushed him.

After England, they'd head back to the States.

Lee felt giddy herself about seeing Ireland but held back. "I'm sure it will be everything you've imagined and more."

"It's unfortunate Jackie had to miss it."

"Yes, she loves Ireland." Lee worried they were grasping for small talk. Or was it just her? Struggling to focus and keep up with Jack? The buzz from those drinks began to take hold and make her feel light-headed.

"But I'm not disappointed that you're here."

Jack's remark gave her a small start and she met his gaze as he moved closer.

"It's not often that we get the chance to be alone."

Her pulse throttled and compromised her ability to think. Usually, she enjoyed his company. They shared the same wry yet sharp wit and often made each other laugh. Tonight, though, she couldn't deny the tension between them.

"I want you to see something."

She followed as he entered his suite through the adjoining door. He opened the door to the balcony and waited for her to join him. The cool evening breeze enabled Lee to snatch a fresh breath but didn't bring the clarity she suddenly craved.

Jack took her hand and placed it on the railing. "The view is magnificent, isn't it?"

Lee continued to inhale, subtly, and nodded. Berlin glittered below, but her focus waned.

"Breathtaking." She had both hands on the rail to steady herself.

"Let's make the most of this night."

He put one hand on the nape of her neck. With the other, he slid the zipper of her dress down. Her breath caught as the dress separated and he spun her around. Speechlessness held her voice hostage as he took her into the room, undressed her, and eased her onto his bed.

WHEN SHE AWOKE, disoriented from the throbbing headache and pitiful sleep, she thought she was rousing from a strange dream. But then came a sudden rush of a flashback. Jack sinking his fingertips into her hips as he pounded her with thrusts from behind. She trembled because it wasn't cloudy like a dream. Didn't feel distant or heavy with uncertainty. Haunting her further were the smells. Jack's liquor-tainted breath hot on the back of her neck. The faded scent of

Old Spice—which Caroline loved to buy him each year for Christmas—mixed with sweat.

Using her thumb and forefinger like a pair of tweezers, she lifted the sheet and peeped her nakedness underneath. The familiar whiff of carnal aroma pinched her nostrils. She knew.

Bolting upright with the sheet now clasped to her chest, she wondered where Jack was. Bathed in soft morning light, the room appeared empty. She clawed through the fog in her mind, trying to recall his itinerary for the day. Had he, or Dave Powers, told her the agenda? Yes, she remembered. Today they headed to Ireland.

She slid her legs over the edge of the bed, about to plant her bare feet on the floor, when the bedroom door opened.

Her body clenched and she gripped the sheet impossibly tight.

Jack entered, showing no signs of having come off a night of drunken, forbidden sex. In fact, he looked well-rested, chipper even, and sharper than ever in a fresh gray suit.

"Glad you're awake. How are you?"

The sentiment surprised her. Rarely did Jack display a caring nature. At least toward her. She tucked her legs back between the cool silk sheets.

"Perplexed. Uncomfortable. Maybe even a bit disturbed."

He twitched his head sideways. "Not what comes to my mind after last night."

"That can't happen again." She was proud of the declaration, even if it sounded weak and unconvincing.

"I'm not sure it needs to." His cheeks puffed from the grimace. "But who's to say." He flashed a salacious look at her. "The desire is there. Always has been. Opportunity, however, is another matter. We took advantage of that last night. Hard to say if it will present itself again."

He stood at the dresser and put on his cufflinks like it was a normal day while Lee grappled with disbelief.

"At any rate, I hope this discourages you from your interest in Aristotle Onassis."

Her jaw went slack. "What on earth does Ari have to do with this?"

"I know you only see him to get under my skin. I don't give much creed to psychologists, but from what I've read, I think the way you behave with him is a misguided attempt for my attention."

Lee thought his hubris was overblown and repulsive. "You must be joking."

"Hardly." Slowly, he lowered himself onto the bed, closer than she liked. "You should keep to your own house, Lee. End this nonsense with Onassis. And when you're struck for a longing to be with a powerful man, well," he patted her covered leg, "I've got a lot of traveling to do next year for my reelection." He stood. Slowly. "She'll be preoccupied with the new baby, and you know she hates campaigning."

Lee stared at him. "Go to hell."

"Feisty. I always liked that about you." He buttoned his suit jacket. "While you're at it, you should make more of an effort with Stas. He's a good man, worth holding on to, and he's not using you the way Onassis is."

Lee drew her knees to her chest and wrapped her arms around her legs. A feeble measure to ward off the insecurity spiking through her. Jack had tapped into her greatest fear—that no man could ever truly love her for who she was. That there were always strings attached or an underlying reason that kept him in her bed. Her first marriage had served as a means of escape from their parents' control for both her and Michael. But the union deteriorated with Michael's drinking and dissatisfaction with his career. Then, while still married to Michael, her affair with Stas had been for amusement and relief from Michael's brooding. But had she and Stas only fallen in love because circumstances and providence forbid it? She didn't know. Nor could she untangle it after a night with her brother-in-law.

When she looked at Jack—really looked at him, not as her sister's husband but as a man who wanted her—she couldn't deny her own attraction for him. Yes, the desire had always been there for her too.

Didn't that make her complicit in last night's romp, no matter how many drinks she had?

Passionate desire was one of her weaknesses, but last night's encounter had the potential to destroy her life if Jackie ever found out, and Jack knew it too.

How would she ever face her sister again?

"I DIDN'T BELIEVE it at first, but..." Lee wiped the tears from her cheeks. "It happened, Jackie. I wish to God it didn't, but it did, and I was too drunk or confused or maybe I just didn't care enough to stop it."

Jackie swallowed the coarse lump in her throat, unable to face her sister, her body trembling. Was it from rage? Or was it the manifestation of having a long-held suspicion turned into a reality?

"I suspected." Not because she distrusted Lee but because she knew Jack. He helped himself to women the way a farmer plucked apples from his orchard, taking what he wanted whenever he wanted it.

One could argue that Lee had been a victim. That Jack's actions had been vulgar and served as an attempt to put Lee in her place, so to speak. Using her the way he did, also allowed Jack to blackmail her against Jackie and to poison Lee's relationship with Ari.

But Jackie put the men aside. She blamed Lee for not holding their sisterhood to higher esteem. One where husbands were off limits, regardless of circumstances and copious amounts of consumed alcohol.

"It was because of what happened in Berlin that I went through with it," Lee said.

"Went through with what?"

"My vow renewal with Stas. He always said we weren't truly married until we exchanged our vows in the church. And he needed that for his father to be proud of him. I had put it off as long as I could, but after Berlin, well, I knew I owed it to you, and to Stas. As if that could make up for what I'd done. I think it also gave Stas confidence that I wasn't about to leave the marriage, even though I already had emotionally. But that night with Jack." Her breath audibly caught. "And there was Bobby. He was part of it too, insisting I stay away from Ari. The pressure and the guilt overwhelmed me. I never would've had the guts to fight for what I wanted."

"I don't think you loved Ari, not like you think you did."

Lee gave her a snide, pinched expression. "We were both raised better than to put our hope in love and romance, weren't we? We married the men who could give us security and the life we dreamed of. That's what we fell in love with, the life we deserved—and that's why you married Ari."

Jackie couldn't deny it. Though part of her loved Ari deeply—she'd kept his name for God's sake—she knew, or suspected, before they wed that Ari wasn't the kind of man who took care of his wife's love for him. No matter how genuine her feelings became. Much like Jack. Ultimately, that was Ari's greatest betrayal to her, all the ways he rejected her feelings and the genuine love she had for him.

"Renewing my vows with Stas affected Ari," Lee went on. "We had talked seriously about me divorcing Stas and moving onto the *Christina* with him. But coming off that trip with Jack and then days later going into that church with Stas, well, it discouraged Ari."

"I don't believe that." Jackie wasn't going to allow Lee to blame her for the misfortunes that plagued Lee, both in her relationships and in her financial status.

"Of course you don't, Jackie, because you think the world revolves around you and that every man is in love with you. Well, I for one can assure you that Ari only married you for the prestige of claiming the widow. Marrying you was achieving the greatest prize known to man at the time. Besides money, the only thing Ari cared about more was making a name for himself and conquering the world in every way he could."

"You're just saying that now to hurt me." But Jackie knew Lee had a point. Ari had the spirit of a pirate. He forged a reputation as a ruthless businessman, as well as that of a suave lover. Both attributes —and his staggering wealth—had attracted Jackie. But Ari didn't want to get married—not until Jackie dropped a subtle ultimatum. One that forced him to close the deal. But it didn't take long for Ari to grow dissatisfied with her and return to Maria.

Had Jackie been wrong to marry him? Would Lee have made him a better wife?

"That's rich, coming from you." Lee laughed bitterly. "I sacrificed my future and happiness because I knew if I married Ari it would look bad, that Jack might not be reelected. I thought I owed it to you, after sleeping with Jack, to give up Ari. But I never would've dreamed that you'd marry him! Have you ever thought for a moment about the humiliation you put me through? Or the pain I endured, letting Ari go?"

She had thought of Lee! But like so many things when it came to her sister, Jackie considered her affair with Ari to be a fleeting fancy. After all, Lee had lost interest in two husbands. What made Ari different?

"And look where it's led me," Lee continued. "I put you first, and I lost out on everything. Now I'm cursed to walk the earth in your shadow, branded as Jackie O's younger sister. Nothing I ever do will be mine in my own right. It will always tie back to you, and I hate you for that!"

Jackie reeled at the emotional gut-punch. "So it's really not about Jack at all. This is about how much you..." What was the point in repeating those words?

"I almost have a mind to phone up Liz Smith and tell her everything about Berlin. I wonder if that's the only way I'll ever get this out of my system."

"Don't you dare!" Jackie's fury spiked. "You can hate me all you want, Lee, but if you do such a thing that further soils Jack's memory, you'll only hurt Caroline and John. For that, I'd never forgive you."

Lee took a step back, as if she realized she had gone too far.

"Let's be honest, Jacks. You'll never forgive me for this outburst and for telling you the truth, because you can hold a grudge like no one else. I might be wasting my breath saying this, but I never meant to hurt you."

Jackie had grown too numb to care. "It's not going to resolve itself tonight. There's nothing else to say." She wanted the onslaught of hurtful words to stop. If she could leap over the edge of the railing and start running, she would have. Anything to get away. But that wasn't an option. It was up to her to amend the scene Lee had made earlier. "We have to get back to the dinner table. I'm sure Mummy is on the verge of being furious by now."

Not that she cared about Mummy.

She cared about nothing and no one in that moment. But those were the words that would end the confrontation. Jackie feared she was on the cusp of fainting and dissolving into the gush of tears that wanted to pour out of her. The sudden crash of turmoil on her heart devastated her. And her throat clenched as a ragged scream swelled and compromised her ability to breathe.

But it didn't matter. A tempest of heartbreak meant nothing when one was disrupting dinner at the home of Janet Auchincloss. Morris. Duty and decorum reigned above all. In truth, that would see Jackie through. Janet's expectations were the only thing that kept her steady. At least on the outside.

Lee turned from her, as if she was through with the conversation, but Jackie snatched her forearm.

"I don't care a thing about our sisterhood right now, but if you ever make any of this public, or if Caroline and John ever find out..." Jackie squeezed Lee's arm as her rage built.

Lee yanked her arm from Jackie's tightening hold. Though her gaze seemed to burn with her own anger, she looked away as a downcast expression washed over her.

They both said nothing as they left the Windmill, leaned into the wind, and trekked across the expansive lawn, back to their awaiting family.

ELEVEN

January 1980

Jackie believed she was entitled to the anger sizzling through her, but Lee's revelation didn't take her completely by surprise. The real impact had come when Ari told her. Just months before he became gravely ill, he told Jackie—with the intent of hurting her—that Lee had slept with Jack in Berlin. Drunk on ouzo, and drunk with grief from the recent news of his first wife's sudden death by suicide, Ari lashed out and seemed pleased he delivered such a crushing blow. For Jackie, that solidified that their relationship was over.

She pretended, for as long as she could, that Ari had fabricated the tale. That it couldn't be true. But the mention of Berlin in 1963 was too specific to ignore. And she knew Jack showed no restraint when it came to bedding the women he wanted. It was just like him, and sleeping with two sisters was probably an equivalent to obtaining stripes in the Navy.

Lee had filled in more details. Having the full picture painted of their drunken night of sex while Jackie was six months pregnant was like having her heart removed with a rusty knife. Living with the confession over the last several weeks had amped her anxieties and tainted her holiday cheer.

Such a rift depended on Lee to make reparations. In Jackie's opinion. But no one knew better than Jackie how detached Lee was from accountability and how she never sought forgiveness from others. She relied on her uncanny ability to switch the blame around and wait for the other person to crawl back to her.

Well, she's going to have quite a long wait for me.

Jackie said nothing, of course, to her children or Tina about what transpired on Thanksgiving, though maintaining a happy front proved demanding and draining. A cloud of gloom threatened to overshadow her. Piled on top of the hurt was the grief of losing her sister, perhaps for good. The shackles of depression weren't far behind. But Jackie knew better than to succumb.

She had to focus on the hope that came with the new year, and she had projects in need of her editing eye.

When Diana Vreeland phoned and asked Jackie when she might get the chance to review galleys for her upcoming book *Allure,* Jackie offered to meet her afterhours at the Doubleday offices. She liked the idea of the two of them having the place to themselves. And working with Diana on another book that originated as one of Jackie's ideas was hardly work at all.

Diana's career had begun in 1936 with a column she wrote for *Harper's Bazaar.* Before long, she was a fashion editor and was even credited with discovering Lauren Bacall. An eighteen-year-old model at the time, Bacall posed for the cover shot in 1943, which was directed by Diana, in what became a striking photograph that helped launch Bacall's acting career.

In 1962 she joined *Vogue* and stayed until she was fired in 1971. From there, she went to work at the Metropolitan Museum of Art as a consultant to the Costume Institute.

For a brief time, Lee had worked as Diana's assistant at *Harper's,* but Diana had been part of Jackie's—and Lee's—social circles for as long as Jackie could remember.

Allure, an oversized coffee table-style book, featured an array of artists and photography. Diana had worked with most of the celebrities and photographers showcased and included her commentary on what each of them brought to fashion, the arts, and life in general.

Working with Diana sometimes reminded Jackie about *Vogue*'s contest she entered in 1951, "Prix de Paris." Requirements were to craft an essay on "People I Wish I Had Known" and to draft a layout of an issue of the magazine. Over a thousand participants submitted, but Jackie's entry won. The prize was a one-year internship where she would work six months in *Vogue*'s New York office, then six months in the Paris office. In all likelihood, the experience would have led to a full-time position. Jackie could have become an editor!

But after less than one day on the job, Jackie turned down the opportunity. Her mother was against it. She warned Jackie that she wouldn't find a husband working for a women's magazine, and she didn't want Jackie returning to Paris for another extended stay—convinced Jackie would make the move permanent. Living in Paris would've been a dream come true for Jackie, but she agreed with her mother. She also didn't want Lee to feel abandoned by her and worried how Lee would fare with Janet without Jackie as a buffer. *A lot of good that did.*

If she were brutally honest, though, Jackie didn't want to work that hard. The fashion industry interested her; the demands and responsibilities of a regular job did not.

Now, as she and Diana flipped through the galley pages of the upcoming book, Jackie knew she'd made the right decision. She had ended up with the career that was ideal for her. Nearly thirty years later.

"Mm." Diana paused and stared at the two-page feature of Marilyn Monroe. "Are you sure you're all right with this?"

Jackie smirked. "How could we possibly publish a book titled *Allure* without including her?"

"You're the editor. You can do whatever you like."

Looking at the two black-and-white pictures of Marilyn only stoked Jackie's pity for her, despite the fact her affair with Jack had become common knowledge.

Maria Callas was also included in the book for her undeniable talent as an opera singer. Both women had passed, and Jackie held no ire toward either of them.

"We want to sell as many copies as possible, don't we?"

Diana nodded. "Spoken like a true professional. You always know the right things to say, Jackie."

JACKIE'S greatest fear became whether or not Lee would divulge the incident to Liz Smith, or another bloodthirsty gossip disguised as a journalist. She clung to Lee's assurance of silence—and deeply hoped that Lee's love for Caroline and John would supersede her bitterness toward Jackie.

Fortunately for Jackie, her blossoming relationship with Maurice was a genuine distraction that silenced the mental bombardment. Over the last six months, he had disarmed her and surprised her. His gifts, always thoughtful, hinted at his wealth but weren't exorbitant like Ari's or one-note like Jack's. Maurice also had a way of discerning her moods and catering to her unspoken needs.

"I can see that you're tired, quite understandable after a morning full of meetings. I'll see myself out and let you retire for the evening. Perhaps enjoy a chapter or two of The Rise of Theodore Roosevelt before bed."

Having a man be sensitive to her sensitivities proved as new as it was unusual. Jackie had never considered how a relationship might exist where a woman wasn't called to stroke a man's ego and serve him.

In turn, she enjoyed trying to please him in small ways, such as learning expressions in Flemish—which she found easier than

Yiddish—and building on her knowledge of Judaism, though Maurice observed mainly Rosh Hashanah and Hanukkah. She shared the progress on her new home, Red Gate Farm, walking him through the bare studs of the main house and taking him on a tour of the property grounds.

During the holiday season, they had seen each other only sporadically, with Jackie traveling with Caroline and John while Maurice spent time working and seeing his children. However, over dinner at 1040 one evening, Jackie shared about the episode with Lee at Thanksgiving. Difficult as it was to relay the scene, even with keeping much of the details to herself, Jackie found being able to share the hardship with Maurice helped lessen the burden of her pain.

One January evening, they returned to Jackie's apartment after a walk in the park, just as a predicted snowfall began. Brandies by the fire warmed them, and after a few minutes Maurice disrupted the pleasant atmosphere when he asked Jackie if she had reached out to Lee yet.

"No." Jackie found the cognac harder to swallow as she suddenly worried that perhaps Maurice thought their failing-out was petty. After all, it was a one-night stand that happened over sixteen years ago. Even Jackie had moments when she wondered if it was worth the upheaval or the resentment.

"I'm not sure if this will help any," Maurice said, "but I have heard, through reliable sources, that her design business is on the brink of failure. Her expenditures are exceeding her income and profits are almost nil. She won't be able to continue much longer at the pace she's going. I suspect this has been a problem for a while and may have been a contributing factor for the outburst she had with you. I only mention it because I don't want you to blame yourself for what's happened. I'm sure you're both hurting in your own way." He held his hands open. "Perhaps there's room for compassion, though I wouldn't dare tell you what to do in this situation."

"I suspected there was more going on with Lee that night." Jackie sipped her drink. "She prefers making people miserable when she's miserable, although I'm usually her favorite target."

On the precipice of another failure. I might've known.

Jackie thought back to a few years ago, when Delacorte Press canceled their contract with Lee for her memoir. They claimed the writing wasn't up to par, and there wasn't enough 'Kennedy material' included. Another blow came for Lee soon after when CBS cancelled her show, *Conversations With Lee Radziwill* after only six episodes. Using a style similar to Barbara Walters's, Lee casually interviewed her guests, but TV executives claimed the show didn't find its audience.

If Maurice was right about Lee's business on the verge of folding —and if her relationship with Newton Cope had fizzled—that would explain her sudden need to drag Jackie down with her. Make her feel as denigrated as she did. That was Lee. Relying on fruitless, low-down tactics rather than addressing problems directly and forging a healthy solution. But had she come to Jackie in need of money to save her business, Jackie would have turned her down flatly and unequivocally, having no desire to serve as a safety net for Lee's financial troubles.

Jackie glanced at the side table where two tabloids currently rested. One of them featured a picture of Lee and Newton with a tear between them, indicating their break-up. But the one she caught sight of showed director Mike Nichols and Jackie in a photo that had been captured after they attended *Sugar Babies* in December.

When she looked at Maurice, she realized he saw it too and averted his gaze.

"You know, the older I get, the less interest I have in squabbling with others." Maurice casually finished his drink. "I'm also not one for speaking where it's not wanted, and if I were overstepping my bounds, let's say, I do hope you would graciously correct me."

Jackie nodded as her curiosity prickled.

"In some regards, I think I'm too old for certain rules, and to be perfectly honest, I wonder if rules set people up for failure."

With a teasing half-grin, she asked. "What are you getting at?"

"Oh, nothing too weighty. But I suppose the poet in me fumbles when it comes down to simply saying what I hope won't be taken the wrong way. You've become quite a beacon in my life, Jackie. I look forward to our dinners and time together more than you know. In fact, I'll come right out and admit that being with you makes me giddy. It's truly a sensation I've never known before. And I'm not overstating when I say there is no one—absolutely no one else—I would rather be with than you."

Jackie braced herself for a proposal—and quickly decided she wasn't ready. Not with an answer or the destruction to their relationship that could follow if she didn't give him the answer he wanted. Her best bet, she figured, was to head him off.

"Maurice—"

"Now," he held up a hand as if to stop her, "please don't worry. I'm making no impositions on you, but it was important for me to let you know how greatly I care about you, and how deeply I'm falling in love. I have no expectation of a duplicate response from you, but I do hope that we may grow even closer in the year ahead."

In that moment, she could breathe again, and yet she was breathless at the same time. Rather than scold her for having a night on the town with another man, Maurice proclaimed his love and devotion to her—and levied no expectations. He didn't say it outright, but she believed his declaration affirmed his intention to date only Jackie. Exclusivity from him but with no strings attached? She couldn't read him perfectly yet, but she suspected the snapshot of her and Mike injured his feelings, and instead of launching an argument, Maurice chose to profess his love and loyalty. A move that stayed true to his mysterious nature and suddenly ramped up her attraction to him.

Jackie reached for Maurice's hand and without a word, led him into her bedroom.

January 1980

WITH TEDDY officially in the running for the presidential nomination, Jackie did her best to follow his speeches and appearances as they appeared in newspapers. Occasionally, in the lounge at the office, she caught news clips of him waving to or addressing a crowd. One of the most talked-about clips involved Joan.

At a recent impromptu press conference, when Teddy and Joan arrived in Iowa to begin campaigning for caucus votes, a reporter opened the session with a question for Joan:

"Mrs. Kennedy, do you believe your husband's story about Chappaquiddick, and if you do, how big of an issue do you think it will be in the nomination battle?"

Unprepared for such a pointed, deeply painful topic, Joan blanched. She managed an answer, confirming her belief in his story and did her best to display her full support for her husband. When Joan left the microphone, Teddy's drawn, stoic visage showed no phony gratitude or a hint of pride in Joan. Only disgust. Three days later, Teddy lost the Iowa caucus in a crushing defeat, leaving Jackie to wonder if there was an ounce of hope left for his campaign.

Jackie tried getting in touch with Joan, concerned over how she was handling the pressures of being under such scrutiny, but despite leaving messages for Joan, they didn't get a chance to connect.

Now, fresh from a trip to Carolina Herrara's studio for a private fitting and selecting pieces from her newest collection, Jackie was feeling more like herself. Also lifting her spirits was her quick trip to Rome for an evening at the opera with Maurice, which he had arranged after their night of intimacy.

The painful confrontation with Lee, scarring as it was, had started to lose its sharp edge. Experience had proven to Jackie that was exactly how life worked. No matter the trauma or the tragedy, time healed. Although the amount of time needed for one to recover was always unknown.

March 1980

ENTERING HER APARTMENT, Jackie grinned as the aroma of the floral displays greeted her. She knew immediately that Marta and the rest of the staff had taken her instructions to heart when she briefed them about preparations for Princess Grace's visit. An exuberant, abundant arrangement of a variety of flowers was a must, particularly because it was a not-so-subtle wink to the publication and accomplishment of Grace's work, *My Book of Flowers*.

Being decades-old acquaintances, Jackie welcomed the opportunity to assist Grace in bringing the book to American audiences. It had already been released in Europe and received much acclaim. Of course, Jackie's bosses at Doubleday were thrilled she leveraged her friendship and helped make the deal happen.

However, Jackie preferred keeping her involvement in projects under wraps as much as possible, which included keeping her name off the cover. A detail she decided to curtail after *In the Russian Style*, wanting her authors to receive all the merit for their work. With Grace's book, Jackie focused primarily on the layout, changing little from the overseas version, which suited her fine. Even better, Grace still had enough star power and awe that having Jackie attend her launch party was unnecessary.

Now, anticipation tickled Jackie since Grace had agreed to lunch at Jackie's apartment.

Before Jackie came along, Grace had known the Kennedy family for years, having met them through Joe during his time in the film industry. In fact, Joe Kennedy had gone to great lengths to steer Grace into Jack's orbit, having interfered with Grace's engagement to Oleg Cassini—who later became Jackie's courtier during her years as First Lady—and encouraged her to see Jack. Perhaps Grace found the Kennedy clan too brash and unrefined, as she never took a serious interest in Jack. Oddly enough, he never gave the impression he "missed out" on Grace.

Years later, when Jack was hospitalized and recovering from back surgery, Jackie lifted his spirits when she asked Grace to don a nurse's uniform before entering his room. Giddy at the idea of the prank, Grace played along, but her acting skills faltered soon after she went to Jack's bedside and told him it was time for his sponge bath. She and Jackie enjoyed a hearty laugh at Jack's amused, titillated expression while he playfully cursed at them for making him flinch from pain as he chuckled.

Jackie giggled again at the memory as she freshened and changed. When she returned to the library, Marta had lunch plated and waiting on trays. Chicken salad with a side of vegetables and pita bread. Simple.

Grace arrived moments later, as scheduled, looking radiant with an updo that showcased her diamond tear-drop earrings and wearing a crème silk blouse and a navy skirt with matching pumps.

Expecting Grace to look regal, Jackie had resisted the urge to match or outdo her guest. Sharply tailored trousers and a light cashmere sweater sufficed. Keeping faithful to the tone of simplicity.

Grace marveled at Jackie's apartment and the lengths she'd gone to with the flower arrangements, the nod to her book not lost on her. Jackie led them into the library. Marta poured white wines as they settled in with chit-chat.

While they dined, Jackie appreciated their endless flow of conversation, from their children to art to the book to future endeavors. She couldn't escape thinking about Grace and Prince Rainier's visit to the White House back in 1961. For reasons unknown to Jackie, Grace had been in an impish mood that day and hardly took her eyes off Jack, as though she were plagued by regrets of not marrying him. Jackie didn't care. Women often swooned over Jack. She was accustomed to it, along with his flirting. That particular day, she worked hard at holding in her laughter. Grace had worn a white hat that resembled a swim cap. Though it may have been considered high fashion in Monaco and other parts of the world, Jackie thought she looked ridiculous. Jack said nothing but Jackie knew he hated it too. He was ravenous with her in bed that night, and she told herself it was because he was grateful that she never made him look like a fool.

Now, with dessert being served, Jackie suppressed the smile that the memory enticed. Rare were the moments when another woman upstaged Princess Grace, and Jackie knew better than to gloat, especially from such an aged recollection. They were different women now, both having raised children who were deemed celebrities or royals from birth—whom the public felt akin to and branded their futures with high expectations.

Jackie picked at her piece of coffee cake and subtly noticed Grace was doing the same. Being the hostess, Jackie fretted over the sudden lag in conversation. As she was about to ask something frivolous, Grace set down her fork and seemed to abandon the ruse of eating her slice of cake. Then, she stunned Jackie by spilling an alarming revelation.

"I don't know that he still loves me." Grace clenched her fist as if the admission were painful to share. "We seem to only speak to one another when we have to, and the same can be said for when we're together. It's just for show. I can't tell you the last time he touched me or the last time we shared a bed."

During her White House days, Jackie had found having a separate bedroom for Jack convenient. Not only for the nights when his flared back pain meant endless movements to find comfort, but also for the late-late nights when politics and duties kept Jack at bay. But Jackie realized the Grimaldis' arrangement spoke more to the disharmony between them.

"Men like Rainier are complicated," Jackie said, "and they like to pretend their wives are not."

"It may sound like the strangest thing," Grace dabbed her mouth with her napkin, "but I think after we had the children, we began growing apart. Oh, he was proud of them, and thank God we had a son, but it's like we picked different roads. He remained faithful to the monarchy, and my heart was for the children. I never gave a second thought to moving to Paris for their schooling. Never. He approved, naturally, and said children needed their mother. I had no intention of building a life without them, but he preferred Monaco. Maybe I was wrong, choosing the children." Solemnity tightened her expression. "He always used to compliment me but not anymore. I know I've changed over the years, and I think it's helped drive him away."

Jackie wasn't insensitive to Grace's sudden discomfort. They were both shackled to the public's expectation of being ever conscious of their figures, even though they weren't immune to the changes that came with growing older. Jackie wondered if her friend felt a jab of embarrassment and intimidation since she had remained svelte into her fifties while Grace no longer had the strikingly slender silhouette of her movie-star days.

Grace kept her gaze pinned on the table. "I think he's disappointed the glamour has faded."

"It's been my experience that men are never happy for long, even when they have no reason to be unhappy. Perhaps it has something to do with being domesticated. They aren't charging into war or sailing off into the sea or venturing into the unknown anymore. It's like they can't be settled."

Grace didn't seem to be listening.

"There are times he likes embarrassing me. When we attend events, he'll sit and talk with other women for most of the night. I don't think he's been unfaithful, but he must know his inattentiveness hurts. A couple months back we were dining out with friends, and I was telling them about my book. He took a flower from the vase on the table and crumpled it onto a plate. 'Voila! Looks like I'm as talented as Grace. I should command good money for my artwork,' he said. We all laughed, of course, but I knew he was mocking me."

Another painful bond they shared. Husbands who humiliated them without a thought.

Jackie touched Grace's hand. "Then let him mock. This book is yours. No one should spoil that satisfaction for you. And if you want, I'm sure you can use this opportunity to do other things."

Grace's eyes lit up and a grin broke the solemn expression on her face.

"And whatever you want to do," Jackie continued, "that's up to you. Perhaps write another book. There are a wealth of topics you could explore, from Monaco's history to the monarchy to entertaining or even parenthood. Or you could start a charity. The important thing is that you find something you love. Something that will let you thrive." *And you won't have time to wallow about your marriage.* "The children are growing up, so it's good for you to focus on yourself. Don't depend on your marriage for fulfillment."

A broader smile emerged. "I should be like you then—and start a new career?"

Jackie straightened, exactly as she'd been taught in etiquette class long ago and sipped her coffee with ladylike perfection. "Well, I don't know if you'd make much of an editor, Grace, but I can see if they're hiring."

May 1980

Jackie,

Exquisite! Simply exquisite is all that comes to mind after reviewing the potential layout for the Tiffany book. I knew pairing you with John Loring for this endeavor would be one of the smartest moves I ever made. John told me you were hesitant at first about the subject matter of table settings, but I hope you are now as excited about this book as I am. I will admit the cover design gives me pause. I still believe it's too dark and moody. However, I'm willing to trust your opinion on this since you were confident that its features are just enough to complement the 1960 publication while allowing this installment to stand on its own. Again, thank you for taking this on, even though I didn't give you much choice in the matter. Blame it all on that fine taste you have.

Best,
Thomas Hoving

TWELVE

June 1980

Jackie was anxious to wrap up items for work and head to Martha's Vineyard for a long weekend. She and Nancy had spent the better part of the afternoon going through mail and prepping correspondence in the living room of Jackie's apartment. When they had almost finished, Jackie's doorman called to inform her that a package had been delivered. Nancy volunteered to sign for it and bring it back up.

Upon reentering the apartment, though, she didn't hide her disappointment when she handed Jackie a box that fit in the palm of her hand.

"All that to-do for this?"

Jackie laughed at her. "I think you'll be surprised."

Nancy fixed her hands on her hips. "Can't be new shoes or a Gucci bag. Probably not even a belt."

Jackie removed the packaging and exposed a navy-blue velvet box. Opening the lid revealed a dazzling pair of diamond earrings.

"Ooh, well, I guess you were right."

Jackie held them up to watch them sparkle in the light. Maurice, being the CEO of Lazare Kaplan International, a diamond firm, had helped her acquire them, and she couldn't have been more pleased, both with his thoughtfulness and with giving them as a graduation gift to Caroline.

"These are lovely, just as I knew they would be." Jackie closed the box. "Although they may not be fitting for the workplace. Fine jewelry rarely is, but I'm sure she'll have plenty of events to attend where she can wear them."

"Do you know what she'll be doing?"

"We haven't had a chance to discuss the details, but I'm so thrilled for her. And working at the Met means she'll be close by."

"It's an interesting choice, working in the film and television department." Nancy tilted her head. "Taking after you a bit, isn't she? More on the journalism side than politics, which is probably a relief."

Jackie appreciated and admired that her daughter was democratic about her decisions, having worked as an intern for Teddy for two summers and spending one summer as a courier for New York's *Daily News*. Caroline once told Jackie she had a passion for photojournalism. During the 1976 Winter Olympics in Innsbruck, Austria, she worked as a photographer's assistant but found her presence served as a distraction. Growing up under the lens of the press had compromised her ability to blend into a crowd.

"Caroline isn't suited for politics, at least not at this juncture in her life. She prefers being productive without being under scrutiny."

"Again, just like her Mum. What about that beau of hers? Do you think there's a chance he'll propose soon?"

"Sooner than one might expect." Irritation laced Jackie's tone.

Nancy's expression wrinkled with confusion.

"He's moved on to someone else," Jackie clarified, "and there's a rumor he plans to propose to this *other* girl. Apparently, he's been seeing her for some time."

"We are talking about the same man, aren't we? Tom, the writer?

The young man *you* set her up with, who she's been dating for a year—"

"Over two years. Yes, that's him."

Nancy shook her head. "How could any man treat Caroline like that? All those years together, why, I thought he was the one. What a rake!"

Although Jackie knew Nancy's reaction held no malice, a pit still formed in her gut. She *had* been the one to introduce the pair over dinner at 1040 one evening. A Yale graduated with a pensive nature and Irish heritage, Tom had been cordial yet shy when he and Jackie met at Doubleday. When she broached the topic of introducing him to Caroline, he remained cautious, but Jackie still detected a twinkle of interest in his eyes.

"Caroline thought he was the one too, and she's broken up about it."

This was the second break-up for Caroline—the second time a man had dropped her flat. Mark Shand, whom she met during her internship at Sotheby's, had been her first love. Several years older than Caroline but well-educated, they spent two years together, exploring the art scene and attending parties before he broke off the relationship.

"Let's do what we can to make her graduation special," Jackie said, "and keep her mind off Tom."

"Well, I know that hits hard. You really wanted to see her married and settled."

A shiver down Jackie's back. Was she clinging to an old-fashioned notion, wanting to see her daughter happily married one day? She couldn't help it. In her view, marriage made sense for young people. Who didn't dream of falling in love? And what was wrong with wanting Caroline deliriously happy?

But Jackie felt like stringing Nancy along.

"Perhaps she wants to devote herself to her career. I've read there are women opposed to matrimony these days."

Nancy arched an eyebrow and peered over the rim of her glasses.

"You want Caroline to forge ahead single? Potentially become a spinster or an old maid?"

"Are you putting yourself in those categories, since you never married?" Jackie pressed her lips together to keep from laughing.

"Some of us are not meant to be domesticated wives. What would you do if I had a grand house to maintain and a husband to answer to? Your life would be in shambles without me."

They laughed, but Jackie couldn't deny that having Nancy as a friend and an assistant had proven pivotal in her life more than once. What would Jackie have done without such a loyal friend? One who knew her and understood her in ways only a life-long friend could.

"There's so much talk about women's rights and empowerment." Jackie gave a half-shrug. "And it's not as though she has to marry." Part of her envied Caroline's freedom. Had she been connected to a family fortune, Jackie wondered if she would've made different life choices. How long would she have stayed on as the Inquiring Camera Girl at *The Washington Times-Herald* newspaper if Jack hadn't proposed? Would opportunities have presented, ones that could have added career growth or led her in exciting new directions?

Strangely, a memory of John Husted unpacked itself from the attic of her mind. John, the first man who proposed to her. She'd accepted, but when her mother learned of John's salary, she discouraged Jackie from going through with the marriage, warning her that a stockbroker's wages wouldn't afford her the life she was accustomed to. Jackie ultimately agreed, but part of her decision was influenced by Jack. They had seen each other sporadically but neither committed to the relationship.

John Husted, on the other hand, pursued and wooed Jackie. Accepting his proposal had been Jackie's way of doing what was expected, and what she thought was a sure-fire way to purge the congressman from her mind. When she broke off the engagement during a car ride to the airport, she had no ready-made plan with Jack. No promises from him that she could fall back on. Yet taking that chance, risking that she might remain single, meant everything.

"You forget who you're talking to," Nancy said, interrupting her thoughts. "I'm not buying this tripe of yours for a second. I know you want that girl married and to one day make you a grandmother."

It seemed a far-off future to Jackie, but she loved the dream of her little family growing.

"Well, the only diamonds in her immediate future are coming from her mother, so it will be a while before we can shop for baby items." Jackie grinned. "That is, if she doesn't end up like you."

Nancy popped a hand on her hip again. "Attractive, self-assured, and completely in charge of her life?"

They laughed again.

"But I will say, this bit with Tom." Nancy shook her head. "Mm-mm. Just goes to show you can't trust a writer."

August 1980

BEFORE TEDDY CONCEDED his bid for the presidential nomination during the Democratic Convention, he had phoned Jackie and told her. She was relieved, primarily for Joan. Teddy shared a poem by Tennyson with Jackie that he intended to read during his speech. Tears glistened her eyes as she recalled Jack quoting those same words.

"I may be done, Jackie."

She waited to see if he would elaborate, if he would admit that he was done vying for the presidency.

Perhaps he didn't need to say it considering the abysmal state of his marriage and the fact he would never be able to distance himself from Mary Jo's tragic death.

"It's best for me to continue to serve in the Senate," he said. "But I wanted you to hear it from me and to know how much I've always appreciated your support. I just wish I could've made you proud."

Her chest pinched with an ache for him. What could she say?

She couldn't help harboring a degree of disappointment in him, but she worried that he could sense it.

"You know I'll always love you, Teddy."

After all, Jackie had never been one to kick a man when he was down. Not even Teddy.

April 1981

RAPTUROUS BEST DESCRIBED Jackie's excitement and emotions when the construction of her new home on Martha's Vineyard was completed. What had been a sheep farm with only a cottage two years prior was now her island sanctuary. Among the white oaks, cedars, and beetlebung trees she had designed and then kept a close eye on the construction of a Cape Cod-style main house, a four-bedroom guest house, and a caretaker's house, all clad in cedar shingles, and a faux silo that included a bedroom, bathroom, and open living area. While working with architect Hugh Jacobson, she insisted every room feature a view of the water.

Although a tennis court and a pool were also added, she left most of the three hundred and forty acres untouched. A subtle nod to honor the Wampanoags who once lived there. Naturally, she left the landscaping in the capable hands of Bunny Mellon, her longtime friend and collaborator for the White House Rose Garden. Blue herons and egrets frequented the two freshwater ponds, and over a mile of shoreline edged her property. The wind-shaped dunes and clay cliffs reminded her of Ireland and her visit back in 1950.

Red Gate Farm, next to her children, her horses, and her career, was her pride and joy. The secluded, coastal setting allowed her to rejuvenate. Two hundred and sixty-three miles from the heart of Manhattan, it gave her the dreamy, stark contrast she wanted when getting out of the city.

And then Joan had called, distressed and crying—perhaps tipsy as well—over what to do about Teddy. Since his failed bid to run for president, Joan had distanced herself from him, moving into her own home. As far as Jackie knew, the press hadn't caught on to their separation. She invited Joan to come and stay at her house on the Vineyard for a week, making her the first person, besides her immediate family and Bunny, to see the newly built home.

Driving the candy-apple-red Jeep she had purchased specifically for the raw terrain Aquinnah had to offer, Jackie picked up Joan at the dock and sped back to the house, intent on giving her sister-in-law an unforgettable visit from the get-go. She chuckled to herself, surprising Joan with her devil-may-care driving style that made Joan cling to the roll bar with one hand while bracing herself against the dashboard with the other.

After her bags were placed in her room and Joan freshened up, Jackie took her through the house and guest house. She walked her through portions of the dunes and showed her Squibnocket Pond. They returned to the main house for the picnic basket she had prepared, then went to the beach. With a little help from the breeze, they flared out a blanket on the sand. Jackie unpacked the fruit, cheeses, crackers, prosciutto, and rosemary sprigs. Joan commented on the breathtaking view as they each made a plate.

"My Jackie, you've done it," Joan said as they ate. "You've created a magnificent home, and it suits you. So earthy and understated, yet cozy and regal in its simplicity."

Jackie smiled. "Sounds like you should write an article for *Town and Country*."

"I imagine you've had a dozen magazines offer to come and do a feature."

Jackie nodded. Since part of Nancy's job was fielding telephone calls, she usually scoffed and remarked at least once a week that she wished the lot of them would take a hint and quit calling and asking for something that wasn't going to happen. Not for any magazine and likely not for any other Kennedys.

Joan looked back at the house. "And I can see why. It's all taste-fully done."

"I'm glad you're here to see it before John brings his friends and has sand scattered throughout the living room and wet, dripping swim trunks hanging in the bathroom. He plans to get a waterbed for his room."

They laughed, but as soon as the merriment subsided, Joan's countenance turned pensive.

"I don't know how you've managed after everything, Jackie. All you've been through, and your wit is sharper than ever. You don't owe anybody, and nobody owns you. I'm envious."

Jackie sighed to herself. "My picture might sell tabloids but I'm not special, and I'm no better than anyone else. I survived, but so have you, Joan, and you're much stronger than you give yourself credit for."

Joan had always been the easiest for Jackie to relate to, although she hated what Teddy put her through. His shameless philandering. Mary Jo's death. Joan's three miscarriages, and Teddy squirreling her away in a rehab center after her drunk driving arrest in 1974.

Ted Jr, her middle child, had been stricken with bone cancer when he was only twelve. Joan had proven to be a dedicated mother, especially when he lost part of his leg to an amputation.

"I wish I could divorce him, Jackie. Walk away for good and have my own life."

Jackie understood her frustration, and she worried that Teddy knew precisely how to manipulate Joan and wreck her confidence. As though he preferred keeping her under his thumb, despite the fact that he, like Joan, was done with the marriage.

"There's no reason you can't do what you want. You have to work for it and work hard at it, but I know you have the kind of gusto it takes."

"I don't know, Jackie." She shook her head. "I'm not good at anything."

"Nonsense. You're a talented pianist, and you're wonderful with children. Why, you could go into teaching and giving music lessons. And I'm sure there are a number of charities that would welcome you on their board. You don't need Ted's permission to do any of those things. And you mustn't discount your sobriety. I've read stories where people share about overcoming their struggles hoping that it might help others who are going through something similar. You could do the same."

When Joan lowered her head slightly, Jackie worried she had embarrassed her by referencing her addiction. Or was her reaction a learned response from Rose Kennedy's scoldings? The woman showed no tolerance or compassion for behaviors she considered a weakness. Joe Kennedy had been the same, and both condemned alcoholism as a character flaw. Was it ironic that Teddy, out of the Kennedy men, was known to drink too much?

"Ted says I'm a failure at everything I do." Joan pressed her lips together.

"You can't keep letting him have a say in your life, not when he's wrong about you and showing little respect. That's just something he says so you won't leave him."

Joan met her gaze. "Should I do it, Jackie, go through with a divorce?"

Jackie was touched that Joan trusted her so much. "I can't decide that for you. But no matter what you do, you should own your independence. If that means staying married and forging your own ways, then so be it. If it means completely severing yourselves from each other, so be it. Make the most of your talents and believe in yourself. That's the most important thing."

Jackie stopped short, suddenly concerned she sounded too much like Stephen Appelbaum, whose book on psychotherapy had been one of her recent projects. A side effect from her career. Though her encouragement was sincere, Jackie had read about co-dependency and knew that Joan would need more than a picnic on the shore to take charge of her life.

Even so, if Jackie and the backdrop of Martha's Vineyard could provide a catalyst for Joan to heal and refresh her self-confidence, she welcomed that chance.

July 1981

BEING tardy had once been a flaw of Jackie's. It wasn't that she ran late; she simply operated on her own time. However, over the years, and especially since entering the workforce, she became mindful of being punctual. Tonight, though, she intentionally arrived late for her dinner with Frank Sinatra.

When she'd reached out to him weeks ago, she opened the conversation with a cheeky barb, asking if he was enjoying a new set of friends since he switched to the Republican Party. Earlier in the year, Frank had gone so far as to host a gala, similar to the one he and Peter Lawford hosted for Jack in 1961, but for newly elected President Ronald Reagan. She risked Frank taking her tease as a criticism, but the gamble paid off. Frank rolled with the intended humor, and Jackie was relieved the ice breaker proved charming rather than offensive.

Before she had a chance to ask, he insisted they get together for dinner.

"We're due for a long chat and some catching up," he said.

A chance to reminisce. Precisely what Jackie hoped for. She wasn't surprised at his eagerness to reconnect, though spending an evening with him would require a deft performance from her. He suggested they dine at one of his favorite spots, and even though she typically veered away from Italian cuisine she readily agreed. A strategic move that aligned with her aim to please him and warm him up for the ulterior motive she had in mind.

Meeting in public furthered her strategy. Under no circumstance did she prefer to be alone with Frank, especially when she considered their past history and the time Frank, drunk on cocktails and confidence, made a pass at her. Bobby had intervened, saving her from Frank's groping hands.

For this endeavor, she was able to shelve her true feelings for him.

When she arrived at the restaurant, the place was void of fellow diners. The staff, presumably, stood in a straight line, their pristine-white coats buttoned to the neck and their heads topped with puffy toques, while Frank stood in front of them. He approached and kissed her cheek.

"I thought it would be more intimate if we had the place to ourselves."

"This is quite unexpected." Jitters threatened, and she was glad she'd told her driver to wait nearby and to call the restaurant in exactly ninety minutes if she didn't appear before then.

"I know how you like your privacy." He held out a chair and she sat. A robust bouquet of lavender hydrangeas and lit votives decorated the table.

"You're so thoughtful, Frank, but all this trouble wasn't necessary."

"Anything for a dear friend."

She forced a pleased smile, certain his dramatics were intended for the staff.

Frank ordered appetizers and drinks, then joined her at the table as the staff dispersed.

"You look ravishing."

She thanked him and batted her eyes. Though she never forgave him for his drunken behavior that night at the private White House dinner she and Jack hosted for him, the years since had softened her distaste toward him. However, she would never be able to separate him from acting as a pimp for Jack, which included hooking Jack up with Judith Campbell.

For tonight, she pretended Frank had nothing to do with the egregious avalanche of revelations about Jack's infidelities.

Her yellow dress with large yellow polka dots had been the right choice. Floor length, long-sleeved, and trimmed in ruffles, its sunshiny color brought pizzazz but no sex appeal. Diamond earrings—a gift from Ari—and light make-up completed her respectable yet off-limits look.

"Let me tell you, I was sure surprised to get that call from you," Frank said. "It's been, what, years since we were last together."

The word *together* made her cringe inwardly.

"I believe it was when I saw you perform in Rhode Island back in '74. It was a whirlwind of a night, if I recall. I was with Peter Duchin and his wife Cheray. We flew in a helicopter from Manhattan to the venue for the show, then we all flew back to the city afterward for dinner."

"Yes, you're right. I could never forget that night, but was it really that long ago?"

She forced a smile. "Oh, I'm sure we've run into each other at events here and there, but it's so easy to get whisked away and trapped in conversations at those things."

"You got that right." He swigged from the glass already at the table.

Jackie wondered how many drinks had preceded her arrival.

"But what a shame. We have so much in common. So many people that tie us together."

Frank had been instrumental in helping Jack win the 1960 presidential election, with both his charismatic ability to work a crowd and his behind-the-scenes connections. If one believed the rumors.

"It's astonishing when you think about it." Jackie sipped her water.

Once Jackie and Jack moved into the White House, Frank had salivated at the hope of dining as their special guest. Jackie relented, but the quiet evening turned disastrous with Frank and various Kennedys becoming inebriated and unruly. Frank eventually fell out of favor altogether with Jack in 1962 when Jack ditched his plans to stay with Frank and spent the weekend at Bing Crosby's estate in Palm Springs. The primary attraction being Marilyn Monroe, who met Jack in the poolside cabana for a "private party". If one believed the rumors.

Outraged, Frank took a sledgehammer to the helicopter pad he had installed specifically for the president's visit.

Frank began a stream-of-consciousness run down memory lane, and Jackie let him. She laughed and punctuated the stories with her own take when appropriate.

When he tired out, she transitioned.

"Frank, I want to ask an awfully big favor of you."

He met her gaze. "What's that, sweetheart?"

"I want you to write your memoir and let me handle the project at Doubleday."

"A memoir, huh? I wouldn't even know where to begin."

"We'd pair you with a ghostwriter, and it would work much like tonight. You would share your experiences, talk about your marriages and...lost loves." Jackie played coy. "Who wouldn't want to read about your upbringing and career? It's so inspiring just thinking about the obstacles you've overcome and how you've known and worked with so many people in Hollywood."

"So that's what this is all about." He cocked a half-grin. "Butterin' me up for one of those a tell-all books."

"Well, you are a living legend, Frank. It's unlikely there will ever be another man whose talent and charm could compare. Why not encapsulate one of the greatest stories yet to be told?"

A wry grin appeared as he leaned back in his chair. "Let's say I agree to this. What's in it for me?"

Jackie suspected Frank would want to try to take advantage of the situation. Since he was already spectacularly wealthy, money would mean little. Instead, she had to appeal to his hubris.

"Isn't it obvious? Another token of immortality."

He laughed and held his arms open. "I've already got that with my music. You've gotta give me something I don't already have." His gaze drifted down to her chest. "Maybe something I've wanted for a long time."

"I can."

His droopy eyes met hers. "Oh?"

Jackie leaned in toward him. "Yes. If you decide to go through with this and commit to the project, I can assure you that we'll be trading phone calls frequently, and that we'll need to spend time together. You could say it might take our relationship to another dimension. Seems like an expression kids say these days."

"I'll say this for you, Jackie, you've given me something to think about."

She was mildly discouraged he didn't accept outright, but knowing he was tipsy, she could at least hope he would make the decision when his head cleared. At the very least, she had done her job, and the next time she sat in a meeting on acquisitions, she could share that she had approached Frank Sinatra about writing his memoir. If Frank ever put ink to paper and signed a deal with Doubleday, perhaps it would also help her entice Diana Ross.

However, if Frank Sinatra had any delusions that a book deal would entitle him to a romp in the sheets, he was woefully wrong.

THIRTEEN

June 1982

"I think it suits you." Jackie remarked after walking through Maurice's new suite at the Stanhope Hotel.

For months he had said he wanted to be closer to Jackie's apartment. Taking the step of moving his belongings had been his own doing since Jackie had remained cautious about encouraging him.

While it was true their relationship had grown and deepened, Jackie was still leery of making a commitment. She liked keeping her options open, although nowadays that existed more in theory than practice. Frankly, she was disturbed by the rise in AIDS cases. Early research suggested those engaging in casual sex with a variety of partners were more likely to be susceptible. Not that Jackie was sleeping with anyone else, but the risk of contracting a vicious disease—now known to kill people—wasn't worth the gamble.

"Should we celebrate tonight?" Maurice asked. "I could order up entrees from Mortimer's, if you're in the mood for steak."

"I didn't realize a move was worthy of Mortimer's on a Tuesday." She had no reason to feel a bit edgy, especially with Maurice, but she couldn't shake it.

"Well, I was also thinking of your promotion to senior editor. That's worthy of a dinner cruise on the yacht with a fireworks display."

Jackie arched an eyebrow. "Should I get my shrug then?"

He chuckled. "I can't say I planned that far ahead. Forgive me?"

She laughed with him and relaxed. That was Maurice. Charming, light-hearted, and thoughtful to a T. "How did you already know about my promotion?"

"I read the trades and keep my ear to the ground for the latest news." He winked. "But I'm ecstatic for you and very proud, my Jacqueline."

Her cheeks tingled from the rush of heat. She was proud, too. A promotion and a raise, all on her own work and merit. Maurice's recognition added to her joy. Jack had been proud of her for the unexpected impact she had on voters, mainly attributed to her beauty and style. Ari had been proud having the most desirable woman in the world at his side like a prized thoroughbred. Neither man fully appreciated her intelligence, though, and both would have felt their manhood threatened by a successful working woman as a wife. But Maurice wanted her to shine and gladly stepped out of her spotlight.

"Do you ever find our relationship odd?" she asked.

"How so?"

"I wonder, why do we work so well together, when others think we're a mismatch?"

"That's quite simple. *Others* will always want you to choose a Cary Grant type of a man. Debonair. Effortlessly romantic. Classically handsome."

Physical appearance didn't hold the clout with Jackie that *others* thought it should. For her, an interesting and complex man with various tastes, one who was a forward thinker and liked taking certain risks, truly excited her. Maurice checked those boxes, and he was substantially wealthy. An important factor she couldn't deny.

She was surprised, though, that since she had been about town with Maurice, the tabloids labeled him as her escort or companion. No issue seemed to be raised about the fact he was married. Or Jewish. How had she circumvented such criticisms?

She smiled. "I suppose it's a good thing I like disappointing others' expectations."

July 1982

Jackie,

As you've probably already heard, I'm moving ahead with the divorce. It will be one of the hardest things I've ever done—if not the hardest—but I know it's for the best. I wanted you to know how much our time together at your beautiful home has meant to me, and that you helped me find the courage to take care of myself. If it wasn't for you, I don't know how I'd move forward with my life. My children have been so supportive and understanding. I'm sure you can imagine the encouragement that's given me. I've started working with the Pine Street Inn homeless shelter as well. It breaks my heart there is such a need, but I hope I can make a small difference. I'm also getting more involved with the Boston Symphony—and I can't tell you how alive it makes me feel, getting in touch with music again. For the first time in a long while, I'm excited for what lies ahead, and I owe much of that to you.

All my love and devotion,
Joan

September 1982

PRINCESS GRACE DIES IN MONACO

Princess Grace of Monaco—who rose to worldwide fame starring in such films as *To Catch a Thief* and *High Society*—died Tuesday night in a Monte Carlo hospital, a day after she was injured in a car accident. A statement from the royal palace said the 52-year-old princess died of an "intracerebral vascular hemorrhage" after suffering leg, rib, and shoulder fractures. Upon hearing the news of her death Prince Rainier was said to be inconsolable. A memorial service will be forthcoming.

January 1983

REGRET OVERWHELMED AND BLINDSIDED JACKIE. As she sat in the office of Janet's doctor, with Lee by her side, such a bombardment was the last thing she expected. But trembling there in her seat, she wished Janet had agreed to a complete check-up sooner. Whether a few months would have made a difference, Jackie didn't know. Even so, she longed to go back in time. For one, she would have loved her mother better, though she wasn't sure how or what she might have done differently. Now, having discovered the cause of Janet's forgetfulness and sharp mood swings was harder than Jackie had imagined. Harder than not knowing.

She also regretted not having resolved or at least addressed her aperture with Lee. Now wasn't the time, but having allowed the distance between them to grow, she decided, was a mistake. Lee's indiscretion with Jack still bothered her, but not as much as the fact they both kept moving on, living their lives without needing each other.

But today was about Janet and her diagnosis.

Alzheimer's disease. Jackie only had a general idea of what the disease entailed, and no idea what it meant for her mother. Taking his time, while Janet waited in a separate room, the doctor thoroughly explained how Janet's mental capacities were slowly failing, how that would lead to physical limitations, and eventually, death.

Afterward, he satisfied Jackie's questions, though in her state of bewilderment, she wasn't able to be as thorough as she wanted. Lee, on the other hand, seemed paralyzed by the news and raised only a handful of concerns.

Before he excused himself from the room, the doctor said they could take some time to discuss matters while he checked on Janet. He told them that when they were ready, he would bring her in to share the results with her.

In the silence that followed, Jackie kept her composure as her emotions ratcheted.

"If you ask me, it's all ridiculous." With her arms tightly folded, Lee looked even smaller in stature. "According to everything he said, there's nothing they can really do for her, except ply her with pills and hope for the best. And no matter what they do or don't do..."

She's going to die.

"It is quite shocking nothing can be done. Maybe we could take her to Europe and see if there are alternatives." Jackie's enthusiasm waned before she finished. She realized her mother was probably in no condition for extensive travel or able to endure testing and experimental treatments.

Lee rubbed her forehead. "I don't know, Jacks. Maybe."

Jackie nodded, not knowing what else to do.

"So the memory lapses will worsen, and one day she won't remember who we are? How do we sit back and watch her deteriorate? God, this is awful. How can it be so hopeless?"

"It doesn't seem possible."

Silence beat.

"I'll arrange for her to have a nurse in the house with her on a daily basis." Jackie drew a breath. "And when she needs more...help, I'll see to it that her needs are met."

"It's more than I can do for her."

Jackie couldn't discern if Lee meant it as a bitter remark or one laced with gratitude. Though she didn't know the current state of Lee's finances, Jackie saw Lee's penthouse had been featured recently in *Architectural Digest* and heard that her design business experienced a boost from the exposure. New clients had reached out to her, and if the rumors were true, Lee's creative spark had been revived.But even if Lee's bottom line was on the upswing, Jackie wouldn't dream of asking her to pony up money for their mother's care. And for a change, Jackie wasn't pestered by bitterness for being the one to take on the financial responsibility.

"On top of all this dreadful news, I suppose we'll have to tell Bing," Lee said.

Bingham Morris, stepfather or not, hadn't crossed Jackie's mind, but she knew Lee had a point.

"I wonder if there's a way to use this to our advantage. Perhaps we can tell him that the best thing is for him to leave Mummy alone, that she needs the people she's most familiar with and has known the longest."

"Oh, Jacks, you're terrible. Besides, Bing might argue that he's actually known Mummy longer than we have."

Lee chuckled softly, which lightened the tension for Jackie. She wanted to wallow in that carefree feel, with each of them laughing and making fun of Bing. From the gaudy straw hats he wore to the weathered overalls she couldn't purge from her mind.

"Do you really hate him that much, Jacks?"

Hearing the word *hate* reminded Jackie that it was best not to let her guard slip. That she and Lee weren't the chummy, giggling sisters they once were.

"He doesn't know how to take care of her, and I don't understand why Mummy thinks she needs him around."

"It's like we've come full circle." Lee sighed. "Mummy couldn't stand any of our choices in men, and here we are, griping about her choice in a husband. The irony is just too rich."

Ironic indeed.

Equally baffling for Jackie was the way they acted unscathed, as though Lee's confession had never occurred. But Jackie knew it spoke to the way they had been raised. To bury their true feelings and uphold a public image for the sake of one's reputation. Janet had disciplined them well.

But Jackie wanted to believe that today's sad news, shattering as it was, laid the groundwork of hope. Hope that she and Lee could heal and forgive and one day restore their relationship. Because she missed her sister. The one who had been there through her trials and heartaches and joys.

Her mind drifted back to when she lost Patrick. Miserable and alone in her hospital room, the only thing she'd craved was her sister. Although Lee had never miscarried or lost a child, Jackie wanted to bury herself in Lee's embrace. When Lee arrived from London, sometime in the gray dawn hours of night and walked into the room, she said nothing. She slipped from her shoes and carefully climbed into bed with Jackie. Dulled from pain medications, Jackie felt like a ragdoll that had been torn into pieces. Lee laid her head against Jackie and whispered, "I love you, Jacks." Agonized as she was, Jackie knew she would find the strength to recover, thanks to her sister's love.

And weeks later, she invited Jackie to join her on Ari's yacht...

Now, if there was any hope of repairing the hurt, Jackie believed Lee had to want it as much as she did. Jackie had no way of knowing Lee's feelings without a deep, honest conversation, and if they ever dared to plunge into those murky, treacherous waters, would it be worth stirring up those pains once again?

Jackie wondered what it would take for each of them to feel

whole, able to completely forgive, and desire a healthy relationship. How far would they go and how hard were they willing to work to save their sisterhood? Because for the first time, Jackie might live with the shambled remains before she worked at it alone.

February 1983

Dear Jackie,

I can't bestow enough gratitude to you for attending my launch party for <u>Maverick in Mauve</u>. Who knew your interest in Aunt Florance's diary about her life as a young woman in the gilded age would lead us here. Even as a historian myself, I find it baffling at times to gauge what might enrapture the attention of people these days, but your keen belief that her story was worth sharing won me over. Your stout support sparked my own enthusiasm for turning her diary into artwork. The time you took to select every picture and determine the layout and flow of the story was magnificent.

However, I will admit that when Nancy called to tell me you wouldn't be attending the publishing party because there would be too many reporters there for your liking, I'm proud that I found enough favor—and persuasion—with you to change your mind. Or was there a little pressure from Johnny Sargent? I know how bosses can be. Clearly, I have no regrets in selecting the Museum of the City of New York for the event. It was money well spent to rent out the space, and I'm sure you agree. Thank you for coming early, waylaying my nerves, and for being among the last to leave.

We may not be close in the traditional sense of relations—and our relation is only as tight and close as the strands of marital connections allows, thanks to our beloved Hughdie, may he rest in peace, but having this opportunity to work with you has given me the chance to encounter a different side of you. To say I found you insightful with your comments is an understatement. Combined with the depth and breadth of your professionalism, and your guidance throughout the process, you've given me a memorable experience.

Lunch soon? Anywhere, please, besides that dank little office of yours again. Granted, the sandwiches you had delivered from Katz's Deli were tasty, but sitting and eating on the floor one time was enough for me.

Sincerely the best,
Louis Auchincloss

June 1983

WHEN IT CAME TO JOHN, there were no small accomplishments as far as Jackie was concerned. As he strode across the stage and received his degree in American History, having completed his studies at Brown University, she thought her feet might leave the ground as her pride swelled.

There had been distractions though. Temptations that had threatened to derail his success. For one thing, he smoked pot. Jackie made the discovery in his room at Red Gate Farm. She confronted him and had since then banned him and any of his friends from staying in the main house. John claimed he only partook occasionally and used it as a means of relaxation. Jackie wanted him to have nothing to do with an illegal substance and warned him of the dangers of such recreational drugs. John seemed to take her comments in stride, acting agreeable, though not reassuring her he wouldn't touch the stuff again.

John had blossomed into a rugged, devastatingly handsome young man. No longer lanky and awkward, he'd trimmed his floppy mop of hair, as Jackie called it, and seemed to transform overnight. Naturally, the tabloids took notice and featured John often, usually playing football shirtless with his friends in Central Park. Jackie was exceedingly grateful that he didn't seem to date a lot of different women. Sally Munro, a beautiful brunette, was his steady girlfriend during his years at Brown. As far as Jackie knew.

Further reassuring was the fact he'd been accepted into NYU for law school. But it terrified her. John had gotten by with help from tutors, and Jackie worried law school would provide his greatest academic challenge.

For now, she shelved her concerns. John had graduated and they were on their way home to celebrate. Marta had insisted on throwing John a party at 1040. She took care of all the decorating and preparations, wanting to do everything herself as a gift to him. Aside from family, John was allowed to invite close friends with Jackie's approval. Caroline created a video montage of John through the years, which Jackie adored. Maurice squeezed her shoulders when tears welled in her eyes. Adding to her joy was the fact Lee, Anthony, and Tina joined them.

Later that night, when the party was over and everyone had gone to bed, Jackie quietly made her way to the kitchen. She imagined Marta was asleep, exhausted from her loving efforts, but Jackie treaded carefully. Plus, she wanted to pick through the leftovers by herself. There had been so many wonderful dishes, and Jackie had shown restraint while company was present. Now that she was alone, she could savor whatever she wanted. In moderation, of course.

Nibbling on a cherry-glazed lamb chop, she gasped when the kitchen light flicked on.

John laughed softly as he squinted and took in the sight. "You too?"

Jackie had placed an assortment of covered plates and dishes on the kitchen island. She shrugged. "I can't have Marta insulted and thinking we didn't love all the food."

"Good thing I'm here to help." John plucked a fork from the silverware drawer and scooched the gingerbread ring and applesauce toward him as he plopped onto a stool at the kitchen island. He dug out a generous bite. "Mmm. Nobody cooks like Marta."

"It is a delicious problem." Jackie, forever her mother's daughter, whether she liked it or not, took plates from the cabinet for them to use. "Today was very pleasant."

"It really was. I had everyone in the world that I love most in the same room."

A bit of an exaggeration, Jackie knew, but not by much.

"I take it that means there's no lady currently in your life?"

"No one I care to bring home."

Jackie squirmed slightly at the implication and decided playing dumb was the best option.

"So there is someone?"

"Maybe the best way to put it is that part of my life is often complicated."

Jackie nodded. "I can understand." But could she, really? Did she know the pressures he endured from every side?

John was now a young adult. A vibrant man with the world at his feet but an uncertain future ahead. There would be law school, of course, but then what? It probably bothered Jackie more than him, not having the details ironed out.

But she wanted to focus on their current topic. John's private life. Naturally, she didn't want to intrude, but as his mother and a woman, she felt it her duty to thoughtfully educate him about women. Tonight wasn't the first time she tip-toed around the subject, and when it came to John there was no way around the awkwardness. It wasn't as though she could send him off to Uncle Teddy for sound advice on relationships. She was all John had, and she wanted to be a source he could always count on. But how did mothers talk sex with their sons?

It was different with Caroline. Like Jackie, she was reserved and didn't trust easily. With a solid head on her shoulders, she wouldn't fall for flimsy flirtations or men with only one intention. Jackie also felt safe in the assumption that Caroline knew how to take care of herself sexually.

John was another creature altogether. Affable, social, and adventurous, sometimes to the point it teetered on dangerous.

"What I meant to say, John, is that I know you have so many challenges before you, and you must be careful when it comes to letting people get close to you."

He smiled. "I know, Mummy. You probably worry too much about me."

"Probably, but I can't help it. I want to make sure you understand how to treat women." Her nerves began to spike.

"You don't want me to use women the way my father did."

His boldness stunned her slightly.

"I'm not perfect, Mummy, and I know you know that. And maybe it sounds insincere, or like a guilty person claiming he's innocent, but I'm not like him. Not in that way, and I don't want to be."

That John would use women for pleasure, and that women would be willing to be used, had been one of her greatest fears.

"I'm thankful to hear that." She truly was, despite her voice sounding weak and mousy.

"I want to fall in love someday and get swept up in a great romance and I want it to last forever."

His heartfelt wish made her smile.

Then he set down his fork. "Can I ask you something, Mummy?"

"Anything, dear."

"I don't mean for this to sound cruel, and I'm not asking to hurt you, but what was it like, living with...the way he acted?"

Now was her chance to prove she meant what she just said. That she genuinely wanted to be a source he could count on. It was best that he came to her and not solidify his opinions of his father based on rumors and tabloids. Jackie owed him the truth, at the very least, no matter how personal and embarrassing it might be for her.

"Humiliating. We rarely spoke about his actions, and it was impossibly hard not to, given its frequency in our lives. For a long time, I thought all men were careless, but your father...I hope it's not too harsh for you to hear, but there were days I hated your father." The words felt too bitter and demanded correction. "No. That's not fair. I hated his behavior and that he excused himself from self-control. He put his carnal desires above everything. He risked his position, his reputation, and he gave no thought to what he was doing to me, or the tarnished legacy he was leaving to you and Caroline."

And he didn't live long enough to suffer any of the consequences.

After the assassination, Jackie fully believed Jack's womanizing died with him. That none of his affairs or trysts, or his penchant for hookers, would become public knowledge. So she romanticized the nation's dead hero with Camelot. Only, the sin demanded exposure, and Jackie was the one to endure the on-going agony of the steady stream of revelations. Every account like another trip down Dealey Plaza.

Joe and Rose crossed Jackie's mind. The way their marriage mirrored hers and Jack's in some ways. Joe's unfaithfulness set a tone for Jack. Taught him that the "right" woman knew how to tolerate indiscretions. But Jackie saw no purpose in dragging their example into the conversation. She trusted John was wise enough to make the connection without her needing to sound bitter.

"You know, we used to talk about going to Ireland after his second term." The memory coaxed a smile from Jackie. "He hoped to be the US ambassador there one day. We would move there and you and Caroline—" she stopped short of saying *"and Patrick"*— "—would have grown up there, and we both loved that future. But if he would've...continued, I don't know that I would've stayed with him."

She watched John's face as he mulled over the implication with his jaw set and his eyes sharpened with concentration. Maybe she had gone too far.

"I was afraid how much you and Caroline saw, especially when he had women join him in the pool at the White House. I didn't want you two to grow up thinking that was acceptable, or to resent me for not doing something about it."

"Do you mean that?" he asked. "You would've divorced my father?"

She couldn't say yes, but she couldn't say no. The fact was, she didn't know what kind of woman she would've became if Jack had lived.

Maybe she was wrong about herself. Would she have stayed? She couldn't forge an honest, pure answer.

"I didn't like harboring that resentment toward your father."

John nodded, and she hoped he understood.

"If we're being fair, one thing to think about is the fact Jack Kennedy wouldn't have tolerated a disloyal wife, you know."

"I think that's fair." John paused, then, "What about Ari and the rumors he wanted a divorce?"

Jackie had no chance to mask her surprise. Had she opened a Pandora's box and gone wrong with her intention to foster raw honesty?

"You know Ari wasn't well. He never got over losing Alexander in that awful plane crash." Truth be told, she hadn't fared any better in her marriage to the Greek tycoon. He'd remained devoted to his paramour, Maria Callas, after his nuptials to Jackie, and when his dissatisfaction with the relationship combined with his grief and deteriorating health, he became a different man.

But John knew all that. Her attempt to stall an answer couldn't have been more transparent.

"Yes, Ari wanted a divorce. He had started drawing up papers with his lawyer, but it seemed he kept changing his mind. Whether it was about me or conditions in the will, I don't know."

To her surprise, John reached over and put his hand on top of hers.

"I'm sorry, Mummy, for all you went through. You deserved to be loved so much better."

FOURTEEN

August 1983

Nancy poked her head into Jackie's office at Doubleday after returning from lunch.

"I saw your note. What's up?"

"Tucky, good, you're here. Come in and close the door."

Nancy stepped in and shut the door. "Sounds a bit mysterious."

"I am keeping a secret of sorts. For a little while longer." Jackie reviewed the notes she'd written on her legal pad. "I'm meeting with Steve Rubin and John Sargent in an hour, and I wanted to run this by you before I go in there."

"The big boys, huh?" Nancy sat. "Working on a new proposal?"

"Yes."

As Nancy settled in the chair across from her desk, Jackie was struck once again with that fleeting reminder that she needed to see about replacing the worn-out chair. The squished thin padding and faded tweed fabric weren't the impression she wanted guests to have.

"Well, that's hardly a secret in this industry."

Jackie smiled. "Maybe it's not a secret as much as it is a surprise."

"Is it Frank? Did you finally get him to commit?"

"No." The memory of her dinner with Frank zipped through her head. They hadn't spoken since. "Someone much better than Frank."

Nancy's eyebrows jumped. "Better than Frank? Have you resurrected Elvis?"

Jackie laughed. "I'm serious, Tucky. If I manage to land this deal, then Doubleday's bottom line will be strong and healthy for at least a year or two."

"I'm going to expect a hefty Christmas bonus in that case. Who is it?"

Jackie leaned across her desktop. "Michael Jackson."

Nancy's face puckered and she shook her head. "Isn't he the kid with a squeaky voice? The one who sings with all his brothers?"

"He's launched out on his own. Are you telling me you haven't heard of his music or that album of his that's breaking record sales?"

"Sammy Davis Jr and Smoky Robinson are my Motown favorites."

"Michael Jackson is Motown inspired, but they classify him now as pop rock."

"Pop. Rock." Nancy's expression seemed dubious and contemplative. "Like the candy?"

"You could say that."

"I don't envision you as a big fan of such music, so where's the interest coming from?"

Jackie couldn't deny it. Her fondness for classical music and jazz ran deep. Though she did listen to The Rolling Stones and the Allman Brothers on occasion. She also couldn't deny—but wouldn't admit—her disappointment in failing to convince not only Frank to pen a deal but also Diana Ross and General Norman Schwarzkopf. Signing Michael Jackson would make up for the loss of all of them. She hoped.

"It was John's idea. He watched a television special a few months back where Michael performed. Since then he's been listening to his album nonstop and says the young man is an artistic genius. I started doing my own research and found that he's on track to having the highest selling record of all time. He's only twenty-five, but since he's been in showbiz since his childhood, I imagine he could write a compelling book."

Nancy considered that. "Oh, I don't know, Jackie. Younger celebrities these days are...complicated. Are you sure you want to put yourself out there for him?"

"Absolutely. This is one instance where I hope to use my so-called fame for something worthwhile." Saying it out loud strength-ened her flimsy conviction. She wanted this deal, and she was willing to step out of her comfort zone to make it happen. "I'm going to convince the big boys to let me set up a meeting with him and fly out to California."

"Pulling out all the stops?"

"Every one of them. Let's just hope Mr. Jackson is a history buff and a bit of a fan."

———

A MONTH LATER, during her visit to Michael Jackson's home in Encino, California, Jackie did her best to charm the singer while keeping their meetings professional. She found his child-like behav-iors unexpected. What grown man intermixed skipping with dance moves? Or kept a collection of Care Bears? When he introduced her to his pet boa constrictor, Muscles, she sensed that he didn't get the surprise and shock-value he wanted when Jackie reached out and patted the silky-smooth creature. Having been around John's pet snake, Mick, also a boa constrictor, had cured her of squeamishness. Not that she mentioned it to Michael.

He spoke about his upcoming tour, his plans to build a carnival-like estate where children could come to play, and how flattered he was to have the First Lady approach him with the project of writing an autobiography.

Jackie's head spun, but her well-seasoned veneer didn't reveal her discomforts when he sat too close and acted too familiar for her liking. Her resolve also didn't give away her newfound concerns about whether or not he was capable of focusing and seeing the project through, especially when he mentioned his preference for crafting more of a coffee table style book with glossy pictures of him on stage rather than giving readers a behind-the-curtain peek into his life.

Of course, Jackie knew she could rely on other staff members to step in and help when it came to hammering out details. Her main focus would be the content, and she was set on making sure the young man gave enough insights that would propel the book to best-seller status.

But based on her brief interactions with Michael Jackson, she was worried Nancy was right. Working with him already seemed to require a delicate balance. And she couldn't tell if he truly was playing the role of eccentric artist or if he was that unusual. Hope-fully, when it came to the work, he would drop the act or put aside his idiosyncrasies.

Complicated indeed.

December 1983

TYPICALLY, Jackie looked forward to her annual Christmas party. A gathering of her family and close friends at her apartment proved relaxing. Exchanging gifts brought joy and laughter. Idyllic memories were created and stored in her heart.

John and Caroline would be there, naturally, along with Ed, Caroline's boyfriend.

Lee and Tina couldn't make it, but Anthony would be there along with Maurice's children and a few of Jackie and Maurice's good friends.

But tonight, jitters plagued her. She fiddled with her cuticles, giving her nerves a necessary outlet, though she couldn't pinpoint why she was pestered with such worry.

Would it really create a fuss, announcing—no, sharing—that Maurice was moving into her apartment? He'd been her companion for years. They were both exclusive now, his gentle love having won her full devotion. Living together as a couple made sense to Jackie, and unlike her mother, she didn't need a marriage license to validate her decision.

Maurice joined her in the dressing room of her bedroom.

"Are you almost ready, my darling?"

She blushed as she closed her eyes and nodded.

Maurice paused and seemed privy to her hesitations. "If you're concerned or having any second thoughts, we don't have to say anything. Perhaps telling the children individually over lunch or while we're at the Vineyard would be better."

"No, it's fine. I'm just being a touch foolish."

He stepped back and regarded her. "You're worried about what they'll think."

"Partly, I suppose, but it's silly. I'm entitled to live my own life, just like I've raised them to do. But I know they want what's best for me and for me to be happy."

"Nothing could give me greater pleasure than knowing I make you happy." He took her hands in his and tenderly kissed her cheek.

No one had loved her like Maurice. He didn't despise her independence and he put no demands on their relationship. Though their sex life lacked the frequency she'd known with Jack and the nearly obsessive passion that began her marriage to Ari, Jackie believed the trade-off was worth it. Maurice never displayed a temper, enjoyed sipping Chardonay as they read Proust, and loved the opera and ballet as much as she did. He was protective yet not overbearing. Trustworthy with her finances and intuitive when it came to her emotions and needs. And Maurice Tempelsman did not chase and sleep with other women.

Plus, they were the same age. Technically, Jackie was older by almost a month.

"If I'm not mistaken, you're fretting over the inevitable question," he said.

Again, she nodded. "They're bound to ask if we're getting married."

"What upsets you, having to justify that?"

She pondered the question for a few moments, equally interested in her own conviction and response. Much of her life had been dependent upon marrying the right man at the right time. But now, having a career and more money to her name than she ever dreamed possible, the pressure of obtaining a husband was gone. Fully replaced by the freedom of her personal choice.

For the first time in her life, Jackie was confident in setting aside what convention dictated and doing what she wanted.

She drew a breath and affectionately squeezed Maurice's hands. "Nothing has me upset. I suppose I just needed a minute to think on it, and to hear it out loud."

Pride beamed across his face. "Then my darling, let's get ready to welcome everyone to our home."

February 1984

Dear Mrs. Onassis,

How I hope you are already enjoying our inside joke. Even on paper I can't escape referring to you as Mrs. Onassis. My job of introducing you during our receiving line—although you're the last woman on earth who needs an introduction—has taken root. I digress! My real purpose here is to thank you, once again, for your stalwart support in our efforts to save St. Bartholomew's Church. I find it odd that we have to butt horns with a church committee. However, I suppose if a development firm were dangling fifty million bucks in front of me so they could build a high-rise in my garden, I might cave too and chuck notions of preservation. It was so wonderful of you to testify at the hearing, all the way in Albany I might add, against the Flynn-Walsh Bill. Leave it to greedy, sneaky developers to attempt to craft legislation that exempted religious entities from preservation laws. Makes me wonder what the world is coming to. At any rate, we are indebted and grateful once again for your above and beyond support to save the architectural integrity of this fine city.

Until our next receiving line,
Gill Brendan
Municipal Arts Society

April 1984

EASTER WEEKEND always revived the plentiful memories Jackie had made with the Kennedys, especially when her children were young. Like Christmas, Easter was always celebrated in Palm Beach. Coloring and hiding eggs for the bounty of grandchildren to seek and find was as messy as it was joyful. Sunday started with mass at St. Edward's Church, then back to the estate for the enormous table spread Joe and Rose insisted upon. Family games commenced on the lawn afterward and were followed by rounds of tennis or laps in the pool.

As with most functions and holidays now, Jackie didn't partici-pate with the Kennedys. Not that she wasn't welcome, but since marrying Ari she had been liberated from making the Kennedys a top priority. Even after his passing, the arrangement still suited her.

Caroline and John, along with many of their cousins, had outgrown hunting for eggs anyway.

Her most personal bond was with Joan. Jackie still spoke to Ethel and the Kennedy sisters too but on rare occasions. Within the core family, she remained closest with Teddy, bound by so many tragedies, but nowadays he only seemed to phone with urgent matters.

This time had proved no different.

"It's Mother," Teddy said as soon as she answered.

Noting the stress in his voice, Jackie exclaimed, "No! Is she dead?" Then regretted the immediate assumption and her clumsy, insensitive delivery. But she had never known Rose to be ill or struck by maladies. She kept a strict routine of swimming in the ocean, playing golf, and daily walks. A solid example of good health. Being active and fit only came secondary to her daily attendance at mass.

"She's had a stroke."

Suddenly, Jackie was transported back to December 1961, when Joe Kennedy had returned from a round of golf complaining about a headache. The hitch in his demeanor and loss of rosy color in his cheeks prompted Jackie to telephone the family doctor. Joe protested and lay down on the couch. A short time later, Jackie found him unresponsive and telephoned for an ambulance.

Joe had suffered a massive stroke that left him unable to speak and confined to a wheelchair for the last seven years of his life.

Not again.

"They aren't giving her much hope because of her age. The next forty-eight hours..." He choked up and didn't finish the sentence, but Jackie understood.

Teddy recovered and went on to say he didn't expect Jackie to come, especially since there was little chance Rose would regain consciousness or live through the night.

But Jackie, with Caroline and John at her side, flew to Palm Beach and joined the family vigil.

In Rose's bedroom, muffled sobs and bowed heads lent to a somber atmosphere. No one spoke to each other, only stared with swollen, teary eyes as Rose slept. Jackie had never seen the matriarch look so frail and vulnerable. When she clasped her hands together in prayer, she didn't know what to pray at first. A recovery seemed impossible, so Jackie prayed for God's will to be done, exactly what Rose would've wanted.

Caroline decided to stay while Jackie returned to New York with John the next morning.

In the days that followed, Caroline, who held a loving attachment to Rose and several of her Kennedy cousins, became entangled in what resulted in another family tragedy.

When David Kennedy, the fourth child of Bobby and Ethel, showed up at the house to pay his respects to his ninety-three-year-old grandmother, he quickly became belligerent when family members suspected he was high on heroin and refused to let him into Rose's room. He left but returned hours later, still in an agitated state, and was asked to leave.

The next morning, Caroline, concerned for him, went to his hotel. She hoped to find him in a better condition and wanted to help him. Knowing what it had meant to her to be with Rose, she aimed to take him back to the house with her and allow him to visit Rose. But her knocks on his hotel door went unanswered.

Back at the Kennedy estate, she phoned Jackie and told her what had happened. Jackie called the hotel and asked for someone to check on David. A staff member entered the room, after no answer, and found David face down between the room's two beds, dead.

David's addiction issues with heroin and alcohol had been known among the family and treated for years. News of his death deepened the sadness shrouding the Kennedys, but Rose defied the odds and hung on.

FIFTEEN

August 1984

I n an attempt to avoid being stuck alone with Bing while she stayed at the Castle, Jackie took her morning coffee in the kitchen. She expected Janet Jr, Lewis, and their youngest, Alexandra, to sleep a tad late since they had arrived the day before from their home in Hong Kong. She preferred chatting with the two staff members Janet had retained since transitioning from living in the big house at Hammersmith Farm to the Castle. In truth, she would've preferred conversing with a blank wall rather than Bing.

While the staff prepped breakfast, Jackie noticed a TV had been added in the kitchen and played the morning news broadcast. When she glimpsed the picture of Truman Capote that suddenly appeared above the newscaster's shoulder, she moved to the set and turned up the volume.

"Once again, for those who have just joined us, famed writer Truman Capote has died. According to the coroner's report, Capote passed from complications of liver disease. He was staying in Bel Air at the home of Joanne Carson, ex-wife of late-night talk-show host

Johnny Carson. Capote was known for his literary works *Breakfast at Tiffanys* and *In Cold Blood*. In later years he gained attention for his public scandals, which included a scathing article in *Esquire* published in 1975 that exposed secrets of rich and famous socialites he befriended. When asked for comment about Capote's death, Gore Vidal, a longtime rival simply said, 'It was a wise career move on his part.'"

Stunned, Jackie reflected on her own friendship with Truman. The times his razor-sharp wit amused her, as well as his penchant for gossip. But when she replayed his betrayal—that rant David Susskind allowed on his show—and Truman's public attempts to humiliate her, the tinge of remorse she felt changed to indifference.

She turned from the TV and realized Lee hadn't called. If Truman had passed at the height of his relationship with Lee, years back, when they were practically inseparable, she would've been devastated. Perhaps inconsolable. Lee's silence on the matter told Jackie that the friendship had died years ago.

Jackie decided to burn no more thought on Truman. She finished her coffee and followed the staff with their serving trays to the dining room. Her tension mounted with each step as she hoped Bing wasn't there, stuffing a napkin in his shirt collar and patting his chest, which Jackie had seen him do before a meal. But she stole a cleansing breath and assured herself it didn't matter. Janet Jr was there, and nothing would spoil their time together.

JACKIE MADE sure to keep her work schedule light during the month of August to minimize distractions during her sister's annual visit.

Living in Hong Kong since marrying Lewis Rutherfurd in 1966, Janet Jr had spent a month at Hammersmith Farm with her parents almost every year since. She taught French at the Chinese University of Hong Kong for two years and served as stockholder and advisor for the venture capital firm her husband co-founded and managed. More recently, she'd founded the League of Women Voters overseas chapter.

Jackie couldn't have been prouder of the young woman Janet Jr had become and watching her as a strict but gentle mother only deepened her admiration. Unlike Jackie, and Lee, Janet Jr had an easier relationship with their mother. Rarely had she heard their mother raise her voice with Janet Jr, and to Jackie's knowledge, their mother refrained from slapping her in the face. Jackie attributed it to her mother's age, being more experienced and calmer at thirty-seven, when Janet Jr came along, than she had been at twenty-one, when Jackie was born. Of course, Jackie also took her mother's husbands into account. Black Jack Bouvier probably had no business being a husband while Hughdie was the epitome of reliability and chivalry. Even though she endured a heavy hand growing up, Jackie never held that against her sister and loved Janet Jr immeasurably.

Unlike Lee, who showed little interest in their younger sibling.

During breakfast, Jackie helped Alexandra, who was bright-eyed, full of questions and observations, and had trouble sitting still. Jackie marveled at how long and curly her niece's hair had grown, and her sprouting vocabulary. Naturally, Jackie had brought a satchel full of books for the three-year-old and a scrapbook with pictures of her travels to Israel. The trip had been in 1978, for the opening of a Jewish museum at Tel Aviv University, but she was certain she hadn't shared the pictures with her family.

In between keeping Alexandra entertained and focused on eating, Jackie noticed that Janet Jr only nibbled a piece of toast. And was she paler than usual, or was Jackie imagining things?

"It's such a beautiful day out," she declared. "Why don't we head to the beach, then spend the afternoon waterskiing?"

Yusha and Lewis heartily agreed. Janet said she would join them at the beach, then bring Alexandra back to the house while they skied. Alexandra hopped from her chair and excitedly took her nanny's hand so she could change and get ready. The men fell into a discussion about current stock prices, and Janet began rattling off the itinerary of events she had planned for them.

Jackie kept a subtle eye on her sister. She couldn't pinpoint what was off, but her imagination suddenly perked up. What if Janet Jr was unexpectedly expecting again? Jackie suppressed the giggle that wanted to escape and clung to the hope that was it—that Janet Jr was battling morning sickness and wondering precisely how to tell the family.

Yes, that had to be it. And nothing worse.

ONCE THEY WERE out on the boat, and Jackie got her fill of racing, riding, and skimming the waters, she traded places with Janet Jr.

"I'm sorely out of practice," Janet Jr said. "Yusha should go next."

Her hesitation gave Jackie pause, but she ignored it and pressed. "Nonsense. It will all come back to you once you dive in."

Janet Jr conceded, but once she was in the water, she struggled to place the skis on. When she was finally ready and took hold of the roped handle, she seemed out of breath and struggling against exhaustion.

Concern pinched Jackie as Yusha maneuvered the boat ahead. Janet Jr gave a thumbs-up when Yusha looked over his shoulder. He throttled the engine. Janet Jr popped up on the skis, but, in Jackie's mind, couldn't have looked more like a novice. The rope wobbled, and Janet Jr didn't stand straight. Within minutes, the rope snapped from her grasp, and she smacked into the water. As the boat slowed and prepared to turn around, Jackie waited for her sister's head to bob through the surface, but she didn't show.

"Hurry, Yusha!"

Catching a glimpse of Jackie's furrowed expression, he seemed to understand her urgency and sped the boat back to where Janet Jr had been. They found her, treading water with only her face above the surface. Jackie jumped in and bolstered her upward. Yusha and Lewis pulled her onto the boat, but she seemed listless.

Slumped on her hands and knees, she coughed up water and appeared on the verge of passing out.

After climbing aboard, Jackie draped a towel around her.

"What happened, dear?"

Janet Jr fell sideways onto Jackie. "I just don't know. It's like every ounce of my strength has left me."

Jackie looked to Lewis. "We should get her to a hospital."

"Maybe she just needs to lie down."

"I think she should see a doctor." Jackie didn't want to say more, but ever since she'd greeted Janet Jr and held her in her arms, something felt off. She no longer wanted to pretend that it was due to jetlag or perhaps a mild headache. Or the joke she created in her head that she was possibly pregnant. Jackie had to know what was wrong with her sister.

With no further objections, they returned to the house, dried off and dressed. Careful and attentive with his wife, Lewis kept close to her side as they made their way to Newport Hospital.

Janet Jr was admitted, and various tests commenced. Hours dragged by as a wicked waiting game commenced. The late afternoon turned into evening. Jackie, Yusha, and Lewis, not wanting to leave, though they were told test results wouldn't be in until tomorrow, decided to stay the night. Slumped in chairs, they made the best of the arrangement, not that any of them expected much sleep.

By morning, stretches and strong coffee were in order. When Jackie telephoned her mother, she could only say they were still waiting for news from the doctor. She didn't dare mention that her sister, now confined to a hospital bed and on an IV, seemed increasingly afflicted with weariness.

When the doctor finally summoned the family to a private waiting area later that afternoon, Jackie, racked from sleeplessness and trying to keep her mother placated, trembled. Yusha, perhaps sensing Jackie's need for comfort and support, put a protective arm around her and squeezed. When they traded glances and perfunctory grins, she suddenly feared the worst.

"I'm sorry to tell you this," the doctor said, "but we've found that Janet has lung cancer."

"That can't be!" Lewis's voice snapped sternly, breaking the stunned silence. "She's never smoked a day in her life."

"It's rare and uncommon, yes, but I'm afraid it's true. In fact, it's quite advanced."

"What are you saying?" Jackie was breathless from the shock.

"I recommend having her transferred to Boston. There, she can begin treatment, but from what I've seen," he sighed, "there doesn't appear to be much hope."

"This is preposterous!" Lewis exclaimed. "We brought her in for not feeling well and you're telling me that she's dying! She hasn't been sick, and she just turned thirty-nine. None of this is possible!"

Jackie went to Lewis and threw her arms around him.

"I understand your hurt and confusion, Mr. Rutherfurd," the doctor sympathized, "and please, feel free to get a second opinion, though I suggest she reserve her strength for treatment. She's going to need it, and she's going to need all of you."

THAT EVENING, Lewis stayed at the hospital while Jackie and Yusha went home to Janet. Desperate for the false sense of peace that showering and a sensible meal would provide, Jackie wanted to collapse when she walked into her mother's home. But she couldn't. On the drive back, she and Yusha had discussed what they would tell Janet and agreed that for now, it was best to keep the bleak news vague. At least for the evening's dinner.

Alone in her room, Jackie let the sobs come and the tears flow. She needed the release because she knew once she changed and joined Yusha, her mother, and little Alexandra at the table, she wouldn't be able to look into her niece's eyes—those beautiful, innocent eyes that reminded her of Janet Jr's—without the grief mounting. An outburst, especially in front of her mother during dinner, would not be acceptable.

Jackie needed to be strong for her family. After all, Lewis had the more difficult task of telephoning his sons, Lewis Jr and Andrew, and preparing them for what lay ahead. Though they were grown and off to university, Jackie knew the boys would be devastated.

Before she left the hospital, Lewis asked Jackie to tell Janet, believing the news would be best coming from her.

Pain constricted in her chest, though, when she thought of Alexandra. She was only a toddler and had no hope of understanding the loss. Of course, Jackie reverted back to her days with John after the assassination of his father. His endless questions coupled with his inability to understand Daddy had gone to Heaven to be with Patrick because he was lonely.

She shook her head slightly, trying to hush the recollection of John's little voice. Alexandra and her mother needed her focus. Numbness threatened to set in, but Jackie resisted knowing that would do her no favors. Her niece and mother deserved better, and she would summon every ounce of strength she had while hoping the doctors in Boston might find a way to save her sister.

AFTER DINNER, Jackie, Yusha, and Janet gathered in the living room. Alexandra had enjoyed her meal perched on Jackie's lap. After a hug and a kiss, she relinquished Alexandra to her nanny.

Then, with carefully measured words, Jackie explained to her mother that Janet Jr needed to be moved to Boston for further testing before a solid diagnosis could be made. She and Yusha promised they would take her to see Janet Jr tomorrow. To Jackie's surprise, Janet didn't launch an assault of questions, and Jackie worried she was grappling with her own issues.

Finally settled on the sofas, with slices of pound cake and a freshly brewed pot of coffee before them, Jackie took a scrapbook from the bookcase. Revisiting memories, she hoped, would soothe her mother. The first few pages featured snapshots of eighteen-year-old Lee at her coming out dance.

A proud smile creased Janet's face. "Such a beautiful debutante. All of you girls were remarkable and graceful, but I think your sister is an exquisite beauty."

"She truly is, Mummy."

Seeing the images reminded Jackie that Lee had yet to be informed about Janet Jr. In the back of her mind, Jackie began rehearsing the call she needed to make to Lee. Although Lee and Janet Jr weren't very close, Lee never took tragic news well.

But now, as Jackie flipped through the pages of the scrapbook with her mother, the ache in her chest lessened. Watching Janet smile and share snippets of stories and details from the pictures was the relief she needed. But when they turned to pages featuring photos of Jack, her breath caught. Rarely did she spend time going through her past, even though, thanks in large part to Joe Kennedy's sense of history, there were endless captures of Jack on film. Immortalized for the world, looking youthful, to a degree, and unaware of his fate.

Seeing Jack rattled the well-boxed grief she kept stored away for him. Pictures of Jack always transported her back to their days in the White House. Summers on the Cape. Lunching on the *Honey Fitz*. Euphoric times that she hadn't known since. But on the tail of those highs came the crescendo of humiliation. Pestering reminders of Jack's infidelities. His penchant for the young interns and other women he saw on the side. Then came the rushing pain of losing him.

Jackie fought back the melancholy as she focused on the images in front of her.

"Oh, remember this, Mummy?" She pointed to a snapshot of Jack stepping from *Marine One*, the presidential helicopter, after it touched down on the lawn of Hammersmith Farm. The press had dubbed her mother and stepfather's estate "the summer White

House" since Jack visited regularly. "You used to love going out to greet Jack whenever he arrived on the helicopter. Although you complained that it always ruffled your hair."

Janet nodded. "It always made such a racket and upset the dogs and horses." Her gaze lingered over the photo. "But tell me, Jacqueline, who was Jack?"

SIXTEEN

November 1984

Having longed to return to the Virginia countryside for ages, Jackie finally arranged to have her horses stabled at Bunny Mellon's estate, Oak Spring Farm, and joined the Middleburg Hunt Club. Life's constant state of melancholy had given her the prod she needed—the reminder of how short and fleeting life could be, and that in the space and time she was given, it was up to her to create her own happiness where she could.

She returned to her annual tradition of riding during Thanksgiving week. Unlike in a true fox hunt, Jackie's riding club didn't pursue a live fox. A rider started out ahead of the group, dragging a ball with the scent of a fox on it through the meadows. The run and imaginary chase was more about the thrill than an actual hunt.

Jackie welcomed the moments of rushing through the forest with a cool breeze brushing her cheeks. She only wished Janet Jr could know such relief.

A shimmer of light had presented itself though. Last month,

while enjoying a cruise on the *Relemar* with Maurice, John, Caroline, and Caroline's boyfriend Ed, Caroline had announced that she and Ed were engaged. Champagne bottles were popped, and Jackie couldn't have been more elated as Caroline shared the story of how Ed proposed at his parents' chalet in the Berkshires the previous weekend. A lively discussion followed. They would need an event planner, a church, a reception hall, and a mountain of security.

Caroline expressed that she wanted her reception at the Kennedy compound on the Cape because she wanted to make it as easy as possible for Rose to be part of the festivities. Nothing could've pleased Jackie more. Even though Rose was now confined to a wheelchair and her speech was challenged, she proved what an indomitable figurehead she was with her unrelenting will to live.

In Jackie's mind, there was no question who would design Caroline's dress. Over the past several years, Jackie had forged a fast, genuine friendship with Carolina Herrera and her husband Reinaldo. Jackie would keep her involvement and her opinions to a minimum. She wanted the day to be completely Caroline's dream and unlike her own wedding where the Kennedys and her mother made most of the decisions for her.

Her thoughts about Caroline's wedding were interrupted as dark clouds rolled in and rain began to speckle. The weather report made no mention of precipitation. Not that it would have kept Jackie away. Light showers soon became heavy rain and compromised visibility. The hunt quickly soured as the dogs were helpless in the downpour.

Jackie tilted her head back and let the rain wash over her. Within minutes she was soaked to the bone, but she didn't care. As Frank galloped back to the stable, the chill in the air combined with the cold rain. She *did* care about contracting pneumonia and knew she needed to shed her wet clothes as soon as possible.

With Frank in the care of the stable hands, she walked briskly to the guest cottage, her usual spot at Bunny's. A crackling fire awaited inside. An unexpected yet welcome surprise. Had Bunny gotten wind of the fact she and the other club members were drenched? She gave it little thought but locked the door. Standing in front of the fireplace, she began the laborious task of peeling off her wet clothes. Her gloves, hat, boots, jacket, undershirt, jodhpurs, socks, and intimates piled on the hearth. Completely naked, she braced herself against the mantle as the warmth radiated over her and began to dry her damp skin.

If she were in danger of catching a cold—as her mother might warn—she didn't care. Few were the moments lately that revitalized her so.

As the shivers subsided, she tried combing her fingers through her wet hair, but it was useless. Only a shower would help. She turned, letting the flames blaze against her backside, when suddenly, the bedroom door opened.

Startled, Jackie drew herself in and covered her nudity, best she could, with her arms. Adrenaline surged through her until she glimpsed the man's face in the firelight.

"Maurice, what are you doing here?"

"I didn't mean to frighten you, my darling. I thought you would notice my overcoat hanging up when you came in." He pointed to his charcoal-colored Burberry on a nearby peg.

Aside from the fire and a small table lamp, the living room was shrouded in grays. She hadn't seen it.

"I finished a meeting early and planned to surprise you. I hope that's all right."

"Of course." Laughing put her at ease.

A wide grin puffed his cheeks as he perused her from head to toe. "Must have been an interesting ride today."

"We got caught in a storm."

"Lucky for me." He looked her over once more. "And quite appropriate, if you ask me, since we have cause to celebrate."

"Oh?" A spark of delight eased the spike of tension.

"Why don't I fetch your robe and pour us both a drink first."

"Do I have enough time to shower and change?"

"You may have whatever you want, darling. If you're going to such lengths, I think I'll phone the main house and see if they might craft a small dinner for us."

She grinned. "We're not at the Carlyle, dear."

"No, but we're on Bunny Mellon's property. The main house isn't far. Do you think her staff isn't equipped to service us? And when I tell them it's for you, why, I'm certain they will go to any length to ensure your satisfaction. Come to think of it, I'll ask for their best Bordeaux."

"Wine, dinner by the fire." Jackie sashayed to him and shrugged a bare shoulder as she slid her fingers along his silk tie. "Can you at least give me a little hint what we're celebrating?"

He put his hands lovingly around her waist. "Lilly has granted me a *get*. It's a Jewish divorce. There's no legal weight behind it, but it means we're spiritually severed. That's more important to me than a bunch of documents stamped by a court."

"So, you're a free man?"

"Well..." Desire pooled his eyes as he drew Jackie closer. "I happen to belong to someone."

"Indeed you do." She whispered in French.

Holding onto his tie, Jackie tugged him in for a kiss.

January 1985

IN THE WEEKS THAT FOLLOWED, Jackie hid her heartbreak best she could, when doctors in Boston shook their heads and said there was no change in Janet Jr's grim diagnosis. She agreed to undergo intense rounds of chemotherapy, despite the lack of guarantees or a trace of confidence from her doctors. Jackie suspected her sister did so to appease Lewis, and because no other choices existed.

Further compounding Jackie's grief and distress was the unexpected death of her former friend and lover.

By the time Jackie spoke to his wife Pamela over the phone, she had already heard from other friends and had seen snippets on the news that David Ormsby-Gore, officially known as Lord Harlech, had died.

Her romance with David had lasted only a few months. Not nearly as long as the tabloids played it out, which was often the case. Although he had served on the board of trustees for the development of Jack's library, he lived in Great Britain and was an active member of the House of Lords, which hampered the chances for he and Jackie to see each other regularly.

David had been another example of a man she gravitated toward because she found him comfortable and familiar. While Jack was president, David served as ambassador to Great Britain. He and Jack were solid political allies and forged a friendship outside the bonds of politics, which had given Jackie the chance to get to know him informally.

When David phoned her in 1967 with the tragic news that his wife Sissie had died in a car accident, Jackie deeply empathized with him. She understood the grief that came with the sudden loss of one's spouse and found herself drawn to David.

Her first relationships after losing Jack reflected a pattern. They were men she already knew well and loved. Bobby had been first and foremost. Though an affair with her brother-in-law violated convention and sacraments, Jackie was convinced their intimacy was the only way she survived the depression. Then she grew closer to Jack Warnecke, the architect whose design helped saved Lafayette Square in DC, a historical preservation project. Warnecke had also worked for several years on Jack's gravesite at Arlington. Then came her time with David.

Content when they were together, though not enthralled, Jackie attributed the demise of their relationship to a single sheet of paper.

She found a discarded note intended for his daughter in the waste-basket of their adjoining hotel rooms during their goodwill trip to Cambodia in 1967. In the letter, David complained that Jackie always ran late and exhausted him with her neediness. He also didn't like the constant attention surrounding her. The secret admissions were upsetting, but Jackie realized she had no intention of marrying David. When she ended their relationship, months later, she made no mention of the note.

Learning that he'd died—and from complications and injuries sustained in a car crash—had stolen Jackie's breath.

After her tears subsided, Jackie composed herself and phoned Teddy. Together they made plans to attend the service in Wales. Jean and a handful of other Kennedys joined them.

The night before the memorial service, Pamela hosted dinner for Jackie, the Kennedys, and over a dozen other dignitaries and friends. To everyone's dismay, perhaps Jackie's especially, Teddy became drunk and unruly.

Pamela pulled Jackie aside. "You must do something about him."

"I'm so sorry, Pamela. He is getting out of hand, but there's nothing I can do with him, not when he's this far gone."

"Yes, you can. Get him out of here."

Jackie knew she was right. The longer he stayed and the more beer he consumed, with side shots of Penderyn whiskey, the worse he would become. But handling an inebriated and disorderly Teddy wasn't her forte.

"I...I just don't know what to do exactly."

"You and the sisters should encourage him to go."

"I don't know if he'll budge, if he's not ready."

Pamela's eyes widened. "We've got to try something."

Jackie nodded.

They rejoined the table. Jackie leaned into Jean and whispered her concerns about Teddy. She also told her how upset Pamela was by his behavior.

"She wants him removed."

Jean swallowed hard. "Is she going to have him thrown out?"

"No. She wants us to persuade him to leave. Now."

"Oh, Jackie. I've never fussed with Teddy when he gets like this."

"None of us have." Anger tinged Jackie's voice. "But we've got to try before he gets any worse."

With careful prodding, Jackie and the Kennedy clan worked together getting Teddy out of Pamela's home. Help from the younger Kennedy men, Jackie's nephews, proved most effective. Together, they all but carried him out.

Somehow, the next morning, Teddy appeared unscathed. Jackie and the others made no mention about his behavior, knowing he probably didn't remember and wouldn't take accountability for it anyway. Now that he was sober and subdued, she put the incident to the back of her mind.

At the service, she focused on David and their time as friends and, later, lovers. How could it be that she was mourning the loss of another man she held dear?

And when she was on the brink of losing someone else she deeply loved.

———

SINCE THE RUTHERFURDS didn't have a home in the States and Janet Jr needed to stay close to the Dana-Farber Cancer Institute, where she received treatments, Lewis arranged for his wife to stay in a nearby care facility. Jackie did her best to make the space feel more like a cozy cove than a medical institution.

With permission from the staff, Jackie gave the room personal touches. A small display of family pictures clustered on the bedside table. Satin sheets and billowy pillows covered the bed for added comfort, and Jackie made sure her sister had a fresh satin nightgown and robe daily. Since she couldn't easily transport food from Marta,

Jackie saw to it that Janet Jr had healthy, delicious, meals prepared by local chefs and delivered.

And to help Janet Jr recover from her bone marrow transplant, Jackie gave blood transfusions when needed.

Exceedingly difficult for Jackie, and even more so for Janet Jr, were the effects of the treatment on Janet Jr's body and appearance. She lost her hair, and the whittling of her weight seemed to be the only constant for her. Jackie brought a bag with a couple of wigs and head wraps, an assortment of make-up, and a variety of nail polishes. Not to fuel any sense of vanity, but to help her sister feel normal. Some days, that only happened when, lying weak in bed, she could wiggle her fingers and smile at her brightly colored nails.

Each time she visited, Jackie took her outside. When Janet Jr was weary from treatment, Jackie pushed her in a wheelchair. If Janet Jr was up for walking, Jackie held onto her the whole time. As the winter months settled in, snowy and cold, Jackie didn't waver in her determination to get Janet Jr out of the sterile confinement of the care facility's walls and able to scarf the fresh, brisk air, even if it was only for a few moments.

Janet and Lee came to accept the inevitable and were part of the rotation of visitors that included Yusha, Janet Jr's three children, and, occasionally, lifelong friends from Newport. Fresh flowers were delivered often from an array of friends and colleagues who couldn't make the trip.

Jackie found time with Alexandra proved the hardest. Youngsters, she believed, weren't made to endure hospitals or places where they were considered too loud and surrounded by too many things they weren't allowed to touch. Bodily pains and injection sites made it difficult for Janet Jr to hold her little one. Jackie and others tried incessantly to anticipate and accommodate Alexandra's boredom and movements, but bouts of tears usually erupted.

One evening, Jackie had dozed off in her chair when her sister's groans awakened her. She set aside the manuscript on her lap, surprised it hadn't slipped to the floor and scattered across the white linoleum, and went to Janet Jr.

"Should I call for the nurse to come? Do you need your pain medicine?"

"No," she said through the obvious discomfort. "I just need a minute."

Jackie was continually impressed by Janet Jr's strength and her will to fight the disease raging through her. She gripped Jackie's hand fiercely until the intensity passed. Jackie, still holding on, reached for a damp washcloth with her free hand and patted her sister's face, hoping the coolness soothed her.

"Are you sure I shouldn't get the nurse?"

Janet Jr shook her head. "Those pills always make me sleep. I want to stay awake a while." She turned toward the window. "Watch the snow fall."

Jackie couldn't blame her. Even against the milky gray afternoon, the thick white flakes looked beautiful. Janet Jr relaxed into her bed and released Jackie's hand.

"Thank you."

Jackie kissed her sister's cheek and watched the snow fall with her.

February 1985

THOUGH JACKIE usually didn't spend time at her house on Martha's Vineyard apart from the summer months, she was desperate for a respite from recent events. David's funeral—exacerbated by the debacle Teddy created—and Janet Jr's illness kept her in a worn, frazzled state.

But Massachusetts in the throes of winter didn't evoke cheer. Squibnocket Pond was frozen and dusted with snow. The ducks and herons were absent, and the refreshing summer breeze had been replaced by an icy wind.

Still, it was better than the hospital room where her sister lay dying.

After a warm bowl of clam chowder, she was set to retire for the evening, but the phone's sudden, sharp ring beckoned. On the other end, a frantic John Sargent, Doubleday's president, chimed in.

"Jackie, glad I finally caught you."

A mild headache thumped as she slightly regretted making her phone numbers available to her boss. But who was she kidding? She had known John for ages; he probably had her numbers somewhere.

"It's a bit late, John. What couldn't wait until morning?"

"I just talked to Michael. He wants to pull the plug on the book."

Jackie palmed her forehead. Working with Michael Jackson the last two years, even in a peripheral role, had been more than she bargained for. He had gone through two ghostwriters and failed to produce the book by the deadline. Rather than squabble and risk losing the deal, Jackie and Doubleday had renegotiated terms. At that point, she believed they were close to getting the manuscript. Once they had it in hand, she was determined to get it polished and ready for its print run.

However, when the draft was completed, Jackson claimed he didn't have time to read it since he was on tour. An editor from Jackie's team joined him in Australia and read the manuscript aloud to him. The notes and feedback he offered from those reading sessions were incorporated. And now he wanted to cancel the whole thing?

"But why? It's nearly finished." *Finally.*

"He says it's too personal and he's feeling exposed."

"It's an overreaction. We already discussed this with him previously."

"I'm just telling you what he said tonight."

A pause lingered, and Jackie knew she and John were keeping their personal opinions about the pop star's lack of professionalism to themselves.

"Can you call him, Jackie? I think he'll respond better to you."

His hope in Jackie's persuasiveness wasn't unfounded, she knew. Despite the complications he provided as a client, Jackson frequently expressed his admiration for her. She recoiled inwardly, though, when he lumped their fame together. Not out of superiority but out of the fact that she never had a desire to belong to the people. As far as she was concerned, her contribution to history was complete and fulfilled the day she and her children moved out of the White House.

Michael Jackson, on the other hand, regularly took the stage in exchange for money. In Jackie's eyes, he owed his faithful fans.

Jackie didn't pretend there was another option. As much as Michael Jackson's naivety and neediness had drained her and her team, she would phone him. Because once again duty called, and Jackie refused to go down as one who shunned her duty.

―――――

ALTHOUGH HER BRIEF escape to her home at Martha's Vineyard didn't prove as therapeutic as she hoped, Jackie would be the last to complain. Her call to Michael Jackson got him back on track and revived his enthusiasm for getting the book finished.

The following week, Nancy handed her a packet before she left for Boston and her weekend vigil at Janet Jr's bedside.

"There's a nice article in *Architectural Digest* you'll want to check out." Nancy tapped the sheathed magazine with her finger. "It's by their new editor-at-large, Lee Radziwill and features Rudolph Nureyev's apartment. Nicely done."

Jackie took it, not sure what to say. Anger flared sometimes when she thought about how little Lee had done for their ailing sister. But she knew that was Lee and dwelling on it or letting anger toy with her was pointless.

Over the months she had spent at Janet Jr's bedside, Jackie treasured the fact they had talked about everything. From their marriages and spouses to the differences in their childhoods, to their fears and regrets. And yet, Jackie believed there was so much more to say. And there were so many things Jackie was afraid to say, such as, "How will little Alexandra cope without her mother?"

Today, Jackie brought a bouquet of daffodils to liven up the room. She placed them in a vase near Janet Jr's bedside.

"Maybe spring will come early now."

Janet Jr smiled.

Jackie made quick work of readying her sister for their outside visit. Once they were in the fresh air, Jackie steered the wheelchair to the pond out back. Sunshine and temperatures had been generous of late, thawing the water's surface and warming their faces. Somewhere close by, a cardinal serenaded them.

"I hope you and Lee will be good to each other," Janet Jr said. "I always envied the bond you two shared. All I had was Jamie, and we both know how that turned out."

Jackie agreed but said nothing. The youngest of their blended, expanded family, Jamie filled the role of black sheep effortlessly. For Jackie in particular, he'd fallen out of favor in the mid-seventies when he agreed to a tell-all interview with Kitty Kelley, who released an unauthorized biography about Jackie years later. He claimed he had no idea the session would be used for a book and that he said nothing disparaging about his half-sister, but Jackie no longer spoke to him. Since they had never been close, shutting him out was easy.

When it came to Lee, Jackie had no solution. She wondered if Janet Jr had a sixth sense, bringing up Lee when Jackie had just been ruffled by her, though only in her mind.

"I think one of the worst things that happened to us was that our children grew up," Jackie said. "When they were younger, we always made time for birthdays and spent the holidays together. It's complicated now that they're off on their own travels and living lives apart from us."

Jackie had become a hard-core believer in the notion. Regardless of any friction or upset between them, she and Lee always came together for the children. They were faithful to the vow they made at the dawn of motherhood, that their children must grow up together, and that meant summers, vacations, and life milestones were always shared. Now, if Caroline, John, Anthony, and Tina had a schedule conflict, then she and Lee would let it go at that.

But there was no need for Janet Jr to be exposed to the agonizing details.

Janet Jr turned and fixed her gaze on Jackie. "Promise me one thing. That no matter what it is that's come between you, you'll work through it."

Tears began to well in her eyes, but Jackie stole a silent breath and held them back. How could she not promise her dying sister, and yet, how could she keep such a promise?

March 1985

Janet Auchincloss Rutherfurd died last Wednesday at a Boston hospital of cancer at the age of 39. A resident of Hong Kong, Mrs. Rutherfurd was a half-sister of Jacqueline Kennedy Onassis and Lee Bouvier Radziwill.

She was the wife of Lewis Polk Rutherfurd, an international financier based in the Far East. Her parents were Hugh D. Auchincloss Sr. and the former Janet Lee Bouvier, the mother of Mrs. Onassis.

Mrs. Rutherfurd was educated at Washington's Potomac School and Miss Porter's School in Connecticut and studied music history at Sarah Lawrence College.

Her debut in 1963 and her wedding in 1966 to Mr. Rutherfurd, then a Princeton senior, were highlights of the Newport social season. After the marriage, the couple moved to Hong Kong where Mrs. Rutherfurd became an adviser and shareholder in her husband's enterprise.

In Hong Kong, she was a founder of one of the first overseas chap-

ters of the League of Women Voters and served as its president last year.

She is survived by her husband; two sons, Lewis Jr. and Andrew; and a daughter, Alexandra. A funeral service was held Tuesday at Trinity Church in Newport, Rhode Island. A memorial service in New York is being planned.

The New York Times, Obituary

SEVENTEEN

April 1985

Part of Jackie was furious with Lee for not attending funeral services for Janet Jr. Lee claimed it was too painful for her. Jackie was tempted to lash out at her and ask her how she might feel, not having the support of her entire family if she were ill. She wanted to scold her for being so selfish and for not thinking about the toll Janet Jr's death had taken on their mother.

She could have at least been attentive and caring toward Mummy.

But Jackie would be the last to ignite a confrontation and widen the divide between her and Lee.

Maurice's observation on the matter encapsulated her emotions best, "I think your sorrow is deepened by the fact this tragedy didn't bring you and Lee closer together. Not like before."

She and Maurice took Lewis and Alexandra to the airport when it was finally time for them to return to Hong Kong. Curbside good-byes weren't easy for Jackie, especially since Lewis couldn't say for sure when they would visit, though he hoped to make it back for Christmas. She squeezed Alexandra tightly and breathed her in, then made sure she had her little bag, stuffed with the Oreos, crayons, and coloring books she'd bought her for the plane ride. When Alexandra kissed her cheek, Jackie blinked back tears.

She and Maurice watched them until they entered the terminal, then they returned to their limo. As their driver eased into traffic, Jackie slumped in her seat.

Maurice reached for her hand. "This might not be the proper time to bring up the matter, but I think you should reconsider Ethel's offer."

Shortly after Janet Jr's passing, Ethel had phoned. Having heard the news, she expressed her sympathies and invited Jackie to have lunch with her at Hickory Hill, her home in McLean, Virginia. Genuinely touched by Ethel's sincerity, which hadn't always been prevalent in their relationship, Jackie thanked her but made no promises.

"It might do you both good."

For the most part, Ethel had never been a source of *good* for Jackie. From the outset of when she and Jack began dating, Ethel had been quick to poke fun at Jackie. Her 'big' feet, her Debutante of the Year title, her preference for French cuisine, and so forth. They also had strikingly different personalities. Ethel was boisterous and energetic like the Kennedys, while Jackie was content to be alone, reading or dabbling with watercolors.

But they'd both lost their husbands tragically. And just last year, Ethel had lost David to a drug overdose. Perhaps Ethel reaching out was meant to be a turning point for them, and wouldn't it be cruel if Jackie didn't give it at least one chance over lunch?

She sighed as she looked at Maurice. "You're right. I'll give her a call as soon as we get home."

Anything to distract me from this heartache.

WHEN JACKIE ARRIVED at the Hickory Hill estate, memories bombarded. Jack had purchased the house in 1955, convinced that he and Jackie would fill the nearly thirteen thousand square-foot home with a large brood of their own. But a year later, after failing to win the vice-presidential nomination at the Democratic Convention in Chicago—followed by the loss of Arabella—Jack sold the home to Bobby and Ethel, who had already welcomed five children.

Inside that house, Jackie had packed a bag and left Jack, set on divorcing him. Their separation proved temporary, though tenuous, but Hickory Hill easily reminded her of the lowest point in her marriage to Jack. Perhaps subconsciously, those factors played into why Jackie never visited.

She packed away the unpleasantries as Ethel welcomed her.

As they settled in the dining room, Ethel pointed out that she'd instructed the caterer to draw inspiration from French cuisine. Jackie was touched by the loving gesture and inwardly adjusted to the fact the house was no longer overrun with noisy, unruly children and large, unruly dogs.

Also meaningful for Jackie was the fact Ethel didn't mention Janet Jr's passing because Jackie didn't want to rehash and relive the excruciating details of her sister's illness and death.

Over coq au vin and steamed vegetables, they spent most of their lunch catching up on the children. A lengthy task for Ethel as a mother of eleven and now grandmother to an ever-expanding group. But Jackie sensed that tug of sorrow when there was no mention of David. Had they been closer, Jackie might've reached over and squeezed her hand. As it were, such an action seemed too personal, even though loss and grief were the very reasons Jackie had made the trip.

For a moment, she regretted not making a greater effort to be there for Ethel when Bobby was killed. Who better to understand her despair? But at the time, Jackie had been shamelessly self-absorbed. Her relationship with Ari at the forefront, and Bobby's death, in a tragic way, had released her from his disapproval.

There had also been her injured pride. After Bobby had made his formal announcement that he would seek the democratic nomination for the presidency, Jackie had been genuinely excited for him and the solid chance he had of being elected, even stating, 'It's really going to happen, isn't it? We're going to be back in the White House. Oh, it's going to be wonderful.' Ethel had corrected her immediately and said, 'What do you mean *we*?' It had been Ethel's not-so-subtle way of icing Jackie out of their political spotlight—a punishment for Jackie's affair with Bobby—and the final indication that their intimate relationship was over. Jackie took the barb and knew she deserved it.

Two months later, Bobby was dead.

Their relationship had dissipated for the most part by 1968, but deep feelings for one another remained. Though Jackie had feared for his life—and told him so—she knew nothing would keep him from running for the presidency. Not the enemies he'd made or, least of all, his own fears. She had accepted losing him.

"I heard about the book you're working on with Michael Jackson," Ethel said. "Quite impressive, and a departure from your usual topics."

Jackie forced a smile to hide the surge of uneasiness. Michael Jackson was one of the last things she cared to discuss. And although Ethel probably didn't intend to make Jackie suddenly feel defensive, the comment reminded her that Ethel had a knack for rubbing Jackie the wrong way. But Jackie would let nothing raise her dander today.

"We are very excited about the project." Her standard, public relations reply. "Not that I can say much about it."

"Can't spill the beans on any of his secrets just yet."

"Something like that."

Ethel smiled and apparently took the hint Jackie didn't care to talk about the singer. "So, from what I've read, it looks like you and Maurice are settling down."

Jackie clenched her jaw for an instant. Ethel should have known better than to tread onto the sacred ground of her personal life.

Yes, when we're not dabbling with "shrooms" and enjoying our swingers group, we're 'settled down'.

Oh, what she would've given to be able to drop such a statement just to witness the sheer horror on Ethel's face—then take it back as though she'd never said it.

"Settling down does seem to be an affliction of growing older." Jackie suppressed the brimming regret of having agreed to this lunch. Ethel had never been a source of comfort for her, so why had she put faith in today's visit? What did she think she was going to gain from Ethel of all people?

"What about you? Are you still seeing Andy?"

As soon as the words left her mouth, Jackie wished she could take them back. Mentioning Andy Williams was a low blow—and uncharacteristic of Jackie—since Ethel and Andy both publicly claimed their friendship was platonic.

But Ethel, grinning, seemed to take the remark in stride. "You've been reading too many gossip rags."

Touché

"It does get lonely though." Ethel's expression turned somber. "I still talk to Bobby. At night, sometimes before I fall asleep. I'll tell him about something that happened with the children or grandchildren. And sometimes I even forget he isn't there in bed next to me. I roll over, reaching for him, but my hand only finds his cold pillow."

Jackie said nothing as shivers cascaded over her. How she remembered those nights and her own longing for Jack!

"And to think," Ethel continued, "June will mark seventeen years of living without him. Next year, I'll have spent more time as his widow than his wife."

The temptation to squirm prodded Jackie, but she resisted—and continued with her impish mood.

"Haven't you wanted better? To break away from that widow's mold?"

Ethel arched an eyebrow. "Because he was so unfaithful to me?"

What could Jackie say, knowing that she had been one of the

many—supposedly—Bobby had cheated with? Was that what this lunch was really about? An admonishment—a confrontation—for the way she'd wronged Ethel.

"I forgave him. Before he committed to run for the presidency, he said he needed my full support. I couldn't believe it. He had no reason to doubt my devotion. But I realized that wasn't it. He was asking me, without coming right out and asking me, to forgive him. And I did. Of course I did, because I could never love another man the way I loved him, no matter what he'd done to our relationship."

Jackie understood. She also could have sunk into the plush carpet. How was it possible that empathy and embarrassment blazed within her in equal measures? And what kind of response did Ethel expect?

"But don't you want to move forward, Ethel, and find a way to create your own happiness?"

Her smile returned. "Who says I'm not happy? I'm not like you, Jackie. I'd never have the gall or the guts or the gusto or any other adjective I needed to forge a new identity if that's what they call it nowadays. I only cared about being a wife and mother. Bobby might say it's a moot point now, and he'd be right, but," Ethel sighed, "I forgave everyone. Maybe not in word or deed—" she stole a glance at Jackie "—but in my heart and through my faith. I never would have thought that was possible, letting go of that bitterness. But that's what moved me forward, as you said, and honestly, that's what brought me happiness."

———

THE AMTRAK RIDE from DC to Manhattan was scheduled to take three and a half hours. Jackie wondered if she needed longer than that to process the revelation that dawned on her at Ethel's home.

If Ethel was capable of forgiving Jackie for sleeping with her husband, for whisking him away on vacations while Ethel was pregnant, for using him emotionally and physically to heal her grief, then how could Jackie not forgive her sister for the one night she slept with Jack?

She could argue that Lee's betrayal cut deeper because they were sisters, but her talk with Ethel illuminated a fact she couldn't deny—Lee's betrayal was a moot point now.

Maurice had been right to encourage her to go and see Ethel. Jackie couldn't wait to share how their afternoon had shifted her insights—and possibly helped liberate her from her own shackles of bitterness.

May 1985

NOT ONE TO TAKE HER promise to Janet Jr lightly, Jackie phoned Lee and invited her to stay at Red Gate Farm, saying they owed it to themselves to get away and reconnect after all that had happened. Perhaps her hope of repairing their relationship should have been more subtle, but Jackie didn't care. Lee readily accepted.

Realizing that she'd never taken accountability for the hurt she'd caused Ethel with her affair with Bobby had been profound for Jackie. She had been awash in grief, oblivious at first and later insensitive to the fact she had contributed to Ethel's pain as a jilted wife. A role Jackie had lived and knew well. How had she managed to separate and distance herself from *wife* to *the other woman* without a thought to the damage she was contributing to Bobby and Ethel's marriage?

Jackie had also let go of the belief that mending their split depended on Lee launching a thousand apologies. She even discarded the mental image she had crafted of Lee on her knees with tear-stained cheeks, begging for forgiveness.

Why—*why*—did a part of her want Lee to suffer? She didn't understand it. Not completely. Yes, she wanted her sister to pay a price for what she'd done, but to what end? There was no penalty or degree of punishment that would undo what had happened. And, selfishly, she wouldn't have endured a pinch of agony to appease Ethel.

But that was what her time with Lee at the Vineyard was about. Abandoning blame. Mending the broken bond. Moving forward.

Not that she expected them to sit across from each other, hold hands, and express their regrets. Women of their caliber—or was it dysfunction—were as complex as they were indirect.

When Lee arrived yesterday, they held each other in a long embrace. Lee said she was sorry, and Jackie knew she meant for avoiding Janet Jr's illness and funeral. Jackie had nodded, which indicated she accepted Lee's apology, combined with her weakness, and assured her that nothing else needed to be said on the matter.

Over dinner they mainly discussed their mother and the toll losing Janet Jr had taken on her. Lee noted how their mother had handled difficult changes well of late, including her former home operating as Camelot Gardens, a public museum people could tour for seven dollars. Hammersmith Farm also now served as a venue for wedding receptions and private parties. Jackie still couldn't believe it but said nothing. Lee promised to phone and check on their mother more often, a decision Jackie was pleased to hear.

Today, with the sun beaming in a cloudless sky, they played tennis before taking a swim in the ocean. Afterward, weary and worn, they trudged up the beach to their awaiting towels.

"I can't tell you how much I needed this getaway, Jacks." Lee sighed and wrapped herself in a plush towel before sitting on another already laid out on the sand.

Jackie did the same—and hid her smirk. Lee had officially closed her interior design business, and her life consisted mainly of dinner parties and shopping, Jackie assumed. Hardly stress-inducing. But perhaps writing about lavish homes for *Architectural Digest* was trying. Jackie wouldn't ask.

"You know I'm seeing someone."

Jackie didn't but it wasn't a shock to hear.

"His name is Richard Meier," Lee went on. "He's an architect. In fact, he's working on the Getty Center in Los Angeles. A brilliant man, really, a true creative, but he's by far the busiest man I've ever known."

"I've heard of him. He won the Pritzker Prize last year. Quite an honor."

"Yes, so he's in high demand. Between his work, spending time with his children, and all the traveling he does, he's stretched thin."

Jackie heard what her sister wasn't saying: *I'm not his main priority.*

"He manages everything well, but he's so disciplined and structured. Why, the inside of his refrigerator is so ordered and immaculate it's intimidating. I refuse to touch it anymore."

Jackie already suspected the relationship didn't have much steam but wouldn't say so.

Lee became contemplative. "He's nothing like Peter."

Jackie paused and wondered if she meant Peter Tufo or Peter Beard, both were old flames.

"Maybe it won't amount to anything, but we lunched together several weeks ago."

"You'll have to elaborate for me, Pekes. Which Peter?"

Lee smiled. "Peter Beard. Would you believe he reached out to me? He said he was going through old photos and found several of me at Montauk. Oh, we must have talked for an hour that day."

"Does this mean a reconciliation is in the works?"

Her sudden cheer downgraded. "No. Friendship is best. Although he's still so handsome my knees quake when I see him. He's going through a divorce though from that model."

Jackie snickered to herself. Of course, Lee was too proud to mention Cheryl Tiegs by name.

"Despite what happened between us, he is a wonderful man. And it's such a relief to lay aside the anger and resentment."

A sense of fresh hope washed over Jackie. "Yes, Pekes, it certainly is."

October 1985

JACKIE SCURRIED from Doubleday's office doors to the curb and tried not to draw attention to herself as she hailed a cab. Now was not the time to be recognized or approached by a well-meaning stranger who had long admired her. After ducking into the taxi that pulled up, she told the driver to head to Lenox Hill Hospital.

She wasn't one to pray the rosary, unlike her more devout Kennedy relatives, but she did pray.

Dear God, please let him be all right.

Worry strangled her threadbare faith. Losing Janet Jr, two husbands, some friends, her precious babies...she wanted it to be enough. Enough heartache that she somehow deserved to have this *one* thing in her life.

She closed her eyes and drew in a deep breath. Who was she to question Providence?

Still, she didn't want to imagine living without Maurice. They had created a life she loved. For the first time in her all her years, she was part of a relationship with no complicated trade-offs. Maurice didn't pretend to own her, and he made no demands on her. He loved her for the woman she was, and she trusted him completely.

When his doctor had called, only moments ago, and told her that he admitted Maurice for chest pains, suspecting he may be having a heart attack, her mind fathomed the worst scenario. The doctor assured her they were taking good care of him, and he was stable, but Jackie needed to see him for herself.

At the hospital, she ignored the wave of shivers, and pushed away the memory of her father. His final days were spent there, dying from liver cancer. Jackie had stayed by his side, tortured by the regrets of having let their relationship grow cold and distant.

She made her way to the coronary care unit. The sight of Maurice in a hospital bed, attached to an assortment of tubes and monitors, gave her pause. His eyes were closed and his head resting against the pillow while his mouth hung slightly open. The scene reminded her too much of Janet Jr's final days.

She entered the room quietly, not wanting to disturb him. Despite her stealth efforts, Maurice batted his eyes and brightened when he saw her.

"Oh, I'm so sorry to wake you." Jackie went to his side and put her hand on his shoulder.

"Nonsense." He placed his hand on top of hers. "Are you all right? I preferred to phone you myself, but they wouldn't let me. I was worried what they may have told you."

Jackie relayed what the doctor said.

"Test results are pending, but the doctor thinks I've had a mild heart attack." He patted her hand. "I don't want you to worry, my darling."

"Maurice, how could I not worry?" Her own heart still pounded frantically, but she was relieved he was awake and sounding like himself. "This is very serious. You know, when we get home, we need to make changes. I'll speak with Marta about creating healthier meals. Brisk walks in the park, and perhaps we can work on a swimming regiment—"

Wicked coughing erupted, and Maurice clutched his chest.

Jackie tensed. "Should I get the doctor?"

Maurice waved his hand, as best he could.

When the cough had subsided, Jackie poured him a cup of water from the pitcher on the side table. He sipped, then handed back the cup and nodded.

"I'm fine now, thank you."

Jackie eased into the chair at his bedside.

Maurice reached for her hand. "Darling, please don't look at me that way."

"I can't help it. I'm...scared." She bit her lower lip, realizing she was wrong to burden his condition further with her worries.

"We'll get through this. I'll just be off my feet for a bit, but we won't miss opening night for Tosca. Our seats are magnificent, and I know how much you've been looking forward to Franco Zeffirelli's interpretation of the story."

"That's the last thing on my mind. I would swear off the ballet if it meant saving you and restoring your health."

"You're wonderful, my darling, but it won't come to that."

As they laughed together, Jackie relaxed in her chair. Being with him eased her concerns.

"Tell me the story again, about how we met."

Maurice smiled. "You like that, don't you?"

She nodded. "You craft it perfectly."

"Well, we'll have to turn back time to the late 1950s. One of my lawyers and good friend, Ted Sorensen, knew I had a lot of clout and had groomed a great deal of connections in Africa. Back then, there was much tension on the continent, especially when it came to Americans. Ted wanted me to meet a young man he had high hopes for, Jack Kennedy. In particular, Ted knew I was the ideal man to introduce him to Sir Ernest Oppenheimer, who controlled the De Beers Diamond Consortium at the time. So I arranged the formal get-together.

"To my pleasure, you accompanied Jack. He was a smart man, bringing you along, because he knew you would easily charm Ernest, and you did. We were introduced for the first time, and I had quite the challenge keeping my eyes off you. Not only were you a perfect beauty, a rival to any stroke Botticelli put to canvas, you also couldn't have been more feminine in your mannerisms. When you spoke with Ernest, I knew immediately that you'd done your own homework on him, trading just enough German with him to leave an impression. Admitting that you knew very little of the language won him over.

From that very moment, I was enraptured, not only because you were the most striking woman I had ever seen, but also because I sensed what an intelligent woman you are. I was smitten."

He stroked her hand with the pad of his thumb.

"I remember that day. How I almost decided not to speak German in case my accent was wrong. The last thing I wanted to do was offend Mr. Oppenheimer. Jack was antsy about the meeting, and I knew if I made too many mistakes, he would have second thoughts about my being an asset to him."

"Fascinating, isn't it?" he mused. "The different angsts we each experienced on that day. But tell me, what is your first recollection of me, where I finally broke through those barriers of yours and you considered me a true friend?"

She considered that. "I would have to say when I would slip away from Washington and attend the ballet with you and Adlai in New York. Adlai would call and ask if I minded that you were joining us. Knowing you wanted to come gave me a little thrill, because you were so interesting and slightly mysterious. And when we were together you were always the one to open doors or hold out my chair. Do you remember?"

Maurice laughed. "Of course. It may sound coarse since we were both married and forbidden to pursue a romantic relationship, but in some ways, I consider those evenings our early courtship. Anytime I caught wind that you were in the city, I phoned Adlai and asked if I might tag along for the evening. It was fortunate for me he was usually agreeable."

"There was one time when Adlai couldn't make it, but he said I'd be in good hands with you. I wasn't worried. By then, you were familiar. You'd been to dinners at the White House, and I felt I knew you outside of the business persona. But that night, we went to a dumpy little theater on the Lower East Side, and the performance had been cancelled because a water pipe had broken. You didn't let it faze us. We got into a cab, and you said there was an exhibit one of your children had attended and I must see it. What you didn't realize was that the live models were only wearing paint. The look on your face! Oh, you were horrified, and I completely understood because what would you tell Adlai when he asked you about it later?"

"Horrified is right." He chuckled. "There I was with the president's wife in what some would describe as a shady setting, only a step up from a nude bar. I was worried someone might recognize you and alert the press."

"But I assured you it would be better if we walked through the gallery and simply acted like everyone else around us. Leaving abruptly could've drawn attention."

"And you were right. Your instincts in such circumstances are always right."

"And I appreciated that you stuck it out, even though you were uncomfortable."

"I couldn't help it," he said. "Naked bodies posed and sheathed in paint. *That* should've induced a heart attack. At least the experience taught me to be more aware when it came to the label of contemporary art."

"It probably made you wary of your children's recommendations too."

Laughter bubbled between them.

"Afterward you took me to a lounge for a nightcap. It was very dim and had the feel of a speakeasy."

"Intentional on my part, no doubt. I'm sure by then I had perspired through my suit."

"That was the night we became true friends," she told him. "I think we got to see a different side of each other, and perhaps seeing a couple dozen people naked for the sake of art bound us together. I don't think I told anyone about that evening, and there's something about keeping little secrets that intrigues me."

Maurice winked. "Don't I know it."

For Jackie, their friendship became more valuable through the years, after Jack and during her marriage to Ari when the trips to New York became more frequent as her marriage steadily soured.

Maurice was one she could call upon for an escort to the ballet or opera. He mastered discretion and protected Jackie's privacy as he had a knack for standing just far enough from her to escape the lens of nosy reporters when they were out. Being married also worked to his advantage and lumped him into that platonic group of men who were often seen about town with Jackie.

When she took stock of their friendship and how it had evolved, she nearly teared up, fearing the unknown and what could lie ahead for him. Was she on the brink of losing him?

"You've always had a way of taking care of me. Now it's my turn to look after you. I don't want you to worry about a thing. Whatever the doctor says we need to do to get you healthy again, that's exactly what we'll do."

Somberness tinged his expression.

"Jackie, I want you to know, no matter what happens from this day on, that my time with you has been the greatest in my life. Living together, seeing you in the morning, sharing our coffee, perusing the newspaper, planning our special days together, traveling, seeing you in every nightgown you own, your kiss before retiring at night, all of it. Every moment I've ever spent with you has meant so much."

Whether it was on the peripheral or at the head of her dining table, Maurice had occupied a place in Jackie's life longer than any other man. He was also the only man she was close to who hadn't humiliated her. His financial advice and maneuvering had made her wealthy beyond her dreams, and his company brought her peace. Unlike the men she committed herself to in marriage, Maurice was cognizant of her needs and allowed her the freedom to discover and nurture every layer of the woman she wanted to be without feeling threatened.

She wasn't ready to let him go, and she would do everything in her power and means to help save him.

April 1986

INTEROFFICE MEMO

Jackie—Congratulations! You've done it! We got the manuscript from Michael Jackson today. He had it delivered, and I cannot tell you how good it feels to finally have this in hand. Will be sending it your way soon for proofing and edits. –Steve

---

July 1986

Jackie dear,

Just a quick note to congratulate you on the perfect wedding day for your precious daughter. I always knew she would make a stunning bride. How is it that the curly-topped toddler who used to tap and run her little feet in the halls of the White House has already grown into a confident, accomplished young woman? I see a great deal of you reflected in her poise. And I must say that Carolina outdid herself in crafting both Caroline's gown and your mint-colored dress. Clever of you to wear those white gloves once again. The fashion elite will commend and applaud you for giving them another taste of— dare I mention it—Camelot. Don't be surprised or injured when they come for those bridesmaid dresses though. What droopy floral sacks! I know you didn't have a thing to do with them, but wedding photographs are eternal.

From what I hear, Edwin Schlossberg is somewhat of a mystery. A few of my former colleagues commented how impressed they were with his work on exhibits at the Met, but others weren't quite sure what he does exactly. As long as

they're in love and he takes care of your girl, I know you'll be
satisfied.

May this union bring you all much happiness.
DV

———

June 1987

JACKIE DECIDED to walk the nearly two miles to Le Cirque,
where she was meeting Lee for an early dinner, convinced the exercise was what she needed to soothe her frustrations.

A newly hired editor, a man she hadn't met until she stepped into
his gleaming corner office at Doubleday, had been dropping unflat-
tering earwigs into various people around the office about one of Jackie's projects that was coming up for release. His grumblings were
aimed at Jackie, though she couldn't fathom what the man had
against her professionally that caused him to tell Steve Rubin, and
others who would listen, that 'Those Tiffany books are a waste of
time. Most of our readers aren't dining in palaces or entertaining
washed up artists who are past their prime.'

Steve Rubin had popped into her office, told her everything the
man had said, and laughed.

"Just goes to show he doesn't know how much money those books
bring in." Steve read her humorless expression. "Now, don't worry.
He's new and needs to learn some of the ropes. Besides, don't you
give me beef about doing those books?"

Her cheeks reddened. There had been times when her zeal had
wavered—after all, how many books about Tiffany did they really
want to publish? But she and John Loring had complete creative
control. Jackie was proud of every book they turned out and each one
seemed to improve from the last.

She knew Steve was right. The books practically sold themselves and were consistent hits. Since John was the Director of Design for the brand, he had enough clout that he didn't need Jackie to attend the release parties, and her name didn't need to appear on the books.

But Steve had just phoned her at home to let her know that Doubleday had decided to host a huge launch party for their latest installment, *Tiffany's 150 Years*, in an attempt to rival Martha Stewart's book *Weddings*, set to release next month. Steve wanted to ensure Jackie's attendance. Naturally, she agreed to be there— anything for work.

She'd phone her cousin-by-marriage and author Louis Auchincloss, who had written the introduction for the book, and would make sure he could attend with her. Still, the sudden inconvenience annoyed her, and she blamed the new editor. And Martha Stewart.

As an aside, *The Tiffany Wedding* was already in the works and slated for publication next September. Jackie was excited about that endeavor and had told John in one of their meetings, 'We'll show Martha how it's *really* done. A bride nowadays shouldn't feel bound to rules and traditions that have no meaning for her. We're going to set brides free from others' expectations and encourage them to trust their tastes.'

Feeling more at ease, despite the grip of the late afternoon humidity, Jackie made it to Le Cirque faster than she'd expected. After she was seated, Lee joined her a short time later.

Jackie wanted to saturate herself in the new-found ease of being with Lee. Unlike in the past, Jackie wasn't preoccupied with what she could or couldn't tell her sister. Sitting together, laughing and chatting, with no pretenses wedged between them, was freeing.

But such delight ended up giving Jackie pause. Rarely had there been times when an unresolved, heady issue didn't exist between them. Could such peace last?

Lee wasted no time in launching off the conversation.

"It feels like I'm trimming the fat in my life. Last year it was ditching Richard, and now, I plan to cut ties with *Architectural Digest*."

"Oh? I thought you enjoyed the position. It wasn't as though you were committed to a work schedule, and they gave you such freedom."

"Yes, but I think I tapped out my resources, and it doesn't interest me anymore." Lee laughed. "Like Richard."

Jackie sipped her water. "So what does interest you these days?"

"I'm getting involved with an Italian."

Jackie's expression turned coy.

"Not like that," Lee corrected. "I'm becoming a brand ambassador for Giorgio Armani."

"Which entails what exactly?"

"Wearing the free clothes they send me and attending parties and functions around the world. So whenever I'm photographed at a posh event, I can tell them I'm in Armani. The exposure helps build the brand, and they pay all my expenses. Imagine getting paid to travel and look chic."

Envy sparked within her, but only for a fleeting moment. Jackie certainly didn't care for being hounded by photographers about what labels she was wearing, though she primarily favored Carolina and Valentino.

"You know, Jacks, it's the first time in a while where I haven't been attached to a man, yet I feel optimistic and hopeful about the future. It's been ages since I've felt so satisfied with who I am, where I'm at, and the open road of possibilities ahead."

To Jackie, her sister's life seemed unstable. Fledgling and uncertain. But she wouldn't tarnish Lee's new-found confidence—or dare ask who was paying her bills.

June 1987

WITH A RAISED GLASS OF CHAMPAGNE, Steve Rubin addressed Jackie among the standing crowd in the conference room.

"To our esteemed senior editor, Jackie Onassis. Here's to all her hard work on *Moonwalk*, which is exceeding expectations and already on its way to selling half a million copies. You're an asset to the company. Oh, and best of luck with the follow-up book. We hear Michael Jackson can't wait to work with you again."

Mild snickers and laughter accompanied the ting of clinking glasses as Jackie and her team drank to the toast. Steve, Nelson Doubleday Jr., and James McLaughlin, Doubleday's new president, had recently shared the news that Jackson's memoir had skyrocketed in the three months since its release. This was the formal recognition for her and her editorial team. The book was her highest-grossing project, one that put Doubleday in a solid financial position for at least a year.

Blockbuster or not, Jackie didn't consider the book a favorite. Although she'd convinced Michael to open up about his difficult childhood and relationship with his father, which included shocking revelations of abuse, she knew he watered down the truth when it came to his plastic surgeries. He admitted to having two nose jobs and the creation of a cleft chin. Other changes in his appearance, he claimed, were due to puberty and his vegetarian diet. Jackie let him have his way. One could argue she crafted an elegant yet ambiguously disguised poke at Michael in the opening sentence of the introduction he *insisted* she write.

"What can one say about Michael Jackson..."

Pleased as she was with the book's success and the recognition from the higher-ups, she had no intention of working directly with him again on a new project.

EIGHTEEN

June 1988

G rand Jackie. That was the name Jackie and Caroline had decided her granddaughter Rose—and all future grandchildren—would call her. In Jackie's opinion, none of the typical monikers suited her, and she had no intention of fitting into the traditional mold of a grandmother. She wouldn't teach her grandchildren how to bake. Wouldn't knit booties for them or craft blankets since she had no skill or talent.

Instead, she would fill their nursery with books. All the books Caroline and John had loved when they were little and a trove of new children's books she had discovered, especially since working as an editor.

At Red Gate Farm and at 1040 she planned to dedicate a room where artwork could be created. Fingerpaints and markers would be used. Spills and messes could be made. When her grandchildren were older, she would teach them about art and help them learn French. She hoped her passion for the opera and ballet would prove contagious and infect them too. One day, she envisioned, she would gather them all up and travel to her favorite places. Paris. Ireland. Russia. India. Yes, Grand Jackie would show them the world.

But for now, as she cradled baby Rose Kennedy Schlossberg, she marveled at the newborn and the fact her daughter was now a mother.

Also wonderful and worth a celebration was Caroline's graduation from Columbia Law School. Jackie was awestruck at the incredible woman—and mother—her daughter had become.

September 1988

THROWING a party for someone she had never met before veered from the norm for Jackie. But it was the least she could do for Lee and her new husband, Hollywood director Herbert Ross.

Although Lee's design business had folded and freelance design projects no longer held her interest, she'd made a great deal of contacts and new friends on the West Coast and ventured back frequently. When she told Jackie about Herbert and their engagement and why-should-we-wait-nuptials, Jackie had déjà vu. Would Herbert Ross turn out to be another Newton Cope? A man Lee fancied for a while, became engaged to, and called it off last minute? Of course, Jackie had played a minor part in the disintegration of that relationship when she vehemently told Lee to get a prenup that guaranteed her a hefty allowance from day one of the marriage.

But no. Lee and Herbert went through with their "I dos" on September 23rd.

Flippantly, Jackie had offered to host a dinner celebration at her apartment after the ceremony. She made good on that promise, though, and with Maurice at her side, happily welcomed the intimate gathering of family and friends. And met the man for the first time on the day he became her brother-in-law.

But truthfully, it was a wonderful occasion. Jackie hoped her sister had finally found a lasting love like she had with Maurice.

"You don't like him, do you?"

Jackie startled. She didn't realize she'd been staring at Lee and Herbert while swept away in her thoughts. John, suddenly at her side, jolted her back to the moment.

"What gives you that impression?"

"For one thing, you've hardly spoken to him, apart from the token congratulations and welcome to the family bit." John slid a caviar-topped cracker into his mouth and chewed. "And you seem to casually migrate out of whatever room the newlyweds are in."

A mild shudder glided down her spine. She didn't realize her son was such a keen observer.

"Shouldn't you be taking an interest in the young ladies here?" Regret grasped her the moment the words left her. She had worked hard to raise John as a man who respected women and didn't view them as pieces of candy, all there for his taking. Unlike his father.

Currently, he was dating Christina Haag, a young woman he had known since his prep school days who had also attended Brown University. Jackie liked her, though she couldn't gauge how serious John was about her. They also seemed to experience periods of what the tabloids called, "on again, off again," which made it even more difficult for Jackie to pinpoint her son's availability status. She had learned not to ask, as she had with Caroline when she dated, but to let him come to her whenever he wanted to talk.

Jackie switched topics. "If you're not careful the next thing you know the press will be calling you a momma's boy or using some other psychological insult right beside your Sexiest Man Alive title." She couldn't resist the giggle that arose.

"I think I like 'momma's boy' better. Has some substance to it."

They laughed together.

"So am I right?" he asked. "You don't like the guy, and you have your doubts about the relationship."

Jackie had no desire to encourage him. "There are times I feel I hardly know your auntie anymore." Her gaze returned to the library. Lee and Herbert were still standing by the fireplace talking to Rudolph Nureyev. She couldn't isolate the emotion nagging her, but it was akin to disappointment. Although she and Lee had improved their relationship since Janet Jr's passing, it wasn't what Jackie had hoped for. They weren't chummy. Lee always seemed busy but with what exactly Jackie didn't know. Putting forth that initial effort of truly mending their rift had been hard for Jackie, and Lee didn't give her the credit she wanted for bringing them back together. Perhaps it was selfish of Jackie, still wanting 'recognition' that *she* was the better sister. But she couldn't help it.

She noticed John staring at the couple now, and she wished she could've mined his brain, tapped into exactly what he was thinking.

"They probably need their space. You know, the way couples do at times."

John cracked a smile. "If that's your way of asking about Christina, you're losing your touch, Mummy."

"I wouldn't dream of such a thing."

John leaned in close. "Tell me something though. What do you think of *her*?"

He gingerly pointed to a tall, lanky blonde Jackie didn't recognize from behind.

"Who is she?"

"Daryl Hannah. She has a part in *Steel Magnolias*, that film coming out, directed by none other than auntie's new man."

Jackie knew the name and supposed she had seen a movie with her in it somewhere. But watching her now, with her hair long and stringy, a dress that was too short, and a manly sounding laugh, Jackie's first thought was *frumpy*.

Naturally, she couldn't say that. Or tell her son she hoped he would do better. Coming from a mother such words only amped a man's interest and clouded his judgement.

The actress turned, perhaps sensing that John was staring at her. She wiggled her fingers at him and smiled.

Jackie suspected they already knew each other since she didn't make a sudden beeline in John's direction.

"I think I'm going to check on our guests and make sure everyone is enjoying the champagne."

Maybe tomorrow I'll call Christina and invite her to lunch...

ATHENS, Greece – Relatives of shipping heiress Christina Onassis attended a somber funeral mass Friday with friends, government ministers, and a crowd of about 5,000 people.

Onassis's body, which arrived Thursday in Athens from Buenos Aires, Argentina, was kept overnight in a small building in the compound of an Athens cemetery, guarded by three police officers.

The shipping heiress died November 19th, leaving the family fortune to her 3-year-old daughter Athena, who was not present at Friday's ceremony.

Attending the mass was Onassis's fourth husband, Thierry Roussel, members of the Onassis family and friends from the shipping community to which the heiress and her father, Aristotle Onassis, belonged.

The coffin was later flown to a northwestern area in Greece in preparation for its transfer by road and ferry to the island of Skorpios, owned by the Onassis family. Christina Onassis will be buried near the grave of her father, who died in 1975, and her brother Alexander, who died in an air crash in 1973.

Jacqueline Onassis, widow of assassinated President Kennedy and stepmother to Christina Onassis, did not attend the mass.

Despite heavy rain, police lined the square outside the church, and a crowd of about 5,000 watched from balconies, nearby apartments, and sidewalks. Mourners threw chrysanthemums on the casket as it was carried from the church after the mass.

UPI, November 25, 1988

December 1988

JACKIE DIDN'T LIKE it when her mother drank too much. Now that Janet was on a regimented schedule of medications, Jackie warned her that consuming alcohol was a poor choice and likely to cause complications. But she was learning, painfully so, that there was nothing more stubborn than a mother resisting well-meaning advice from her daughter.

Perhaps it had been a mistake, Jackie mused, to combine Janet's birthday celebration with an early Christmas party. Was it too much for Janet now, having most of the family over? Janet proved moody over dinner, complaining the lobster bisque was too watery and the steaks were over cooked. After, when she opened her gifts, she hardly reacted and uttered little thanks. Now that Janet had rebuked her daughter's warning about having another drink, Jackie made the snap decision to end the get-together.

"Let her do what she wants." Bing said after tossing back a swig from his bottle of bourbon. "There isn't much to her life these days, so what harm can it really do."

Jackie entertained visions of removing him from the house and locking the door. Magically, he would disappear on the other side.

"I think I know what's best for my mother."

Bing seemed to consider that as their gazes held. Whether he was in no mood to argue or didn't care to uphold the phony assumption that he took care of Janet, Jackie didn't know. But she was glad he simply nodded and decided to head back to his place. Never had she been more grateful that her mother and Bing had the sense to keep their own homes when they married. Jackie could practically *shoo* him away since the couple didn't live together full-time.

Small favors.

She politely encouraged the rest of her family to head home. Caroline offered to stay, but Jackie told her she could handle it.

"Besides, you need to get little Rose to bed."

Caroline conceded. She and Ed gathered Rose's bevy of toys and accessories before they left.

With the help of the household staff, Jackie managed to get Janet changed and into bed. Even so, Janet seemed unable to settle down. Jackie blamed it on the eventful evening. A houseful of guests, cake, and presents had probably overstimulated her. One highlight of the night had been getting a picture of the four of them—herself, Janet, Caroline, and baby Rose. How much more time they had to spend together no one could predict, and Jackie knew to savor such finite moments.

With Janet Jr's illness and her mother's decline, Jackie had also refined her patience and skillset as a caregiver. She called upon that now, as Janet fidgeted at every turn and seemed to be difficult merely for the sake of being difficult. Jackie reminded herself what Janet's doctors had told her, that some of her behaviors and mood swings were beyond her control. And they would only worsen over time.

"It's getting late, Mummy, and you need your sleep," Jackie told her.

"Don't speak to me like a child."

Humiliation pulsed over Jackie. She tamped down the urge to walk out and leave her mother in the hands of others to be tended to. Quietly, she thanked and dismissed the nurses to their rooms for the night. Her sense of duty prevailed over the temptation to give in to her sudden anger and the fact that Janet showed no appreciation for all Jackie had done. It didn't matter that Jackie had spent the money to ensure quality care. That she made sure medications didn't run out. Or that she followed up with the doctors when she couldn't attend appointments.

Most of all, she was never going to get an apology from her mother for the strict, harsh upbringing she and Lee endured that included sharp slaps to the face when either of them rebelled or disappointed her in the slightest.

No thanks would come to Jackie for never entertaining a thought about tucking Janet away in a home or an asylum now that Janet was increasingly incapable of taking care of herself.

But Jackie did none of those things for personal gratification. She did them because she harbored no animosity or need for vengeance. And because no one could ever say, "She's just like her mother."

"Would you like me to get you a sleeping pill?"

Sitting on the edge of the bed, Janet fussed and fluffed her pillow. "No. But I can tell you I'm not waiting up for him."

"Who, Mummy?"

"Your father, of course."

Jackie didn't know what to say. Her parents' acrimonious divorce had played out nearly fifty years ago, and her father had passed thirty years ago.

Janet's brow furrowed. "Maybe I have it wrong, and he isn't due home until tomorrow night. Yes, I believe that's right. It's tomorrow night. Oh, all the traveling he does to Cuba, who can keep up really?" She pulled back the covers and slid into bed.

Jackie adjusted the lights and tentatively tucked her in.

"Business, he says. He's always down there for business, though I can't imagine what business he's conducting in another country." She gripped the covers. "It's not as though I'm a fool, Jacqueline. I know what really goes on down there. The drinking. The gambling. The women. Oh, he is such a scoundrel!"

"Please, Mummy, don't upset yourself." A pang of grief hit Jackie. Her father had cemented a soiled reputation and deserved every bitter word Janet spoke. But Jackie loved him and still missed him terribly.

Janet huffed. "You're right, of course. He may be a brute, but he always comes home, doesn't he?" A thin smile appeared. "And he brings you and Lee such delightful gifts. Remember the dresses and the bracelets? The hairbrush was my favorite. The one with the pearl handle. Remember?"

Of course she did. The brush was still one of her prized possessions and always reminded her of her father. She had taken it with her to Paris for her year abroad. In fact, the hairbrush had gone on most of her travels. How could her mother remember such a minute thing and forget that they were divorced...that Black Jack Bouvier was long gone...

"Rest now, Mummy."

Janet sighed. "Yes. Just let me close my eyes. A little refresh, that's all I need. Jack will be home soon."

NINETEEN

NEW YORK—Caroline Kennedy Schlossberg has received notice that she passed the New York state bar examination.

The daughter of President John F. Kennedy and Jacqueline Onassis took the test in February under her maiden name and passed on her first try.

Los Angeles Times, May 3, 1989

June 1989

I know it's awful to say, and I know we'll never get to see or speak to Mummy again, but I feel so relieved."

Jackie looked at her sister, who stood at the living room window of their mother's home staring out at the bay. Numb and hollow from the last several days, Jackie understood Lee's sentiment. When Janet's doctors had phoned and informed her that Janet's passing was imminent, she and Lee kept vigil at their mother's side until her last breath. Her deterioration was over. For that, Jackie was grateful.

Now, just the two of them remained after everyone from the funeral reception had dispersed. Jackie wondered what life would look like going forward. No more memory slips to help Janet through. No more bouts of anger and frustration from her. No more calls from nurses or doctors regarding her condition. And no more Bingham Morris.

Perhaps it was selfish of Jackie, but she savored the fact that she was on the verge of never having to see or deal with the man again. Thanks to the prenup, which kept their homes, possessions, and finances separate, no legal wranglings would follow. That assurance deepened Jackie's sense of relief.

But a spat of spite tingled in Jackie. Lee had been the least inconvenienced, the least burdened when it came to Janet's decline. Excusing her from their sister's care was one thing. But Jackie couldn't recall an occasion when Lee had been called upon urgently to take care of Janet or her needs. Or a time when Lee had volunteered. Jackie, Yusha, the nursing staff Jackie had hired, and even the dreadful Bingham, at times, had comprised Janet's core support system. When Lee did visit, she complained how stressful it was for her, tolerating Janet's mood swings and correcting her lapses.

Jackie knew voicing her grievance, though, would serve no valuable purpose.

"I feel like we lost Mummy years ago. That day in the doctor's office when they diagnosed her." That familiar despondency flared within. "None of us were the same."

"God knows it's true." Lee left the window and sat on the couch but didn't seem at ease. "Losing one's parents is expected, I suppose."

Jackie wouldn't admit it, and she imagined Lee wouldn't either, but to know they were free from their mother's criticisms brought respite. However, reality crept in. No matter how old she grew and regardless of her mother's physical presence, Jackie knew that Janet's voice would live in her head forever.

"I've read that you and Maurice are live-ins now."

Lee's comment made Jackie stiffen. She couldn't discern whether Lee meant it as a jab or a segue into a new area of conversation. Lee hadn't been present at the Christmas party dinner, the night she and Maurice shared that they would be living together. And Jackie didn't make a point to inform Lee.

"One of the tabloids had your picture on it. Something about you shacking up with the diamonds merchant."

"We're happy with the arrangement." Jackie despised how sanitized her words sounded.

Lee arched an eyebrow. "Does that mean I won't be returning the favor of hosting a post-nuptials reception?"

"We don't need to be married to have what we want." Jackie bit her lip, certain she sounded too defensive. She knew she didn't have to justify her choices to anyone, but old habits surfaced.

"Who would have thought my sister would prefer living in sin, as they say, over getting married. It's so modern of you, Jackie. It surprises me, though, you choosing Maurice. I thought something would come of your affair with Mike or even Peter, but not Maurice."

Jackie's cheeks blazed. She had managed to keep her flings with both men under the radar. At the very least, the friendship she had cultivated with each man likely helped blur the lines of her involvement. Or so she thought.

Her relationship with Peter Hamill, a journalist and a friend of Bobby's, was short-lived. Though she found him stimulating intellectually, he was prone to bouts of brooding and had a pathological dedication to his writing, both fiction and nonfiction. Complacency set in quickly, and Jackie had no interest in competing with a man's work. Not anymore.

Her time with film director Mike Nichols proved more layered and complicated. Primarily when it came to guarding her privacy. Mike's career didn't allow him to scuttle away to Martha's Vineyard for weeks on end. He was social and worked closely with a variety of actresses. Though she didn't count herself as insecure, Jackie didn't want to couple with a man whose job included him working with naked women at times.

"You don't approve of Maurice?"

Lee laughed. "Not that it would matter. He just seems...too buttoned up. A genius when it comes to doing your taxes, but..."

Jackie couldn't blame her for not finishing the sentence. Had Lee really spent time picturing Jackie and Maurice behind closed doors?

If she were honest, Jackie would have to admit she'd struggled with moments of insecurity. When she was married to Ari, there were times he wasn't pleased with her. It often occurred when they were entertaining guests. Ari would criticize her, in front of everyone, for not dressing up or wearing enough make-up or bringing up dull conversation topics. She would either play it off and act like his words didn't humiliate her. Or she would ignore his remarks. One time, she left the table. Such incidents usually resulted in the two of them sleeping separately. Alone in her room on those nights, Jackie had wondered if Ari preferred Lee over her when it came to sex. Sometimes she even worried Ari would toss out such a remark during one of his outbursts, but he never did.

Now, hearing Lee criticize Maurice's prowess in the bedroom, she had an ornery thought.

I won't have to worry about Lee sleeping with him.

Lee stood and poured herself a drink. Half a glass of straight vodka. Then she returned to the couch. "You know, Jacks, every time we go through something like this, I always think, well, this is the worst of it. Nothing else can happen that could be more painful or difficult. But I'm lying to myself, aren't I?" Her eyes glistened with tears. "Because one day, it's going to be you or me on that deathbed."

Since losing their sister, the same thought had haunted Jackie. Which of them would go first? And how much longer did they have together?

"It's not easy to think about."

"No." Lee kicked back a drink. "I'm terribly selfish, you know, and I don't want it to be me, sitting there, holding your hand, trying to figure out what on earth to say." She finished the vodka. "And I don't want to be the one sick and dying, because I'm so afraid..."

Jackie agreed and had felt the same but didn't want to say so. Perhaps for her, the real fear was being too raw and vulnerable, even in front of Lee.

When Lee broke into sobs, Jackie went and sat beside her. Crying with abandon had always been a faux pas for the sisters, and an overt display of sorrow in public was not to be tolerated. Of course, those had been their mother's rules.

"I know I've been awful to you at times, Jacks, just horrible," Lee went on. "And I can't promise I won't make more mistakes, but God knows I'd give anything to fix all that's gone wrong between us."

Jackie didn't know how to counter the emotional paralysis within. She feared Lee expected her to do the same, to confess her own missteps where Lee was concerned and beg for forgiveness. That wasn't Jackie. But at the same time, a boldness surged inside her and she was no longer afraid to be honest.

"Lee, you know I don't care about the past anymore." She meant it. Or thought she did. Although she had been accused of icing people out of her life once they hurt her or crossed a line, Jackie saw it as self-preservation. If a friend—or even a half-brother—gave interviews about her, wrote books, or gossiped about her with others, it only made sense not to speak to them anymore. A violation of her trust had consequences.

With Lee it was fiercely complicated. Jackie loved her and, in some ways, had been closer with Lee than either of her husbands. Finding out that Lee had slept with Jack had been the deepest betrayal. She blamed Lee, not Jack, mainly because Lee should have known better than to trust Jack.

But time, as it always did, had a way of lessening the sting. Jackie came to realize that clinging to blame meant nothing. She thought she was entitled to be angry by a matter of virtue. That her unblemished commitment to Jack made her pious. Practically canonized her.

Her lunch with Ethel also helped her realize that forgiveness was more meaningful, more powerful than the emptiness of being right—or thinking she was right.

Lee's relationships turned out disastrous and ended in divorce. During her marriages to both Michael and Stas, Lee had not remained faithful. Neither had her husbands. That summer, in 1963, when Lee was fooling around, having a not-so-secret affair with Ari and spending more time on his yacht than with her husband, that seemed to be the pinnacle of her brazenness. She ignored Janet's disapproval and Jackie's concerns—and even Jack and Bobby's anger about it.

But that was Lee.

Again, it took time, but Jackie saw her own ideals didn't make her spotless. And self-righteousness was a poor substitute in place of a sister she loved.

"Jack and Ari are gone. They shouldn't come between us." Jackie considered mentioning that neither man loved them the way they wanted, but that was a truth that might only deepen their scars. "We are better women now. Maybe because of them, or in spite of them."

Lee, now settled down, took tissues from her purse. "Things will never be the same."

Whether Lee meant their relationship or in general because of Janet's passing, Jackie couldn't discern.

"No, they won't."

"And there's nothing we can do about the whole thing." Lee patted the tissue under her eyes. "We have no say, no control over how much time we have left or how we might go. The unknown is maddening and awful."

"There's plenty we can do." Had this been the moment Jackie had waited for? That point of sheer brokenness where they could finally rebuild their bond?

A tinge of bewilderment flashed in Lee's puffy eyes. Jackie took her hand and laced their fingers together.

"We can love each other and look out for each other right now. Let's make the most of whatever gift of time we have. There's no need to waste a day on worry."

"You're right, of course. You always know what to say, Jacks."

Since her enthusiasm seemed to fall flat with her sister, Jackie prickled with suspicion and an ache of disappointment. All the tears weren't because Lee missed their closeness.

"There's something more, isn't there? What is it, Lee?"

She rubbed her forehead. "It's Anthony. He's been diagnosed with testicular cancer."

Jackie felt like she had been drained of emotion due to the last few weeks, but hearing her beloved nephew was stricken with cancer landed like a horse kick to her stomach. Was that why he had left right after the funeral service? In her immediate recollection of him from earlier that day, she couldn't recall him looking poorly, but she hadn't been fully attentive.

After working as a producer for NBC Sports, which took him to Calgary, Canada, to cover the '88 Winter Olympics, Anthony had recently joined ABC. Staying in the vein of producing, he now worked on Primetime Live. Like John, he led an active lifestyle and even ran the New York City Marathon. Factors that made it difficult for Jackie to believe he had been diagnosed with cancer.

Just like Janet Jr.

"He said they caught it in time, and he'll be receiving excellent care, but I don't know." Lee struggled with the words. "What if he's not telling me everything? How do I prepare myself to lose my son?"

As much as she wanted to crack and wallow in the misery of Lee's news, Jackie couldn't. She couldn't imagine losing her beloved nephew.

"It won't do you any good to think like that, and it certainly won't help Anthony. You've got to be strong for him. He's going to need his mother."

Lee's chin dipped. "It's one of my biggest fears, that no one really needs me. Or loves me."

"I love you, Pekes. I always have. Through everything. And I always will." Jackie wrapped her arms around her and pulled her in tight. "We're going to get through this as a family."

She meant it. Every word. But she hoped Lee couldn't feel her trembling and didn't sense how terrified Jackie was for Anthony and his journey ahead.

———

August 1989

JACKIE WAS among the few and was one of the last to visit Diana Vreeland at her bedside in her home. Diana's declining health in recent years had forced her to pull back from the social scene as well as her involvement with the Met.

Shortly after Jackie's final visit, Diana was transported to Lenox Hill Hospital, where she died from a heart attack.

TWENTY

March 1990

"Oh, Jackie, come quick. You must see this."

Intrigued, Jackie followed Nancy back to her office. When she entered, the large bouquet of gerbera daisies snatched her breath away. Long-stemmed and arranged in a glass vase, the snow-white flowers resembled pinwheels.

"How beautiful! Who are they from?"

"That's what you're not going to believe. Read this." Nancy handed her a small card.

"'Nancy, thank you for a pleasant afternoon. I hope to see you again soon. Regards and affection, Richard.'"

Nancy clasped her hands together. "Richard. As in Richard Gere. He sent me flowers. Oh, as if I hadn't already fallen head over heels for the man, and he does this! I was so worried when he was here the other day that he probably thought I behaved no better than a lovesick schoolgirl."

Jackie raised her eyebrows matter-of-factly as she handed back the card. "You fawned over him terribly. Bringing every assortment of tea, arranging three plates with finger foods, brushing off his chair before he sat, and offering to run out if he preferred something else. You practically suffocated the man."

Smiling, glowing, Nancy said, "I was hospitable and making sure he was comfortable."

"Draping the napkin over his lap was a bit much."

Nancy popped a hand on her hip. "You may not have seen or appreciated his performance in *American Gigolo*, but I for one was transfixed, and he was riveting in *An Officer and a Gentleman*. Those eyes of his and that smile, oh, it gets me every time."

A wry grin curled Jackie's lip. "Yes, I'm sure that's what you enjoy most."

Nancy blushed.

"Well, he did seem amused by your attention, Tucky. I suppose he's used to women going gaga over him."

Nancy scoffed. "I wouldn't say I was gaga, just friendly—yet professional. You should give me more credit since I was only doing my best to help woo him into signing a book deal. You played the intellectual part with him, asking all those questions about his religious practices. It was very clever of you, exploring the possibility of a book on Eastern spirituality as an alternative to writing his memoir."

Jackie nodded. "He seemed receptive, but actors can be hard to read." Although the meeting had gone well, and Jackie was certain she and Gere had charmed each other, she reined in getting her hopes up. The editors-in-chief wanted to add another big-name celebrity to their list, and when Richard Gere was mentioned during a meeting, Jackie agreed to reach out to him. Their time together waylaid any concerns she had about duplicating her experience with Michael Jackson. Richard seemed more down to earth, less paranoid, affable, and probably didn't have a chimpanzee at home.

"And Richard must not have been *too* put off by my behavior. He did send me flowers."

Nancy sighed and took a moment to admire the arrangement

before looking back at Jackie—and clearly noticing the impish expression she recognized all too well.

Nancy straightened and crossed her arms. "You didn't."

Jackie spun on the heels of her leather Gucci loafers and left the office, laughing softly.

May 1991

"HAVE YOU SEEN THIS?" Nancy showed Jackie a statement in *Publisher's Weekly*, and read it aloud, "Main Street Books acquired a yet-to-be-titled book by Joan Kennedy, former wife of Senator Ted Kennedy, to be published sometime next year."

Jackie nodded. "Yes, we talked about it a while back when she came for a visit. That was before the divorce. I told her it might be good for her to find her own projects. It would give her something else to focus on."

Jackie had hosted Joan again at Red Gate Farm back in 1989, roughly six months after her last DUI. Joan had crashed into a fence in a suburb of Cape Cod. Fortunately, only the fence suffered damage. Her license was suspended for forty-five days and a rehab stint in Saint Luke's Roosevelt Hospital was required.

Jackie had suspected that Joan would have a harder than usual time with her divorce from Teddy. Further complicating matters had to be the fact that her children had grown up and didn't need her as much. Knowing, too, how Joan struggled with self-confidence, Jackie's compassion for her had soared.

During her most recent visit to Red Gate Farm with Jackie, Joan seemed better and more dedicated than ever to maintaining her sobriety. She also mentioned that she was starting to work on a book designed to enhance a child's love for classical and piano music, Joan's specialty.

Reading about Joan's success now, Jackie beamed for her dear friend.

"Didn't Steve Rubin give you grief about this?" Nancy asked.

"He said he was surprised I wasn't working with her, but I told him it was better for Joan to have an editor who could push her and crack the whip when needed."

"I suppose that makes sense. Working with a deadline changes relationships."

Jackie groaned. "Compounded by how close you are and how much you care about the person."

Nancy's expression brightened. "Oh, speaking of Joan, that reminds me. Gloria Steinem called. She wanted to know if you would pass along Joan's contact number for an interview."

Jackie smirked to herself. *Gloria should know better.*

"If she calls back, tell her Joan and I aren't in touch."

December 1991

JACKIE RELISHED the chance to enjoy an evening at her apartment with just her and John. She was exceedingly proud of him and all his accomplishments in the last year and a half. Passing the bar—finally—after two failed attempts. Going to work at the Manhattan District Attorney's Office and winning his first case in August. In her view, he was firming his foundation and discovering the trajectory he wanted his life to take.

His affair with Daryl Hannah had run its course, but to Jackie's dismay, his relationship with Christina Haag also ended.

John had brought over a pizza loaded with toppings. Unlike her son, and practically every American, Jackie wasn't a huge fan—and certainly didn't care to have it on a regular basis. But since John made the effort, she'd tolerate a slice of mushrooms, peppers, and sausage atop greasy cheese and sauce.

They ate in the kitchen because Jackie insisted, fearful a slice might slip from John's plate and ruin one of her rugs. Marta had left on the small television on the counter. Though Jackie and John were focused on their conversation, the newscaster's sudden mention of William Kennedy Smith caught their attention. When the reporter finished the segment, Jackie turned off the set.

"I can't believe the trial starts tomorrow."

"I didn't realize." Jackie swallowed hard but hoped John didn't notice. She had to tread carefully on the topic and measure her words.

"I plan to attend."

"Oh, John. Do you really think that's best?"

"He deserves his family's support."

Jackie drew in a breath and resisted the temptation to point out that William Kennedy Smith, Jean's son, had plenty of *other* family members who would be attending the proceedings.

"You don't want me there in court, do you?"

It aggravated her, to a degree, when John pressed for the truth. But how could she fault him when that's exactly what he'd learned to do?

"I'm worried it's not wise for you to publicly associate yourself with this."

Back in March, Teddy and his nephews, Patrick and William, had visited a bar in Palm Beach, not far from the Kennedy estate. By closing time, the men were inebriated but two young ladies were willing to drive them home. The next day, one of the women claimed William had raped her when they went for a walk on the beach.

"You think he's guilty," John said.

"I'm not involved, John. Nor do I care to be." The sharpness of her tone surprised them both. "It's a delicate matter."

John nodded. "Maybe it's best we don't discuss it."

Jackie agreed but said nothing. What good could come from the conversation? She had a hard time believing a young woman would falsely accuse a man of rape, and she didn't want to defend her stance. The accusations had merit in her view. Plus, Teddy was involved. Considering his behavior in recent years—being photographed having sex on a boat, drunken episodes at DC restaurants, getting caught half-naked with a lobbyist, and well-known for sexually harassing women in the workplace—who wouldn't believe the charges? Uncle Teddy had proven, consistently, that a Kennedy got away with everything.

"I do have some good news." John rifled through a stack of papers he'd brought with him until he found the sheet he wanted and handed it to Jackie.

It was a letter from an editor at *The New York Times* commissioning him to write a piece for the travel section. Specifically, an article detailing his kayaking trip with three friends last year in the Aland Islands that almost turned tragic. John had saved one of his friends from drowning when the kayak capsized.

"That's exciting, John." Jackie recalled how breathless she felt hearing him recount the harrowing story—and how grateful she was no one was hurt.

When some of John's papers slipped to the floor, Jackie helped pick them up. She noticed a pamphlet with the title, Sky's The Limit Flight Academy. Her chest constricted as she looked at her son.

"John, are you taking flying lessons?" She gave him the sheets she'd gathered and sank back onto her chair.

He pressed his lips together and paired it with the cautious-uncertain expression he'd mastered as a tyke whenever he was caught doing something wrong.

Just as she couldn't tell him not to go to the trial, she couldn't prevent him from learning to fly. Although it had been one of his long-held desires, Jackie had her reservations.

"John, I've never told you this, but sometimes, I have this terrible nightmare where something awful happens to you in a plane." She casually slid her hands under the table to hide the fact they were shaking now. "You know I'm not superstitious or anything like that. I only mention it because it's plagued me more than once. I've never had a problem with you scuba diving and exploring shipwrecks or any of your other pursuits. But please don't fly a plane. I...I..." Words failed her.

John reached over and put his hand on her shoulder.

"Mummy, I don't want you to worry."

She refused to be an overbearing mother or one who metered out her love based on how well her children pleased her. But in her heart, she wanted John to promise her that he would never pilot a plane.

Tears brimmed as pieces of the nightmare flashed in her mind.

John saw her mounting distress. He embraced her and whispered, "I'll put it aside for now, Mummy. Don't upset yourself."

She squeezed her eyes tightly shut to force the images away. At the same time, she relaxed in John's arms. It wasn't the exact words she ached to hear, but his tender compassion for her concern was reassuring. For now.

TWENTY-ONE

June 1993

Before Christmas, when Jackie and Maurice were discussing and proposing travel destinations for the summer, he told her he wanted to see France.

"But I want to see the France you love," he said, "not just Paris."

France held a dear place in Jackie's heart. Not only was her ancestral home there in Pont Saint-Esprit, which she had toured after her academic year at the University of Paris and the Sorbonne, but much of the countryside also held memories for her. She'd spent several weeks in the early summer of 1950 traveling with Claude de Renty, her roommate and daughter to Madame de Renty, her Parisian host. Together, she and Claude toured castles and hamlets, visited distant relatives of Claude's, and embraced rural living. They washed their clothes and bathed in streams like true bohemians. Not that Jackie had a desire to repeat those particular experiences.

And then there was Paris. Before she shared Ari's apartment on 88 Foch Avenue, and before she was an honored and celebrated guest of Charles de Gaulle as America's First Lady and Jack's wife, there was Jackie's Paris. The wealthy, handsome bachelors vying for her affections. Sneaking from the de Renty home so she could meet a mysterious stranger and explore the catacombs late at night. The masquerade ball, the botched proposal, and the betrayal of a classmate. Most memorable for her was the romantic night in a rowboat on the Seine—and getting arrested for public nudity. Arrested but released without being charged.

Not that Jackie had shared those detailed memories with Maurice.

Nothing could have thrilled her more, though, hearing that he wanted to experience France with her.

With that in mind, Maurice arranged for them to travel by barge down the Rhône River with stops at Provence and Camargue. They arrived in time for the feast held in Saintes Maries de la Mer, a commune believed to be where the three Marys—Mary Magdalene, Mary Salome, and Mary Clopas—fled after witnessing and sharing about Jesus's empty tomb after His resurrection. According to the legend, the Marys left the Holy Land to avoid persecution, and throughout the ages, were honored with individual celebrations across the area.

Jackie and Maurice enjoyed strolling the beaches and spotting the wild horses.

In Paris, they had enjoyed an early dinner with Claude. Married to Bernard, an attorney, she was now Claude du Granrut, mother of five, and after working in politics, then journalism, she returned to politics and worked as the vice president of the regional council of Picardy.

Naturally, Jackie and Claude reminisced about their college days.

"Oh, Claude, is it possible those times were really forty years ago?" Jackie exclaimed as they relaxed on the veranda at Claude's home, trying to catch her breath after hearty laughs. A slight discomfort arose in her stomach, which had hampered her appetite, but not enough for Claude and Maurice to notice.

"It's impossible, yes." Claude sighed then sipped the fresh coffee that had just been served. "If you're up for it, I can take you to see Mother tomorrow afternoon."

"That would be wonderful! Do you think she will remember me?"

Claude nodded. "Oh, of course. How could she forget *Jack-leen*, especially after you became so famous. For years she bragged to friends about having been your host mother. But she is getting on. Ninety-four now, with good days and not-so-good, but I'm sure she would love to see you. We won't stay long. She has been through a lot, and with the tragedy, well, I feel that's been especially hard on her."

"Tragedy?"

Claude stared at her. "You mean you don't know? Oh, it was everywhere. You'll have to bear with me. It's been two years, but I don't think I've had to tell anyone the whole story—and I must warn you, it's awful. Beyond your worst imagination. You see, Ghislaine was murdered."

Jackie gasped. "Oh, I'm terribly sorry, Claude. I had no idea."

Claude relayed the story. How Ghislaine, her older sister, had married again in 1965 to a man named Jean-Pierre Marchal, owner of a car supply company. He died years later, leaving Ghislaine a wealthy widow. Then, after she disappeared one summer afternoon, friends began a search for her. Shortly thereafter, she was found dead in a locked cellar of her villa outside of Cannes. Part of her skull had been crushed, her throat slit, a finger cut off, and her body stabbed ten times.

Dabbing away tears, Claude told how a gardener was suspected primarily because *Omar m'a tuer* was found written in Ghislaine's blood in the cellar. Translated, the inscription read, *Omar has kill me*. Moroccan born and illiterate, Omar Raddad proclaimed his innocence. Defense experts pointed out that the message should have read *Omar m'a tuée*, (Omar has killed me) and it was unlikely Ghislaine, a French-speaking native, would have made such a grammatical mistake. Regardless, Omar Raddad was convicted and awaiting sentencing.

Jackie and Maurice sat speechless and dumbstruck.

"Utterly heartbreaking, Madame Ganrut," Maurice finally said. "It's unimaginable what you and your family have been through. My deepest sympathies to you."

"Oh, Claude..." Jackie embraced her, and they both wept for Ghislaine.

THE NEXT DAY, Jackie and Claude visited briefly with Madame de Renty while Maurice stayed at the hotel and tended to business matters.

With the news of Ghislaine fresh on her mind, Jackie had no way of separating her own sorrow from her grief for the countess. Jackie assumed Madame de Renty still remembered her based mainly on her pleasant disposition and the endearing smile she shared each time she looked at Jackie. Claude retold various memories from the time Jackie stayed with them, and the countess nodded but didn't add her own take or embellish the stories. A dullness seemed etched in her eyes. From the passing of time and a long lifespan or from having endured a horrific loss? Whether or not the tenderhearted Guyot de Renty actually recalled their time together, Jackie couldn't say, but she was grateful for the brief visit.

After they left the care home where the countess lived, Claude asked, "Have you been in touch with Paul?"

There was no reason for her cheeks to tint, but Jackie was powerless against it. Perhaps it was because Claude was among the few who knew about her history with Paul.

"Yes, I reached out to him before we came. Maurice and I are heading to Courances tomorrow to see him."

"Wonderful! I know he'll be thrilled to see you."

"You should join us!" Jackie said.

Claude shook her head. "I wouldn't dream of intruding on your time together."

Jackie darted a coy glance at her. "We were never lovers, you know."

"A shame. I'll always wonder what would've become of the both of you if you had gotten romantically involved."

They laughed, and Jackie couldn't have been more grateful for the chance to visit with her good friend.

JUST AS SHE REMEMBERED, the Château de Courances could still rival the Palace of Versailles. To a degree.

"Darling, you'll have to explain to me one day why you didn't fall for the man who owns this estate," Maurice said as they drove onto the property. After a beat he added, "On the other hand, it may be best I don't know."

"It's very impressive. But wait till you meet Paul. He's so personable and down to earth."

Count Paul de Ganay didn't disappoint. With a full head of silver-white hair, he was still as strikingly handsome as he had been in his twenties. At least to Jackie. Years as a polo player and an active lifestyle had kept him trim and fit. He welcomed both of them warmly and said lunch awaited.

Piscine pêche cocktails, made from peaches grown on the property's orchard, Paul noted, were served. Enjoying the fresh baked baguettes, niçoise salad, and seared scallops with leeks was secondary to Paul's exquisite company.

After they finished, Maurice looked at Paul. "Would you mind, sir, if I borrowed a private room for a while? I need to make some phone calls to a few of my associates overseas."

"Of course. I will speak to Jacques, and he will see to it that you have everything you need."

Jackie excused herself to the bathroom. Although she and Maurice didn't discuss it beforehand, she suspected his business matters weren't urgent and he was giving her a chance to visit with

Paul alone. As usual, Maurice proved generous with his thought-fulness.

When she returned to the dining room, Jackie found Paul by himself.

"I take it that Maurice may be a while," he said. "Jacques is crafting some mint grapefruit mimosas. Should we enjoy them on the patio?"

"That would be lovely."

Paul escorted her outside, where a table awaited, draped in a crisp-white linen that breathed and billowed in the afternoon breeze. An assortment of pastries were arranged on a large plate next to a centerpiece of fresh purple irises. After Paul held out her chair, Jackie sat. Jacques must have been right on their heels, as he was already filling their crystal flutes.

Jackie sighed happily as the sun's rays warmed her face and bare arms. "I still remember the night of your family's autumn ball."

"The night we first met."

She noted the affection in his voice but wanted to tease him. "It was awful."

His expression contorted, making her laugh.

"Awful because Claude and Madame de Renty insisted I wear that rumpled peach frock they rummaged from a closet."

Paul smiled. "In my memory you looked ravishing in that dress."

She could have been be wrong, but Jackie recalled only wearing a similar color one other time, during her trip to India in 1962 with Lee.

"I was overwhelmed that night. Crowds can intimidate me and make me feel vulnerable. I came out on this very patio to escape and catch my breath."

"And I was thrilled to find you out here alone."

"I don't know what I would've done if you hadn't saved me from my nerves."

He sipped his drink. "Your shy nature was one of the things that drew me to you that night."

Exhilaration bubbled within Jackie as the memory replayed in her mind. "Remember how we watched everyone from out here, and how you filled me in on all the shameless gossip?"

"I recall warning you about Philip."

"Yes, Philip." Jackie tasted her mimosa as she revived those aged, stored memories of a man who had been one of France's wealthiest bachelors. He'd taken a strong interest in Jackie and attempted to woo her. "How is he?"

"The same since the last time you asked about him. Richer than ever, still dabbling in government affairs and probably making his wife miserable."

"And Marceau?" In truth, Jackie only asked after Philip because it was polite and expected. She cared nothing for him, especially with the way their relationship ended.

But Marceau was a different story. He had enraptured her heart like no other man. From their night in the catacombs to their morning together painting the sunrise at the Trocadéro, Jackie had been enamored by him.

Paul relaxed in his chair and laced his fingers. "I've only seen him a handful of times over the years. He always wants to know about you. I suppose one could say he's found happiness. At least the best he could do after the two of you departed."

She hoped Paul wasn't offended as her cheeks turned crimson. Hearing that Marceau asked about her thrilled her in ways she couldn't describe and validated the feelings she'd once had for him. Her blush deepened, though, when she recalled the time Marceau posed nude for her art class.

"You know we were never together," Jackie said.

"Neither were you and I, yet here we sit. Perhaps my pining for you is why I never married. Settling for any other woman wasn't possible for me." He laughed good-naturedly while Jackie's blush held. "Some connections, my dear, are deeper and go beyond the physical."

Jackie agreed. A secret part of her heart would always hold a torch for Marceau. In some ways, Paul too.

"But enough about your old beaux. I want to hear about you." Paul smiled warmly. "Tell me all about this position of yours, and why in God's name are you so thin?"

JACKIE WISHED she would've had the stamina for a stop in Ireland after they left France. But considering she wasn't even up for a brief stayover in Monaco, to at least see Prince Rainier and pay her respects, the decision not to visit Ireland was best.

Surely, time at the Vineyard would restore her. Aside from enjoying visitors and her grandchildren once a week, her only other plans included reading manuscripts on her patio in the morning light. Punctuated with sailing on the *Relemar*. She also made a mental note to look into herbal remedies for boosting one's energy.

September 1993

AFTER JANET JR'S PASSING, Jackie dearly missed their time together in Newport. To help ease the loss, she began hosting an annual Labor Day picnic at Red Gate Farm. Conveying how important the get-together was to her, she ensured that Caroline, Ed, and John made the weekend with her a priority. Normally, she wasn't one to make demands on others, but she had no qualms imposing the invite on them. Holidays and occasional dinners and visits weren't enough, especially now that Caroline had given her two more grandchildren, Tatiana and John, whom they called Jack.

Jackie also invited neighbors and friends she'd made since living at the Vineyard, including Carly Simon, who had become a close friend. So close, in fact, that they had worked on three children's books together and had another one in the works.

Jackie was exceedingly grateful Caroline always came with the children. She and Ed had crafted a quiet, private life, splitting their time between Manhattan and Long Island. Jackie's weekly playdate with the girls included a variety of activities. When they were in Manhattan that meant going to the park and usually a trip to Serendipity for ice cream, provided they were good—and they were always good. Little Jack was only eight months old, and Jackie knew she couldn't handle all of them on her own. But at the Vineyard, where the pace was slower, she spent time with her grandchildren on the beach, in the pool, and exploring the dunes. On the days she had little Jack, her strength to keep up seemed to deplete rapidly.

At Red Gate Farm, after they roasted lobsters over a campfire, which John loved to be in charge of, they ate coleslaw and roasted corn on the cob. The children preferred chocolate chip cookies for dessert, but Marta was happy to also make Caroline's favorite, a chocolate roll.

Playtime on the beach commenced. Jackie loved encouraging the girls' creativity. If they weren't digging through the sand looking for dinosaur bones or a long-forgotten buried treasure, they were building castles with moats where mermaids swam.

When the sun began to sink, John danced and chased the girls. Jackie loved their infectious laughter, especially when John pretended to fall, and they piled on top of him. He tickled them until they couldn't breathe. The day ended with all of them gathered around the dying fire making s'mores.

Jackie was the happiest she had ever been.

TWENTY-TWO

October 1993

Seated between President Clinton and her dashing son for the rededication ceremony of the John F. Kennedy Presidential Library and Museum, Jackie burned inwardly with embarrassment.

Although she was exceedingly proud that the library's foundation had successfully raised money for and built an expansion, she was most pleased with their decision to revamp much of the exhibits and content in an effort educate the younger generation who had grown up after Jack's passing. Intensifying her pride was the fact Caroline, who served as the library foundation's president, had participated and contributed to the overhaul and renewal.

Her embarrassment stemmed from her hair. Dry and brittle, it lacked its usual luster. She was flustered with herself that she hadn't been to the salon beforehand for a conditioning treatment. Standing outside the library in the receiving line for President Clinton hadn't been ideal with the wind whipping through it. As she and her children, along with other Kennedy family members, made their way inside to their seats on a platform, the best she could do was simply swipe it from her face. She worried reporters would notice. After all, the press lived to capture moments of celebrities and politicians tripping on a carpet or spilling coffee on themselves or looking haggard if they didn't apply enough make-up.

She told herself not to be so sensitive. Too much concern would show on her face. And today she was under the lens. Someone was bound to write an article about her fading looks. The gall! She'd had a facelift. Had jogged and walked enough miles to cover the entirety of Central Park several times over. For God's sake, must a woman spend her whole life obsessed with her appearance?

Careful thought had gone into her suit. A dark green jacket over a black skirt. Gloves and layers were needed to camouflage her stick-thin figure. She had enough hubris left—perhaps tangled with body dysmorphia—to appreciate having remained svelte into her sixties. Criticisms embedded from her mother long ago—"We *pick* at dessert, Jacqueline, we don't *eat* it"—and occasionally nourished by timely comments from Rose Kennedy—"How will you ever be able to fit into that gown before the inaugural ball after having a baby?"—amped her dependence on cigarettes and helped her craft habits to control her weight. Habits she formed so long ago.

Now, she concentrated on keeping a stiff posture in her seat. Her expression pleasant but vacant. Such tasks were more arduous than they used to be. Teddy took the podium, causing her to realize her focus was lax.

John leaned over during Teddy's remarks. "You all right?"

What had caused him to ask?

She nodded and gave her public smile, not too wide and not too thin.

But a hidden fib lurked in her gesture. Ever since her trip to France, she felt off-kilter. Not jetlag. The best she could figure was that traveling zapped her more than it used to, and there were the demands of her job. *Paris After the Liberation*, a nonfiction work she adored, was approaching its deadline and took most of her attention lately. Perhaps she hadn't taken enough time to simply rest. That made sense, didn't it?

An hour later, relief glided over her as the speeches concluded and the staff prepared to open the doors for the public. Having toured the library privately last night with her children and other Kennedys, Jackie shook hands with the president once more before she and John slipped into their awaiting car. Caroline, with Ed at her side, stayed to take part in the planned activities.

"I thought you'd be more excited about today." John waved at the crowd as they left Columbia Point.

"Last night was more enjoyable." Sitting on display while people gave speeches fell into the category of obligations she didn't like. Necessary at times but stale.

"True." John nodded thoughtfully. "But you don't seem like yourself today. Is something wrong, Mummy?"

She couldn't look at him. A strange fear began to pester her. Warned her that if she were even a little honest about how she'd been feeling lately, she would break down and tell him everything. Part of her wanted to do exactly that and fall into his arms of comfort and reassurances. But she was his mother. She couldn't burden him or—God forbid—alarm him, especially when she had no way of explaining anything.

"There is a matter I've been wanting to discuss with you and Caroline, but it's such a challenge getting the three of us in the same room anymore." Not a complete lie, but she hoped he wouldn't see through her ruse.

"Oh?"

"Yes, it's about the Peapack house. I think it's time to put it in your name and Caroline's name. It may sound silly, but Maurice had mentioned a while back that nowadays it's more prudent to have property transferred over beforehand than when it's in estate. Oh, I'm probably muddling this up, but I hope you know what I mean."

John's expression seemed solemn but not distrusting. "I understand, and he's right."

"Good. I'll tell him to get the paperwork started then."

"Just the Peapack house?"

She picked up on the hitch of doubt in his question.

"For now. We'll see how it goes, but don't worry, I have my will all taken care of."

"Whatever you say, Mummy."

A genuine smile burst through when she noted his carefree demeanor. That was the John she loved and couldn't resist. But a fleeting thought disturbed her happiness with her son.

Was this how it started with Janet Jr? When did she suspect something was wrong, and did she know—did she know—*before the doctors found that it was cancer, did she already know she was dying?*

November 1993

THIRTY YEARS.

The length and depth and breadth of time was too much for Jackie to comprehend. Three decades. Unlike past anniversaries of November 22nd, this one felt weighty to Jackie. She'd lived more of her life as Jack's widow than beside him as his wife.

Just like Ethel.

There had been no delusions for her, that she and Jack would grow old together. Not when she kept vigil at his bedside, twice, assured by doctors that he wouldn't survive back and spinal surgery. He recovered, miraculously, but he was also afflicted with digestive issues, an ulcer, Addison's disease, and later, suffered from the early stages of osteoporosis, brought on by the steroids he took to subdue symptoms from his failing adrenal glands.

Had their motorcade made it through Dealy Plaza, through the dull-gray tunnel ahead, and on to the luncheon at the Trade Mart, would Jack have lived to see the other side of fifty—or sixty?

That was merely one of the questions Jackie contemplated, but she didn't want her sorrow to dominate. Joining her riding club proved to be the ideal solution. Getting up before dawn and perched in the saddle gave her a purpose. A much-needed focus. Because staying in Manhattan for the weekend was out of the question. Documentaries, news specials, articles, and the awful footage from the Zapruder film would be everywhere.

Lee had left a message on her answering machine yesterday. "Sorry I won't be there for Thanksgiving. Herbert insisted we join his children in LA. A full holiday dinner spread in a beach house where it's eighty-five degrees outside almost strikes me as sacrilegious, but the worst part will be that you're not there. Unless you call Bunny and arrange to fly here on her jet. I won't discount the possibility. Just know that I'm thinking of you, Jacks. Talk soon."

Jackie had learned to be more flexible with Lee. They both led different lives than decades earlier, and now that Lee had remarried, Herbert was her priority, as it should be. Jackie found Lee's message touching, and having her back in her life, with no more underlying strife between them, meant the world.

Jackie would call her later, after she changed and settled in at Red Gate Farm. Caroline, Ed, John, and the grandchildren were coming for dinner tomorrow. That was all she really wanted and needed. The best distraction to keep her mind off Jack.

Jack...

She tapped her heels into Frank's flanks, urging him to go faster once she noticed how far she was slipping behind the pack. Frank acquiesced and the brisk wind slapped Jackie's cheeks. She shut her eyes for a moment and welcomed any sensation that tamped down her flared-up sorrow. But suddenly, Frank's swift gallop was interrupted. He gave a short, sharp whinny. Had his hoof dipped into a rabbit hole? Or was he spooked by a possum or badger? Jackie didn't know. She was only aware of the brief, jarring second where she was somehow jolted from the saddle, lost hold of the reins, summersaulted, and slammed down upon the cold, damp ground.

"THIS IS WONDERFUL, ISN'T IT?"

Her vision clouded, but Jackie found herself wearing the raspberry-pink Chanel suit sitting next to Jack on the jump seat of the convertible Lincoln, her pillbox hat perched and pinned atop her head.

Crowds, as far as the eye could see, lined both sides of the motorcade. People stood almost close enough to touch. Children topped their fathers' shoulders, waving a small American flag in one hand and the other at her and Jack. Pigtails on young girls bounced. Women clutched their chests. Men beamed. Exuberant and cheering, everyone moved in slow motion.

Jack turned to her and smiled. In a split-second, every ache and longing she'd experienced since she last kissed him rushed back into her chest. She thought the pain was about to crush her from the inside out.

"Aren't you glad you didn't wear the sunglasses?"

She moved to touch him, but her limbs were too heavy.

"Jack, we must get out of here—" The words she needed to warn him, to save him from what was about to happen, wouldn't come.

"It's all right, Jackie."

"No, it isn't." Slowly, she swiveled her head, thinking she might reach for the driver, tap his shoulder and urge him to go faster, but no one else was in the car with them.

"I've waited a long time to see you, Jackie."

Her focus returned to her husband. "Oh, I've missed you, Jack."

"It's been hard."

"Yes."

"There isn't much time."

A pit formed in her stomach as she feared Jack would be shot again.

But he reached over and squeezed her hand. She cursed those stark-white kid gloves, wanting nothing more than to feel his skin on hers.

"Be strong," he said.

"But I don't want to."

He turned his attention back to the crowd as he began to fade.

"Jack, take me with you."

She tried to move but couldn't. She tried to raise her voice, but no sound came.

Everything went blank.

"MRS. ONASSIS, CAN YOU HEAR ME?"

Jackie opened her eyes and blinked against the fluorescent lights and the confusion swirling in her head.

Where's Jack? She couldn't articulate the words.

"Mrs. Onassis, can you see me? Can you focus on me?"

Blinking, she made the effort to look at the stranger.

"What..." was all she managed. Her dry throat hampered her words.

"Just relax, ma'am. I'm Dr. Feldman. You're at Memorial Hospital." He poured her a cup of water from the bedside pitcher and handed it to her. "You took a bad fall from your horse and were unconscious. Do you remember what happened?"

She put her hand to her forehead and needed a moment to think. Riding. Yes, she'd been riding. Frank. Then...she didn't know.

But then there was Jack.

Dr. Feldman proceeded with various questions. Each one helped Jackie's consciousness clear and assured Dr. Feldman she didn't have a head injury. There was no need to mention her beautiful moment with Jack and have him explain it away. She wanted nothing more than to close her eyes and return to him, even though she knew there was no way for that to happen.

Preoccupied with her new longing, she realized the doctor had touched her arm.

"I'm sorry. What did you say?"

A sympathetic grin appeared. "When you were brought into the emergency room you were examined for injuries. No wounds were found, but you do have swelling in your groin."

Heat zipped up her face. Being examined while she was unconscious seemed inappropriate—especially in her groin area. But she was in a hospital, surrounded by medical staff. She considered peeking at the area but didn't.

"Are you being treated for that, Mrs. Onassis?"

A bit of color tinted his cheeks as well.

"No. I wasn't aware..." She'd noticed the swelling but gave it no attention, thinking it would go away as swiftly and as mysteriously as it appeared. Plus, the approaching anniversary of Jack's death had distracted her.

"I see. We'd like to keep you overnight for observation."

"Oh, is that really necessary?" Most of the time she'd spent in hospitals had been as a family member, not a patient. The idea of spending the night—*being observed*—made her uncomfortable. "I'd much prefer my own bed."

"It's a precaution. You were unconscious for thirty minutes, which gives us reason to be concerned. Before today, how have you been feeling?"

His query provoked memories from her trip to France. The stomach cramps and body aches. More recently there had been the rededication ceremony where her head had been a jumble of thoughts and her body felt alien to her. How did she relay that to this man, who wasn't her regular doctor?

"Fine." She paired it with a shrug, as if that could disguise her fib.

He nodded and seemed resigned to the fact she didn't relent details. "I'll see about getting you released then, but I want you to promise me if anything changes with your condition, you won't hesitate to come back immediately."

Jackie nodded.

"Good. Let's also get you started on a round of antibiotics. I'm going to presume the swelling is related to an infection. It should clear up in a week or so. In the meantime, I recommend you make an appointment with your general practitioner and have a full work up done."

"Thank you, Dr. Feldman. Yes, that's just what I'll do."

Her relief over going home proved strong enough to subdue her concerns over the swelling and being unconscious. At least for the moment.

December 1993

THOUGH SHE TOOK the medication Dr. Feldman prescribed, Jackie didn't make a point to see her doctor before the holidays arrived. Surely, the matter could wait a few more weeks. The pure joy of experiencing her grandchildren as they opened presents bolstered her energy. So much so, she thought the antibiotics had done the trick.

However, during her Caribbean cruise with Maurice after Christmas, strange symptoms began to plague her again. Soreness in her chest when she breathed too deeply. Pains in her stomach that compromised her ability to eat much. The ever-present exhaustion. And the swelling in her groin had lessened but was still there. She did the best she could to downplay her discomforts the first few days of their vacation, not wanting to ruin the outing for Maurice, but the persistence of the aches became too much for her to hide.

Lounging on the deck near the pool with her head wrapped in a scarf and wearing dark sunglasses, she set aside the book she brought. Her mind didn't want to focus.

Maurice, careful with the two steaming mugs he carried, joined her.

"I thought a cup of tea before lunch might hit the spot. The ship's nurse assured me that ginger and peppermint are ideal for a cranky stomach."

She thanked him before taking a few sips.

"I was thinking, my darling, perhaps it would be best if we headed back early."

Jackie considered protesting but why would she when those were the words she needed to hear? "Maybe I'm not suited for traveling anymore. Could that be it? I've turned into a homebody. We should see about getting rocking chairs next, I suppose."

She appreciated that he laughed at her attempt to make light of the situation.

"I can't explain it, Maurice, but I want things simple."

"You've always been that way, my darling. Although you may splurge when it comes to your wardrobe at times, you prefer things streamlined."

"The only thing I really want is to spend time with my family. It's like a deep yearning I've never known, yet I don't want to intrude on their lives."

He nodded. "I know precisely how you feel. There aren't enough holidays."

"Something like that." The boost to her spirit started to wane as her insides churned against the tea. "Honestly, Maurice, I don't understand what's wrong with me."

He slid his hand onto the back of her neck as a comforting gesture. She stiffened when his hand came upon another swollen spot, but he didn't address it. Whether he didn't want to make Jackie more self-conscious or was afraid of his own worries manifesting on his face, she didn't know. She detected the look of concern in his eyes, despite the shade of her sunglasses, though, and was grateful his instinct was to say nothing.

"I'll arrange for us to leave at the next port. We'll get you home, and we'll get you to the doctor. In the meantime, I don't want you to worry. They'll pinpoint what's troubling you, then we'll get it taken care of. You'll get rested up and back to your vibrant self."

She wanted to saturate herself in his positivity. His gentle ways and encouragement provided the boost she needed.

"You're right. Once I see a doctor and identify what's going on, all will be made well."

TWENTY-THREE

January 1994

Jackie's doctor subjected her to a thorough exam, ordered a panel of blood tests, and had her undergo a CAT scan. When the results were in, Dr. Neelam Ashanti's office called and scheduled an in-office meeting.

The morning of her appointment, Maurice squeezed her hand as she sat across from him at the table, stirring her coffee endlessly and staring into nothingness. He didn't bother with faulty assurances when their eyes met, only looked at her lovingly and with a silent promise they could get through anything.

She ended up skipping the coffee, and they headed to Dr. Ashanti's office inside the New York Hospital Cornell Medical Center. Trembling slightly, she took her seat and couldn't recall the last time she'd felt so vulnerable.

"Mrs. Onassis, the results of your scan are concerning," the doctor began reluctantly. "The swelling you've been experiencing is your lymph nodes. Our first call of duty is to order a biopsy. I want to do it today and get it to the lab as soon as possible."

Her urgency scared Jackie.

"What do you think it is?"

She shook her head. "I'm not going to speculate. There are too many possibilities. Could be a staph infection or worse. The biopsy will tell us exactly what we're in for."

Jackie looked to Maurice then back to Dr. Ashanti.

"Should I be worried?"

Dr. Ashanti glanced at the floor. "Be prepared, and you'll want to tell your family. Going forward, you'll need their support."

———

DAYS LATER, the biopsy revealed a diagnosis. Non-Hodgkin's Lymphoma, a type of cancer. Jackie wasn't familiar with the disease.

"It's a cancer affecting the lymphatic system," Dr Ashanti explained. "The cells in your biopsy were what we call primitive stage. This type of cancer can be highly malignant, and without treatment could spread to other parts of the body. You'll want to start chemotherapy immediately."

Cancer...cancer. The only words she heard.

Jackie swallowed. "What are my chances, doctor?"

"Every patient is different. Current studies show a survival rate of fifty percent."

She didn't like the sound of the odds, but it was her own fault for asking. Putting faith in a statistic was foolish. Now if she could only erase it from her mind.

On the other hand, there was Anthony. He had undergone treatment for testicular cancer and had gone into remission. There was hope.

Maurice cupped a hand on her shoulder. "Whatever the odds, you'll beat them."

"Absolutely." Her thoughts strayed to Janet Jr and how she was given no hope at the outset. Jackie refused to make the mistake of feeling sorry for herself. Although she was older than her sister had been, Jackie had a fighting chance. She would make the most of it without complaint. "Now, when do we start treatment?"

IF THERE HAD BEEN a way for her not to tell her children, Jackie would have faced the battle ahead privately. Maurice discouraged the idea from the start, however, and before her first treatment, she invited them to her apartment for dinner.

While they dined, Caroline and John seemed especially upbeat and chatty. Memories surfaced from when they had been a family of three. Gathered around the table on a school night, long before boarding school, college, and travels took them in different directions. John usually entertained them with some little ditty or song bite while Caroline and Jackie always went along with snickers and laughter.

Now, they needed a bigger table. Jackie lived for the times when they were all together. The rapid-fire conversation, the stories they shared, mixed with the children's curiosities and giggles. Those little voices delighted her soul.

How she loved them all!

What Jackie would have given to preserve that night. To keep it pure and unspoiled by the news she had to tell them.

After dinner, on the floor of her living room with baby Jack in her lap, she told Caroline and John about her diagnosis and upcoming treatment. The words came easier than she had imagined. A strange tinge of pride teased her, until she saw her children's faces.

Tears welled in Caroline's eyes. "I—I didn't think it was that serious. When you said you were going to the doctor—"

"Yes, darling, I know. It's not what I expected either, but I'm going to be fine. From what they've told me, the effects of the chemo will be the worst of it. But once we get past all that, it may take a little time, but I'll recover."

"Is that what they said?" John stood and handed his niece to her father. "The doctor's exact words?"

The hitch of anger in his voice surprised Jackie.

"More or less."

He ran a hand over his face, then splayed his hands as if he were explaining something carefully. "I need to get this straight. They promised you that treatment would fix everything?"

"Well—"

"They actually said that you'd be cured."

"John." Maurice's sharp but gentle whisper seemed to go ignored.

Jackie slightly despised the fact that John was making the moment harder on her. At the same time, she loved him even more because she glimpsed the fear in his eyes. It told her how afraid he was of losing her. Knowing how much her son loved her almost broke her heart. She had not anticipated his reaction, but she promised herself she wouldn't cry tonight. That she wouldn't fall apart in front of the people she loved most. She needed to comfort them and ease their fears, not create a greater burden.

But when he knelt beside her and delicately put his hand on her back, she felt her resolve crack. She kissed the top of her grandson's head and fought back tears.

"Please, John. It's going to be all right." Though she only managed to whisper the words, she believed them. "A few months and all will be well."

LATER, as Caroline, Ed, the grandchildren, and John prepared to leave, Jackie regarded her performance that night as credible since she didn't end up a sobbing mess. But she knew she failed to instill confidence in her children. Long embraces before they left both soothed and frightened her. What if, in the days ahead, she couldn't put forth a strong front for them? She dashed the thought aside.

A new discipline needed to emerge. One where she gave no

tolerance to negative thoughts or what ifs. Though it was probably natural for people to dwell on their mortality in such situations, she believed it to be wasteful. She would remind herself to focus on enduring the treatments and getting on the other side. Simple enough.

Now, as her grandchildren reached for her, tucked into their puffy winter coats, she held them. Oblivious to the somber mannerisms of the adults, they hugged and kissed their Grand Jackie like they always did. For that she was grateful.

After they were gone, Maurice offered to make her tea and toast before bed, but she politely passed. She didn't say it, but she didn't want to be taken care of until she had to. Not that Maurice's gentle thoughtfulness went unappreciated.

They retired to her bedroom, and Maurice made sure she had a fresh glass of water for her nighttime medication.

"I have one thing left to do tonight."

"You could wait till morning." Maurice lowered his head after he said it. Jackie suspected he had forgotten, only briefly, that she began her treatment tomorrow. She couldn't fault him for that since it felt as though everything was happening so quickly.

"I think I'll sleep better…"

Maurice nodded, then kissed her cheek. "I'll leave you to it." He bid her goodnight as he headed to his bedroom, an arrangement they liked.

She readied for bed first, unsure if she was procrastinating. After she fluffed and propped up her pillows, she got in bed and brought the phone to her lap. She stared at the numbers. A phone call would be best. It would save them both from the dramatics sure to play out between them. Maybe Jackie just didn't want to see the look of pity. Anguish and disbelief were sure to accompany it, but pity, well, she didn't want to endure that.

A cigarette. Yes, that's what I need. Just one…

But she heard the doctor's voice in her head. Now was the best time to kick the habit. She doubted that, given that it had been part of her life since she was, what, fifteen or so. But the satisfaction she had always known eluded her now. She abandoned the idea.

At the same time, she considered putting the phone back. Forgetting the whole thing. Perhaps Maurice was right. She could wait until tomorrow.

But the harsh reality was that news of her condition would spread like wildfire once a reporter caught a whiff. She wanted to be the one who let the cat out of the bag, and only when she had to.

Tonight, she had to.

Jackie picked up the receiver and pushed the numbers to call Lee.

"JACKS, NO!" Lee exclaimed at hearing the news. "I—I can't lose you. Not now."

Jackie had no idea how long they stayed on the phone together, chatting quietly. Lee needed to know every detail. From when Jackie first suspected she was ill to her diagnosis and treatment regiment. Much like Caroline and John, Lee went through an array of emotions. Disbelief and anger were primary, but Jackie found a strange comfort when they wept softly together. The choke of emotion led them through a scattering of memories, which led to happier tears for Jackie.

She wondered if she should have told her sister in person. Lee had outdone herself, surprising Jackie by offering to go to the doctor and the clinic with her. A true departure from Lee's usual response of shying away from one who was sick. Gently, Jackie resolved her from any obligation to accompany her since she herself didn't know what she was in for.

Jackie dared to believe their reconciliation was solid and complete. Their jealousies and rivalries felt obliterated, and Jackie felt wrapped in an abundance of Lee's love, thanks to her reassurances and expressions of wanting to be there for her. Tender as the moment was between them, an ache of regret surfaced, making Jackie wish she had told Lee in person so she could have rested in a long embrace from her sister. Because no matter what lay ahead, Jackie knew she could endure it now that she was secure in Lee's love for her.

Perhaps that will be the good that comes out of this.

THE HARDEST PERSON TO TELL, Jackie found, was Marta. Though she ran 1040 with precision and high standards, her tough exterior dissolved and her deep affection for *Madam* reduced her to a sobbing mess.

Caught off guard, Jackie was touched. She did her best to assure Marta that she would overcome the cancer, and Marta agreed and committed to helping her any way she could.

At Doubleday, she told Nancy in private, and was thankful Nancy didn't show an outward display of emotion. Jackie despised the aspect of plunging those she loved into turmoil.

Later, when she told her bosses and editorial team, she fared better and almost felt detached from the difficult news. Perhaps the fifth time around made it easier. But she still had others to tell. Ted and the Kennedys, Bunny...

"I'll have to reduce my workload a bit, but nothing drastic." Jackie addressed her coworkers in the same conference room where she'd enjoyed so many accomplishments and achievements in her career. Surely that would bring her luck. "I just don't want to hold up any pertinent projects. Once I finish the treatments, I can jump back in full steam."

Jaws were slack and heads nodded as the news settled over them.

"We're all pulling for you, Jackie." Steve Rubin, who possibly knew Jackie best among those gathered, seemed to speak for the group.

Jackie appreciated the support and said as much, finishing with,

"Oh, I'm sure by the time spring rolls around we'll all be making jokes about this."

SURPRISINGLY, Jackie didn't thoroughly despise the new routine that took shape over the next few weeks.

Treatment was once every three weeks. Maurice accompanied her, and when they arrived at the clinic with the sunrise, he went in first to make sure no one else was in the waiting area. Then he retrieved Jackie from the car and held her hand as she, wrapped in a head scarf and wearing a pair of her thick, dark sunglasses, ducked inside.

The day after chemo, she felt fine. However, the following day made up for it with fatigue and nausea. Medication alleviated the nausea, but there seemed little she could do to battle the exhaustion. When her body demanded rest or naps, she gave in, certain that she would bounce back faster once her cycle of treatments ended.

Doctors also warned that her hair would fall out.

"I may need a wig then," she decided aloud. *Perhaps I could try being a blonde.*

Her duties at Doubleday weren't as interrupted as she expected. She kept working, though primarily from 1040, or during chemo sessions since she joked with a friend that it allowed her more time to read.

John left his position at the DA's office and rented an apartment down the street. When he told Jackie that he wanted to accompany her to future doctor appointments, she drew a line. His urge to protect her and his assertiveness charmed her to an extent, but she needed her privacy. And she was prepared to dig in her heels if he attempted to dominate her and insist he be there. She tamped down the streak of fury that threatened and reminded herself that in the best ways, John was like his father and uncles, a man who believed in taking action, propelled by his love and passion for her.

He called or stopped by every day. When the weather wasn't bitingly cold, they went for walks. Sometimes Caroline and the children were able to join them too. Mainly, they kept to the path around the reservoir in Central Park since it was close to home and Jackie had learned that her stamina could deplete quickly. She didn't mind a light snowfall but was looking forward to spring when the rhododendrons would begin to bloom along the walkway.

"You know, if we're not more careful, the paparazzi are going to pick up that something's different," Jackie pointed out one day.

John looked at her. "Because a son can't spend time with his mother?"

"It is unusual nowadays, isn't it? I'm supposed to be perturbed you don't call me enough, and you're supposed to be off conquering the world and wooing young ladies."

He shook his head. "Those are the last things on my mind."

Although she liked being a priority in John's life lately, sadness pinched her. She didn't want to burden him or keep him from doing the things he loved. Luckily, the winter months meant time off from his usual pursuits of diving, swimming in the ocean, and kayaking. There'd been no mention about flying lessons, and Jackie wouldn't dare ask.

"But I have been thinking about other things," he said. "Such as what I might really want to do with my life."

Appropriate, Jackie thought. Given the circumstances they had been thrust into. In addition, John wasn't an erratic young man. He'd spent his twenties rounding out his education, despite the bumps served in the Peace Corps, travelled, and became a certified diver.

Still, an ache lived in Jackie's heart when it came to John. Unlike Caroline, he quietly lived with the expectation that one day he would run for president. Though his Kennedy family never pressured him, Jackie knew it stayed in the forefront of his mind. The American public already had an unquenchable interest in everything John did. When he introduced Teddy at the 1988 Democratic Convention, his first major address, the hall nearly shook with applause, leaving little doubt how people felt about him and his leadership potential. Mostly, people wanted him to recapture and continue his father's legacy, which had been cut short. Jackie understood, but better than anyone, she knew John was not Jack and wondered if he feared disappointing the masses more than actually running for office.

"What might that be?" she finally asked when he didn't elaborate.

"I never wanted to continue directly in my father's footsteps. It's important to me to carve my own way. Whether or not that means running for office one day, I'm still not sure."

His admission brought a degree of relief because if he did seek election, she dreaded the increase in public scrutiny of him.

"Right now, I'm more attracted to the arts and the influence media has on culture."

She didn't know where he was going with such a declaration, but she wondered if he'd rehearsed his delivery. His mention of the arts reminded her of *Winners*, the play he starred in back in 1985 with Christina Haag, his former love. Though the production was purposely short-lived and by invite-only tickets, Jackie understood his interest in acting. When he was growing up, various artists had invested in his life. Peter Beard, Andy Warhol, and Rudolph Nureyev. She and Caroline did not attend the play, to avoid all attention falling on them, but Jackie read every review about his performance—which was mostly praised—and had no doubt in his abilities. However, privately, she told him acting wasn't a viable profession for a Kennedy heir. John took it well, as if he already knew but needed to hear it out loud.

"I'm thinking about starting a magazine. One that combines healthy discussions about current issues and creates content that engages everyone in politics."

Jackie didn't know what to say.

"Remember when you told me how dinners used to be for my father and his family growing up? Everyone was encouraged to come to the table with topics to discuss, and sometimes those dinners turned into heated debates?"

Memories of such evenings at Hyannis Port revived. Bobby and Jack getting into heated exchanges over the best way to build foreign relations or the best campaign tactics. Eunice and Teddy also chimed in with their own ideals, and Joe had mastered playing devil's advocate, which usually riled somebody sooner or later. She hadn't thought of those times in ages, and it brought a smile as she nodded in response to John's question.

He continued. "I want to recreate that, only I want to inject it with style and panache. Elevate the way we discuss politics without making it too high brow or an unchecked free-for-all."

"Starting a magazine is quite ambitious." She wasn't sure she could muster enough enthusiasm on the spot. Such an endeavor required a lot—from start-up costs to building a staff to luring in advertisers and so on.

"I'm not interested in easy, and I'm attracted to the idea of not only producing something that isn't out there but also owning it and putting my name on it."

Equally stumped and intrigued, Jackie had nothing to offer in the way of advice. How would the public receive such a magazine? Would it unleash disappointment?

A touch of light-headedness struck, causing her to put a hand to her forehead and slow her pace.

John reached for her other hand and led her to a bench nearby for them to sit.

"Can I do anything?"

She closed her eyes and focused on her breathing. "I'm sorry. I just need a moment is all."

"You don't have to apologize or feel embarrassed about being sick."

Her instinct was to snap a reminder that she wasn't *sick*, just hampered, and that it was only temporary, but she realized that was precisely the kind of reaction John was trying to save her from.

Breathing came easier as she inhaled slowly and deeply.

"I suppose we wouldn't have this moment otherwise."

He gave a half-grin. "That's one way to put a positive spin on things. And you're right, if this were last year, we'd both be at work or going about our business shuffling through the city." He placed his arm around her shoulders and lovingly squeezed her closer. "We'd be busy like the masses. Running on empty and chasing nothing."

Jackie's balance slowly restored, but rather than complying with the urge to get moving she resisted. A gray mist slowly shrouded the skyline, adding to her peace. She rested her head on John's shoulder.

"I suppose I should keep up this ruse a bit longer then."

———

AFTER HER NEXT TREATMENT SESSION, Jackie asked Maurice to make a special stop on the way home.

"Are you sure, my darling?" he asked.

His concern stemmed from the fact he wouldn't be able to go in and assure privacy for Jackie before they entered. At least that's what she assumed. Or perhaps he preferred their routine of getting her home and in bed for a nap. But like a fussy toddler, Jackie didn't want to lie down.

When Maurice looked to her for a definitive answer, she nodded.

He drove down to Eighty-ninth Street and turned into the parking lot of the church of St. Thomas More, Jackie's parish. Though she no longer considered herself a regular church goer, she recently began to feel a pull on her heart to return. Perhaps it was natural, she thought, for one to eventually face her mortality and prepare. As best she could, anyway.

With Maurice beside her, she slipped into a pew and knelt while Maurice sat. Silently, with her head bowed, she recited the prayers she knew. Memories of Father Leonard revived. The connection they made when they first met in Ireland in 1950 had meant a great deal to her. Letters they shared over the next thirteen years that sustained her and her faith as she became a young wife to Jack. His prayers and references to scripture anchored her as their marriage struggled. When she lost Jack, she craved the chance to speak with him, but an illness that led to his passing snatched him away.

Loss. There is so much loss in life.

She decided not to dwell on it. Instead, she prayed for her children and grandchildren. She asked for more time, though she couldn't say how much time would be enough.

If only I could see John married and become a father. That's all I ask.

February 1994

Jacqueline Kennedy Onassis has non-Hodgkin's lymphoma, a treatable form of cancer of the lymphatic system, and has been undergoing chemotherapy for about a month without interrupting her personal routines or duties as a book editor, a family spokeswoman said yesterday.

"She is undergoing a course of treatment and there is every expectation that it will be successful," the spokeswoman, Nancy Tuckerman, said in an interview. "There is an excellent prognosis. You can never be absolutely sure, but the doctors are very, very optimistic."

The lymphatic system, composed mainly of lymph nodes and other tissues in the neck, armpits and groin, is a major component of the body's immune system. Non-Hodgkin's lymphoma, which is more common and can be more difficult to treat than Hodgkin's disease, is a painless enlargement of lymph tissue that can damage the immune system and eventually be fatal if unchecked.

The American Cancer Society says that non-Hodgkin's lymphoma, whose cause is unknown, will be diagnosed in 45,000 people in the United States this year, most of them over 50, while

Hodgkin's disease will be found in only 7,900. The society says 52 percent of those with non-Hodgkin's lymphoma will live at least five years, while the survival rate for Hodgkin's disease is 78 percent. The rates are higher for those whose cancers are localized and diagnosed early.

Ms. Tuckerman said Mrs. Onassis, who is 64 years old and has enjoyed robust good health virtually all her life, was found to have the lymphoma after going to a doctor with flu-like symptoms. She said the disease was apparently in an early stage and chemotherapy alone was prescribed.

Citing Mrs. Onassis's well-known desire for privacy, Ms. Tuckerman declined to identify the doctor who made the diagnosis or the medical institution where she is being treated. Moreover, because the prognosis appeared to be excellent, she said there would be no further reports on her condition.

Ms. Tuckerman, a lifelong friend and confidante of the former First Lady, said Mrs. Onassis, a senior editor at Doubleday, has continued to work three days a week at the office and two more days at her Manhattan apartment, reading and editing manuscripts. Mrs. Onassis edits about a dozen books a year, primarily nonfiction dealing with the performing arts, especially ballet and music.

Mrs. Onassis continues to see friends socially and her family, including her grandchildren, Rose, Tatiana and Jack Schlossberg, the children of Caroline Kennedy Schlossberg, and on weekends goes often to her estate near Peapack, N.J., where she rides horses, Ms. Tuckerman said.

She said Mrs. Onassis had decided to disclose the diagnosis of lymphoma because there had been "speculation and rumors" about her health recently. She said Mrs. Onassis "saw a doctor almost immediately" after coming down with the flu-like symptoms. The condition, she said, was "not too obvious at first because she was in such good health."

Excerpt from *The New York Times,* February 11, 1994

———

March 1994

IN MARCH, Jackie endured another battery of tests, including an MRI. Days later, she again found herself seated across her doctor's desk, steeling herself for the words printed on the papers inside the plain folder Dr. Ashanti brought into the room. Maurice shifted in his seat, indicating, she supposed, that her grip on his hand was stronger than expected, though he didn't complain.

"Mrs. Onassis, I wish I had better news," the doctor said once she joined them. "Although the lymphoma in your neck, chest, and abdomen has cleared, I'm afraid your spinal cord and cerebellum show signs of being affected."

Dr. Ashanti continued, but Jackie's attention had already drifted away with a deluge of thoughts. Would she ever get to ride again? Feel the wind and speckles of rain on her face? No more sailing on Narragansett Bay. No more travels. Though she had nothing to whine about, considering she had seen so many beautiful parts of the world, she wished she had been more cognizant of every detail. That she would have loved it more. Pain flared in her chest though when she thought of her children. Did this mean she wouldn't get to celebrate any more of her grandchildren's birthdays? That she wouldn't see John get married and have a family of his own?

"Mrs. Onassis?"

She flinched back to attention when Maurice squeezed her hand.

"Oh, I'm sorry. What were you saying?"

"I was explaining that there's still a chance. If you're in agreement, we can get you started on a new, experimental medication, but it requires having a shunt inserted into your head. It's a safe procedure but may sound frightening, having doctors drill into your skull. The shunt enables medicine to be injected directly into the sites and the administration of aggressive doses..."

*Aggressive doses...aggressive treatments...*just like Janet Jr.

When the doctor finished her thorough explanation, Jackie glimpsed Maurice's blanched expression, then looked at the doctor.

"Let's do it."

March 1994

LEE AND TINA brought Jackie several Hermes scarves that she could wear as head wraps since she'd lost her hair. Tina, like Marta, struggled seeing her aunt diminished. Jackie did her best to put up a front and to make light of her health battle. She even teased that with her new treatment, she might be turned into a bionic version of herself. The attempt at humor was lost on Tina, but Lee played along, adding that next time she would bring belts from the department store in case Jackie became equipped with gadgets.

By the time they left, Jackie was weary, which was exacerbated by her worry that Tina was taking her condition so hard.

Days later, she signed her final will and testament.

TWENTY-FOUR

March 1994

J ackie knew, regardless of how awkward the conversation would be, she needed to ensure that her preferences were known for her funeral. She sat down with Nancy and Maurice, confident they would faithfully adhere to and carry out her detailed plans.

"Whether it must happen sooner or later, I want it simple." Jackie wasted no time diving into the difficult conversation as soon as Marta had left them with a plate of pita chips and pâté. "I want the same casket as Jack."

She handed Maurice a brochure. He opened it to the dog-eared page and looked over the listing. "The Seven Ten model. Hmm. What it may lack in aesthetics, it makes up for in quality. The African mahogany is beautiful. Classy and timeless but quite expensive. A perfect choice, I would say. Leave the task of ordering it to me."

Jackie nodded. "As for floral arrangements, I want lots of greenery. Ferns are probably ideal with white flowers."

Maurice listened while Nancy scribbled notes and murmured, "No parade or fireworks."

"I don't mind telling you that I hate the idea of a funeral home and being on display."

"So no live satellite feed?"

Jackie traded glances with Maurice before laughing hysterically at Nancy's remark.

"But I will say, in all seriousness, that reminds me." Nancy pointed her pencil at Jackie. "What if you held an Irish wake?"

Jackie looked at her. "Meaning what exactly?"

"We skip the funeral home. Loved ones come here to pay their final respects, then we button you all up, and head to the church for the service. Hmm. After that I suppose we'll need to get you to Washington, but we can figure that out. Hosting the wake here also helps with security measures. We won't have to worry about anyone sneaking in and snatching you."

Jackie laughed harder than she had a moment ago. "Can't you just picture someone taking my corpse for ransom! Maurice, if that happens, don't you dare pay them a dime! Oh, and make sure I'm not in a designer dress and only wearing fake jewelry—perhaps from that collection they sell on television."

Nancy cackled with her while Maurice hesitated. Then he said, "My darling, your sense of humor is downright wicked, and I love you for it."

IF THERE WAS one thing Jackie had done right, one thing she cared to be remembered for, next to raising her children well, it was her planning and execution of Jack's funeral. Despite her grief and traumatized state, her initial thought was to replicate President Lincoln's funeral.

Jack had lain in state in a closed casket atop the catafalque used for Lincoln in the East Room. Black crepe draped much of the room, a traditional sign of mourning, though, and not a detail Jackie created. Only family and select others were allowed visitation, while Marines stood guard.

Public viewing was permitted the next day, after the coffin was moved to the Capitol rotunda. Over a quarter of a million people filed by and paid their respects. Then the next day, the day of the funeral, Jack's body was carried by a horse-drawn caisson down Pennsylvania Avenue. As it passed by the White House, little John saluted his father. A riderless horse, named Black Jack, with boots inserted backwards into the stirrups, was led by a handler and proved a bit rebellious. Jackie, with Bobby and Teddy by her side, and a multitude of leaders and dignitaries as well, walked behind the procession to St. Matthew's Cathedral, where the funeral service was held.

The Secret Service had objected to her desire to walk down the street for a mile, claiming security for her and the others would be nonexistent, making them vulnerable to another potential attack, but Jackie insisted.

Then it was on to Arlington. A detail that pitted her against the family. Knowing her husband had become an icon to the American people, even though his term as president was short, Jackie envisioned his grave as a living memorial, complete with a burning eternal flame. The Kennedys wanted Jack in the family plot at Brookline, but Jackie convinced them, "Jack belongs to the people."

In overseeing the design and construction of Jack's gravesite, she had picked her own burial plot and grave cap.

Thirty years ago, she couldn't imagine how her life would unfold without Jack. In fact, she dreaded the dawn of each morning and for months wanted nothing more than to join her slain husband. But now, feeling trapped in a body that had betrayed her and being ravaged with doubts about her survival, she wanted more time.

Sulking about her fate was useless, and she preferred not to dwell on things out of her control. One of her main concerns was ensuring that those she loved and cared about could be comfortable around her and not afraid that they would say or do the wrong thing. Jackie hoped by confronting matters and having a frankness, she would give death a run for its money.

With such thoughts fresh in her mind, and while Caroline and John settled at the table, joining her for lunch, Jackie announced,

"When the time comes, whenever that may be, I want my grave cap to read, 'Jacqueline Bouvier Kennedy Onassis.'"

Caroline and John traded glances.

"I know what you both must be thinking, and that's why I wanted to make it clear and discuss it with you. That way there can be no argument later about whether or not it's what I wanted."

"You don't owe anyone anything," John said.

The firmness in his remark was what Jackie expected, along with the mild push-back. She knew he was referring to Christina Onassis's stipulation that Jackie keep Onassis as her last name. It had been a term she agreed to in her settlement from Ari's estate. But Christina had passed, and perhaps John was indicating that no one else would hold her to that pledge now.

"You're exactly right, John. I'm under no obligation. It's my decision."

"But—"

"I understand you may not want to hear this, but I have given it plenty of thought. Ari was a good man. Just like your father, he had his faults. Both of his children are gone, and everything rests on his granddaughter now. I'll never be separated from the men I married, though I know many prefer to think of me as Mrs. Kennedy. That's fine. But I created a life I loved as Mrs. Onassis. Ari never would have approved of my career, but he's been with me through every book I've worked on. So has your father.

"I also want you to consider what the press would say, if I dropped Ari's name. They would think I was getting my revenge, or that I was bitter over the difficult parts of our marriage, or that I regretted being his wife. None of which is true. I'll not have anyone thinking one of the last things I did was insult a man I was married to. It's not who I am."

"That's an interesting point, I suppose." John looked to Caroline, as if he were waiting for her to launch a protest that Jackie would listen to, but Caroline, with her hands folded in her lap, seemed resigned.

"Besides, I've grown attached to it over the years." Jackie hoped her genuine smile eased their discomfort. "Upholding and adding to your father's legacy is up to both of you now, and I know you'll continue to make us both proud. After all, you're Kennedys."

John sighed. "All right, Mummy."

"Good. It's settled then."

Though she did wonder if Jack would return to her in another dream and chide her for making him lie next to *Onassis* for eternity.

April 1994

WHEN JACKIE COLLAPSED and was taken to the hospital, doctors discovered the steroid treatment she was undergoing had created a tear in her stomach lining. Surgery was required to repair the ulcer. Further tests determined that the chemo administered through the shunt in her head was not preventing the cancer from growing and spreading. A bone-marrow treatment was suggested, but Jackie declined.

When she returned to 1040 to rest and recuperate from the surgery as best she could, Lee was there waiting.

At first, Jackie dreaded having to explain the recent details and developments—having to face Lee and admit that she was going to die—but something in Lee's eyes told her she didn't need to. Somehow, Lee already knew.

Lee took over for Maurice and helped Jackie change and settle into her bed. Maurice kissed Jackie's forehead and left them.

Lee said, "I brought you something, Jacks."

Jackie hadn't noticed the large box sitting at the end of her bed until Lee opened the lid and withdrew a blanket. Reds, yellows, oranges, and greens had been woven into a sharp pattern that looked distinctly tribal.

Lee held it up against her body. "It's from Peter. He brought it back for you from Africa. Kamante's tribe made it."

Blissful memories washed over Jackie like that first time the tide would hit from the ocean after a winter hiatus. Peter Beard had been a dear friend for decades. He used to join Jackie and Ari and the children on the *Christina*. During their times together, he taught them about animals and photography. Showed them how to create collages and how to take fun, yet calculated risks.

Jackie had written the afterward for Peter's book, *Longing for Darkness*, which featured stories by Kamante, a young boy of the Kikuyu tribe who became Karen Blixen's cook and close friend during her time on a coffee plantation in Kenya. *Out of Africa*, penned by Blixen in the late 1930s, detailed the seventeen years she spent working the farm and included her marital woes, and the trials and failures that plagued the endeavor. When the book was released in 1937, it became a bestseller. Decades later, it was made into an award-winning movie.

Lee draped the blanket on top of the covers already on the bed.

"It's beautiful. How thoughtful." Jackie moved her hands over the fabric.

"Yes, Peter can be a prince when he wants."

"I'm glad you two reconciled."

Lee nodded and sat in a chair by Jackie's bedside. "The friendship was worth saving. We share so many unforgettable times, although I can't help cringing when he sends me his Christmas card. There's always a handprint or a doodle in his blood."

Jackie shrugged. "He's an artist who's stayed true to his signature, unconventional as it may be."

"Yes, it's definitely Peter." Lee looked Jackie over, as if she were taking stock of her condition. "You know I don't know how to do this, Jacks."

"This is where you make me promises. That you'll stay close with Caroline and John. Watch the grandchildren grow. Be there when John gets married. Snuggle his little ones for me. Maybe check on Maurice from time to time."

"I'm not sure the sun will have a reason to come up anymore, if you're not here."

The small chuckle Jackie managed shot pain through her abdomen. She recovered quickly. "Now, Pekes, you know that's not true."

"I am worried that the best of my life is over."

"Nonsense. Knowing you, you'll take over as editor of *Cosmopolitan*, open a gallery featuring your watercolors, and start a line of designer gowns and handbags."

Lee puckered her lips. "Hmm. I never thought of handbags." She scooched closer and reached for Jackie's hand. "I do have a bright spot of news. Anthony is getting married this summer."

"Oh, that's wonderful."

Anthony had visited her often, bringing books and sometimes photographs from his travels. There were times he choked up, his emotions getting the better of him seeing Jackie ill, but to Jackie, it only bonded them more. She couldn't have been happier for him, hearing that his life was moving forward so blissfully.

On the heels of such good news, Jackie added, "You might become a grandmother soon."

"We'll see. They're both busy with their careers. It's not like when we were getting married. By the time they decide about children, I may be too old to be a grandmother. Who knows." Lee's playfulness faded. "Anthony is worried the cancer will come back, and I'm not certain, but I think he's having some symptoms."

"Well, he can't live in fear. He has to do what he wants and what's right for him."

"You're such a know-it-all, Jacks. And God knows I'm going to miss everything about you."

"One day, we'll have eternity together, Pekes. I'll go ahead and set things up, like I used to do with our dollhouse before we played. Everything in its place. Then I'll tell you it's ready and surprise you with how creatively I've arranged it." She tried to smile. "Just do your best to make sure you don't come too soon."

JACKIE STOOD on her balcony and braced herself with the railing. Being on her feet and out of bed were liberating. So was being outside. She inhaled deeply, wishing the smells of the city had enough strength to float up fifteen stories and meet her. Exhaust fumes, bags of trash awaiting pick up, jackhammered particles of concrete, newly poured asphalt. And the more pleasant aromas. The hot dog-scented steam from a vendor's cart. A fresh batch of bagels. Pizza just out of the fire-roasting oven. Not that she enjoyed those often, but she missed everything about the city she loved. She missed living her life.

A few minutes more of savoring the breeze on her face and arms —she'd worn a short-sleeved shirt—and flapping her head wrap, of savoring the view of Central Park in full springtime blooms, then she stepped back inside.

Marta was waiting with a sweater to cover her. Nancy was there too. Together, they safeguarded Jackie as she made her way to the library. With great care, she eased into a chair by the fireplace. Marta helped position a pillow behind Jackie's head and covered her with the blanket from Lee, then she propped up her feet on an ottoman.

"Lunch is almost ready, Madam."

"Marta, could you whip up something for dessert?"

A lightning-quick exchange of glances between Marta and Nancy followed. Was it because Jackie only allowed dessert with lunch when it was a special guest, or because both women knew Jackie's appetite was compromised and at best she could only manage two or three bites?

"There is still some mango ice cream left," Marta said.

"Oh, perfect."

Marta nodded and left them.

Nancy sat next to Jackie, having pulled over another ottoman. "Are you sure about this?"

Jackie looked at the stack of letters and papers on the side table beside her. For the last several days, she and Nancy had sorted through a multitude of her personal papers, letters, and correspondence with various world leaders, heads of state, and politicians.

"Yes. I want the peace of knowing these won't end up as a tell-all book someday."

"But you can give them to Caroline and John to keep. They're practically historical artifacts."

Jackie smirked. "It's *my* history, and I don't believe anyone else is entitled to read any of this. Not even Caroline and John. They shouldn't know *everything* about their mother anyway."

"I suppose." Nancy sighed. "It just feels like we're desecrating the *Mona Lisa*."

Jackie laughed, though part of her agreed. "You're so dramatic, Tucky. Now, let's start the fire."

May 1994

"DARLING, LET ME HELP YOU," Maurice said when Jackie couldn't lift her arms high enough to place the scarf around her wig. He draped it perfectly and gently tied it under her chin.

"Do I look all right?"

Of course, she was asking him to look past her face, now gaunt from weight loss and lack of sun. She had done what she could to camouflage her thin frame—beige wool trousers, a matching trench coat, even though the temperature had stretched into the upper sixties. What she really wanted to know, was did she look convincing? Would she fool the waiting photographers and the public into thinking she wasn't deathly ill?

"Lovely, as always," he said.

Jackie detected the hitch in his voice. He wanted to protect her and possibly dissuade her from doing this. On the other hand, he knew her well enough to know that once she made up her mind to do something, the ideal recourse was to go along.

She had given the matter serious thought, and like many times before, this was what she wanted—to control her image. The public image she had manufactured and curated for decades. This would be her final act. One last peek, unless God had a change of plans.

Jackie slid on a pair of her oversized, dark sunglasses.

"Then I'm ready for my walk in the park."

———

DAYS LATER, pneumonia took advantage of Jackie's weakened state. Tests confirmed the cancer had invaded her liver. Treatment efforts proved ineffective as cells had spread and grown in her brain and spinal cord. Radiation and other treatments were suspended, per Jackie's wishes.

Upon returning home from the hospital, Jackie became confined to her canopy bed. Attached to an IV for fluids and pain meds, she soon required a ventilator to assist with her breathing. Before she slipped into a coma, those closest to her visited and paid their last respects while a Gregorian chant, played by monks of Santo Domingo de Silos played in the background.

Caroline, John, and Maurice were at her bedside when she took her last breath.

———

May 20th, 1994

"Last night at around 10:15pm, my mother passed on. She was surrounded by her friends and her family and her books, and the people and things that she loved. She did it in her own way, and in her own terms, and we all feel lucky for that. Now, she is in God's hands. There's been an enormous outpouring of good wishes from everyone both in New York and beyond, and I speak for all of our family when we say we're extremely grateful. Everyone's been very generous. I hope now, you know, we just have these next couple days in relative peace. Thank you all very much."

John F. Kennedy Jr's statement
to the press outside of 1040 Fifth Avenue

EPILOGUE

Dearest Jacks,

Time is an evil bandit of sorts. It's been over a decade since we said our goodbyes. That seems impossible. Wasn't it only yesterday we were meeting for lunch at The Colony? Then again, I could say the same for the summer days we rode our horses and played at Lasata or met Mummy for tea at the Plaza. It couldn't have been that long ago we were up half the night wrapping Christmas presents for the children or whisking them away for a vacation at Bunny's estate in Antigua. Yet that's precisely what I mean about time. It's deceptive, isn't it?

Of course, I know it seems trite and trivial, writing a letter you'll never read, but I need this. Let me pretend for a while that we're going to sit together, perhaps cross-legged on the floor with a roaring fire warming a room on a chilly night...

A day hasn't gone by where I haven't thought about you or been reminded of you. So much has happened—well, I should say, the worst has happened. We lost John. Beautiful, loving John.

Your darling John fell in love and married. I will say, what a striking young woman he chose, but whether or not you would have approved is hard to determine. In the time they were together, they had their troubles, though I never knew specifics, only the tabloid speculation. But I've never seen him so captivated as he was with Carolyn.

They died in a plane crash, along with Carolyn's sister Lauren, on their way to Rory's wedding.

Jacks, it was the most heartbreaking thing. During those days when the plane was missing, I cried uncontrollably at times, thinking how you were right—how you begged him not to fly because you feared for his safety. But I suppose he was John to the end, a risk-taker and perhaps over-confident where he shouldn't have been.

You want to know what almost did me in? If I can pen the words... Anthony was ill at that time. In fact, his cancer had returned again and was terminal. John spent a lot of time with Anthony that summer, looking after him and desperate to cling to every day with him, just as we all were. It may sound morbid, but John wrote Anthony's eulogy with Anthony's help. They tried to keep a sense of humor about it, but John broke into tears a few times. So did Anthony. I found comfort in the fact they had each other, even though their time together was ending.

When we lost John in July, so unexpectedly, their roles reversed, and Anthony gave a moving, difficult tribute for John as we stood on that boat—forgive me, I can't recall the name—with Caroline holding the urn with John's ashes. Carolyn and Lauren's parents sprinkled their daughters' ashes. We left them all at sea.

Anthony followed John in death a few weeks later.

Tina, Carole, Anthony's wife, and I have managed, but we're shattered on the inside. I'm thankful you didn't have to endure losing John.

I hear Maurice is doing well. He moved to a grand hotel. We brunched together a couple of times after you left, but without you there was little common ground. As far as I know, he isn't seeing anyone.

Caroline continues to thrive in everything she does. Oh my, how I wish you could see her children. Rose favors you with her wide-set eyes and luscious brown hair. Her spunk too.

Herbert and I parted ways. Nothing scandalous occurred, but not long after our divorce, he passed. I suppose I was never meant to be a widow—or a life-long wife.

Tina and I are doing well. We've learned to be gentler with each other. Or perhaps I have finally realized what a treasure she is to me. I care nothing for pettiness or squabbles. Tranquility means more to me than it ever has.

I will say, there is one bit that would please that devilish sense of humor of yours to no end. The press and the gossips had a field day with your will and your mention of leaving no provision for me. They all believed you cut me out because of Ari and went on about how it was your means of revenge. I laugh to myself when I hear that drivel or any reference to our rivalry and fractured relationship. Just shows how none of them ever knew you—just the way you wanted it. And no one has ever been the wiser about the trust you established for me before you departed. Another stroke of your genius. We fooled them all!

I bought an apartment in Paris and split my time between there and New York. I like to think that's exactly what you would have done. You know what it reminds me of? <u>One Special Summer</u>, the scrapbook from our trip to Europe that we had published. I may do something *similar with some of my photographs. Creating another book and basking in cherished memories has an appeal—but don't worry, Jacks, I'll keep our secrets safe and tucked inside the broken pieces of my heart.*

All of my love always,
Lee

———————

Her eyes they shone like diamonds
I thought her queen of the land
And her hair, it hung over her shoulder
Tied up with a black velvet band

"Black Velvet Band," a Celtic folk song
Jackie heard in a pub during her 1967 trip to Ireland.

AUTHOR'S NOTES

This book is a work of fiction. Although this story revolves around real people and real events, it is a fabrication of the author's imagination. Certain events portrayed in this tale are intentionally false. However, the tragic death of Ghislaine de Renty Marchal is true.

ACKNOWLEDGMENTS

Once again, I'm grateful for the chance to work with the talents of Hannah Linder, Catherine Posey, and Christy Distler. They are vital in bringing together various elements of this book and making it shine. Big thanks to my friends at Buckeye Crime Writers. As always, I"m thankful for my family and their support along this journey.

~MK

ABOUT THE AUTHOR

A founding member of Buckeye Crime Writers, Mercedes King is a Columbus, Ohio, native. With a degree in Criminology from Capital University, she enjoys combining her love of pop culture with history and exploring the depths of deviant behavior. Since her stories often mix fact with fiction and are shaped by not-so-distant decades, she refers to many of her works as Modern Historicals. In 2016 and 2017, Mercedes was a finalist for the Claymore Award. When she's not elbow-deep in research, reading, or enjoying the local bike path, she might be at Wrigley Field or sinking her toes into the sand somewhere along Florida's coastline.

BOOKS BY MERCEDES KING

The Jacqueline Bouvier Kennedy Onassis Collection

Jackie's Paris

Jackie's Camelot

Jackie's Greece

Jackie's New York

Historical Fiction Titles

A Dream Called Marilyn

Plantation Nation

Crime Fiction / Mysteries

Every Little Secret

Grave Secrets

Columbus Noir

Newsletter subscribers receive a FREE e-book for joining. Sign-up here.

Printed in Great Britain
by Amazon

46072262R00189